MW01446175

Dear FairyLoot Readers,

Ever since I was a child, I have dreamed of sprawling worlds and magic, of tales full of adventure and epic quests ... But above all, I've longed for books where girls and women take centre stage as the heroes of their own stories.

This desire, I've come to realise, is the thread woven through every book I write. It's a theme I'm compelled to explore again and again.

Within these pages, you'll meet Wren, a heroine who carries the weight of the past on her shoulders; who has been underestimated and overlooked. This book, and the series that follows, is her response to a realm that tried to silence her. It's her rise from the ashes of a broken place.

Feminine rage is a glorious thing, and all my heroines possess it in spades, far more openly than I've ever dared to in my own life. It just so happens that sometimes the monsters and villains in fiction are far less terrifying than the realities we face out there in the real world.

This book is a tribute to every reader who has ever felt underestimated. It's a reminder that your voice matters, your anger is valid and your story deserves to be told.

Here's to making your mark, rewriting the narrative and becoming the hero of your own tale.

The mind is a blade. Keep yours sharp and carve your own fate.

Signed by Helen Scheuerer

This edition published by Bramble in collaboration with FairyLoot

Iron & Embers

BY HELEN SCHEUERER

The Legends of Thezmarr
Blood & Steel
Vows & Ruins
Fate & Furies
Shadow & Storms

The Ashes of Thezmarr
Iron & Embers

HELEN SCHEUERER

IRON & EMBERS

THE ASHES OF THEZMARR
BOOK ONE

BRAMBLE FairyLoot

First published 2025 by Tor Bramble
an imprint of Pan Macmillan
The Smithson, 6 Briset Street, London EC1M 5NR
EU representative: Macmillan Publishers Ireland Ltd, 1st Floor,
The Liffey Trust Centre, 117–126 Sheriff Street Upper,
Dublin 1, D01 YC43
Associated companies throughout the world
www.panmacmillan.com

ISBN 978-1-0350-6741-1 HB
ISBN 978-1-0350-6742-8 TPB

Copyright © Helen Scheuerer 2025

The right of Helen Scheuerer to be identified as the
author of this work has been asserted by her in accordance
with the Copyright, Designs and Patents Act 1988.

All rights reserved. No part of this publication may be reproduced,
stored in a retrieval system, or transmitted, in any form, or by any means
(electronic, mechanical, photocopying, recording or otherwise)
without the prior written permission of the publisher.

Pan Macmillan does not have any control over, or any responsibility for,
any author or third-party websites referred to in or on this book.

3 5 7 9 8 6 4 2

A CIP catalogue record for this book is available from the British Library.

Midrealms map by Alec McKinley
Drevenor map by Melissa Nash

Typeset by Palimpsest Book Production Ltd, Falkirk, Stirlingshire
Printed and bound by CPI Group (UK) Ltd, Croydon, CR0 4YY

This book is sold subject to the condition that it shall not, by way of
trade or otherwise, be lent, hired out, or otherwise circulated without
the publisher's prior consent in any form of binding or cover other than
that in which it is published and without a similar condition including
this condition being imposed on the subsequent purchaser.

Visit www.panmacmillan.com to read more about all our books
and to buy them. You will also find features, author interviews and
news of any author events, and you can sign up for e-newsletters
so that you're always first to hear about our new releases.

*To the women who rewrite the rules, one page at a time.
Your potential is the plot twist the world never saw coming.*

REGARDING REFERENCES TO PLANTS AND POISONS

*Some are true, some are not.
It's safest not to guess which is which.
Don't try this at home.*

PROPHECY

'Gold will turn to silver in a blaze of iron and embers, giving rise to ancient power long forgotten'

– PROPHECY FROM
THE SEER QUEEN OF AVEUM

Dorinth
Delmira
Thezmarr
The Mourner's Trail
The Bloodwoods
Hailford
The Chained Islands
Harenth
The Broken Isles
Ciraun
Naarva
The Scarlet Tower
The Veil

THE MIDREALMS

LEVEL ONE

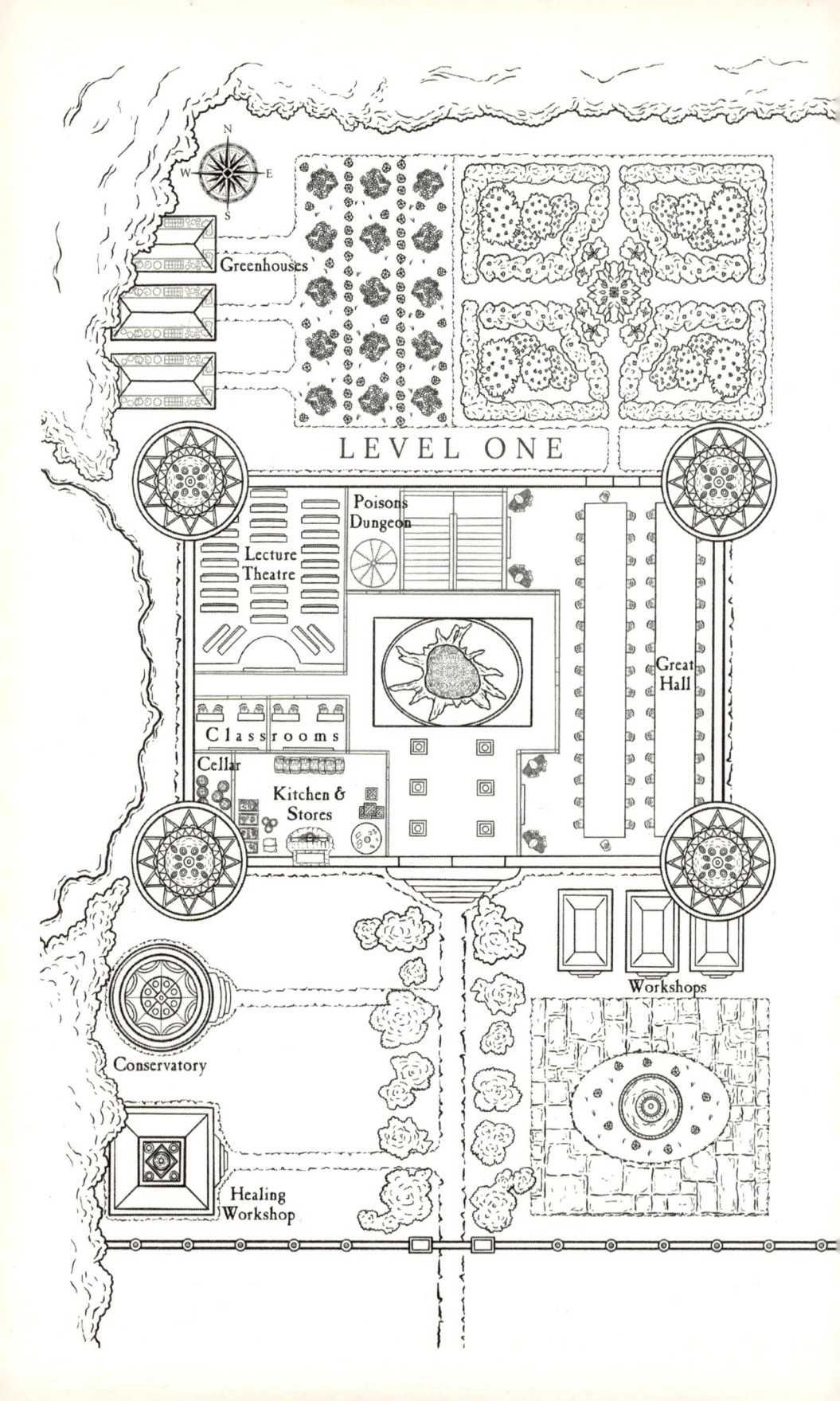

Greenhouses

Lecture Theatre

Poisons Dungeon

Classrooms

Cellar

Kitchen & Stores

Great Hall

Workshops

Conservatory

Healing Workshop

LEVEL TWO

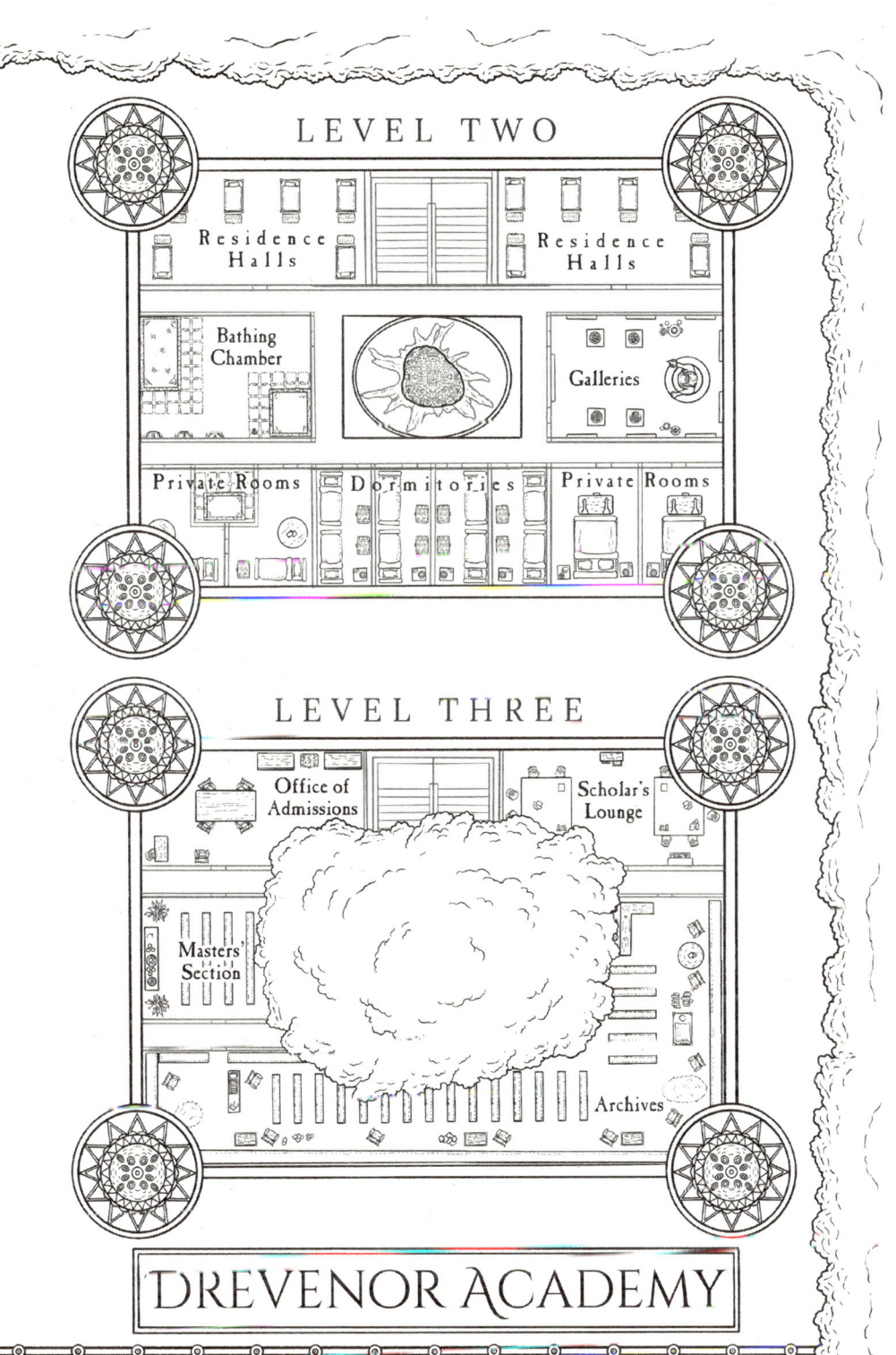

Residence Halls

Residence Halls

Bathing Chamber

Galleries

Private Rooms

Dormitories

Private Rooms

LEVEL THREE

Office of Admissions

Scholar's Lounge

Masters' Section

Archives

DREVENOR ACADEMY

A RECENT HISTORY OF THE SHADOW WAR

The Shadow War, a conflict that reshaped the very fabric of the midrealms, reached its brutal conclusion a mere five years ago at the fortress of Thezmarr. This war, unprecedented in its savagery and evil, left an indelible mark on our lands and people.

Its origins can be traced to the shocking betrayal of King Artos and Princess Jasira of the Kingdom of Harenth. Seeking ultimate power and control, father and daughter utilized their considerable magical prowess and political influence to amass an army of nightmarish creatures, primarily composed of shadow wraiths and the dreaded rheguld reapers. These entities, born of darkness and hunger, swept across the midrealms, leaving devastation in their wake. Countless innocents fell victim to dark curses, their fates a testament to the war's unnatural cruelty.

In response to this overwhelming threat, the kingdoms of the midrealms set aside their long-standing differences to form an allied force that rallied behind the legendary Warswords of Thezmarr.

The war culminated in a devastating battle at the fortress of Thezmarr. This bastion, long revered as impregnable, became the stage for the final act of the conflict. The allied forces clashed with the monstrous horde, leaving every stone of the courtyard stained red with blood.

While the midrealms ultimately emerged victorious, the cost was staggering. Entire regiments were annihilated, noble houses extinguished and swathes of land rendered uninhabitable by lingering dark magic.

In the aftermath, the midrealms faced unprecedented challenges. The conflict had depleted not only lives but also resources, leaving treasuries bare and fields ravaged. A generation of orphans and displaced peoples struggled to find their place in a world irrevocably changed.

The very geography of the realm was altered, with the fall of the Veil – a *barrier of mist that had long defined the borders of the known world – revealing uncharted territories ripe for exploration . . . or conflict.*

As we mark the fifth anniversary of the war's end, the midrealms continue to grapple with its consequences. The shadow of Artos and Jasira's betrayal looms large, a reminder of the price of corruption and the ever-present threat of darkness.

CHAPTER 1

Wren

'The difference between poison and cure is simply a matter of dose'

– *Toxic Tales: Chronicles of Lethal Elixirs*

IF POISON WAS a woman's weapon, then Wren Embervale was a woman through and through. It was an art she'd relished in the five years since the shadow war, a mantle of revenge she'd taken up against those who'd played their part in spreading the darkness that had cloaked the midrealms for so long.

The stain of what they'd done had lingered. Time had not yet closed all the wounds the war had left. But slowly, the world had found its rhythm once more.

And so had Wren.

The noble houses, the politicians . . . Corruption was a disease that ran rampant through them all, and slowly but surely, Wren had been cutting it out: one by one, dose by dose.

And that was what had brought her to the opulent parlour before her now. Thick rugs covered much of the marble floor; the papered walls were clad with gold filigree frames and oil paintings. The furniture was upholstered in decadent emerald-green velvet. An overly large bird cage hung on a stand in the far corner, empty.

Perching herself on the edge of a lounge, Wren tucked loose strands of her bronze hair back into her messy bun and secured it with her favourite pin.

She waited.

Lord Briar started as he strode into the parlour. 'Who are you?' he spluttered. 'Who let you in here?' He stared at the jagged scar down Wren's throat, eyes narrowing.

Suppressing the urge to trace the line of marred skin, Wren smoothed her apron over her simple linen gown, mindful of the belt of tools and vials at her waist. Not that it mattered, but the scar made her recognizable – the storm-wielding heir of Delmira from the war. She watched her mark as the realization dawned on his ruddy face.

'I know who you are,' he said, straightening his shoulders, his gaze still lingering on her ruined flesh. 'I know what you did . . .'

Wren gave an impatient sigh. 'You'll have to be more specific.'

'It was *you*. At the end of the war. You *murdered* the former Guild Master of Thezmarr,' Lord Briar declared boldly.

'Executed,' Wren corrected him, watching as Lord Briar's maid brought a large jug of water and poured him a glass. She waited until the woman left before she spoke again. 'I hope he wasn't a friend of yours?'

It was no secret that she had disposed of the traitor in the fortress. She remembered it as though it were yesterday. A simple workshop, an assassin's teapot and a quiet conversation that led to the creation of her ledger of marks.

The birthplace of the person she's been for the past five years: *the Poisoner*.

It had been her first taste of vengeance, though not the last.

The midrealms thought Elwren Embervale had sought revenge for her fallen sister and then faded into obscurity, a recluse hidden away in the ruined lands of her ruined kingdom. An heir without a throne; an heir who'd refused a crown. But Wren didn't concern herself with what the rest of the world thought. Her business was her ledger, and striking another name from it.

She spoke louder this time. 'I said, I hope he wasn't a friend of yours, my lord?'

'Not a friend. Of course not.' Lord Briar drank his water, downing it in several large gulps before smacking his lips and refilling his cup. 'But he deserved a trial.'

The smouldering fortress flashed before Wren's eyes, the blood running in rivers between the cobbles, the lashes of shadow and forks of lightning cleaving through the air. 'He deserved *death*.'

It was always the calmness of her expression that triggered her marks' panic, and she'd be lying if she denied that some small, broken part of her enjoyed it, revelled in it.

There.

Wisely, his throat bobbed. 'Why are you in my house?'

Wren didn't move. She didn't need to. 'You almost single-handedly funded the enemy's archery force. You provided Artos with information that saw countless innocents die.'

'Lies!' he blustered. 'I had no affiliation with anyone on the wrong side of the war.' He looked around wildly. 'Guards!'

'They're indisposed. It's amazing what a few drops of poppy extract can accomplish,' she told him conversationally. 'As for the wrong side of the war . . . I think you know all about that. Before he died, Osiris told me the names of all the so-called noblemen Artos had in his pocket. Guess whose name was top of the list? Guess who I've waited five years to meet?'

Lord Briar scrambled back.

Wren almost laughed. 'You think I'd make an attempt on your life right here? Don't be ridiculous, Lord Briar. I did that days ago.'

The man paled, guzzling more water. 'Then you failed.'

'Did I?' Wren raised a brow. 'Thirsty, aren't you?'

'It's a warm day.'

'Not particularly.'

Lord Briar shook his head, looking into his glass. 'You can't have—'

'Oh, you're quite right. The water is uncontaminated.'

The nobleman had begun to sweat profusely.

'Your mistress' cosmetics, on the other hand . . .' Wren said thoughtfully. 'Well, they're another story.'

'What . . . what have you done?'

'A little mixture of henbane, datura and nightshade added right into the paint she uses for her lips . . . Your lovely companion was given an antidote, of course. It's not her fault you're a treasonous bastard.'

Lord Briar scrambled for the water jug, wrenching it from the table and drinking straight from the vessel.

'The thing about that combination,' Wren continued, 'is that a few days after exposure, the subject experiences an unquenchable thirst. To the point where . . .'

Lord Briar collapsed with a wretched gasp.

'. . . they drink water in excess, increasing the speed at which the poison enters the bloodstream. How much water have you had today? Or yesterday, for that matter? Either way, it'll look like an accident. Just like all the rest.'

Lord Briar was on all fours, veins bulging in his neck, eyes wide with horror.

'This time, a tragic choking. Perhaps pneumonia if they bother to look at your lungs.' Wren sighed. 'Then it's simply a question of what kills you first . . . The toxins, or drowning.'

There was no sound from the nobleman. He lay in a puddle of water and spit, his eyes lifeless, staring into the void.

There was a mastery to ending life; a discipline that she'd come to know intimately. And there was a beautiful balance in the creation of something so delicate and yet so deadly.

'Drowning it is, then.' Wren got to her feet and reached down to slide his family crest ring from his index finger. Pocketing it, she made for the door. She was eager to leave the city of Hailford behind her.

And so, the poisoner disappeared into the night.

CHAPTER 2

Torj

'I pledge my sword and my life to
the protection of the midrealms'

— *Warsword oath to the Furies upon the Great Rite*

BONE CRUNCHED BENEATH his knuckles. Torj Elderbrock withdrew his fist only to drive it back into his opponent's nose with another satisfying crack.

A garbled moan sounded as blood sprayed across the tavern floor.

The crowd around the makeshift fighting ring in the Laughing Fox groaned in unison as coin exchanged hands and pints were refilled. Only moments ago, Torj had been among them, almost drowning in drinks. Lots of drinks. And toasts, countless toasts, to the lightning-kissed, storm-blessed, silver-haired Bear Slayer.

'Had enough yet?' Torj asked his rival.

In answer, the man took a messy swing at his face, missing by some distance and losing his balance.

Torj sighed, unsatisfied. He'd started the brawl because the bastard had groped one of the Fox's waitresses. He'd kept fighting because he liked it, though he felt sorely underchallenged.

When he was moving, when his fists were flying, he could forget. But in those quiet moments in between, the past would rush back to him and he would be right there, on the battlefield, five years ago.

Pure, unadulterated power hit him. The sheer force of it was utterly terrifying. Bolts of lightning sparked in his very blood and the taste of rain kissed his lips. A storm, furious and wild, surged in the air around him, channelling through him and his war hammer as he leapt from the fortress wall and into the bloody maw of death itself.

The strike of the hammer with his Furies-given strength shattered the hold of darkness, the impact singing through his bones, along with more storm magic than he thought ever possible. He couldn't contain it—

The drunkard landed a hit to Torj's jaw.

Revelling in the contact, the Bear Slayer surged forth, the crowd going wild around him as he lifted his opponent up by the front of his shirt, the fabric tearing under the strain. The man whimpered and kicked out, and Torj dropped him like a sack of grain with a noise of disgust.

As he exited the ring, several patrons clapped him on the back and offered him more drinks, but he waved them off. Needing a moment, he leaned against the bar, pushing a stray lock of hair from his brow. Five years ago, it had been as golden as the sun; now it was as silver as the moon. His hand came to rest on his tattooed chest, the ink marred by a web of lightning-shaped scars from that same fateful day. He rubbed the old wound, still feeling the echo of that power beneath his skin.

Five years since the very essence of her had been seared into his flesh.

A lot could happen in five years.

The first time he'd seen her after the shadow war was three months after the final battle. Their band of unlikely companions had reunited within these very walls over roast boar and tankards of sour mead. Cal Whitlock, Torj's former apprentice, had just passed the Great Rite, joining the ranks of the Warswords. Thea Embervale had just captured her Tverrian stallion – a Warsword rite of passage well worth celebrating. And Kipp Snowden . . . Well,

Thezmarr's chief strategist had been doing what he did best: making a nuisance of himself. Even Torj's fellow seasoned Warsword, the once brutal and moody Wilder Hawthorne, had embraced Torj like a brother.

Despite all they had been through, Torj thought there was hope at last. And when Wren Embervale's gaze lingered on him from across the table, he was sure of it.

So when she ducked away from the revelry, he followed.

He should have left her to steal a moment to herself.

He should have given her time.

He should have done a lot of things.

But he hadn't been able to stop himself from approaching her in that quiet corner . . .

Three months after the shadow war
Four years, nine months ago

'What is it that you want, Bear Slayer?' Wren demanded.

'I've made no secret of what I want.' Tension corded every muscle as the words spilled forth, words he'd been holding in since the moment he'd seen the fiery alchemist. 'You,' he said. 'It's always been you.'

A delicate pink flushed her cheeks, her stormy eyes darkening with the unmistakable haze of lust, her tongue wetting her lips. She leaned in, her hands coming to rest on the broad plane of his chest, his heart hammering wildly beneath their heat. Had she ever touched him before? Not like this. There was no forgetting the force of her.

'Then let's get a room,' she murmured, her attention dropping to his mouth. 'Let's settle this thing between us.'

Desire coursed through him like a current of fire, hot and demanding, rising as he closed what little gap remained between them, pressing her to him. He nearly moaned at the feel of her. For how long had he imagined this very moment? Taking her in his arms, taking her to his bed? He breathed in the heady scent of her, spring rain and jasmine—

But then, her words registered. 'Settle?' he asked.

Wren fixed him with a challenging stare. 'Yes. There's clearly an attraction here. I'm not fool enough to deny it, but you're a Warsword. And I'm the woman who poisoned your former Guild Master. Our paths don't align.'

'Says who?'

'Says me,' she replied.

Torj felt the world slide out from under him as he stepped back. 'Wren . . .'

But she shook her head, a muscle feathering in her jaw as she seemed to fight something within. 'I have nothing left to give you, Bear Slayer.' Her words were raw, her anguish bleeding through.

Torj's heart broke for her. She had lost a sister and her two closest friends in the most violent way only three months before . . . He sometimes woke in the middle of the night, his mind echoing with the cry that had fallen from her lips as she'd seen their heads on spikes.

'I know you're hurting,' he said gently.

'You know nothing about me or how I feel,' she told him, her voice hard. 'If what I offer isn't enough, then this is where I leave you.'

Torj nearly choked on the shock. 'And what is it that you're offering? So there is no confusion between us?'

'One night.' She didn't look away, didn't blush as she spoke the words.

Torj went incredibly still. 'One night in your bed?'

'Whose bed doesn't matter.'

Torj sucked in a breath. Of all the ways he'd imagined taking her, this had never been one of them.

He passed a hand over his face, buying a moment to compose himself.

'Then this is where you leave me,' he said, voice low and gravelly. Wren blinked. 'What?'

He looked at her, truly looked at her, taking in the loose tendrils of bronze hair framing her face, the freckles scattered across her nose, the jagged pink scar that ran the length of her throat from where they'd faced the darkness together in battle.

He wanted her, desperately, like a dying man longing for a cure.

But Elwren Embervale had taken her heart off the table.

And now, so would he.

'One night is not enough,' he told her.

It wasn't often he forgot his place in the world, but as he walked away, he had to remind himself: she was the heir of Delmira. It was a fallen kingdom, but she was still a queen by blood. And he was a warrior, nothing more.

CHAPTER 3
Wren

'For centuries, magic in the midrealms has been contained to those with royal blood. The only exception being the power gifted to Warswords by the Furies'

– *The Midrealms Chronicles*

For half a decade, Wren had been playing the long game, doing what the legendary warriors of Thezmarr could not: cutting out the rot left in the wake of the war. The work did not end simply because the final battle had been won, and Wren worked *hard*.

As she rode through the night back to her ramshackle cottage in Delmira, lightning illuminated the horizon. Wren shuddered. The storm was not of her making. These days, her magic was erratic – fickle. Part of her wondered if she'd somehow broken her power in those first months of wandering the moors of her ruined kingdom. Lost and raw with grief, she had ravaged the lands further with her storms. Delmira had withstood the brutal onslaught, her lightning scorching its earth, her rain flooding its rivers . . . Part of her had wanted to wash the ashes of war from the kingdom, and part of her had simply lost control.

Now, the storm crackled above her and brought the taste of rain to her lips. With it, a flood of memories came rushing back, threatening to drown her.

A vortex of dark magic tore open within the very core of the conflict, swallowing creatures, warriors and innocents alike. Their screams were mercilessly stifled as they were sucked into the maw of the insatiable abyss.

And then there was him.

The golden-haired Warsword hurtling towards the black void, war hammer raised above his head.

Time stilled, the breath between life and death.

On the nearby parapet, Wren shot out a hand without thinking, power blasting from her fingertips and channelling into the great warrior's weapon. The iron absorbed her magic, the force of her storm, sparks igniting and racing through the runes on the Warsword's hammer.

Wren's heart lodged in her throat, a scream falling silent on her lips as the man drove monster and darkness into the ground, a swirling vortex of shadow surging for them both.

In that moment, she knew fear like nothing else. The bitter taste of it on her tongue, the panic tearing at her chest like a caged animal, the cascading rhythm of terror growing wilder with every heartbeat – until the shadows dissipated, and revealed the sight beyond . . .

The Warsword had sealed the portal. He knelt on one knee in the ruins, braced over his hammer, sparks flitting along the iron.

When he lifted his head, a whimper escaped Wren.

For the golden-haired warrior was no more. He had been kissed by lightning and thunder, and scorch marks blackened the ground where he knelt. Thrumming with power, he stood. His hair, now silver, caught in the wind as he squared his shoulders.

His gaze, now as dark as the shadows he'd vanquished, went straight to Wren.

Wren came back to herself, shaking and alone. Her grip on the reins was vicelike, her spine slick with sweat in the aftermath of the memory. Dawn was breaking on the horizon at last, though the light did little to comfort her now.

Torj Elderbrock, the Warsword now known across the lands as the silver-haired Bear Slayer, a saviour of the midrealms, had haunted both her dreams and waking hours for half a decade. They hadn't shared so much as a kiss, but he was the storm beneath her skin that wouldn't abate.

A familiar unbroken stretch of yellowed grass greeted her, and the fallen kingdom of Delmira welcomed her home with its dark irony. *A poisoned land for a poisoner* . . . The kingdom had fallen long before the shadow war and was still in ruins, refusing to grow even the hardiest of crops across its hilly plains. It was no wonder the lands remained uncultivated and uninhabited.

It suited Wren just fine. She preferred solitude, and with her battered residence obscured by the thick, unruly foliage and gnarled trunks of an ancient forest, the rest of the midrealms left her well enough alone.

At long last, her cottage came into view, and her shoulders relaxed at the sight. A moss-covered thatched roof sagged over crooked timber beams, while patches of ivy clung to the worn facade. The glass panes of the windows were fogged with all manner of alchemy Wren had experimented with over the past year. Hopping down from her horse, she unsaddled the beast and led it to the water trough, imagining a simple meal before the fire and some time to work on her latest poisons.

Inside, she took Lord Briar's signet ring from her pocket and placed it in the small wooden box with the others: a pendant bearing the Riverton family crest, a pocket watch belonging to the late Baron Alderich, a gold-framed monocle from Lord Malvoth, and a silver inkwell encrusted with rubies, engraved with Lord Renard's initials. Beneath these, there were more. A delicate silver filigree brooch in the shape of a swan. A small, intricately carved ivory figurine of a mountain drake, its eyes inlaid with tiny emeralds. A bronze coin bearing the face of a foreign king.

Closing the lid with a snap, Wren set about lighting the fire. Soon, warm amber light spilled across the room, illuminating the clutter. However dilapidated, this place had always offered her a sense of solace—

A tell-tale creak sounded from beneath the window.

Wren palmed a poison-tipped dagger and whirled around.

Someone was here.

CHAPTER 4
Torj

'The fortress of Thezmarr has always been home to the most elite warrior training programme in the midrealms. It sits on the edge of the world, hemmed in by jagged mountains and savage seas'

– *A History of Thezmarr*

A SHADOW DARKENED the space beside Torj at the bar.
'Get your shit together.' Wilder Hawthorne, his fellow Warsword, already had a pack slung over his shoulder.

Torj downed the fire extract the bartender had placed in front of him. 'What are you talking about? We're not due to leave until—'

'There's been an attack.'

Torj's gaze snapped to his friend's. 'Who? Where?' he demanded.

'King Leiko.'

'Is he alive?'

Wilder nodded. 'Several Guardians were stationed there. They managed to get the king to safety and quell the attack. Audra has called all Warswords back to the fortress for a briefing.'

All Warswords – another change the post-war years had brought about. Torj flexed his hand, feeling the Furies-given strength coursing through his veins. Ballads were sung about their kind –

tales of immortality, of beings forged rather than born. Sometimes it didn't feel so long ago that there had only been three of their kind left in the midrealms. Now, there were thirteen elite warriors who had passed the Great Rite, the series of deadly trials crafted by the gods themselves. Thirteen who bore the steel symbol of crossed swords on their armbands, who answered to no one but the Guild Master. Thirteen who guarded what remained in the wake of the shadows. To summon them all back to the guild was telling.

'Audra suspects something larger than a lone assassination attempt?' The web of scars prickled across Torj's chest.

Wilder motioned for him to get up and follow. 'Won't know 'til we're back at Thezmarr.'

They crossed the tavern and made for the rooms above, uneasiness stirring in the pit of Torj's stomach. The midrealms were still rebuilding, still recovering from the war. As the story of the late King Artos' treachery had bled across the lands, peace between the kingdoms had been fragile to say the least. A royal at the helm of such devastation made for fractured trust between rulers and subjects alike – and now an attack on a king, after everything they had been through?

Perhaps Audra is right to call us all back to Thezmarr.

Torj opened the door to his room, revealing a chaotic state beyond.

'Cal!' Wilder barked in the direction of the bed. 'Move your sorry arse. We're leaving.'

To Torj's utter surprise, Callahan Whitlock, his former apprentice-turned-Warsword, sprang from the mattress as though someone had poured a bucket of ice water over him.

Unfortunately, he was naked.

More unfortunate still, he dislodged not one, but two women who were nestled in the blankets, both shrieking in surprise. The sound did nothing for the ache forming behind Torj's eyes.

'The fuck, Cal?' he said through gritted teeth.

'Sorry, sorry! We came back this morning – Albert gave my room away—'

Wilder shielded his eyes in disgust. 'Because you haven't paid your tab!'

'Kipp was supposed to sort it—'

Wilder snorted. 'You should know better by now.'

Shaking his head, Torj entered the room and started collecting his things. He travelled light, so he made quick work of his pack and shouldered his war hammer.

'Where's Thea?' he asked Wilder, noting her absence from his side. The couple was usually inseparable, a longstanding source of pain for Torj. Though he did not begrudge his friends their happiness, he'd given up his own dreams of a future like theirs long ago.

'She left early,' Wilder replied. 'Wanted to be there for when—' He cut himself off.

'When what?' Torj demanded.

Wilder snatched up Cal's bow and quiver of arrows, shoving them into the younger Warsword's chest before turning back to Torj. 'You'll see.'

Swearing under his breath, Torj left the room and, not waiting for the others, made his way back down through the tavern.

He didn't know why he kept coming back here, not when it forced him to remember. Not just the night at the Fox with her, but the two times he'd seen her since – each encounter worse than the last, leaving a bitter taste on his tongue, leaving him cursing the poisoner from Delmira.

But the truth was, she was everywhere. And the memories stayed with Torj long after he'd left the Laughing Fox and saddled his horse. They stayed with him long into the journey across the Harenth border and onto the Mourner's Trail that led to the fortress of Thezmarr.

As he approached, the strange power that had lingered under his skin became restless. For half a decade, he'd held it off by hunting down monsters and travelling across the seas, but now . . . something had awakened it from its slumber. He hated it. Hated the reminder of her and what she'd done.

No matter how much he fucked and fought, he couldn't get her out of his head. In his stronger moments, he clung to the rage that burned deep within. In his weaker ones, it was the flutter of her pulse beneath his thumb, the brush of her lashes against the tops of her cheeks that came back to him.

He had tried. Tried to be something more to her, to comfort her, and in the end, Wren had chosen her own path.

He'd been right to walk away. He knew it in his bones.

But if he'd been right, why was her lightning calling him home?

CHAPTER 5

Wren

'The "assassin's teapot", often referred to by alchemists as "the Ladies' Luncheon", was designed in the workshops of Thezmarr'

— *A History of Thezmarr*

In the corner of the room, an auburn-haired, long-limbed troublemaker was lounging in her tattered armchair. Resting his growler of mead atop a tower of old books, her sister's friend, Kipp Snowden, grinned at her.

'Long time no see, Elwren.'

With her hand still on her racing heart, Wren gaped at him. Time had been good to the strategist – his lanky frame had filled out over the years, and there was a roguish handsomeness to his crooked smile. A dull ache formed in her chest as she marked the changes. She could only imagine how different she looked through his eyes.

'Kipp,' she managed hoarsely. 'How long has it been?'

'Four years,' he said, taking a swig of his drink. 'At the one-year anniversary memorial at Thezmarr.'

That day was a blur to Wren, but for the Warsword at her side, and his warm, strong arms around her as she sobbed. She pushed it from her mind, as she had done every day since.

'What are you doing here?' she asked with a shake of her head, reaching for a bundle of dried herbs hanging from the rafters.

'Trying to get rid of me already?' Kipp pressed a hand to his chest dramatically before draining the rest of his mead. 'You wound me.'

Wren rolled her eyes and set about weighing florets of lavender. 'How did you know I was here?' She'd made damn sure her whereabouts weren't common knowledge.

'I have my ways,' Kipp said with infuriating slyness. 'Forgive me for thinking you'd appreciate a visit from an old friend. What did I do to deserve such a frosty welcome?'

A pang of guilt shot through Wren. She sighed, looking up from her work. 'Can I offer you something? Tea, perhaps?'

Kipp snorted. 'As if I'd ever accept a cup of tea from you.'

Wren hid her smile. The teapot she'd invented, which she'd used to poison the former Guild Master of Thezmarr, had earned her the moniker that had followed her ever since.

'Now,' Kipp went on, 'mead, ale, fire extract, wine, I'll accept.'

'I can poison those just as easily.'

'Not even you would ruin good liquor.'

'Perhaps not,' she allowed, wiping her hands on her apron and turning towards one of the cabinets on the far side of the cottage. There, she rummaged through the various bottles and concoctions before pulling out a flask and tossing it to Kipp. 'Knock yourself out.'

'Why does it sound like you mean that literally?' He raised the flask to his lips all the same. 'How go the alchemy studies?'

The question was like a blow to her gut. She glanced up, narrowing her eyes. 'Hard to study when you've been turned away from the only academy in the midrealms.' Tasting bitterness on her tongue, she turned away to rifle through a row of vials.

Wren had previously studied alchemy at Thezmarr, as most orphaned girls of the midrealms had. There, she'd found she not only had talent, but a passion for it as well. While her sister Thea's greatest pride had always been the might of her sword, Wren had always felt at home amid the subtler weapons of plants and potions.

After the war, she had discovered that Drevenor, the ancient academy for alchemists, had been reopened. Great masters had returned from beyond the Veil, new intakes of students recruited and ushered in to carry on the work of its forebears. Wren had desperately sought to be one of them.

And for five years, she had been denied.

Each rejection had come with a single reason: *No letter of recommendation.*

All Wren had done for the midrealms during the war, all her studies at Thezmarr – it hadn't been enough. Her former mentor, Farissa Tremaine, had refused to provide her with an endorsement.

'You are not yourself, Elwren,' the older woman had said. *'To send you to Drevenor now would make a danger of you. More so than you already are.'*

Wren clenched her jaw at the memory. She was more herself than she'd ever been, and her work ought to have been revered, not used against her.

Kipp was watching her with interest. 'Farissa hasn't budged, then?'

There was no keeping the note of resentment from her voice. 'Not an inch.'

'You don't think she has a point?'

'No.'

If she wasn't going to get peace and quiet, she might as well do something productive. She located the ingredients she was after: oil of ambrosia, apple seeds and dried bluebells, and returned to her workbench to survey the chaos before her.

'I still don't understand why you're here instead of at Thezmarr,' Kipp declared, swinging up onto his feet and perusing the cluttered cottage.

Wren watched him warily as he took in the tables groaning under the weight of yellowed tomes with worn leather covers, and the array of entangled roots and vines carpeting the uneven stone beneath his boots.

Kipp grimaced at the sight of a juvenile arachne preserved in a jar. The spider-like monster's many legs had curled around its abdomen in death. 'The fortress has got to be better than this.'

'It's not,' Wren said, gripping the edge of the table to still the tremor in her hands as images came back to her in violent flashes. The war-torn courtyard. The lashing shadows. The vortex of wind and rain at her fingertips. Her friends, Sam and Ida, with their heads on spikes, their eyes missing, tears of blood staining their cheeks. She could still taste the broken cry on her lips as her gaze had fallen upon them, the women she'd grown up with.

She was back there again. A ragged gasp escaped her, and Wren felt the sharp crunch of stone digging into her knees as she collapsed in the rubble beside the sister she'd only just come to know. Her eldest sister, Anya, was dead. And all Wren could do was clutch her lifeless hands.

'Wren?'

Kipp's voice was distant as the flashbacks dug their talons deeper into her mind, into her heart, and the unstable storm magic in her veins surged in response.

A jagged claw tore through the flesh at her throat, missing her jugular by a hair's breadth. Fiery pain lanced across her skin, and hot blood spilled down her front – hers, she realized distantly. She stumbled over a pile of rubble, lightning still surging at her fingertips.

'Wren,' someone gasped. 'You have to stop the bleeding—'

Torj. He was there. Lifting her magic-tipped fingers to the open wound at her throat. She struggled against him, but white-hot agony seared her as the Warsword cauterized the laceration with her storm power.

'I'm sorry,' he murmured. 'I'm so sorry—'

'Wren?' Someone was shaking her by the shoulders. 'Wren?'

It was the note of panic in Kipp's voice that wrenched her from her memory with a stifled gasp.

'What the fuck?' Kipp exhaled shakily, peering into her eyes, still grasping her upper arms. 'What *was* that? Are you—'

'Fine. Perfectly fine.' Wren turned away to catch her breath and wipe her clammy palms on her skirts, trying to hide the tremors. Outside the cottage, the wind howled ominously, enough to rattle the windows.

'That your doing?' Kipp asked, frowning at the storm breaking outside.

'Believe it or not, I'm not *always* responsible for the weather.' But Wren went to the window anyway and peered out at the darkening clouds sweeping across the crescent moon beyond the treeline. Her magic flickered in warning.

She had barely touched her power since she'd used it to pour her grief into the lands here. It was rare she wanted to. The cursed thing was unpredictable. There were times where she couldn't stop it coursing through her, tugging her towards something she couldn't see, filling her with the same all-consuming sensation she'd felt as her lightning surged through that iron hammer belonging to the Warsword.

Gathering herself, she turned to Kipp, arms folded over her chest. 'Tell me why you're here.'

Kipp took a long, fortifying pull from the flask. 'About that . . .'

CHAPTER 6

Torj

'Thezmarr has been the training ground
for every notable warrior in history. Novices
known as shieldbearers must pass the initiation test
to become Guardians of the midrealms, sworn to
protect the kingdoms. Very few Guardians hear the
call of the Great Rite. Fewer still pass its trials
to become a Warsword'

– *A History of Thezmarr*

Four years ago

A YEAR HAD passed, and they still hadn't taken the gods-damned spikes down from the walls. Torj knew that would be the first thing Wren noticed when she arrived, the first of many things that would tempt her to turn on her heel and run as far from the fortress as she could.

He winced as he rode through Thezmarr's gates, hating that after nine months, his thoughts were still of her. How she was, what she was doing . . . He hadn't seen her since that night at the Laughing Fox, since those willow-green eyes had pierced his own, and that delicate hand had rested against his chest.

'I have nothing left to give you, Bear Slayer.'

Wren had already started down a dark path, even then. And the whispers he'd heard since had only fuelled his worry for her. But he'd respected her wishes, kept his distance. He'd accepted the Warsword assignments that took him as far afield as possible.

But now, the dead called him back. And the black banners of mourning welcomed him home.

It had been one year since the end of the shadow war, and in the days of fragile peace, the new Guild Master, Audra, had ordered a memorial service to take place.

'You're late,' Talemir Starling said as he emerged from the stables, smiling warmly.

Torj swung down from his horse and embraced his fellow Warsword. 'Then so are you.'

'It's Ryland's fault.'

'That's right, blame the child.'

'Always do.' Talemir clasped his shoulder. 'I want to ask you how you are, but we really are late. The proceedings are down on the Plains of Orax.'

Together, the pair of Warswords headed beyond the Bloodwoods to the fields down by the cliffs where they'd lit funeral pyres a year ago. Wren had spoken over Anya's body then, had told them all how her sister had been *'a mosaic of contradictions, a blend of darkness and light'* . . . Torj couldn't help but think she'd been prophetic in that moment. Perhaps she had known even then what she would go on to do.

'Can you believe it's been a year?' Talemir said as they approached the plains.

'I don't know,' Torj said honestly. 'Sometimes it only feels like yesterday we were fighting monsters in that courtyard. Sometimes it feels like decades ago. And I don't know which worries me more.'

Talemir made a noise of agreement.

Torj peered through the trees, his pulse quickening with sudden nerves. He nearly balked at the sensation. He didn't get nervous.

And yet here he was, nervous to see Wren Embervale after all this time. He had known she'd be here. Wren's sister Thea had let slip in one of her letters that she'd badgered Wren into attending. But knowing and actually seeing her were two very different things. He hated the part of himself that wondered if she was looking for him too.

He and Talemir joined the gathered crowd, and Torj clasped his hands solemnly before him as Audra's words rang out across them all. His eyes wandered over the sea of black clad figures, their faces etched with the same tired grief that he felt in his very bones.

In the front row, he spotted Cal, his former apprentice. Cal had wielded his bow with deadly precision on the battlefield, a fierce glint in his eyes. Now, those same eyes glistened with unshed tears.

Cal's best friend Kipp stood beside him, all traces of his usual devious grin wiped from his face, his head bowed in respect. Beside them was Thea, wearing her Warsword armour as always, her bronze hair braided, her hand holding that of Wilder Hawthorne, who towered next to her.

Torj's gaze drifted to the left, where a group of veterans were clustered together, their battle-scarred faces grim. He spotted Vernich, the retired Warsword who he'd despised for the longest time before they'd fought side by side. The older warrior caught his eye and nodded, a silent acknowledgement of the blood they'd spilled together.

The breeze picked up, carrying with it the briny scent of the sea below. It seemed almost cruel, Torj thought, for the day to be so beautiful when they gathered to mourn so much ugliness and death.

Audra's words were lost to the wind, and Torj had even less chance of hearing them as he spotted a familiar head of bronze hair at the far edge of the crowd. His heart seized.

Wren.

Even from this distance, he could see the tension in her slight frame, the way her fists clenched at her sides. She stood with the rulers of the midrealms, and he was reminded with a jolt that as an heir of a kingdom, that was indeed where she belonged.

As though sensing his gaze on her, she turned, ever so slightly, her eyes locking with his.

For a moment, he couldn't breathe.

And then she dipped her chin in recognition before turning back to the ceremony. She offered nothing more, not so much as a second glance.

Torj felt as though the wind had been knocked out of him.

Beside him, Talemir let out a quiet whistle, looking from Torj to the Delmirian heir. 'Still haven't figured it out, then?' he asked under his breath.

'Nothing to figure out,' Torj muttered.

He knew he was kidding himself, for he hadn't taken his eyes off Wren since. She stood stoically as her sister, Anya, and her friends, Ida and Sam, were mentioned by name, dubbed war heroes by Audra herself as the mournful notes of a lute played. All around Wren, people were crying, leaning on one another, sharing their grief, their trauma from the war.

Not Wren.

Wren stood still and silent.

But when the eulogies and tributes ended and the crowd dispersed, she was nowhere to be seen. Dozens of people gathered around Torj and Talemir to pay their respects, but Talemir gave him a gentle push.

'Go find her,' he said, and barred the well-wishers so that Torj could slip away.

⁃

He found her in a secluded herb garden, tucked away in the Bloodwoods. There, she sat in the dirt, hunched over her knees, her body wracked with sobs. The sound was like a knife to his already bruised heart, and without thinking, he went to her.

'Wren . . .' he said softly.

She started, jumping to her feet, hastily palming her tears away. He knew she hated for anyone, even – or especially – him, to see her this vulnerable.

'What are you doing here?' she demanded, her voice raw.

He came closer, though he didn't reach for her, not yet.

She took a trembling breath and turned away to hide her face. 'Just leave.'

'I can't,' he said simply.

Wren stared, her face falling, as though his sincerity had devastated her. What else had she expected him to say?

And then a broken sob escaped her, and her legs buckled.

Torj caught her as she fell to the ground, drawing her to his chest, wrapping his arms around her. Nothing had ever felt more right, not as her arms slid around his waist, and her chest rose and fell against him as she tried to suppress her grief.

'It's alright to cry,' he murmured, his palm rubbing circles between her delicate shoulder blades. 'It's alright.'

Wren hiccupped against him, her whole body shaking. She clung to his shirt as it grew damp with her tears. Torj stroked her hair, clinging to the precious feeling of being the person to hold her when she was at her most vulnerable. Could she feel the thundering of his heart?

'I won't leave you like this,' he told her.

'Everyone leaves.'

'Not everyone,' he said, ignoring the ache in his own chest. Seeing her like this broke him, but there was also a small part of him that was relieved. It gave him a glimmer of hope – hope that she was allowing herself to *feel*, to grieve after so long. And the fact that she trusted him to be the one to hold her as she did? It meant more to him than he could say.

And so, despite how they'd left things last time, Torj didn't let go.

'They're gone,' she wept into his chest. 'Ida and Sam . . . Anya . . .'

'I know,' he murmured against her hair.

Wren cried herself hoarse, cried until she was trembling against him, until her short, shallow gasps became steady breaths once more.

'Where have you been?' she whispered. He could feel the heat of her pained words against his wet shirt.

'I thought you wanted me to stay away,' he said gently.

A broken laugh left her lips. 'What I want hardly matters now.'

'It matters,' he told her fiercely. 'It *always* matters.'

She looked up at him then. Her eyes were red-rimmed, her skin pink and blotchy, and yet she was still the most beautiful woman he had ever seen.

'Do you ever think about our last conversation?' she asked, wiping her face with her sleeve and drawing back from his embrace to study him.

Always. Torj felt her stare like a brand as she scanned his silver hair, the scar through his brow, and the V of tattooed skin his open shirt revealed, a hint of marred flesh there too.

He forced himself to keep his voice even. 'What about it?'

Tears were caught in her long lashes, bringing out the vibrant green of her eyes. She blinked up at him. 'What could have been . . . ?'

For nine months, *what could have been* was the one thought he'd tried to fortify himself against. The one thought that had haunted both his waking and dreaming hours. He had imagined it so many ways. He pictured them laughing in a tangle of sheets, her smile pressed against his bare skin, her hair fanned out across his chest. He fantasized about her legs spread beneath him as he drove into her wet heat, moans of pleasure on her lips. He had seen himself showing her his homeland, and all the darkness that came with it. No matter which way he pictured it, there had never been any hope of just one night, of walking away from her afterwards.

'Do you?' he asked at last, noting that she was watching him carefully, as though she might read the thoughts in his head by the expressions flickering across his face.

'I wonder if your outlook is still the same . . . ?'

Torj tensed. 'Yes.'

She broke away from him, the cold air sweeping in all too quickly.

'Pity,' she said, suddenly detached, her grief locked away once more in that box she buried deep.

Hurt lanced through Torj then, but he steeled himself against it, against her. 'I won't be your distraction, a balm to an open wound,' he told her. 'I can't give you what you want.'

'Clearly,' she replied.

A noise of frustration escaped him. 'I want to, Wren. Believe me. But the way you're coping . . . You think I don't know what you've been doing? I would know your methods anywhere. These poisonings have your name all over them . . . And I can't condone that path. It will destroy you.'

Eyes flashing, Wren rounded on him. 'I'm already destroyed. What's left but to take the corrupt down with me?'

Despair hit Torj like a blow. Was that what she truly thought of herself? He gripped her shoulders. 'Don't say that. I've seen what you can do, what you're capable of. You have so much to offer the world.'

'I do. Justice. Vengeance.'

But Torj shook his head. 'More than that. There's still light in you yet, Wren. I see it.'

She laughed, hollow and pained. 'You see what you want to see.' She shoved him away. 'There's no light any more. Only darkness.'

'Wren . . .' He reached for her, but she slapped his hand away.

'I don't need your pity,' she hissed. 'Just stay away from me, Torj. Far away.'

She looked around wildly, shaking her head at the sight of the bleeding trees, at the Mourner's Trail beyond the crest in the terrain, and then, finally, at him.

'Gods,' she muttered. 'This place is a poison. I'll never come back.'

And with that, she left.

Heart fracturing anew, Torj stared after her, understanding for the first time that where she was going, he could not follow.

She needed to face her monsters alone.

And only once she'd fought them amid the flames could she rise from the ashes.

CHAPTER 7

Wren

'Is it Thezmarr that's toxic, or is it me?
The longer I stay in the fortress, the harder
it is to tell the difference'

— *Elwren Embervale's notes and observations*

WREN HAD *SWORN* she'd never go back, and as she stood before the gates of Thezmarr, she remembered every single reason why. Kipp had refused to tell her the reason behind her summons, only that if she refused to accompany him to the fortress, the Guild Master had threatened to send Warswords to retrieve her – something Wren naturally wanted to avoid at all costs. But as a stable hand led her and Kipp's horses away, and the memories came barrelling into her at full force, she wished she had taken her chances with the warriors instead.

Sam, Ida, Anya... Their deaths had been the end and the beginning of so many things. The end of who she had been, the beginning of this new version of herself. Dark and uncompromising. Unfeeling and cold. Had it always existed? The monster within? Perhaps it had, and the shadow war had soldered it into place, into an unyielding part of her.

For a moment, it was as though it were yesterday. The screams echoed in her ears, the sickening scent of burnt hair from the shadow wraiths thick in her throat . . . The sight of Anya's lifeless body, and the flash of silver hair followed by the streak of an iron war hammer.

I have seen that gold will turn to silver in a blaze of iron and embers, giving rise to ancient power long forgotten . . .

Wren, Thea and Anya had been there when the Seer Queen of Aveum had spoken the premonition aloud, and Wren had watched as it came to pass before her very eyes. She'd allowed the Warsword to wield her power, an action that had set the wheels of fate in motion . . .

Though the scorch marks on the ground were gone, the past formed before Wren, so sharp and visceral she could feel the gush of blood from the wound at her throat.

'It has a long way to go yet,' a familiar voice said, hauling her back into the present.

Audra, the Guild Master of Thezmarr, stood by the gates, waiting. She wore dark riding leathers and a heavy cloak. Her hair was secured in a tight knot at the back of her head, and her glasses were perched on the end of her nose as always. Audra looked much the same, and it was this that jarred with the newness of the fortress around her.

As the fog of Wren's mind cleared, she realized the gates before her were not the original ones. Of course they weren't. Much had been destroyed in the final battle for the midrealms; and now, even years later, it was still in the process of being rebuilt. There were no spikes on these gates, no rubble piled within a courtyard littered with bodies. Only stonework and scaffolding.

'It's so different,' Wren murmured, craning her neck to take in the rest of the courtyard, suppressing the shudder that threatened to wrack her body.

Audra studied her. 'It will always serve as a monument to those we lost. To honour all of them and what they sacrificed.'

It took all of Wren's willpower not to flinch under the Guild Master's gaze, not to glance at Kipp for reprieve. 'I don't want to talk about them,' she said, busying herself with straightening her apron and adjusting the belt of tools and tinctures around her waist.

Audra was still watching her. 'And therein lies the problem, Elwren.'

Resting her hand on the strap of her oilskin satchel, she lifted her chin and faced Audra. 'Why have you summoned me here, Audra?'

The Guild Master's expression was unreadable. 'Follow me.'

As Wren started towards the steps, Kipp elbowed her. 'If you need a minute, she'd understand,' he whispered.

'I don't need a minute,' Wren replied sharply. She needed a *lifetime*, though still she worried it would not be enough.

'Gods, you Embervale sisters are stubborn,' Kipp muttered, following her up the stone stairs.

Inside, the Great Hall was much changed. Where three great monuments had once stood in reverence to the great war goddesses, the Furies, there was a gaping hole in the rafters. The ceiling had not yet been fully repaired. There were no high seats at the head of the hall, only rough sheets of timber resting on logs felled from the Bloodwoods, creating makeshift tables. Yet however different it looked, it was still the same place where Wren had broken bread with Sam, Ida and Thea for the most formative years of her life. It was still the place that she'd called home since she was an infant.

Struggling to swallow the lump in her throat, Wren crossed the cavernous hall, trailing after Audra. They had reached the doors on the other side of the hall when a blur of movement caught her eye.

'Wren!'

A familiar body crashed into hers, arms flinging around her neck and drawing her in hard.

Wren stiffened, unable to remember the last time she'd been touched. But a second later, she sank into the embrace. 'Althea Nine Lives,' she murmured into a bronze-and-gold braid.

Wren drew back just enough to glimpse Thea's face, bright and full of life. She had only seen her sister a handful of times over the past few years, and Thea had only grown more beautiful, more vibrant. Wren's heart swelled at the sight. The war might have broken her, but it had forged her sister anew, and she couldn't have been gladder for Thea's happiness.

'Where's your other half?' Wren asked, not quite ready to let her go just yet.

Thea beamed. 'On his way. I wanted to beat you here, so I rode ahead.'

Wren huffed a laugh. 'Of course you did.'

Kipp nudged his way between them and swung an arm over Thea's shoulder. 'Where's Cal?'

Thea rolled her eyes. 'Getting another stern lecture on boundaries and propriety, last I heard.'

Kipp looked crestfallen. 'I missed something that warrants a lecture like that?'

Wren watched the exchange unfold with an air of uncertainty. Things felt the same as they always had, but so much had changed.

'I'm sure it won't be the last,' Thea reassured him. 'He's taken one too many leaves from your book—'

Audra cleared her throat from the doorway. 'Your reunion can wait,' she said sternly. 'Althea, I trust you can escort Elwren to Farissa's quarters? She can fill you in.'

Wren blinked. 'Farissa? What does she—'

But Thea was already tugging her by the sleeve towards the corridor, leaving a disappointed Kipp by the door. 'Come on.'

Wren didn't need an escort; she knew the way to her former mentor's quarters like the back of her hand. She had spent years wearing a path in the stone pavers back and forth from the alchemy workshops below. Still, she let her sister lead her right to Farissa's door.

Thea squeezed her shoulder. 'Farissa will explain everything. I've got to meet the other Warswords, but we'll talk later?'

Wren nodded, watching as she strode back down the hall, out of sight.

Slowly, Wren faced the door, and raised her fist to knock.

'It's open,' the familiar voice called from within upon hearing the noise.

Steeling herself, Wren pushed the door inwards, and sucked in a breath.

Farissa's quarters were as cluttered as her own, every surface covered with scrolls, vials, jars with specimens floating inside, stacks of books, and the occasional animal skull. Her former mentor was hunched over her workbench, as she often was, and she didn't turn around as she greeted Wren.

'It's good to have you back, Elwren.'

'I'm not back,' Wren replied. 'Not for good.'

'No, I don't suppose you are.'

At last, Farissa faced her. She looked older than Wren remembered, with deep lines etched in her weathered visage and her bushy chestnut hair, streaked with grey, swept back into a low bun.

'Audra summoned me here,' Wren ventured woodenly. 'Told me you'd explain . . .'

Farissa sighed. 'You haven't forgiven me, then.'

It was no question, so Wren saw no reason to answer. Instead, she waited.

Nodding to herself, Farissa gestured to the workbench, where a sword lay across a sheet of linen. 'There has been an attempt on King Leiko's life in Tver. He's alive. Our Guardians managed to take this from the scene.'

Without thinking, Wren came closer. A strange film of something coated the steel of the blade; it smelled faintly of oranges. In its presence, Wren's magic, however unstable, seemed to shrink back, burrowing deeper within her.

Interesting, she thought as the hint of power receded from her fingertips.

'You feel it?' Farissa asked, watching her. 'Your sister could as well.'

Wren didn't want to talk to Farissa, not after everything her former mentor had taken from her. Five times she'd been denied that letter of recommendation. Five rejections from Drevenor. Five years of having her future dangled out of her grasp . . .

But curiosity came naturally to any alchemist, and Wren's had been piqued.

'What is it?' she heard herself ask, not taking her eyes off the strange substance.

'A form of alchemy we've never seen before,' Farissa answered. 'Weaponized and used specifically against a royal of the midrealms to subdue his magic.'

Wren blinked slowly. 'How . . . ?'

'From the limited study we've done, and from King Leiko's recount of the events . . . In the presence of this alchemy, royal magic is weakened – stifled enough that the royal themselves becomes vulnerable. With their power impaired, an attacker can get close enough to strike . . . and when they do, the alchemy can transfer to the wound itself, interfering with the royal's magic, even if it's not a killing blow.'

'What happened with King Leiko?' Wren said, schooling her features to remain neutral.

'He suffered a small cut to his forearm,' Farissa told her. 'But he felt his magic react to it – *withdraw* was the word he used. His powers have not been the same since. We don't yet know how lasting the effects will be.'

'How did the attackers get past his guards in the first place?'

Farissa sighed. 'That is for Audra to investigate. It is this unknown alchemy that concerns me. Wars have been started over less, Elwren.'

Wren's breath caught in her throat, her stomach bottoming out. And yet the words she forced from her lips were flat. 'That doesn't explain why I'm here. Especially after you've made your thoughts on my talent for alchemy so crystal clear.'

'It was never your talent in question,' Farissa said quietly, pulling on a leather glove and taking the weapon by its grip, tilting it so the strange substance shimmered more clearly in the torchlight.

'We may never have seen this kind of thing before . . . but it reminded me of you. Of your work during the war.'

Wren ground her teeth. 'Whatever you need to say, Farissa, just say it.'

'You weaponized alchemy for us in battle. And more than that, you once made a substance to mask Thea's power. You made manacles that could suppress a Warsword's strength. You have succeeded in understanding elements of alchemy that others have not . . . So we want your help discovering what exactly this new substance is. And whether we can create an antidote.'

Wren's blood ran cold as Farissa met her gaze.

'The midrealms need you, Elwren. Drevenor needs you.'

CHAPTER 8

Wren

'Both wolfsbane and nightshade are known for their interference with the heart'

– *Elixirs and Toxins: A Comprehensive Guide*

Two years ago

THE MIDREALMS NEEDED her to do this, needed her to strike another name from her ledger.

Edmund Riverton.

Wren crept through the shadows of the manor, her dark cloak concealing the vial of poison clutched in her hand. The high-ranking nobleman's lies and publications about her fallen sister had only been the start of his treachery during the war. He had also made generous donations to fund King Artos' experiments with shadow magic in the Scarlet Tower. Experiments that could have spelled the end of the midrealms as they knew them.

Edmund Riverton. She savoured the name on her tongue.

She had something special in store for this one.

Wren paused outside the study, twirling the vial of poison between her fingers. It was a concoction of her own design, and its debut was going to be spectacular.

Taking a steadying breath, she reached for the door handle—

'I wouldn't do that if I were you,' a familiar husky voice murmured behind her.

Wren spun around, poison-tipped dagger drawn, to find Torj Elderbrock leaning casually against the wall.

To her dismay, her breath caught at the sight of him. Time had been unfairly good to him – all six-foot-five of him. His shoulder-length hair was worn half-up, half down, with a lock of silver tumbling over his forehead. He was even more devastating than she remembered . . . Strong, dark features and a square, chiselled jaw covered in stubble gave him a brutal edge, as did the new scar he bore: a thin line slashed through his right eyebrow.

He didn't look away. As though they weren't outside her mark's study, as though there was all the time in the world, his eyes traced her face, her own scar, her body . . . which grew taut under his stare.

It had been two years since she'd seen him last, at the memorial where she'd broken down and sobbed all over him. She refused to flush at the embarrassing memory. A mistake. A moment of weakness.

But she was weak no longer.

'What are you doing here?' she hissed, sheathing the small blade at her belt.

'Stopping you from committing another murder,' he replied dryly.

Wren rolled the vial of poison between her fingers. 'That's no concern of yours.'

'I'm afraid it is.' Torj stepped closer, his broad frame now blocking her from the study door. 'Thezmarr is building a case against Riverton. Has been for years. Then he's to be put to trial.'

'Consider this me cutting out the middleman,' Wren said between gritted teeth, making to push past his massive frame.

Torj didn't budge. 'I don't think so.'

Her eyes narrowed. 'Still held tight on Audra's leash, I see. Some things never change.'

The Warsword's jaw tightened. 'And some things do. Look at

you, Wren. What happened to the woman I once knew? The one who fought for justice, not vengeance?'

'She died with her sister,' Wren snapped, her grip tightening on the poison. 'And her blood is on Riverton's hands.'

'Don't make me stop you by force,' Torj said, his voice low and deadly.

'You wouldn't.'

Danger flashed in the Bear Slayer's eyes. 'Try me.'

Wren's hand flew to her belt, not to her dagger, but to a vial of sedative—

But Torj was faster.

In a blur, he had her hands pinned to the wall behind her, his body braced over hers. 'I won't let you do this.'

Wren strained against his iron grip, her strength no match for his Furies-given power. 'Why? What's it to you? You know as well as I do that he deserves the fate he gets.'

'That fate is not up to you.'

'Care to bet?' she taunted, despite being completely immobilized. 'You're not here just out of the duty-bound goodness of your heart, Bear Slayer. What's his life to you?'

Torj recoiled at her words, which only served to confirm her suspicions.

'Well?' she said.

'People are whispering about the Poisoner. It's only a matter of time before they put two and two together – the Delmirian heir who poisoned the former Guild Master of Thezmarr and the person striking down those linked to the war.'

'All of those deaths were reported as natural. Or accidents,' she said lightly.

'There are those who know better.'

'Indeed there are. Which is how I know your concern isn't for justice, or for my reputation alone.'

A vein pulsed in his neck. 'If I deliver Riverton to Audra, she'll grant me a permanent post beyond the midrealms.'

'Are our kingdoms too small for you now?' she sneered.

'Fifty kingdoms would still be too small with you sucking up all the air,' he snapped.

Movement sounded from within the study, and both of them tensed.

When there was no further disturbance, Torj leaned in close. 'So you see, I won't be letting you poison him.'

Wren met his eyes defiantly. 'Perhaps not today.'

Torj's grip on her wrist tightened, and he smacked it against the wall, the shock and impact causing her to release the vial of poison she was holding.

She watched in horror as it fell from her grasp and tumbled to the floor, shattering across the timber.

Forgetting the mark beyond the doors, she let a noise of rage escape her. 'You—'

'Me,' Torj said grimly, forcing a damp cloth over her mouth and nose.

Wren struggled against him, but there was no stopping the sharp aroma and bitter taste. It was a double betrayal, for she knew exactly who'd supplied the Warsword with the tranquillizer.

Light spilled from the study door as Riverton at last came to investigate the commotion. But it was too late, for Wren's body was falling, her eyes fluttering closed.

And when she lost consciousness, it was with curses for Torj and Farissa on her lips.

·

Wren's mouth tasted of sawdust when she woke on the cold hallway floor of Edmund Riverton's manor.

Both the Bear Slayer and her mark were long gone.

With a groan, she sat up, body aching from a night on the hard, unforgiving surface. The remains of her shattered poison vial lay a few feet away, the shards of glass glinting in the soft morning light filtering through the windows.

A dark laugh bubbled from Wren at the absurdity of it all. How she – the Poisoner – had allowed a warrior brute to drug her. How after all her careful planning and experimenting, her ledger still had one name too many.

Getting to her feet, Wren dusted herself off and shook her head at the audacity of the Bear Slayer.

If that was how he wanted to play it, then that was how they'd play it.

But whatever the Warsword did, Edmund Riverton was a dead man walking.

CHAPTER 9

Torj

'My blood, my steel, are yours. I vow that in the end of days, I will answer the call'

—*Warsword oath to the Furies upon the Great Rite*

Two years ago

TORJ SAT ACROSS from Edmund Riverton in the prison carriage, the rhythmic clatter of hooves against cobblestones filling the silence between them. Weeks had passed since he'd thwarted Wren's assassination attempt on the nobleman, and the satisfaction of that victory still lingered.

Her mark sat whole and unharmed before him, on his way to face trial for his crimes. At last, Torj's work had earned him the post he'd coveted for years – a permanent position beyond the midrealms, far from the shadows of his past.

Wilder and Thea had asked him not to go, arguing that there was still much to be done in the wake of the war, that the remaining kingdoms still needed him. But Torj was weary. He wanted to see what realms afar had to offer. Tales of other-worldly magic, of cyrens and sea drakes, fascinated him. He'd even heard rumours of immortals with eternal youth and pointed ears . . . All of it had him yearning for a different kind of adventure.

After all this time, it was finally within his grasp. He only had to deliver Edmund Riverton to his justice.

The carriage lurched over a pothole and Riverton's face paled as they drew closer to the heart of Harenth's capital city, where his fate would be decided. While the infamous Scarlet Tower had been destroyed, a new prison had been built in its place to hold those who had committed war crimes, and it would likely house one more inmate by the end of the week. As such, Torj couldn't quite blame his captive for blanching.

But as he watched Riverton, a sense of unease crept over him. It wasn't just that the nobleman's face had lost its colour; his breathing was now laboured.

Suddenly, Riverton lurched forwards, his bound hands clawing at his throat as he gasped for air.

'Guards!' Torj shouted, surging to his feet and bashing a fist against the window.

Riverton collapsed, his body convulsing on the floor.

The carriage ground to a halt. Its door flung open as the guards rushed to investigate.

'Get a healer!' someone called.

A sickening feeling of dread settled at the pit of Torj's stomach as he knelt beside Riverton, watching his body twitch in familiar spasms. Commotion sounded on the streets outside, but Torj didn't look away as his prisoner's seizures slowly stilled, a vacant expression frozen on his face.

Reaching out, Torj searched for a pulse, but found none.

Edmund Riverton was dead.

And it was only then that Torj noticed the family crest pendant the prisoner had worn since his rescue was gone. How long had it been missing?

A shout of fury left Torj's lips, and he sent his clenched fist flying into the back of the carriage seat. The upholstery split, its stuffing spilling out, feathers floating down onto Riverton's lifeless body.

Wren.

༄

Audra looked up at Torj from behind her desk, no doubt marking the rage that darkened his expression.

'Riverton's dead,' he told her flatly. 'Poisoned on the way to his trial.'

The Guild Master dropped her quill, outrage flashing in her eyes. 'What?'

Torj didn't repeat himself; he simply waited for the inevitable.

'How did you let this happen?' Audra demanded, getting to her feet. 'How *could* this happen?'

'Wren.'

'I thought you handled her months ago.'

'I did,' Torj said, fighting to keep his cool. 'I stopped her assassination attempt. I took Riverton into custody. She must have found a way to get to him under our protection.'

Audra was shaking her head in disbelief. 'There were no disturbances reported? Nothing out of the ordinary?'

'No.'

Torj watched her pace across her study, her spectacles low on her nose, her brow furrowed.

'This is a disaster,' she muttered. 'Did it occur to you that *you* might be blamed? Having been in the carriage with him when he died?'

It hadn't. How could he have been so stupid, to think that he'd be above suspicion? The prisoner had died in his fucking arms.

'Why have *you* allowed this to happen?' The words burst angrily from his mouth. 'Why has her poisoning been tolerated until now? You've clearly known what's been going on.'

'Because until now, Elwren's actions, however vengeful, have aligned with the values of the guild. In many ways, she has done what we could not, without starting a civil war.'

'And Riverton? What was so different about him? Why did you deem *him* worthy of your intervention?'

Audra's expression hardened. 'He had information we wanted. Information that died with him, thanks to you.' She studied Torj with an unflinching, discerning gaze. 'You know what this means . . .'

Torj had the sinking feeling that he did.

'The offer of your post beyond the midrealms is rescinded. Immediately.'

Torj's stomach bottomed out. '*Audra*—'

She lifted a hand to silence him. 'That predicament aside, the deal was that you deliver Riverton to his trial to face justice. You failed, Bear Slayer. I have no choice but to grant that post to someone else now.'

Torj opened his mouth to argue, to give voice to all the furious resentment bubbling to the surface, to rage against the injustice of it all. But instead, he pushed the loose hair from his brow and shook his head. 'She's a fucking lost cause.'

Audra's eyes were still on him. 'Perhaps.'

'There's no "perhaps" about it,' he told her angrily, heading for the door.

Audra's voice followed him. 'Life has a way of coming back around on us, Torj. The wheels of fate are always turning, and sometimes, the people we least expect can be the ones to steer us back onto the right path . . .'

But with his dream of a post abroad shattered, and his Warsword reputation now at stake thanks to the Poisoner, Torj turned and fixed Audra with a cold, hard stare.

'If I never see her again, it will be too soon.'

CHAPTER 10
Torj

'Time does not, in fact, heal all wounds'

– Bear Slayer, Warsword of Thezmarr

'Elderbrock.' Audra's voice rang out across the war council chamber. 'A word.'

All around them, Warswords were filing out of the crammed space, squeezing around the same mahogany table that had always been there and shooting Torj pitying looks.

'What's that about?' Wilder muttered at his side, pulling back Thea's chair for her.

Over the past hour, Audra had confirmed what Wilder had told him on the road: that the King of Tver had been attacked in his own castle. An attempt had been made on his life, with a substance that had thoroughly unnerved their Guild Master. And Audra was not easily unnerved. In fact, Torj hadn't seen her so uneasy since the war.

The laws of the midrealms stated that an attack on any royal was an attack on all royals. Audra had given her orders: additional protection for the rulers of the midrealms, an increase in Guardians stationed throughout the kingdoms . . . But it didn't explain why she might need to talk to him in private.

'When I know, I'll tell you,' Torj replied in a low voice, eyeing the decanter on the nearby shelf with longing. It already felt like a fire extract kind of night.

When the last person left the chamber and the door clicked closed, Audra motioned to an empty chair. 'Sit.'

Tension bunched the muscles between his shoulders, but Torj did as the Guild Master bid.

'I have a special assignment for you, Elderbrock,' Audra told him, taking the seat opposite his, her expression as hardened as ever. 'One that might see you granted that post abroad you've wanted for so long.'

He didn't dare to hope, not after having his hopes dashed so many times before. 'I'm yours to command, Guild Master.'

Audra reached for the decanter and a pair of glasses, pouring a generous dram of amber liquid in each before sliding one across the table to Torj. 'I'm glad to hear it.'

Torj put the glass to his lips and relished the burn of the liquor down his throat. 'What is it this time? Trouble across the Veil border again?'

'It's a little more local than that,' Audra said slowly, taking a sip of her own drink.

Torj shifted in his chair, suspicion unfurling within. 'You're not usually one to drag things out . . .'

'True,' she agreed. 'I need you to take on one of the royal protection roles.'

'Where?'

'In Naarva.' Audra downed the rest of her fire extract. 'We'll be sending one of the royals there shortly and I will not leave them undefended.'

'Do you expect more attacks like the one on King Leiko?'

'An attack on one ruler is an attack on all rulers, so say the laws of the midrealms. It's just a precaution, but a necessary measure.' She hesitated before she spoke again. 'I need you to guard Elwren Embervale.'

Torj's glass froze midway to his mouth. 'Absolutely fucking not.'

Audra stared him down. 'What did you say?'

'I said, *absolutely fucking not*, Audra.' He put his drink back on the table, the taste suddenly bitter on his tongue.

'Were you not listening to the debrief just now?' Audra snapped. 'The rulers need to be protected.'

'She's not a ruler.'

'She's an *heir*,' Audra countered.

Torj raked his fingers through his hair. 'Trust me, Wren Embervale needs no protection. She's more likely to cause the trouble than be in danger herself. You know that better than anyone.'

'You will protect her, Elderbrock. It's an order.'

'Order someone else,' he said coldly. 'She hates me, and I'm not overly fond of her either. She's the one who lost me that post abroad in the first place, remember?'

Audra simply waited.

'Why not Thea?' Torj demanded, the Guild Master's silence only fuelling his frustration.

Audra shook her head. 'If the threat extends to royal bloodlines then to place the sisters together would make them the ultimate target. Thea has royal blood too – she will need to watch her own back.'

'Someone else, then. Cal. One of your new Warswords.'

'No.' Audra's voice matched her iron will. 'You *know* her. It was *you* who knew at the turn of the war that she was a threat. It was *you* who guessed what she had planned for the former Guild Master. You seem to be able to anticipate her . . . unpredictable nature.'

'Clearly not well enough. As you pointed out yourself after the disaster with Edmund Riverton.'

'Let's hope you learned your lesson then.'

'You can't be serious, Audra,' he implored.

'Have you ever known me to joke, Elderbrock? Your dislike of her only solidifies you as the best candidate. A bodyguard fraternizing with their ward is strictly forbidden, but with your hostile history, you'll no doubt be able to keep yourself in check. Or do you disagree?'

Torj was ready to hit something. 'I assure you, the last thing I'd ever do would be to get involved with Elwren Embervale.'

'Good,' Audra said. 'That makes this simple. She is going to Drevenor Academy, and you will protect her. There will be no need to interfere with her training and studies; your duty to is address outside threats only. Guard Elwren and the post abroad is yours.'

Torj had heard enough. He shoved his chair back and made for the door. Audra may have been the Guild Master of Thezmarr, and though it was his duty to obey her orders, there was one thing firmly in her way, one thing saving him from this Furies-forsaken nightmare of an idea.

'She'll never agree to this,' he told her.

Audra, however, didn't falter. 'Leave that to me, Elderbrock. The only thing I need to know now is: will you?'

CHAPTER 11

Wren

'The true weight of names can never be measured'

– Elwren Embervale's notes and observations

WITH FARISSA'S WORDS still echoing in her mind, Wren found herself in one of the only surviving alchemy workshops in the fortress. The very one in which she had taken her first life – where she'd poisoned Osiris, the former Guild Master of Thezmarr, with her assassin's teapot.

She could still see the pleading, choking bastard on the floor. The image comforted her. She'd taken her revenge on a man who'd been largely responsible for her eldest sister Anya's suffering – for the hard life she'd lived, torn apart from her family. Because of Osiris and Artos, Anya had been framed as a harbinger of shadow: the Daughter of Darkness, they had called her. Well, Wren had taken up a part of that dark mantle now.

'Is it always so . . . brutal?' Thea had asked in this very room, as they'd stared at Osiris' purple face and blood-lined teeth.

'Only if you make it so,' Wren had replied.

And so, the Poisoner had been born.

She'd leaned into that reputation ever since, had let it shield her from the world, had revelled in the power of it.

'Taking a trip down memory lane?' Audra asked as she entered the workshop, her eyes fixed on the same spot Wren's had lingered on earlier.

'Would you blame me?' Wren said.

'Revenge is a precarious path to walk . . . It is often said that those who seek it should dig two graves.'

Wren's shoulders tensed, her hands curling into fists at her sides. 'Because of him, because of all of them . . . I am older than Anya ever got to be, older than Sam and Ida ever were. Their lives, their futures, were stolen from them.'

'They were,' Audra allowed. 'But no amount of poison will change that now.'

Wren didn't argue. She simply thought of the box of trinkets in her possession, and how the acquisition of each one had offered her some semblance of reprieve.

As though reading her mind, Audra spoke again. 'All that anger has to go somewhere, Elwren. To turn it inwards is to poison oneself as effectively as taking a dose of your beloved nightshade. To turn it outwards is to eventually poison the ones you care for. Either way, a path of destruction is created, and you will be at the helm.'

Wren lifted her chin in defiance. 'So where do you suggest I direct my anger, Guild Master?'

She suppressed the urge to fidget under Audra's gaze. Her former warden seemed to be weighing up her next words, the silence only making room for Wren's unease to fester.

'You spoke with Farissa?' Audra asked at last.

'Briefly.'

The Guild Master pulled a crumpled scroll from her pocket and held it out to Wren. 'Then it's time I gave you this.'

Wren took the piece of parchment and unrolled it.

Dear Elwren Embervale,
On behalf of the esteemed faculty and administration of Drevenor Academy, it is with great pleasure that I extend this letter of offer

to you. Your talents in the field of alchemy and your efforts during the shadow war have been noted, as outlined in Master Farissa Tremaine's recommendation.

In light of recent events, and after careful consideration, we invite you to join our prestigious institution. At Drevenor, you will have access to state-of-the-art foundries and greenhouses, renowned faculty members, and a vibrant community of scholars and practitioners. We expect all our students to uphold our values and rules of discretion, all of which will be detailed in orientation after the welcome gala. Details enclosed.

Please signify your acceptance of this offer by sending a raven to the Office of Admissions no later than the end of the month.

Once again, congratulations on earning your place. We look forward to welcoming you into our esteemed ranks.

Yours sincerely,
Remington Belcourt
High Chancellor

Wren didn't bother to hide the trembling in her hands this time. She simply stared at the letter, at the elegant script telling her that after five years of rejection, her moment had finally come.

'There is one condition,' Audra said coolly.

Wren didn't look up from the parchment, her heart hammering wildly. 'Oh?'

'You will be accompanied by a guard. By order of the Guild.'

Wren *did* look up then, incredulous. 'What?' She was sure she must have misheard, but Audra's mouth was set in a hard line. 'Audra, that's hardly necessary. Why in the midrealms would I need—'

'As per the laws of the midrealms, an attack on one royal is an attack on all. I told your sister for years that she wasn't invincible. Nor are you.'

Wren made to argue, but Audra's glare alone silenced her.

'Am I mistaken?' the Guild Master demanded. 'Do you or do you not wish to attend Drevenor?'

Wren's stomach squirmed. The thought of being under constant surveillance left a bitter taste in her mouth, but it was *Drevenor*. Her youthful dreams of becoming a Master Alchemist were suddenly that much closer.

Her pride was like a sharp rock in her throat, but she swallowed it anyway. 'Who have you assigned to me, then?'

'The very best.' Audra pushed her spectacles up the bridge of her nose. 'Someone who knows how to keep you safe.'

Wren's skin prickled, and her storm magic flickered as if in warning. 'Who?'

'Who do you think?' came a husky voice from the door.

She'd know that voice anywhere. That lightning-kissed hair, those deep-blue eyes, that spark in her chest.

Torj Elderbrock, the silver-haired Bear Slayer, leaned against the frame, exuding an intense energy that seemed to vibrate through the air, through *her*.

Raw. Untamed. Masculine.

A challenging smirk graced his lips. 'I'm your new bodyguard, Embervale.'

CHAPTER 12

Torj

'Lightning can, in fact, strike the same place twice'
– Bear Slayer, Warsword of Thezmarr

IF HE COULD have painted the look on her face, he would have. Incredulity and rage entwined into one frustratingly beautiful package. That alone was almost worth the inconvenience to Torj.

'No,' Wren declared, folding her arms over her chest and pinning him with a glare that could have felled a lesser man.

'I'll leave you two to discuss the particulars,' Audra said, having the good sense not to meet his gaze before pushing past him, leaving the Warsword and Poisoner to their showdown.

They hadn't seen each other since he'd stopped her from killing Edmund Riverton, over two years ago now. She wore the same simple linen gown she always had, its hem muddied, likely from picking herbs in the wilderness somewhere. The fabric brushed over the tops of her sturdy leather boots, the laces half undone.

Anything soft about her had been carved away, and what remained had hardened into steel. The angles of her face were harsher, the glint in her green eyes was more determined, and that wicked scar that ran down the length of her throat . . . It showed the world just how fearless she was.

The web of scars across Torj's heart prickled, as though something lingering in his marred flesh recognized its maker—

'If you've finished ogling me . . .' Wren's ire did not abate. 'I thought you were in the new world, beyond the border of the old Veil?'

Torj didn't tell her that his post had never come to pass. He didn't want to give her the satisfaction. Instead, he offered her another sly smile that he knew would infuriate her. 'Keeping tabs on me, are you, Embervale?'

'You wish, Bear Slayer.' Her words were clipped, ice-sharp. 'What were you thinking? Putting your hand up for this ridiculous job?'

He tensed, the scars over his heart still prickling. 'You think I *asked* for this?'

'Then tell Audra to find someone else,' Wren retorted.

'You think that wasn't the first thing I said to her? But it doesn't work like that.'

The mere sight of her brought back every ounce of anger he'd felt in the aftermath of Edmund Riverton's death, at how she'd so thoroughly screwed him over. And yet, Torj couldn't help it: his eyes travelled over her once more, a sweeping dip from head to toe and up again, taking in the tight cinch of her waist beneath a leather belt that housed a dozen tools and vials – poisons, no doubt. By no means did it make him less furious with her, but there was also the bodice that pressed her breasts together in a way that made his cock pulse alongside his agitation.

Her throat bobbed as though she could sense the nature of his thoughts, the long, white scar shifting with the movement. 'Then tell me . . . how does it work?' Her eyes darted to the floor, to the exact spot where she'd killed Osiris in the most calculated of ways. Torj wasn't likely to forget that. He only needed to be careful she didn't poison *him*.

'You do as I say, and I keep you safe.'

Wren gave a dark laugh. 'Just like that?'

'Just like that, Embers.'

'Don't call me that,' she snapped.

It gave him more joy than it should have. 'Oh? Should I call you something else instead? You've more than earned the title of the Poisoner . . . What's your ledger at now? Seven? Eight?'

A muscle flickered along Wren's jaw. 'Now who's keeping tabs?'

Everyone knew that Thea was the outwardly rebellious sister, the one who had been ruthless and ambitious from the start, but what fewer people knew was that Elwren Embervale was all those things too, only more dangerous. Because no one had known about those traits in her until it was too late. No one except Torj. Torj knew, and he'd learned that lesson several times over.

Since the start of the war and the battles that followed, that brutal edge to Wren had sharpened, and was always poised to cut. She was beautiful as always, but now she was honed like a blade. Torj could feel the heat of her in his chest, beneath those lightning-shaped scars that seemed to answer to her. Without thinking, he rubbed his sternum, and Wren's gaze followed his hand to the triangle of tattooed skin revealed beneath his shirt.

'See something you like?' he taunted.

Those stormy eyes narrowed. 'Hardly.' She pushed past him. 'Just stay out of my way, Bear Slayer.'

Every muscle taut with awareness, he was left alone in the doorway, staring after her, fists clenched at his sides, her scent lingering in the air.

A low whistle sounded from the other end of the corridor. 'You certainly haven't won any favours.' Wilder approached him with a grimace.

'I'm not here to win over princesses,' Torj muttered, trying to force down the temper that had bloomed in Wren's wake. 'I'm here to do a job.'

Wilder snorted. 'Keep telling yourself that.'

Torj fully intended to. He'd spent the better part of half a decade carving a brutal path through the midrealms and beyond, leaving a trail of bloodshed and conquest in his wake. All in a desperate bid to forget the green-eyed poisoner. Now, her magic seemed to flicker deep within him, a lone ember remaining from a battle long past.

'You were supposed to be the wise one. What happened to all those pearls of wisdom you forced onto me over the years?' Wilder's tone was apprehensive.

Torj realized he was still staring down the now empty hall. 'People change.'

'I can see that. Don't let it be for the worse.'

Torj gave a huff of irritation. 'I liked you better when you were a moody bastard.'

'Suppose there's only room for one of those in this fortress.'

'Hilarious.' Torj surveyed his friend, realizing that he carried several books under his arm. 'You studying for something I don't know about?'

'No.' To his surprise, Wilder held them out to him. 'You are. Audra said to give these to you . . . *Vigilance and Valour* sounds like riveting stuff.'

Torj turned the top tome over in disbelief. '*Vigilance and Valour: Tactical Training for Professional Bodyguards* . . .' he read aloud. 'You've got to be fucking joking.'

Wilder clapped him heartily on the shoulder. 'I'd say have fun, but . . .'

'Oh, fuck off, Hawthorne.'

Amusement gleamed in his friend's eyes before he shrugged. 'Maybe you'll be exactly what each other needs.'

'Or maybe we'll kill each other.'

'Or that,' Wilder allowed.

Rubbing his aching chest, Torj sighed heavily. 'I guess we'll see soon enough.'

༄

At dawn the next day, their party of five – Torj, Wren, Farissa, Cal and Kipp – stood on the docks, waiting to board the *Sea Serpent's Destiny* to Naarva, where Drevenor Academy awaited.

After spending the night locked away in her rooms with Thea, Wren had insisted that they slip away without fanfare or farewells. According to her, there was no time to waste.

The sea air was brisk, for which Torj was eternally grateful. His body hadn't cooled down since arriving at the fortress, and he was loath to admit it had anything whatsoever to do with the irritating poisoner at his side.

'I have a suggestion,' he said to Wren.

'Furies save us,' she muttered.

Eyes narrowing, he pushed on. 'We need to get you learning self-defence. Even a few additional manoeuvres could make all the difference. You need to be aware of your surroundings at all times.'

Wren fixed him with a cold look. 'I know the basics. Every Thezmarrian is taught—'

'You mean those little lessons the weapons master gave you when you were what? Twelve?' He laughed.

'I'm not taking lessons from you.'

Torj shook his head in disbelief. 'Thea *begged* us to train her.'

As soon as the words left his lips, he knew it was the wrong thing to say.

Wren's expression darkened. 'I'm not my sister.'

He passed a hand over his face in frustration. 'I've been ordered to protect you.'

'So protect away, Bear Slayer. If I need to use fancy defensive moves, it means you're not doing your job properly. My time and skills are needed elsewhere.'

'Gods,' he muttered.

'Are you forgetting that I'm a storm wielder, Warsword? Or that I saved you more than once during the war?'

His eyes met hers in a blaze of fury. 'I forget *nothing*, Embervale.'

'Could have fooled me,' she countered, her chin lifted in defiance. Torj had seen that look before, when she was battling not only with someone else, but against something within. He knew that feeling well enough himself.

'Look,' he said, forcing down his frustration. 'We've known each other a long time. We go way back, before the war. Don't you remember how we first met—?'

'No,' Wren said bluntly. 'I don't.'

'Liar.' Torj checked his temper. 'I assure you, Poisoner, I like this even less than you, but we have to work together—'

'There is no *we*.'

'There is now.' He wasn't going to let her get away with this. She was being childish, stubborn and a certified pain in his arse. She had cost him his post abroad once before; he'd be damned if he let her do so again.

Wren made to leave, and his hand shot out, grasping hers. Her skin was warm and soft beneath his fingers as they closed over her palm. He had to suppress a gasp of shock.

The touch was electric.

It was the first they'd shared in over two years, and it was charged with every bit of storm power he remembered. Raw energy danced across the lines of his scars, and he ground his teeth against the sensation.

But he wasn't done.

'We are bound together, you and I,' he growled. 'Ever since you blasted me full of lightning in the war, Embervale. There's no undoing it. I didn't ask for that, and I didn't ask for this either . . . But here we fucking are.'

Her gaze dropped to where he held her hand.

'You may not want it,' he breathed, feeling her pulse flutter beneath his touch. 'But you are mine to keep safe.'

A tempest broke in Wren's eyes. 'I am no such thing,' she spat, jerking out of his hold as though burned. She stormed off to where Cal was motioning for their party to board the *Sea Serpent's Destiny*.

A light chuckle sounded at Torj's side, and he turned to find Kipp grinning from ear to ear.

'She really hates you,' the strategist said cheerfully.

CHAPTER 13

Wren

'The human mind holds more poison than any plant'

– Elwren Embervale's notes and observations

THE WORST POSSIBLE place for Wren to be was trapped on a boat with *him*. His presence, constantly in her periphery, was distracting at best, downright infuriating at worst. After all this time, after all the disappointments, she was on her way to Drevenor Academy . . . and now it was being overshadowed by the hammer-wielding Bear Slayer.

Several times, she found herself hauled back into the war years, Queen Reyna's words echoing in her mind more than once: *giving rise to ancient power long forgotten* . . . A shiver raked up her spine. Wren had never told Torj about the premonition, and frankly, she saw no need to do so now. It was all in the past – a past she'd rather forget.

As they set sail, the ever-present current of lightning stirring beneath her skin put her on edge. With him at her side, her magic had awakened to new heights, and all her attempts to suppress it with tonics and potions had failed. It simply demanded to be felt.

In the privacy of her cottage, it was far easier to deal with the aftermath of the battle of Thezmarr and the memories that plagued her at the hint of a particular smell or sound. Here, with a Warsword guard, and Cal, Kipp and Farissa nearby, she felt raw and exposed. She was used to channelling those feelings into her ledger of marks, into planning her next poisoning, but as the *Sea Serpent's Destiny* rocked over the waves, she could do nothing.

A familiar hand offered her a steaming cup – a hand roughened by years of working with chemicals and potions.

Reluctantly, Wren took the tea from her former mentor with a stiff nod of thanks.

'You must be excited,' Farissa ventured quietly.

'I will be, when I get there,' Wren replied, taking a sip and suppressing a satisfied sigh. It was dark and sweet, just as both she and Farissa liked it – a small testament to the countless hours they'd spent together before the war.

'Do you understand why I did it?' Farissa asked, looking out to the foam-tipped waves.

Unexpected tears stung Wren's eyes, and she was keenly aware of the Warsword's presence, only mere feet away. 'Why you denied me a place at Drevenor all these years? Why you thwarted my chances at the one thing I wanted?'

'Yes. Do you understand why?'

Wren blinked back the emotion rising to the surface. 'I was your most promising student. Your apprentice. I worked for you for *years*.'

'You were. And you did.'

'The answer is no,' Wren said, stripping the hurt from her voice. 'I don't understand why you did it.'

'What am I a Master Alchemist of, Elwren?'

'Healing.'

'And what was the specialty we shared at Thezmarr?'

Wren ground out the word again. 'Healing.'

Farissa nodded. 'Exactly. You took what you'd learned about preserving life and made it about revenge. About death.'

Wren stared at her. 'You thought I would let those who funded and benefitted from the war get away with it? Sam and Ida were *brutalized*, Farissa. They were your students too.'

'I know.' Her former mentor sighed heavily, drinking her tea, the lines on her face deepening with resignation. 'You will understand. One day.'

Wren bit back a sarcastic remark. She didn't appreciate being patronized, but Farissa was the only one who'd actually been to Drevenor, who knew what it was like.

'You've never talked about the academy,' she said instead. 'Not in any detail.'

Farissa glanced at her, recognizing the truce Wren had called. 'I took an oath of secrecy. As you will.' She cupped her weathered hands around her mug. 'But as you're soon to be a novice there . . .'

Wren knew Farissa was sharing out of guilt, but she didn't stop her.

'Drevenor had been established for centuries, known for producing the most talented masters in our field. But it disbanded when Naarva fell to the shadow wraiths in the lead-up to the war. Its acolytes spread far and wide across the midrealms and beyond the Veil, some retraining in other trades and professions, others trying to continue their studies, albeit with far fewer resources . . . You know how that went,' she added. 'We did what we could at Thezmarr, but it was always a guild for warriors above all else.'

'I'm well aware.'

'What we didn't know was that the academy fell under Talemir Starling's protection. Even during the war, it was not ravaged like the rest of the lands. It was being re-established even then, under the cloak of darkness. And the masters who were still alive, still practising, returned to open its doors once more.'

'And you?' Wren asked, wondering how much salt Farissa would add to the wound. 'Have you been back since?'

'Yes. I've taught healing there on and off for the past few years.'

'And yet you kept me out.' Wren swallowed the lump in her throat and tossed the dregs of her tea over the side of the ship. 'Imagine where I'd be, had you not stopped me.'

'I do, Elwren. Every day,' Farissa said sombrely, meeting her gaze. 'And it terrifies me.'

Wren clenched her jaw. 'So why now?'

Farissa's answering expression was grim. 'Because the alternative terrifies me more.'

Clouds gathered on the horizon, and Wren could almost feel the incoming rain on her skin. It made her all the more restless. The conversation with Farissa simmered in her mind like a potion bubbling over a flame. The bitterness that lingered in Wren's chest was almost painful, and yet, she could not move past it. She paced up and down, finally making for the starboard side—

Only for a towering mass to block out the weak midday sun and follow her across the deck.

She clicked her tongue in frustration, coming to an abrupt halt and spinning on her heel to face the Bear Slayer.

'You're being ridiculous. Can I no longer move a few paces on my own? What's next? You'll follow me to the bathing quarters? Rescue me from the soap suds?'

The corner of Torj's mouth twitched. 'Only if you ask nicely, Embers.'

Wren flushed. 'What have I told you about that name?'

'Can't recall.'

A noise of pure exasperation escaped her and she threw her hands up. 'You're impossible.' But as she made for the other side of the deck, the ship lurched over a wave, and she lost her footing—

Strong, warm hands circled her waist, catching her midfall.

'What were you saying about walking a few paces on your own?' His voice rumbled against her as his breath tickled the shell of her ear.

'Get off—'

But as she attempted to push him away, the ship gave another sudden lurch, water slapping against the hull and spilling across the deck.

Heat enveloped her, and her face met a hard wall of muscle.

Black cedar and oakmoss, she realized, the scent washing over her as Torj held her tightly, his arm around her back while he gripped the rigging with the other. He pulled her close as the ship rocked violently beneath them, sea water still spraying up from below.

His body was a shield. A safe harbour.

And Wren wouldn't stand for it.

Ignoring the heave and pitch of the vessel, she twisted out of his grip and lunged for the railing.

'Embervale,' he shouted over the roar of the waves and calls of the crew. 'Get below deck.'

'I'm fine where I—'

His expression turned mutinous. 'I wasn't asking.' In a blur of movement, he was suddenly there, his hands on her, lifting her—

'*Don't you dare*,' she hissed.

He tossed her over his damn shoulder.

'I vowed to protect you at all costs,' he growled, carrying her to the ladder that led to the cabins below. 'Even if it's from your own damn stubbornness.'

Wren's cheeks flamed as she realized their little display was visible to everyone on board. 'I'm going to murder you in your sleep, Warsword,' she hissed.

But the Bear Slayer only gave a dark laugh as they descended below deck. 'I'd welcome some sleep, Embers. So be my fucking guest.'

She kicked her legs and flailed against his hold to no avail. His grip was iron – not enough to hurt, but immovable.

'If you'd done some self-defence, you might have been able to free yourself,' he said, approaching her cabin door.

In a fit of rage, Wren summoned her lightning and sent several pulses into the brute of a man.

'That's cute.' He didn't so much as flinch. 'It almost tickled.'

And with that, he threw her onto the bed and slammed her door on his way out.

Wren stared after him for a moment before she screamed into her musty pillow.

CHAPTER 14

Wren

'The true alchemist fears not the crucible, for within its embrace, even the unyielding may be transformed'

— *Alchemy Unbound*

SHADOWS POURED FROM the vortex at her feet and wrapped around her limbs like ropes. They dug into her flesh, binding her tighter and tighter, cords of onyx lashing at her, the pain bright and fierce.

She screwed her eyes shut as the next onslaught of pain began.

Make it stop, make it stop—

Wren woke with a scream. The sheets were tangled around her legs and she fought to catch her breath, a river of perspiration between her breasts.

Her door flew open, pale torchlight from the hallway beyond illuminating the giant mass of a Warsword filling the door frame. He was barefoot and bare-chested, his leathers slung low across his hips and his hammer poised to strike. Eyes wild, he charged inside in a single stride, searching her room with brutal efficiency. His attention went to exactly where the shadows had been in her dream, as though he knew precisely where she'd seen them, where they'd struck her, until at last his gaze fell to where her fists clenched the blankets, and where her hair had come unbound, wild around her face.

'It's nothing,' she croaked. 'Nothing happened.'

Torj crouched beside the bed, resting his hammer across his bare shoulder. 'It's not nothing.' His voice was raw, as though he'd been right there with her, as though the darkness had wrenched screams from his throat as well.

Wren exhaled shakily. Though they weren't touching, he was close enough that she could feel the heat radiating from his skin. The torchlight cast a gilded glow across the warrior: the corded muscles of his neck and shoulders, the sculpted curves of his biceps, the hard sinew of his forearms. Hesitation flickered across his face before he reached for her, and in the quiet seconds between possibility and action, Wren pictured it: being pulled into those arms, pressing her lips to the column of his throat.

It took all her willpower not to lean into him. She had done so once before, and it had left her weak. She hated that his presence seemed to quell that panicked terror inside her.

Wren took a moment to catch her breath, waiting for her heart rate to slow, if that were at all possible considering who knelt before her. For a breath, her fear abated – replaced by something full of fire.

Until her eyes fell to the web of scars marring the flesh across Torj's tattooed chest.

Guilt lanced through her at the sight. She had done that to him.

'Get out.' It was barely a whisper.

He flinched as though she'd struck him.

'Get out,' she said, louder this time.

Torj stood, ridges of muscle rippling, that same intense energy charging the air around them. 'Call a night terror of that magnitude "nothing" again and I'll be guarding you from your bedside next time,' he growled, before slamming the door closed behind him.

With panic still gripping her heart in a vice, Wren reached for the box of trinkets beneath her bed, opening it in her lap.

There, she counted each memento: the gold-framed monocle, the foreign coin, the pendant, the pocket watch, the signet ring, the inkwell, the brooch, the drake figurine, the coin ... She recalled each poisoning with a small sense of comfort. She had taken her revenge; she had wiped the stain of their existence from the midrealms.

Yet it did not keep the shadows at bay.

The next day, Wren spent the early hours of the morning in her cabin, trying to forget the feeling of his hands on her. Each time it had happened, her heart had quickened. Each time, her magic had seemed to recognize its counterpart, stirring up longing she had no business feeling. Two years ago, he'd interfered with her ledger. His antics that night had cost her six months' worth of work and snatched a mark right from her grasp. No, there was nothing to be stirred up but fury.

Resolved to ignore him, Wren dressed and piled her hair atop her head in her usual messy bun, donning her belt of tools and tinctures. She opened the door to find Torj waiting outside her cabin like nothing had happened.

Despite the rage coursing through her, Wren deemed that pretending was indeed the best course of action. At least this way she could deny she had ever imagined the press of his body against hers. Mercifully, the upper deck was bustling with other passengers, which gave her something to look at other than him.

The constant company was grating, be it the brutish Bear Slayer himself or Farissa, Cal, or Kipp. The fresh sea air soothed her, though, shaking loose a piece of herself that she'd kept tightly caged away.

She had barely been resting her arms against the rail for a moment, breathing in the briny breeze sweeping across the deck, when Kipp sidled up beside her, an entire loaf of bread in his hands.

Cal took up the space on her other side with an apologetic grimace. Wren didn't need to look over her shoulder to know that the Warsword was close behind them. She could practically feel the heat of his glower on her back.

'Fancy a bite?' Kipp offered between mouthfuls. 'Baked fresh this morning.'

'No, thank you,' she said, though she couldn't remember the last time she'd eaten.

Kipp shrugged. 'Suit yourself.'

Wren glanced at the strategist warily. 'Remind me again what you're doing here?'

'Rude,' Kipp scoffed, nearly choking on the piece of bread he was chewing. 'But I hear there's an excellent tavern within the academy grounds.'

'Kipp . . .' she warned.

'You ruin all the mystery, Your Queenliness.'

Wren's patience was wearing thin already.

Kipp gave a dramatic sigh, as though she truly was spoiling all his fun. 'Audra believes that as Thezmarr's best strategist—'

'*Only* strategist.'

Cal snorted at that.

'Semantics,' Kipp retorted. 'As Thezmarr's *best* strategist, they think I should have a handle on some of the disciplines being taught at the academy.'

'Like what? I don't see you brewing anything unless it's a new type of sour mead.'

'And what a *worthy* pursuit that would be,' he beamed. 'But no. Thezmarr needs to be abreast of what's happening. I'm acting as an ambassador of the fortress.'

Wren turned to Cal, who cut a fine figure as a Warsword now. 'And you?'

Cal grinned proudly. 'I've been assigned to the protection of a prestigious guest lecturer. I was specially requested.'

Wren's brows shot up. 'Who? Anyone I would know?'

Cal straightened his posture, a hint of satisfaction in his voice. 'He's from abroad, so probably not, but apparently he's very renowned in his circles. Professor Vulpine.'

Wren tried to recall the names on the spines of her books back in her cottage, and those she'd read time and time again during her years at Thezmarr. She shook her head. 'I don't think I know of him. But good for you, Cal. Though, are you sure you can't switch with the Bear Slayer?'

Behind them, she heard the Warsword in question cough loudly into his breakfast.

But Cal was all seriousness. 'I may have passed the Great Rite, but Torj has been a Warsword for *years*. There is no one better equipped to protect you.'

'The vote of confidence is noted and appreciated, Callahan,' Torj called out.

'Suck-up,' Kipp snickered.

'I don't *need* protection,' Wren muttered.

'Anyway,' Kipp said loudly. 'Is there a bar on this boat? Preferably with a bevy of ladies who need entertaining?'

'I did hear that the captain's daughter is eager to meet Thezmarr's best strategic mind,' Wren replied.

Kipp's brows shot up. 'Really?'

Wren couldn't help but laugh, the strangely foreign sound catching her off-guard. 'No.'

Kipp had the gall to look offended. 'That was cruel.'

'You make it too easy, Kristopher.'

She left them on deck, ignoring the shadow of the Warsword who followed at a distance, pretending she didn't notice the way his hand constantly drifted to the scars on his chest.

CHAPTER 15
Torj

'The phenomenon of magical transference, in which the effects of a curse are passed from one individual to another, remains one of the most enigmatic and poorly understood aspects of the arcane arts'

— *Magical Transference*

THERE WAS SOMETHING wrong with his scars. A strange vibration plagued the marred flesh there, as though his proximity to their maker created a constant echo of the power that had once hit that very point.

'Are you alright?' Cal asked, motioning to where Torj had been absentmindedly rubbing the old wound.

Torj looked down, gritting his teeth against the strange sensation. 'It's been bothering me lately.'

'After all this time?' Cal frowned. 'You should talk to Farissa. Maybe she can give you something.'

Torj's eyes returned to Wren, who stood with Kipp a few feet away. The pair were talking in hushed voices while Farissa sat beneath the mast with a book in hand, her gaze out to sea.

She looked up when Torj approached and shifted, making room for him. With a nod of thanks, he sat down beside her.

'I imagine you heard everything between Elwren and me yesterday?' she said.

'Occupational hazard.'

'I'm sure.'

'It was nothing I didn't already know,' he replied. 'For what it's worth . . . I think you did the right thing.'

'I'm glad someone does.' Farissa closed her book, her attention drifting to Wren and Kipp. 'Audra wanted her at Drevenor the moment the war ended.'

That didn't surprise Torj. 'Audra has always had her own agendas.'

'True.' Farissa glanced at him. 'Is there something I can do for you?'

For a moment, he felt ridiculous. The scars were just that – scars. Ones that were five years old, completely healed. And yet . . .

'Do you know anything about magical injuries?' he heard himself ask.

Farissa looked alarmed. 'Who's hurt?'

'No one,' he replied, trying to keep his voice steady. 'Not recently, anyway.'

Reluctantly, Torj turned to face her, ensuring that his back was to Wren and the others as he reached for the buttons of his shirt. He undid the first three, revealing the network of scars that had ruined the ink across his chest.

In the aftermath of the battle, it had been Farissa herself who had tended to the burn-like wound, treating it with an array of salves and tinctures. He barely remembered sitting in the makeshift infirmary, dazed from the fight, in a state of shock from the tether that had temporarily connected him to the beautiful lightning wielder.

'They've been troubling me,' he told the Master Alchemist now. 'They feel . . . alive. Sometimes it's like I can feel it happening all over again. Like I've got . . . *her* storm magic beneath my skin.'

Farissa moved closer, peering at his chest, her brow furrowed as she studied each fork of scarred tissue. 'How long has it been like this? Since Elwren channelled her power through you?'

'Yes – no.' Torj fumbled over the words. 'It blazed like fire at the time. When the battle was done, the scars were there, but it wasn't like this.'

'So the sensation is more recent?'

'At first they were like any other scar, but . . . on and off over the years, I've felt surges through them. I thought it was in my head – phantom sensations, perhaps trauma from the war . . .'

It was the first time he'd admitted it aloud, and it pained him to do so. He often woke in a sweat having dreamed about what might have awaited him on the other side of that dark vortex of shadow. He had been lucky to survive that day, lucky that Wren had saved him.

He cleared his throat. 'Over the last few days, it's drastically worse.'

Farissa tore her gaze away from the scars. 'Magical injuries can be complicated.'

Torj huffed a humourless laugh. 'No shit.'

'They can have harsh side effects that don't present until long after the initial wound has healed,' Farissa told him. 'It could contain an unintended curse. It could have absorbed magic from whatever shadow world the portal opened from . . . Although you're a Warsword, your body wasn't built to hold magic like this – magic specific to the ruling bloodlines of the midrealms. That's why it's passed down the family lines in such a way. It's possible that you were in shock, but now your body is breaking down after containing so much raw power.'

Torj raked his fingers through his hair. 'Great.'

'What did it feel like at the time?' she prompted. 'When it first happened?'

'Power,' Torj said, finding his voice suddenly hoarse. 'Power incarnate.'

Farissa nodded, as though this confirmed something for her. 'There are several older texts on magical injuries that might be able to shed more light on the matter. We're going to the perfect place . . . Drevenor should have what you're looking for.'

Torj nodded, rising to his feet.

'Audra will want to know about this,' Farissa warned.

Torj braced himself against the harsh reality of her words, already coming to regret sharing his troubles. 'Fine,' he said. 'But you won't say anything to Wren?' He didn't need the Poisoner knowing his business – or blaming herself.

'No,' Farissa replied. 'But *you* should.'

CHAPTER 16

Wren

'Within these hallowed halls, the secrets of many realms are yours to discover, but tread carefully, for knowledge is a double-edged sword'

– *Drevenor Academy Handbook*

As the days aboard the *Sea Serpent's Destiny* passed, Wren couldn't help but track the Bear Slayer's movements across the deck in turn. Never far from her side, he was larger than life, a weapon honed by the Furies themselves, and everyone knew it. She had seen the way the crew revered him, whispering tales of his adventures in his wake. And the women . . .

Women of all ages aboard the ship were nothing short of obsessed. There was no missing the way their eyes followed his powerful body as he did his morning training exercises at the bow, no unhearing the crude things they said in the absence of their husbands. They stared at him in a way that made something ugly twinge within Wren, though she did her best to ignore it.

The Bear Slayer, however, took it all in his stride: gracious, modest, and, if anything, a little abashed. It only served to fuel the simpering.

Against her better judgement, Wren commented on it one afternoon. 'Someone's popular,' she taunted, jutting her chin in the direction of a trio of young noblewomen from Harenth.

'Jealous?' Torj bit right back.

Wren kept her mouth shut after that.

Wren's magic was restless, and the current surging through her made it harder than usual to sleep. When she did, she was plagued by nightmares.

One night she woke with tears streaming down her face. The pain blooming behind her eyes told her she'd been crying for hours in her sleep. She couldn't recall the dream – a small mercy – but she felt hollow, as though everything inside her had been wrung out and she had nothing left.

Only when she'd palmed the last of the tears away did she spy the Warsword in the corner of the room with a start.

'I kicked your door in,' he told her. 'And still you wouldn't wake.'

Wren drew a trembling breath, her gaze flicking to where the door was propped against the frame, its hinges lying in shattered pieces on the floor.

'How long has this been happening?' the Bear Slayer asked.

She couldn't stand the gentle note in his voice, the pity. It took her back to that damn memorial service four years ago, when she'd completely lost herself, when he'd held her as she'd sobbed. She hadn't cried like that since. Until now, apparently.

'A while,' she replied at last.

'You're painting me a real picture there, Embers.'

'It's none of your business,' she said, though she didn't have the energy to lace her words with as much venom as she wanted.

'Everything is my business now.'

Wren scrubbed at her face and pulled the blankets up to her

chin, her heart still hammering wildly in her chest. 'You broke my door.'

'I thought someone was hurting you.'

Wren took a deep breath and closed her eyes. 'No one can hurt me any more, Warsword.'

CHAPTER 17

Torj

*'The relationship between bodyguard
and principal depends on trust'*

— *The Guardian's Handbook: Principles and Practices of
Personal Protection*

THE NEXT DAY, his ward was back to her usual self.
'How am I meant to "stay safe" without a door on its hinges?' she said darkly, surveying the damage.

'You won't be needing one,' Torj told her coolly, his back aching from sitting in an uncomfortable chair all night. 'You'll get ready in my cabin.'

Wren glanced up again. 'Get ready?'

'We'll arrive in Naarva within the hour. Then we'll be at the academy welcome gala by sundown.'

Her eyes widened. 'You couldn't have told me this sooner?'

'Oh, so we're telling each other things now?' Torj replied, trying but failing to keep the edge from his tone. He forced himself to take a deep, steadying breath but Wren paid him no more heed.

She was looking from her pack tucked away in the corner to her tattered apron and grey gown. 'I . . .'

It was the first time he'd seen her lost for words, without a sharp retort poised on her tongue. Here stood the woman responsible for losing him his dream posting, for tarnishing a once-stellar Warsword reputation. He should have relished her discomfort, should have savoured her apparent distress.

Instead, he asked, 'What is it?'

Wren's shoulders sagged, her cheeks flushing. 'I don't have anything to wear.'

'Oh,' he said, shifting on his feet. 'Farissa thought of that.'

Wren's brow furrowed in confusion.

Torj motioned for her to follow. 'Come with me.'

In his much smaller cabin next door, he shoved a parcel wrapped in brown paper towards her. 'Farissa said that was for the welcome gala.'

Wren took it with unsteady hands. 'Thank you.'

Shocked at her courtesy, Torj remained rooted to the spot, long enough that Wren blinked at him.

'Do you mean to watch me change?' she asked, incredulous.

'I'll turn my back like a gentleman,' he replied.

'You've got to be kidding.'

'As much as I'd like to throw you overboard myself, I don't joke about your safety, Embervale.'

'Why do you care?' she sniped.

'It's my job.'

With a smug sense of satisfaction, he saw the muscle working in her jaw as she ground her teeth. Though no bolts of lightning danced across her skin, he could feel the storm crackling in the air around them.

'Rage all you want,' he said bluntly. 'I'm not going anywhere.' He turned his back to her, facing the porthole. 'Now get dressed.'

Behind him, Wren made an aggravated noise before the paper rustled.

A beat later, she shoved a wax-sealed envelope into his hands. 'That's addressed to you.'

Torj recognized the Guild Master's sigil in the wax instantly. He turned it over, but movement in the reflection of the porthole glass made him freeze.

His breath caught as the reflective surface revealed the curve of Wren's bare shoulder, and the elegant slope of her long neck. He gripped the envelope, crumpling the edges as he drank in the sight of her smooth skin, desire blooming in his abdomen against all reason. Mouth dry, his hardening cock tenting the front of his leathers, his gaze trailed down her naked spine, to the narrowing of her waist and the swell of her hips.

She's the reason you've been stuck in the midrealms for two years, he chided himself. *She's why you spent weeks explaining how Edmund Riverton died in your custody.*

But no amount of willpower could stop the longing that coursed through him. Gods, what he'd give to trace the contours of her body with his hands, with his tongue . . .

Suppressing a groan, Torj tore his eyes away. He just needed a good fuck, that was all. Between brawling at the Laughing Fox and the briefing at Thezmarr, there hadn't been time for any tension relief.

Adjusting his near-painful erection in his leathers, he cracked the seal on the envelope to give himself something else to focus on. As he was greeted by Audra's precise handwriting, it was as though a bucket of ice water had been tipped over him.

He scanned the contents of the letter twice, then a third time, a pit of dread yawning wide within him as the last three lines blurred in his vision.

Under no circumstances are you to warn Elwren.
Under no circumstances are you to intervene.
Outside threats only.

Swallowing the lump in his throat and ignoring the swish of fabric behind him, Torj rubbed the ache setting into his scars. Silently, he cursed Audra.

'You can turn around now,' Wren muttered.

Torj did – and the wind was knocked out of him.

Wren was breathtaking.

The pale green-blue of her gown matched her eyes and complemented her smooth complexion. It was simple in its design, modest even, but that was just as well, for nothing could compete with her beauty. Torj's heart hammered against his sternum as he drank her in. The bodice hugged her curves in a way that made his balls tighten; her breasts and shoulders were covered by a shimmering gauze.

'You look . . .' Words were lost to him. He cleared his throat. 'You look adequate.'

'Adequate?' Wren stared back at him for a moment before she seemed to come back to herself, reaching for her belt of tools and fastening it around her waist. 'You really know how to make a girl feel special, Warsword.'

'A well-honed skill of mine, to be sure,' he replied without thinking, still staring at her.

'Those lucky ladies,' Wren retorted, though there was an edge to her voice.

That, more than anything, wrenched Torj from his trance. 'I'm not sure that matches,' he said, pointing to the tool belt over the formal gown.

'Who asked you?'

Thankfully, a shout sounded from the upper deck and the bells began to ring, signalling land ahead.

Clearing his throat, still clutching Audra's letter, Torj shouldered both their packs and his war hammer before motioning to the door. 'There'll be a carriage waiting ashore.'

Under no circumstances are you to warn Elwren.

Under no circumstances are you to intervene.

There was nothing he could do. The Guild Master had tasked him with protecting the heir of Delmira, only to have him dress her up and throw her to the wolves.

CHAPTER 18

Wren

'A dram of extract from the root of brown laurel dissolved in liquor can cause hallucinations that please the senses'

– Elixirs and Toxins: A Comprehensive Guide

WREN HARDLY REGISTERED disembarking from the *Sea Serpent's Destiny* and finding their carriage. All she knew was that suddenly, she, Torj, Cal, Kipp and Farissa were rattling through the Naarvian countryside, the verdant fields a blur as the driver spurred the horses into a gallop.

The Drevenor welcome gala awaited, and she had no idea what to expect. Wren had never been to a ball. It was something she, Sam and Ida had joked about when they practised a game they called Dancing Alchemists in their rooms. The game had less to do with waltzes and gowns and more to do with being nimble enough to avoid the knives thrown at their feet, but still . . . A lump formed in Wren's throat as a wave of grief hit, and she fought back tears. Once, they had talked of lavish dresses sweeping across marble floors, and music that made their hearts soar . . . She wondered if the gala would be something similar, and wished that Sam and Ida could be there to see it too.

Gathering herself, she looked out the window and tried to quell her nerves by observing the Kingdom of Gardens.

Naarva had fallen to the darkness years before the shadow war had broken out across the midrealms, but what wasn't commonly known was that the Warsword Talemir Starling had rallied the surviving people to care for the lands and rebuild beneath the very noses of the monsters who sought to destroy it. As such, it was now flourishing, barely touched by the stain of battle.

The scent of rich pine filled Wren's nostrils as the vast fields were swallowed by a dense forest, beams of golden sunlight breaking through the canopy. She craned her neck to peer out the window, where the towering trees seemed to whisper to one another, their branches quivering in the breeze as though greeting the party.

'It's pretty incredible, isn't it?' Cal murmured beside her, peering over her shoulder.

'It is,' Wren agreed, equally awed.

It wasn't long before she spotted the intricate wrought iron fence that bordered the grounds, with lush ivy curling around the bars. As the carriage rattled onwards, not even Cal and Kipp's bickering could pull her focus from the glimpses of the academy beyond. Her heart quickened with anticipation as she spied the ancient stones between the trees.

'Gods,' she murmured as they reached a pair of imposing iron gates matching the ivy-covered fence, adorned with strange patterns and carvings of all manner of plant and creature.

She could feel the Bear Slayer's eyes on her, but she didn't tear her gaze from the entrance. The gates were now swinging inwards with a loud creak, not a sentry or watchman in sight. Their carriage entered the grounds alone as the gates opened before them, revealing the towering building that offered a solemn sense of grandeur, rising from the ground like a titan of knowledge.

They travelled down a gravel road, passing beneath the shadow of the impressive spires and towers. A small gasp left Wren's lips as she took in the ornate stone carvings and the stained-glass windows reflecting a kaleidoscope of colour in the light of the setting sun.

At long last, the carriage came to a halt behind several others, and the party of five exited. Only Torj's rigid presence beside her stopped Wren from wandering straight towards the pair of giant oak doors that stood open at the top of the white stone steps. The Warsword seemed tense, even hesitant.

'What?' she demanded. 'What's wrong?'

His deep-sea eyes slid to hers. 'Nothing,' he grunted.

'Then what are we waiting for?' She motioned to the stairs.

'Am I holding you back by your skirts, Embervale? Or do you need me to carry you again?'

Wren let out a huff of frustration. 'Prick,' she muttered, and lifted the hem of her dress, starting the ascent to the doors.

'Welcome, welcome!' a voice sounded on the landing. Wren spotted a middle-aged woman wearing a colourful tapestry of robes and jangling trinkets, standing in a small alcove beside a table laden with documents. 'Hello there,' she said, smiling warmly as Wren and her companions approached. 'Master Tremaine, how good to see you again. You'll find the High Chancellor and the other masters in the staff lounge.'

Farissa gave her a nod of thanks before turning to Wren. 'Good luck,' she murmured. Wren didn't have a chance to respond before her former mentor disappeared up a spiral staircase.

The robed woman was still beaming at her when she returned her attention to the table. 'Welcome to Drevenor,' she said. 'I'm Celeste Blackmane, the Head of Admissions.'

The woman was too bright and bubbly for Wren, but she mumbled a return greeting, trying to peer over Celeste's shoulder, her eyes drawn to an enormous tree taking up much of the foyer beyond—

'If you could provide your offer letter, please? Then you can get inside and enjoy the gala.'

'Of course,' Wren said, fumbling with one of the pouches at her belt. She produced the crumpled letter Audra had given her back at Thezmarr.

'Elwren Embervale!' Celeste declared as she scanned the piece of parchment. 'We're *thrilled* to have you. Master Tremaine's recommendation caused quite the stir.'

The nape of Wren's neck prickled. 'Oh?'

'According to her, you played a big role in the war. Thanks to you, many—'

'Shouldn't she be getting inside?'

A shadow cast over them both, and Torj brushed up against Wren's side.

Celeste's eyes bulged as she took in the war hammer peeking over Torj's shoulder. 'Oh – you must be her guard, the Bear Slayer?'

'The one and only.' He motioned to Cal and Kipp behind him. 'And that's Callahan Whitlock and Kristopher Snowden, here at the High Chancellor's request.'

Celeste consulted a piece of parchment unfurled on the side table. 'Yes, yes, I see that note here. You can leave your belongings with me, and a porter will see to it that they're taken to your rooms at once.'

Torj dumped their packs unceremoniously on the mosaic-tiled floor. 'There's a trunk in the carriage as well,' he told Celeste. 'Apparently it's fragile.'

'We'll take care of that, Warsword Elderbrock. We're used to transporting delicate items here.'

'Great,' Torj replied dryly, before turning to Wren. 'Shall we?'

Wren made to move past Celeste, but the woman stopped her with a gentle hand on her arm. 'I feel someone should help you with this,' she said in a whisper, 'and it likely won't be one of your male companions. It's rare they know anything about fashion.'

In one swift movement, she removed the pin from Wren's bun, letting her bronze hair tumble down around her face.

Celeste hummed her approval. 'Much better. It makes the angles look much less harsh. What's the point of having such beauty if you don't frame it with these gorgeous locks?'

Only Sam and Ida had ever commented on her appearance and touched her in such a way. Too stunned to move, Wren just stared as the older woman fussed over her, positioning the waves of her hair around her face.

'One final touch, I think . . .' Celeste's hands were at her waist, which spurred Wren into action. She tried to bat the woman away from her belt of tools and potions. 'Now, now,' Celeste chided. 'This just doesn't *work*. The dress is perfect without this clunky thing. You need not worry. I'll send everything right up to your rooms. You won't miss it for a few hours.'

Wren's irritation flared, but she didn't want the academy's first impression of her to be an argument with the Head of Admissions.

'Perfect,' Celeste declared when Wren had been relieved of her belt. She felt naked without it, but Celeste pushed her towards the entrance, and Wren's feet moved of their own accord.

A pair of giant oak doors stood open, revealing a foyer beyond that stretched up into several levels above, where balconies draped in garlands of flowers looked down upon the bustling activity below. But most breathtaking of all was the enormous ancient tree that stood at the heart of it all, tall and proud, its gnarled branches reaching up towards the dome-capped ceiling. Overhead, the canopy spread wide, casting dappled patterns upon the guests mingling below. The tree's incorporation into the design of the building reminded Wren of the stone monuments that had once graced the Great Hall back at Thezmarr, prompting her to wonder if the two sites had shared the same architect long ago.

Kipp appeared at her side. 'Free drinks,' he declared, handing her a flute of something gold and sparkling.

Wren made a point of ignoring the towering Warsword at her back as she accepted it gratefully and aimed her attention elsewhere. The melodic notes of lutes and lyres danced with the gentle rustle of leaves in the evening breeze while servers moved gracefully among the crowd, bearing trays laden with goblets of wine and dishes of exotic delicacies.

'This is *quite* the gala,' Kipp commented.

Wren huffed a laugh. 'Been to many galas, have you, Kristopher?'

'Wouldn't you like to know?'

Rolling her eyes, Wren scanned the array of guests. There were people from all walks of life here, the number far greater than the cohort of alchemists she had expected to study alongside. 'Who *are* all these people?' she murmured to Kipp.

'All the different ranks of alchemist, I presume, and the previous cohorts,' the strategist replied. 'Then I suppose there are the scribes, the researchers, the folks from admissions and administration, scholars, chroniclers, botanists, groundskeepers, and a fair few visiting from the University of Naarva, too . . .'

'How do you know all this?'

Kipp gave her a sly grin. 'As I've always told you, the Son of the Fox has his ways . . .'

Wren shot him a wry look. Kipp had been born in the Laughing Fox, one of the midrealms' most famous taverns, and Kipp's wide-reaching connections were seemingly endless as a result.

'Now,' he went on, 'shouldn't you be off making friends?'

Wren grimaced. The thought of stepping into the crowd and being forced to make polite conversation had her insides shrinking in on themselves. But Kipp was right, as much as she hated to admit it. If there were ever a place to find like-minded individuals to connect with, Drevenor was it.

She put the glass of sparkling wine to her lips, taking a much-needed long sip and relishing the sweet taste on her tongue. *Liquid courage.*

As the first delicious mouthful slid down her throat, Wren recognized the faintest hint of vanilla. For a moment, she savoured it.

Then she realized she'd made a terrible mistake.

CHAPTER 19

Wren

'The best antidote is often immunity created via long-term exposure'

– *The Poisoner's Handbook*

BROWN LAUREL. WREN recognized the effects as soon as her hands started to tingle. The first thing she did was reach for her belt, fumbling with shaking hands for one of several vials that might help with the side effects.

It wasn't there.

'Shit,' she muttered as the notes of music began to take visual form in the air before her eyes. The roots of brown laurel were widely known as hallucinogens across the midrealms, particularly when mixed with liquor.

The world shifted beneath her, and Wren looked around the gala. Throughout the foyer, people were acting strangely. A man with white-blond hair was puffing on four cigarillos at once, going cross-eyed as he watched the smoke drift from their glowing ends. A woman was running her hands up and down her curvy sides, waist-length black hair swaying, as though she couldn't believe her own magnificent shape. Another man was putting on some sort of sword-fighting display with one hand behind his back, only instead of a sword, he used a candlestick.

Panic set in, cold and fast, Wren's knees buckling beneath her.

Breathe, she told herself. *Just breathe. It will even out, it will pass, just keep it together.*

It didn't help that next to her, Kipp, who'd had several glasses of wine already, was dancing in a circle on his own to music that certainly wasn't the melody she could hear. A laugh bubbled out of her.

Gods, no. Not the giggles. She'd heard this was how the effects set in.

Kipp looked up at the sound and gave her a dopey grin. That only made her laugh harder. Furies, when was the last time she'd *laughed*? For some reason, the question only made things funnier. Of all the locations to be bursting into hysterics, the welcoming gala of Drevenor Academy was *not* the ideal place.

For a brief moment, the immense fear of her teachers and peers seeing her like this struck hard – but then the whole foyer was awash with colour, her vision distorting with patterns undulating through the air as she wiped tears of laughter from her cheeks.

Kipp was still swinging his limbs about, but Wren's gaze fell upon the giant tree in the centre of the space, which seemed to have a halo of light around it now. Without thinking, she moved towards it, reaching out in sheer awe as the markings in the bark moved to the rise and fall of the lute's notes—

She tripped on her own feet.

A warm hand closed around her arm, hoisting her up.

Torj.

She stopped in the middle of the gala to stare up at him, his scent so rich she could taste it on her tongue. When had she last let herself look at him? Truly look? The fierce contours of his face were sharpened by his trimmed dark beard. His sea-blue eyes were like a storm calling to her, riling her already unsettled magic—

'Gods,' she heard him mutter. 'Don't look at me like that, Embers.'

'I'll look at you how I damn well please.' Instead of sounding sharp, the words came out slow and sultry.

'You usually do,' he replied, his voice low. 'Just not like that.'

Wren didn't know what he was talking about, but was pleased to find she'd arrived at the mesmerizing tree. She moved her arm, and after what felt like an age, she finally touched its rough bark. The sensation beneath her fingertips was suddenly the most amazing feeling in the world.

'Have you felt this?' she asked the Bear Slayer in wonder, who was watching her with a guarded expression.

There was a glimmer of amusement in his eyes. 'I'll pass.'

'You didn't drink the wine?'

'I did not.'

'You should,' Wren told him. 'It's amazing.'

'I think it's best if one of us remains sound of mind, don't you?'

'No.'

Torj laughed, the sound warm and rich. 'Figures.'

Wren found herself staring at him again, heat blooming in her chest at the echo of his laugh. It was magical. Better than all the music in the world. Better than—

'For fuck's sake,' Torj muttered, his attention snagging elsewhere.

Wren followed his gaze across the foyer to where Kipp was swimming in a fountain. There was a pretty red headed woman splashing alongside him. It seemed like a good idea to Wren. It was getting rather stuffy in here—

'Don't even think about it,' Torj murmured, his voice low in her ear.

Liking how close he was, Wren leaned in, inhaling that intoxicating scent of his. 'You smell good.'

The Warsword actually *groaned* and tipped his face to the ceiling. 'Furies save me.'

It wasn't *her* fault, Wren knew that much. 'They took my belt,' she explained matter-of-factly, swaying to a distant melody. 'I could have prevented this if I had it.'

'I know.'

A loud burst of laughter rang out across the foyer, and Wren looked just in time to see Kipp drag a reluctant Cal into the fountain, water splashing over the sides, the red-headed woman shrieking gleefully.

Just as Wren had made up her mind to dart across the tiled floor to join them, a wave of mist washed over the entire foyer from above. As the cool vapour kissed her skin, Wren slowly came back to herself, the vividness of the colours fading, her feet suddenly firm on the ground.

Mortification set in instantly. She sprang apart from Torj, whose arm she was practically cradling.

Movement caught her eye. On the balcony above ground level, a tall professor appeared, draped in robes of azure and gold. He raised his hands, and silence fell immediately.

'Welcome to Drevenor,' he said, voice clear, cold, and commanding. 'I am the High Chancellor, Remington Belcourt, and today, the dawn of a new cohort begins. You are all here because you were the best of the best in your studies, not just in the midrealms, but beyond what was once the Veil as well. Or so I thought.' Piercing grey eyes scanned the throng before him. 'Congratulations, novices. Each and every one of you has just failed your first test. Not a single pupil caught the dose of powdered brown laurel root in your drinks. Had this challenge been more sinister . . . you'd all be dead.'

CHAPTER 20

Wren

'We walk a tightrope between progress and peril, and it is only through balance that we can hope to achieve true mastery of our craft'

– *Transformative Arts of Alchemy*

WREN DREW A trembling breath, shame burning a hole in the pit of her stomach. After all this time, after everything she'd learned, she'd tossed it all out the window the second she'd set foot in the most prestigious academy in all the realms. Several sheepish looks around the foyer told her she wasn't the only one with regrets.

The High Chancellor continued, his voice apathetic and blunt. 'You were all alchemists in your own right, some even apprentices to great masters. You were the elite where you came from, but not here. Here, you are nothing. Here, you are at the bottom of a vast ladder. What you were before is gone. You are novices now. Nobodies. Until we say otherwise.'

Someone at the back gave a nervous laugh, but the sound was silenced instantly.

This might not be Thezmarr, Wren thought, *but it's just as intimidating.* She didn't take her eyes off the High Chancellor. Remington

Belcourt scanned the hall with piercing eyes, letting his words sink in throughout the throng before him.

'Over the centuries, alchemy has meant many things to many people. Like life itself, it has gone through countless seasons and cycles. First, its purpose was finding the elixir of life, and obtaining immortality, for those foolish enough to seek it. Then came the season of runes, where magical symbols were combined with herbology to imbue objects with power. After that came the era of elements and precious metals . . . Throughout the ages, a common thread has remained at the heart of alchemy: that *knowledge is might*.'

The High Chancellor paused, drawing a weighted breath before continuing.

'Here at Drevenor Academy, we teach the four pillars of alchemy: lifelore, healing, warfare and design. As novices, you will study all of these to solidify a foundational understanding of what our great art comprises. Usually, to graduate from novice to adept takes a minimum of a year, but this year we have accelerated studies and challenges to six months. There are sixty students in your cohort from all around the midrealms and beyond, but there are only thirty places at the next level.' The High Chancellor cleared his throat. 'How do these eliminations take place? Through a series of trials known as the Gauntlet.'

Goosebumps rushed across Wren's skin, and she had to remind herself to unclench her jaw, the muscles there already aching.

'The Gauntlet tests your knowledge of what you have learned here,' he told them. 'This will be the hardest challenge many of you have ever faced. It will carve out the weak and leave only the strong. Consider this the Great Rite of alchemy, and be prepared to give it everything you have, including your life.'

Wren felt Torj's eyes on her, but she didn't let her gaze slip from the upper level.

'If you pass, you will graduate from novice to adept. As an adept, you will narrow your focus to a specialty. From adept, we expect you to work towards the rank of sage. And as a sage, you will delve deeper into that specialty and find subjects you might choose to explore further. Only from there may the title of Master Alchemist be within reach, for a select few of you.'

In the years before the war, Wren had dreamed of becoming a Master Alchemist, and now, the mention of the title had that old yearning rising to the surface once more. It was the one thing she'd wanted for longer than she could remember, the one thing that had been solely hers . . . A hope for her future that she'd had long before she'd become the Poisoner. She had learned a good deal of healing from Farissa throughout the years, but Drevenor was going to open up an entire world of alchemy to her.

The High Chancellor ploughed on. 'Over the course of your time here, you will attend classes and practical lessons, and will take up any challenges as directed by your teachers. Do not let the books and workshops fool you – they are your commanders, and their orders must be obeyed. The masters also have the power to award points.' Belcourt gestured behind him, where several cylindrical glass vessels were mounted to the wall, and beside them, a larger dispenser full of dark gems glinting in the candlelight. 'Each piece of black garnet represents a single point. Your masters will see to it that points are tallied and deposited into the appropriate receptacle each week. In six months, these points will be counted and will determine the starting order for the Gauntlet.'

The High Chancellor pressed his long fingers together in front of his chest, passing another sweeping gaze across his captive audience.

'Rules,' he declared. 'There is but one. Break it and suffer the consequences, ranging from academic suspension and expulsion to criminal trial and the removal of your memories.'

Wren blanched. *Removal of memories?* Was that legal? How was it even possible?

'The fuck . . . ?' the Bear Slayer murmured beside her. 'You agreed to this?'

She didn't answer, just balled the fabric of her dress at her sides.

'Secrecy.' The High Chancellor let the word ring out across the room. 'Drevenor deals in complex alchemy that, in the wrong hands, can lead to disaster. We need only look to the shadow war for evidence of that. You will be required to pledge an oath of secrecy. What is taught here remains within these walls and the minds of our students only. Anyone to break this oath will face the full extent of our academy's retribution and punishment.'

It was not the rule or consequences that had Wren's palms turning clammy, but the mention of the war. Besides those who she'd arrived with, she recognized no one here. Had any of them been present for the battles? For the horrors that had bled across the lands?

A cold sweat broke out across her skin as flashes of violence came back to her. An army of monsters charging across the snow. A frost giant impaling soldiers on the spikes of its club. Kipp lying lifeless upon the ice, the fang of an arachne protruding from his chest, blood seeping from the wound. No number of deep breaths or calming meditations could ground her in the present. She had seen the consequences of misused alchemy in the war herself. She had *been there* when the late King Artos and Princess Jasira of Harenth had used a combination of shadow magic and alchemy to create a force of darkness that had almost destroyed the midrealms. They'd weaponized their own empath magic to rob soldiers of their free will and fear, forcing countless men and women into battle and to their deaths—

The scent of black cedar and oakmoss wrapped around her. A warm, steady hand rested on the small of her back.

'Pick one thing,' Torj murmured, his voice low as he leaned in. 'One thing to focus on. The gaudiness of your High Chancellor's robes? Or perhaps the fact that Kipp hasn't noticed his trousers are undone?'

Wren loosed a tight breath, her eyes darting quickly to Kipp; the front of his soaking trousers was indeed gaping open. A huff of raw laughter escaped her, and in the folds of her gown, her fists relaxed.

Blinking back the tears of relief that stung her eyes, she whispered, 'Thank you.'

A dip of his head was the only confirmation that Torj had heard her.

The High Chancellor was still talking. 'Beyond the walls of our institution, you are free to enter the city and surrounding towns. No doubt many of your tasks and challenges will require it of you.'

The sudden clap of his hands made Wren jolt, her body still recovering from the effects of the brown laurel.

'Your education at Drevenor begins on the eighth bell tomorrow. Get ready to meet your fellow scholars, and your adversaries.'

CHAPTER 21

Torj

'Upon completion of the Great Rite, Warswords are presented with gifts from the kingdoms: a blade of Naarvian steel, a stallion from Tver, a vial of healing springwater from Aveum, armour from Delmira, and an ampoule of poison from Harenth'

– The Warsword's Way

THE DISMISSAL FROM the so-called welcome gala should have come as a relief to Torj, a chance to get Wren out of the chaos. But the mass exodus of the crowd brought with it a new issue: recognition. Along with Wren's scarred throat, Torj's presence at her side was confirmation enough of who she was: the Delmirian heir who'd refused her throne and killed the traitorous former Guild Master of Thezmarr.

There was no missing the attention Wren received as they picked up the keys to her quarters and followed directions through the corridors. Word had spread. Torj heard the whispers as he, Cal and Kipp tried to shield Wren on their way to the student residence halls.

Torj marched alongside her, hanging onto his willpower by a thread to refrain from pulling her close to protect her bodily from the words spilling all around her. It raised his hackles more than he cared to admit. Regardless of his own mixed feelings towards the poisoner, she was still a war hero in her own right. She had fought alongside the warriors of Thezmarr to defend the midrealms. He hated that their eyes lingered on the scar at her throat, that someone had the fucking audacity to point it out as they passed. Torj nearly cracked their head open with his hammer then and there.

To her credit, Wren didn't flinch, didn't falter beneath their scrutiny. She simply walked on, her eyes fixed ahead. Torj supposed five years of poisoning people developed a thick skin.

They took another corner into a throng of people, and this time, Torj did draw Wren closer to his side without hesitation, shielding her with his towering frame. Her skirts brushed his legs, and he tried not to lean into her heady spring-rain scent.

He was beyond alert, tracking every flicker of movement in his periphery, aware of every set of eyes following his charge. To his surprise, she didn't recoil from his side as he'd expected; she let him guide her through the last few twists and turns of the torchlit hallways. Perhaps she was still drugged.

You smell good. Her words came back to him with a rush of heat. Gods, the way she'd looked at him . . . It had tested his self-control beyond belief. He wondered if she'd remember it all come morning.

'Elwren Embervale, as I live and breathe . . .' a voice called from an open door.

Torj whirled on his heel, instantly spotting a handsome young man approaching them from the entrance of a shared dormitory. The man smirked, his eyes raking over Wren's curves.

In seconds, Torj had the head of his war hammer crushing the youth's windpipe, pinning him to the stone wall. The same protective instinct washed over him as it had when he'd seen her nightmares back on the ship. He may not like the poisoner, but it didn't mean he'd let others take liberties with her.

'Who are you?' he demanded.

The man wheezed and struggled against his powerful hold. 'I'm a novice – like Elwren.'

Beside them, Wren clicked her tongue in frustration. 'Stop being such a brute, Bear Slayer. He's not armed.'

'I don't give a fuck if he's armed,' Torj growled, narrowing his eyes as he studied the reddening face of his captive. After a moment, he dropped him, taking a step back and allowing the man to catch his breath and straighten his clothes.

Torj was reaching for Wren to turn her towards the final corridor when the idiot had the stupidity to speak again. 'The name's Jasper Greaves,' he said, his voice a mere croak. 'Can I buy you a drink, Elwren? At the Mortar and Pestle?'

Torj went rigid, his fists clenching once more at his sides. The boy didn't know when to shut the fuck up.

Wren, however, surveyed Greaves with complete boredom. 'No,' she said bluntly, and walked away.

Torj couldn't help his smug sense of satisfaction at that.

'Are you going to attack every potential suitor as well as every threat?' she asked when at last they reached her door.

Torj felt the tips of his ears grow hot, but there was no way she could see that beneath his hair. 'Didn't realize you wanted me letting the suitors through, Embervale. Your demeanour doesn't exactly scream "Court me." But by all means, if that's what you're looking for, say the word.'

Somewhere behind him, Kipp laughed. 'The only company the Poisoner keeps are her plants and potions.'

Wren shot him a glare before fixing her stormy eyes back on Torj. 'Perhaps it's not courtship I want,' she said, fitting her key to the lock in the door.

Torj froze at that, an irrational, icy rage washing over him. He'd been no saint, and he certainly had no claim over the storm-wielding poisoner before him, yet the thought of her with someone else, the idea of someone else's hands on her . . . It made him see red.

'Uh . . .' Kipp cleared his throat awkwardly. 'If we're not needed—'

'You'll wait with Embervale while I sweep the room,' Torj ground out. Leaving Wren in the doorway with Cal and Kipp, he entered her private quarters.

Her belongings had been deposited in a neat stack in the centre of the space. Tucked away in the corner was a single bed, which Torj checked underneath. He scanned the walls for peepholes and anything out of place, and he tested the latch on the window and the lock on the back of the main door. Irritation prickled at him anew. This work was an insult to a Warsword of his calibre. He should have been off hunting down the perpetrators of the attack on King Leiko, or tracking monsters across the midrealms, not playing guard to an entitled poisoner who did what she wanted regardless of the cost.

Wren's fiery gaze was on him. 'You're invading my privacy,' she hissed. 'You have no right to go through my things, to—'

'No right?' He rounded on her, halting his sweep of the bathing room. 'I have *every* damn right. I vowed to protect you, and that's exactly what I'm doing.'

Wren shoved past Kipp and Cal, who were looking increasingly uncomfortable, and entered the rooms with a venomous expression.

'I didn't say it was safe,' Torj snapped.

'You're being ridiculous.'

'I'm doing my *job*.'

Kipp cleared his throat yet again from the doorway. 'Cal and I will be in the tavern if you need us. Sounds like you need to … work some things out.' He gave Cal's arm a sharp tug, leading him away from the storm that was about to break.

That seemed to be all the permission Wren needed to truly explode. 'Ridiculous doesn't even cover it! You're rifling through my things! You're attacking random men in the corridor—'

Torj's rage suddenly matched hers, a fire burning right beneath his lightning-shaped scars. He crossed the room in seconds. 'He wasn't a man.'

Wren's eyes narrowed as she glared up at him. 'No? You're suddenly an expert?'

Torj gave a dark laugh. 'If you need a comparison between a boy and a man, I can definitely help with that.'

Seeming intent on riling him now, Wren pushed further. 'I've known plenty of men, Bear Slayer. Given the attention I've received on the brief walk here alone, I imagine there are any number of them just waiting for a chance—'

Without a second thought, Torj stepped closer. 'Then I'd hope for your sake they know how to make your toes curl.'

He felt the shiver course through her before she severed the contact between them, jerking away. 'Is that what you're known for, then, Warsword? Making women's toes curl?'

'Among other things.' Torj shifted in front of her, forcing her back towards the door so he could complete the damn sweep of the quarters. He could feel the rage vibrating around her, and suddenly he was enjoying himself again. If he was going to suffer her company, she could very well suffer alongside him. 'Why are you asking about my sex life, anyway, Embervale?'

The alchemist blushed furiously, and she shoved past him, her loose hair brushing his shirt. 'I couldn't give less of a shit about your sex life.'

'Keep telling yourself that.'

Fury swept across her face in a deep crimson hue, and Torj thought it rather suited her.

'Get out,' she said bluntly. Apparently, it was her new favourite phrase.

'I'm not done checking here.'

'You are if you know what's good for you.'

'Threatening a Warsword doesn't usually end well for people.'

'Nor does pissing off a poisoner.'

He could see her jaw working as she ground her teeth. His presence in her space, her lack of privacy . . . For someone who had lived in isolation, he knew it was a lot to process, but it was hardly *his* fault. In fact, had she not screwed things up so royally for him with Edmund Riverton, he doubted he'd even be here.

The energy in the room crackled in warning, and Torj supposed he ought to hurry things along before she brought a real storm down on them all. He went to the door in the centre of the interior wall, intending to do a final check of the cupboard before getting the fuck out of there.

Flinging the door open, he froze.

It was not a cupboard.

It was another sleeping quarters.

His.

'Fuck.' He turned back to Wren. 'We've been given adjoining rooms.'

CHAPTER 22

*W*ren

'Peppered broadleaf – an alternative to smelling salts.
The bitter aroma is often used to wake
unconscious patients'

*– From Root to Petal: Understanding Plants
and Their Properties*

OF COURSE THEY'D been given adjoining rooms, because Furies forbid she be able to breathe without her new bodyguard hearing it.

'I'll be through here,' the Bear Slayer said, his face a mask of indifference as he strode towards the door.

Only when it clicked closed did Wren exhale, the tension still tight in her shoulders. What was it about that man that riled her up so thoroughly? What was it about the press of his body against hers that sent her traitorous mind to the filthiest of places? The energy between them was more than any reaction Wren could create in a crucible – two elements coming together to make something else entirely. Something dangerous.

Chastising herself, she swept the loose strands of her hair back, re-pinning her messy bun in place before reaching for the toolbelt sitting atop her pack in the middle of the room. Her fingers found the vial of gilliflower essence and the small jar of henbit nettle, both of which would have countered the embarrassing effects of the brown laurel. Gods, she had been drugged out of her fucking mind.

You smell good... Wren cringed as the memory sent a fresh wave of embarrassment washing over her. The only thing that made it worse was that it was true. Even now, the scent of the Warsword lingered in her rooms, causing warmth to trickle down her spine in response.

It's nothing more than the afterglow of the brown laurel, she told herself. Until tonight, she'd never experienced the drug first hand, but Kipp had confessed that in the hours after ingestion, it tended to have an aphrodisiac effect. Once again, she berated herself for the mistake. It had been beyond stupid.

With her skin tingling and heat pulsing between her legs, Wren looked around the space that would be home for the next six months – longer, if she managed to pass the Gauntlet. The High Chancellor had referred to it as the Great Rite of alchemy – counterpart to the set of trials the Warswords faced to earn their totems and Naarvian steel. Her sister Thea still didn't speak of her own Great Rite to this day.

The room was simple, with a single bed tucked away in the corner beneath a stained-glass window looking out onto the courtyard below, and a private bathing chamber, for which she'd be eternally grateful. Most important, though, was the large workbench that took up much of the space, a single stool tucked beneath it.

Her quarters were entirely too clean and tidy. She needed the chaos of plants, books, and instruments to think. She found the emptiness stifling. No matter. For all the work she intended to do here, she knew it wouldn't be long until the space resembled the vibrant mess of her cottage back in Delmira.

After she had unpacked, she set about making a spare antidote kit from her supplies. If the welcome gala was anything to go by, she'd need all the additional reserves she could get. She also made a mental note to get a decent sample from the blade Farissa had shown her back at Thezmarr. If she were going to create a counter-concoction, she needed something to test with.

An hour later, her eyes were bleary, and her formal gown had begun to itch. Her mind brimming with thoughts of what to expect from her first day at the academy tomorrow, she pushed her boots off at the heel. Sighing heavily, she stripped away her skirts, and at last her bodice, leaving her in a short undergarment that ended at the tops of her thighs. For a moment, she simply breathed, bracing herself against the bench, revelling in the freedom of movement without all the layers.

When more of the tension in her shoulders and neck had ebbed away, she headed for the bathing chamber, hoping there were facilities to heat the water. But when she pushed the door open, she let out a cry of surprise.

The Bear Slayer was standing before the basin, wearing nothing but a towel slung dangerously low across his hips, droplets of water glistening on his skin.

Wren's mouth went dry at the sight. The sheer size of him undressed before her was mesmerizing, as were the ridges of muscle that seemed to cover every inch of his body. Fresh heat surged through her, pooling between her legs as she drank in the hard lines of his sculpted chest, the planes of his abdomen, and lower, the deep twin grooves that disappeared beneath his towel—

'It's common courtesy to knock, Embervale.' The Bear Slayer turned to face her, clutching the towel at his waist as though it might come free at any moment.

'What are you doing here?' she managed, not quite able to tear her eyes away.

Torj raised a brow and jerked his chin towards a door on the opposite wall. 'Along with adjoining rooms comes a shared bathing chamber.'

'What?' she blurted.

'Unless you'd prefer to share one with three dozen students down the hall . . . ?'

Naturally the guild had insisted on adjoining bathing quarters as well. Whatever would happen if she slipped on a bar of soap?

It was only when the Bear Slayer's gaze travelled down her body that Wren realized she was in nothing but her shift, the cool air kissing her exposed skin making her all the more aware of just how much of her was exposed. And with the light of her room behind her, she knew the scrap of fabric left very little to the imagination.

Her first instinct was to throw her hands across her chest, where, against the thin material, her nipples were hardening beneath his stare. But no, she would not be embarrassed. She had nothing to be ashamed of, not even as she felt dampness gather between her thighs.

Torj wet his lips. From the way the Warsword was gripping his towel, his knuckles paling, she wasn't the only one affected.

For a moment, she was back at the Laughing Fox, her hand pressed to his chest as she said, *'Let's get a room . . . Let's settle this thing between us.'*

She had come back to that encounter in her mind over and over, his answer always dousing the flames of her desire as it had the first time.

'One night is not enough . . .'

Now, with a measured breath, Torj seemed to steel himself. He reached for a steaming pail of water at the base of the nearby tub. Corded muscle rippling, he lifted it, pouring it into the bath, the new angle revealing the significant bulge at the front of his towel—

Wren inhaled sharply, her skin suddenly far too sensitive. Silently, she cursed the brown laurel root and its delayed after-effects once again. The man before her was *insufferable*, she reminded herself. A sculpted body, no matter how tattooed and powerful, didn't change that. As misty ribbons rose from the hot water, she bit her lower lip and clenched her thighs together, trying and failing to will away the tension coiling inside her.

When Torj turned back to her, a knowing smirk tugged at the corner of his mouth as he surveyed her. 'What's the matter, Embers? Can't handle the heat?'

Wren couldn't stop herself from fidgeting beneath the brand of his stare. She flushed furiously. 'I . . .'

With a final, blazing sweep of his eyes over her body, Torj reached for the door to his room. 'The hot water is for you.'

And then he left.

Cold water would have been more useful, she thought, trying to shake the furious haze of longing from her mind.

But when she sank into the delicious heat of the tub, not even ironclad willpower could stop her hand slipping between her legs.

CHAPTER 23

Wren

'Blackthorn – an unassuming shrub with long spikes prone to causing severe bleeding. While the tree itself is not toxic, its bark and thorns contain bacteria that cause infection and blood poisoning'

— *An Encyclopaedia of Deadly Plants*

Drevenor was bustling with activity the next morning. Kipp had been right: there were more than just alchemists filling its tapestry-lined halls. Researchers laden with piles of books, groundskeepers with barrows of freshly turned earth, and harried-looking scribes, hands stained with ink and quills tucked behind their ears, all went about their business.

As they passed through the foyer, Wren eyed the vessel of glimmering black garnet stones, the points system a blank canvas in the final moments before the academy swallowed them into its chaos.

'This way, Embervale.' Torj's voice brought her back to the task at hand: getting to Evermere Forest for her first lesson – lifelore.

Wren was loath to admit that were it not for the towering Warsword at her side and his large hand at the small of her back, she might have been swept away in the rush, or panicked by the crush of bodies in the halls. Torj's presence created a barrier around her, as no one dared to bump into him or cross his path. At all times there was a buffer of several inches between her and the next person, and whenever that gap was compromised, a glare from the silver-haired warrior was all it took for the distance to be recovered.

To his credit, the Warsword didn't seem overly happy about their situation either. She could practically feel the crackle of his contempt to match her own. His jaw was permanently clenched, his brows drawn together in a scowl.

Kipp, on the other hand, was practically beaming – far too cheerful for her liking. Cal had left to be briefed on guarding Professor Vulpine upon his arrival, but Kipp was here, chattering away. 'Perhaps it wouldn't kill you to make some new friends,' he said as they passed the grand entrance, its towering stone walls adorned with faded tapestries, opening up to reveal a vast hall beyond. 'I know not everyone can match up to me, but still . . .' He glanced around at the countless people watching her. 'Might be harder than I thought . . . for you.'

'Thanks a lot,' she muttered. Her stomach was churning with nerves, and she wasn't sure she'd made the right call by skipping the morning meal. It was too late to change that now.

The warm press of the Bear Slayer's hand at her back grounded her again. The Warsword navigated the academy grounds with ease, almost as though he'd done a practice run sometime before. Wren watched him from the corner of her eye warily, becoming instantly aware that she wasn't the only one doing so. The lightning-kissed warrior garnered nearly as much attention as she did, though of a different nature entirely. It was just as it had been on the *Sea Serpent's Destiny*: women – and men – of all ages gaping openly at Torj, some of them shamelessly ogling the muscles shifting with every stride.

Wren reminded herself to unclench her jaw. They were free to *admire* whatever parts of him they so desired. She had no claim on him, nor did she want one. She only wished they wouldn't be so tastelessly obvious about it.

The academy grounds were split into quadrants, and Wren and Torj passed by two of them on their way to the northern perimeter – one for the greenhouses and one for the gardens – but she hardly got a glimpse as they hurried to her first lesson. Within Evermere Forest was an eerie grove, bordered by gnarled trees that seemed to twist and reach out with their branches, as though trying to ensnare unsuspecting prey. Each step Wren took was muffled by the thick carpet of dead leaves and moss, while the canopy above was dense, allowing only slivers of pale sunlight to penetrate the gloom. A thick, unnatural silence hung heavy in the air, broken only by the occasional rustling of leaves – and pained moans.

In the centre of the grove, suspended between two ancient, moss-covered trees, hung a man. His arms were outstretched, bound tightly with coarse rope that dug into his flesh. A rag was stuffed into his mouth, muffling any cries for help. His head lolled forwards, but the slow rise and fall of his chest indicated that he was still alive.

Unease bloomed in Wren's gut, goosebumps racing across her skin as she glanced up at Torj. If he was surprised to find a man strung up between the trees here, he didn't show it.

Swallowing the hard lump in her throat, Wren spotted another figure at the edge of the treeline: a straight-backed middle-aged man in all black, a belt similar to Wren's around his waist. Indifferent to the nearby prisoner, he didn't speak, simply watched as more students began to gather before him.

'You're on your own, Embervale,' Torj muttered, starting to peel away from the group.

'Wait,' she ordered, reaching for her belt. Brow furrowed, the Warsword surprisingly did as she bid. 'Take this.' She offered him the pouch she'd made last night.

'What is it?' he asked, turning it over in his large hands; it was smaller than his palm.

'An antidote kit.' Pulling the cord around it so it opened like a book, she revealed several small vials within. 'For some of the most common poisons.'

A flicker of amusement ghosted across the Bear Slayer's lips. 'You worried about me, Embers?'

'Hardly. But I could have used it last night. Makes sense for you to have one just in case.'

'Here I was thinking you liked being the one to patch me up. Or have you truly forgotten the first time we met?'

Wren forced a shrug. 'Must have been an inconsequential day,' she said lightly.

'Whatever you say,' Torj replied, eyes glinting as he pocketed the kit and dropped back from Wren and the class.

Wren's side felt instantly cold.

Another gurgle of pain escaped the man bound between the trees, but she forced herself to scan her cohort. She didn't know what she'd been expecting when it came to her peers, but it wasn't the array of ages that surrounded her now. The faces staring back at her ranged from those in their early teen years to a woman who must have been in her seventies. This was no starting school.

There were a few semi-familiar faces from the gala: the white-haired man who'd been smoking several cigarillos at once, and the man Torj had nearly choked to death with his war hammer in the hallway afterwards. Young or old, the glint in every eye was one of determination, of resilience, and every one of them seemed to meet her gaze with a look of challenge.

What right do you have to be here? they seemed to say.

She'd damn well show them soon enough.

As she surveyed her peers, she met the eyes of a woman around her own age, her striking red hair braided down the side of her face, in the same style as Thea often wore hers. Wren recognized her as the woman who'd been splashing around in the fountain with Kipp at the gala. She offered Wren a grin now, which Wren instantly turned away from in a panic. How long had it been since she'd made a friend? She'd forgotten how.

Their teacher made no move to acknowledge the prisoner, but instead motioned for their attention, holding a crumpled scroll in his hands. 'Good morning, novices. I am Hardim Norlander, Master of Lifelore – the study of living things for alchemical application. You may call me Hardim. Before we delve into the first of the four pillars of alchemy, we must address a matter of utmost importance. As you were made aware at last night's gala, all novices at Drevenor are required to take an oath of secrecy. If you break your oath, the consequences are dire.' He gave them a meaningful look. 'This is your last chance to turn back. For those of you without the backbone to commit wholly to the path of alchemy, this is your final opportunity to leave.'

Several people flushed at the mention of the festivities, and Wren felt a cold sweat break out across her own back, but no one moved.

Hardim surveyed them with an unflinching stare, holding out a curling yellowed scroll. 'You are to prick your index finger and press a dot of blood to this piece of parchment, which reads as follows:

I hereby pledge myself to Drevenor.
I will delve into the dark abyss of knowledge and guard the secrets entrusted to me.
With my body as a shield, my mind as a blade, I will not hesitate to sacrifice.
In my own blood this oath is made.
And with it, I swear fealty, until the academy releases me, or until death claims me.
I am marked forevermore as a steward of this ancient art.
I will protect it and harness it, with all that I am and will be.'

Wren took a pocketknife from her belt and pricked her finger without hesitation. She was the first to come forward to press her blood to the parchment.

When everyone had completed the oath, some with more hesitancy than others, the master rolled up the sheet of parchment and turned to them once more.

'This oath is usually taken in the grandness of our great hall; however, the consequences of breaking this vow are not grand. They are severe. Life-altering. They leave a stain on one's soul.'

A knot of tension tightened between Wren's ribs, and she fought to remain still beneath the weight of Hardim's words.

'Some of you may have noticed that we are not alone,' he said.

As if in answer, the prisoner gave a muffled cry behind his gag, the ropes around his limbs creaking as he struggled against their hold.

Hardim took a deep breath, rubbing his temples before he motioned to the bound man. 'You are about to witness what happens when you break the oath.' The prisoner trembled from head to toe as Hardim continued, his voice stripped of all emotion. 'Meet Bertram. He is an adept who has been with us for three and a half years.'

Hardim approached the prisoner tentatively, as though he'd rather be anywhere else. He removed the gag from Bertram's mouth.

'Three and a half years,' he repeated. 'And recently, you did what?'

'I didn't mean to, I just—'

'You broke your oath of secrecy, correct?'

'I—'

'Am I correct?' Hardim pressed.

The next word left Bertram's lips in a whisper. 'Yes.'

Hardim surveyed their cohort. 'Your fellow alchemist must now face the consequences.'

The lifelore master produced an object from a bag at his feet. It was no bigger than one of Wren's textbooks and looked like a tapestry fitted to a frame, only the threads that passed across its surface seemed to shimmer.

'This is a memory weave. Our Master of Design will tell you more about it at a later date—'

'Please,' Bertram stammered. 'I don't want to lose my—'

'You broke the oath,' Hardim said simply. He held a small vial of green liquid to Bertram's mouth. 'Drink.'

'No - I can't. *Please.* I'll never—'

'There is only one outcome here, Bertram.' Hardim did not lower the vial.

Sweat poured from the adept's brow.

'Don't make this harder than it needs to be,' the Master of Lifelore warned.

With fear and devastation etched on his face, Bertram tipped his head back, allowing Hardim to pour the concoction onto his tongue.

Wren watched, her insides twisting. Almost instantly, Bertram's eyes went glassy and unfocused, all notion of awareness extinguished by the tonic's grip on his mind.

With cold efficiency, Hardim held up the strange object, plucking a thread from its latticework and fixing it to Bertram's temple.

The fibre rippled and pulled. And suddenly, Wren could see images drifting from Bertram's now convulsing form.

Shimmering memories forced their way to the surface: a gala, not unlike the one she'd attended last night; potions bubbling away on a workbench; a vibrant garden of herbs, as far as the eye could see; a maze of deep green . . . Then came Bertram's agonized howls.

Wren gasped. He could *feel* it.

Around her, several people started. A wave of nausea hit her like a blow to the gut. Wren's fingernails dug crescents into her palms as she forced herself to watch the brutal unravelling of Bertram's mind. At Hardim's coaxing, the memories rose faster and faster to the surface, meticulously weaving themselves into an intricate mesh across the object the Master of Lifelore held.

Three and a half years of memories, weaving themselves one by one into the artefact, flaying Bertram's psyche in the process.

Perspiration beaded on Wren's brow, her throat aching from suppressing her own cries of horror as Hardim at last pulled the translucent strand from poor Bertram's temple.

The screaming stopped. Bertram sagged in his bonds with a garbled sound. Shadows gathered in the hollows of his face, the awareness behind his eyes little more than a guttering candle flame.

'Where am I?' he croaked.

Wren's heart was pounding so hard her chest hurt as she watched the Master of Lifelore pack away the terrifying object.

Hardim's gaze was hard as it fell once more to the cohort before him. 'This, dear novices, is the fate that awaits oathbreakers.'

CHAPTER 24

Wren

'May you walk into the maw
of the beast with open eyes'

– *Drevenor Academy Handbook*

A DEATHLY SILENCE descended over the assembled novices as the horror took hold, not only at what they had witnessed, but what they'd agreed to.

Wren heard panicked hyperventilation from someone nearby, saw the white-knuckled grip of the man beside her. All around her, harrowing understanding was writ large on her peers' expressions.

Here at Drevenor, it seemed, terrors were to be embraced without reservation, and oaths were eternal.

The eerie quiet stretched out torturously, broken only by the rasping, laboured breaths of Bertram, still strung up between the trees.

Regret flashed across Hardim's face as he turned back and addressed the cohort. 'Now, for today's lesson. The parchment you just marked with your blood was treated with several toxins – which one, exactly, depends on where you blotted your mark. As I told you: this will be neither easy nor safe. Each time you study lifelore, or any discipline here, you put yourself on the line.'

Wren looked down at where she'd pierced the pad of her index finger, studying it for any signs of what the parchment had been doused in. But there was no redness, no swelling or itching, nothing besides the tiny prick she'd made with her knife.

She needed a moment to think, to run through her mind for poisons that had a delayed reaction time, like the mixture she'd used on Lord Briar—

'For those who think lifelore is the weaker discipline, tell me: can you have life without death?' Hardim continued. 'They are two sides of the same coin, novices, and you will come to know both intimately over the course of your time here. Do not think this will be easy. Do not think this will be safe. Lifelore can test you in ways you couldn't even dream. It is the foundation for all alchemy, no matter what discipline you choose to specialize in, should you make it that far.'

Hardim gestured to the knotted trees around them, where a piece of parchment had been pinned to a trunk.

'You will find no chalkboards and apples in today's lesson. You have been split into teams, as listed here. You will be in these teams for the duration of your novice training, and with these teams you will face the trials of the Gauntlet. You must pass the Gauntlet together or not at all. But today . . . today you will go into the forest and seek the antidote to the poison that has by now worked its way into your skin.'

The cohort was experiencing various reactions already: rashes and swelling, and someone was vomiting into a shrub.

Hardim's voice rang out across the growing chaos. 'Knowledge is the victor over fate. The mind is a blade, novices.'

Wren had seen those words scrawled across the gates upon their arrival, had seen them stitched into the tapestries hanging over the stone walls and stamped atop the coat of arms on every flag. But it was only here, in the eerie forest, on the lips of the Master Alchemist of Lifelore, that they sank deep into her bones.

The mind is a blade . . . and she would hone hers until it was sharp enough to cut the world.

All around her, the symptoms of poisoning were intensifying. She saw bleeding noses, clumps of hair falling out, and in one case, complete delirium.

Wren needed to find her team. They needed to get into the forest, and fast.

'Beyond the laws of the midrealms and the single rule the High Chancellor already set, there are none.' Hardim pinned them with a meaningful stare. 'But as it's your first day, first lesson . . . I'll share a kernel of wisdom with you all.'

Wren leaned in with the rest, eager to absorb any knowledge the Master Alchemist was willing to give them.

His voice was completely deadpan as he said, 'Don't die.'

According to the slip of parchment, Wren's teammates were Odessa Chamberlain, the redhead from Kipp's fountain party, and Zavier Mortimer, a surly-faced young man who looked as though he might spit on the pair of them. Wren didn't wait to enter the depths of the forest, and her two teammates trailed close behind her, the trees closing in around them.

Teams? Truly? She hated that her fate was now tied to two others whose skills were yet to be determined. What if they fucked everything up for her? What if she didn't pass the Gauntlet because of them?

'Slow down,' Zavier called. 'You'll walk straight into a—'

Wren ducked just in time.

A flailing vine shot down from above, thrashing wildly.

'Shit,' she muttered, pushing her hair back off her face and surveying the bizarre plant.

Zavier pushed the thing aside with a long stick, wearing a haughty look. 'You're welcome.'

'I don't need your help,' Wren replied.

He scoffed at that. 'Not what it looked like.'

'Come now,' Odessa implored, coming to stand between them. 'We're a team, right? And we're stuck with each other until at least after the Gauntlet. We need to work together.' She threw her fiery red braid over her shoulder and held out her hand. 'I'm Dessa. Pleased to meet you.'

'You've got to be kidding me,' Zavier muttered, shaking his head. He was perhaps a few years older than Wren and stood straight-backed, his sable hair swept carelessly off his face, which might have been handsome but for his dour expression.

Dessa stuck out her hand in Wren's direction. 'You must be Elwren?'

'Just Wren.' Reluctantly, Wren shook Dessa's hand before she turned to the other teammate. 'And you're Zavier?' she asked, not because she wanted to play along but because she figured he wouldn't appreciate her calling him a sour-faced prick.

'Yes,' he said finally, still ignoring Dessa's outstretched hand. 'Satisfied?'

'Completely,' Wren replied sardonically. 'We can all pack up and go home now, job done.'

'We may as well. You're not going to last a week here,' Zavier retorted. Wren registered a subtle lilt to his words, an accent that she didn't recognize.

'Please,' Dessa implored, motioning to her swollen fingers. 'We have to work out what we've been poisoned with—'

'You've got an acute reaction to Naarvian dogbane,' Zavier cut her off.

Wren's gaze snapped to his. She hadn't been expecting *that*. Naarvian dogbane wasn't a commonly known substance, nor was its antidote . . . but one glance at Dessa's hand, which was already twice its normal size and covered in red splotches, told her that Zavier was right.

'Oh,' Dessa said with a wince, as he motioned for her to rotate it. 'I thought it was poison oak.'

'The swelling wouldn't be like that if it was,' Wren told her, donning the pair of gloves at her belt and inspecting Dessa's hand more closely.

'She'll be fine,' Zavier snapped. 'Find some bitter dock leaf, crush up the stalk, and—'

'I know how to treat a reaction to dogbane,' Wren retorted.

'I should fucking hope so,' Zavier muttered, rooting around by the trunk of a nearby tree before handing Odessa a handful of broad leaves. 'Here. Chew it up, then apply it as a paste to the site of the wound.'

'And you?' Wren prompted, as a means of distracting herself from her own potential poisoning. 'What did they get you with?'

'Wolfsbane.' He turned his palm up and showed her a small blister on the pad of his index finger.

Wren frowned. 'That should be much worse.'

'I've been working on my immunity for years.'

Wren blinked at him. 'To wolfsbane? That would have taken—'

'An extremely high dosage and prolonged exposure, yes.' Zavier motioned to her hand. 'Let's see the damage to you, then.'

She didn't want or need any help, especially not from him. His head seemed big enough already. Unfortunately for her, there were no outward signs of poisoning at the puncture site.

'Well?' he prompted.

'No markings,' she told him reluctantly, holding up her finger.

'And how do you feel?' he pressed. 'Dizzy? Nauseous? Like you're about to lift off and fly?'

She shot him an incredulous look.

Zavier shrugged. 'The welcome gala showed us they're not above drugging us with mind-altering substances. Both wolfsbane and ambrosia can create a sensation of—'

'I know,' Wren ground out. 'You're not the only one who knows about protecting yourself. It's possible I'm immune to whatever I've come into contact with.'

'Either that or you'll die a few days from now,' he said. 'Did Hardim say if the death of a teammate impacts our ability to participate in the Gauntlet?'

Wren opened her mouth to tell him to piss off, but a high-pitched scream echoed through the trees.

The trio froze. More screaming followed, and Wren shared a worried glance with Dessa.

Soon after, Hardim's voice carried through the forest. 'I did warn you this wasn't child's play.'

That seemed to break whatever spell had fallen over them.

Zavier tapped his foot in the leaf litter, his eyes roaming from Wren's face to the scar at her throat. 'Time is ticking.'

Wren's fingers itched to reach for her hairpin and press its poisoned tip to his skin. But to her immense frustration, he had a point. If it was a delayed reaction, there might not be a way of knowing until it was too late.

'If you die and it impacts my chances at the Gauntlet, Delmirian, I'll bring you back and kill you myself,' Zavier said flatly.

'Ignore him,' Dessa said quickly. 'You're not going to die—'

'Not if I get a moment to think,' Wren replied sharply.

Thankfully, Dessa quietened.

Wren closed her eyes and took a breath. She had no difficulty doing so, which ruled out any respiratory side effects and, as such, several poisons at the top of her mind. Pressing her fingers to her wrist and then to her neck, she checked her pulse: also steady, which ruled out another list of suspects. One by one, she went through the most common areas affected by poison with a keen familiarity. How many times had she watched one toxin or another take hold of a mark? Her hands were working just fine; there was no tingling or vibrating in her extremities. Her vision was clear.

Wren was still wracking her mind for answers when she tasted metal on her tongue.

Blood.

She lunged for her toolbelt.

A bleeding mouth meant a daphne plant, likely from the heart of Harenth if it had taken this long to affect her. Fighting to keep her panic at bay, Wren sifted through her assortment of vials. She needed a purgative, and quickly. Her own stores held nothing that would counter the effects now that her gums were bleeding.

Staggering through the forest, she scanned the shrubs and climbing vines, spitting that metallic taste onto the ground. Zavier was already waiting beside the bush she sought, and Wren fell to her knees before the rounded leaves, taking several cuttings with her secateurs.

Ignoring Dessa's questions, she squeezed several drops of sap into her mouth, the insides of her cheeks burning at the contact.

Perspiration beaded at her brow, and within seconds she was on all fours, vomiting.

Dessa was there, holding her loose hair out of her face, rubbing gentle circles on her back. 'You did it!' she said. 'Elwren, you solved it.'

Wren wiped her mouth with the back of her hand, grimacing. 'Just Wren.'

'Well, "just Wren,"' Zavier said wryly. 'You're not as awful as I thought. But you lose points for timing. You should have come to that conclusion much sooner.'

Wren spat onto the ground again, her heart still hammering. 'No one asked you.'

Zavier was twirling a scalpel between his long, elegant fingers, looking smug. Wren's stomach lurched, this time with unease. Zavier clearly knew his lifelore, perhaps even more so than she did. All her life she'd been the best at what she did, but now . . . Zavier might be good news for her chances at the Gauntlet, but he was bad news for her pride.

'Those are a fine make,' Dessa marvelled, eyeing the markings on Wren's secateurs as she took several more cuttings of the purgative plant for her own supplies. 'I've heard they never rust . . . And that the blades never dull? I didn't think you could get that kind in the midrealms.'

Wren's heart stuttered as the memory came rushing back.

'It's not my name day . . .'

'No, but . . .' Torj shifted awkwardly on his feet. 'Just open it.'

Wren slowly reached for the parcel. 'Some sort of weapon, I presume? Perhaps a—'

'Just open it, Elwren.'

Wren unlaced the twine and peeled the fabric back, her mouth dropping open at what was inside: a little pair of silver scissors.

'These are what you needed?' the Warsword asked.

Wren blinked, slowly turning to lift her gaze to his. A powerful wave of gratitude washed over her. She wanted to throw her arms around his neck, to kiss him completely senseless. She knew how hard it was to get a pair of secateurs of this make. She'd been trying – and failing – for years.

She realized she was staring. 'I . . .'

Torj nodded. 'Good,' he said, before walking back towards his friends.

Moments later, Thea sidled up beside her and jutted her chin towards the gift. 'What are those?'

Wren couldn't help but stare after the Bear Slayer in awe. 'They're secateurs,' she said, almost in a whisper.

'What?'

'Remember back in Naarva how I was saying my hand hurt from harvesting the orchids? That I do a lot of intricate work with my hands and they often ache from the repeated motions?'

'It rings a bell.'

Wren shook her head, knowing her sister was full of shit. 'In one of about ten thousand meetings, I suggested that all the harvesters be provided with secateurs, to help with the strain . . . They're a design from distant lands, hard to find . . . I didn't think anyone was listening.'

Thea grinned. 'Someone clearly was.'

'Wren?' Dessa was peering into her face, brow furrowed with concern. 'You're alright now, aren't you?'

'Fine,' she managed.

Zavier scrutinized her. 'You sure? You're looking pale still . . . Maybe you don't belong here after all.'

Wren had half a mind to throttle him, but Dessa sighed. 'We're all on the same team—'

'Can't say I'm thrilled by the prospect,' Zavier said.

'Something we agree on, then,' Wren retorted with a glare.

With their poisons accounted for and treated, they made their way back through the forest in silence. Wren pocketed several wild blooms, hoping to use the plant press she'd brought with her from Thezmarr. She was thinking about blissful solitude when another scream echoed through the trees. This time, Wren couldn't stop herself; she sprinted towards the sound, with Zavier and Dessa close behind.

There, in a small clearing, a young man was rolling around in the leaf litter, clawing wildly at his rash-covered arms, pained cries on his lips. His teammates were nowhere in sight.

'What are you doing?' Zavier hissed. 'Leave him. Another team's failure is a win for us.'

Ignoring him, Wren crouched down, examining the pale, sweating face of the young man sprawled on the forest floor. His shallow breathing and the zig-zag rash across his arms had her rifling through her belt.

Above her, Zavier cursed before dropping down beside her. 'Dessa, find a flat rock,' he commanded their other teammate.

Dessa did as he bid while Wren pulled out dried angelica and activated charcoal to absorb the toxin. When Dessa returned with several flat pieces of stone, Zavier snatched them away, along with the ingredients, and crushed the mixture deftly. Wren raised a brow at him.

'What?' he snapped, carefully tipping the antidote into their young charge's mouth. 'If you insist on making a nuisance of yourself, you may as well do it quickly.' Several long seconds passed as Wren monitored the man's breathing, his struggles subsiding.

'Do you know what happened?' she asked him as his brows knitted in confusion, the colour returning to his cheeks.

He blinked at her. 'They gave me some sort of leaf . . . I had a bad reaction . . .'

Dessa looked around with a frown. 'Who's "they"?'

'I was separated from my team. Another group said they wanted to help me . . .'

Zavier shook his head and scoffed. 'Fool.'

Wren helped the man to his feet. 'You're alright now.'

'Thank you,' he replied, a tremor in his voice.

Zavier made another noise of frustration. '*Now* can we go? We're wasting time.'

They made their way back to the grove. *Poisoning, sabotage, backstabbing, and maiming,* Wren mused. *All in a day's work.* This place was more like Thezmarr than she'd realized.

Knowledge is the victor over fate, she told herself as they made their way back through the forest to where Hardim was waiting. *The mind is a blade.*

There was no sign of Bertram; the trees where he'd been strung up were bare. Their cohort was in various states. Some were covered in dirt, leaves stuck in their hair as though they had fought the trees themselves. Others were clutching injuries of varying degrees, and some were missing entirely.

Hardim examined the teams one by one, shaking his head or making inaudible comments as he went. When he reached Dessa, Zavier and Wren, his expression was unreadable. He surveyed them head to toe.

'A solid counter to Odessa's Naarvian dogbane poisoning,' he murmured with a nod. His gaze fell to the spots of blood on Wren's apron and his nose wrinkled. 'Seems like you could have identified your daphne plant sooner . . . Timing is everything with that one.' Then his scrutiny fell on Zavier. 'An immunity to wolfsbane? Very impressive.' He scanned the trio again. 'Not a terrible first effort. Five points apiece.'

The Master of Lifelore turned away to count the cohort, and when he was done, he sighed heavily.

'The points you have earned today will be reflected in the glass vessels in the foyer by the day's end. In the meantime, I need to revive some of your fellow students. I suppose I shouldn't let anyone die in the first lesson. You're all dismissed.'

Somewhat dazed, Wren and her teammates turned back towards the grounds, but Hardim's voice echoed after them.

'Drevenor welcomes you with open arms,' he called. 'But beware the thorns of its embrace.'

A fleeting smile threatened to break across Wren's lips. She could still taste a trace of blood there.

Zavier was wrong. This was *exactly* where she belonged.

CHAPTER 25
Torj

'Assess the potential threat and be aware of surroundings at all times'

– *Vigilance and Valour: Tactical Training for Professional Bodyguards*

IT TOOK EVERY ounce of Torj's training to stop himself from rushing into that fucking forest at the sound of those screams. He knew it wasn't Wren, but that knowledge didn't comfort him in the least. She was still somewhere in there, without him to shield her from harm.

But Audra's orders had been clear regarding the protection of the Delmirian heir: by no means was he to interfere with her training and studies at the academy – if one could call poisoning a group of novices 'studying'. No, he was to address outside threats only. Though the Guild Master could have warned him – this place was no picnic.

He'd come here with notions of intellectual discussions and potion-making, of picking herbs in the gardens and making tinctures . . . But all those preconceived ideas had been shattered when the whole cohort had been drugged out of their minds on arrival. Thus far, every interaction with the academy and its staff only served to solidify his hunch that Drevenor itself posed as much of a threat to Wren as anything in the outside world. An alchemy academy it might have been in name, but he'd just seen a student exit the woods with their hand nearly severed. He'd seen a man's memories stripped from his mind.

Whatever this place of madness was, it was not for the faint of heart.

He watched the Master of Lifelore pace the treeline until the man glanced up, catching his eye. 'Farissa also spoke to me of your predicament,' Hardim said.

'Which predicament would that be?'

'The magical wound you sustained in the war,' Hardim replied, seemingly unfazed by Torj's less-than-amicable tone.

Torj ground his teeth. He'd thought there would be at least *some* measure of confidentiality between himself and the Master Alchemist of Healing. Apparently not.

'What about it?' he asked coolly.

'Magic,' Hardim began. 'That elusive force woven into the fabric of existence itself leaves its mark upon both wielder *and* recipient. It always has. Wounds born of magic transcend the physical, delving deep into the core of one's being. Unlike mundane injuries, they can fester not only in flesh, but in spirit.'

Torj stopped himself from rubbing his chest, where his scars had begun to tingle. 'So I've heard.'

'I have some contacts you can speak to. People who have experienced similar afflictions, or who are close to someone who has. It may prove a helpful addition to the books Farissa is having pulled for you from the archives.'

Torj brushed a lock of hair from his brow and studied Hardim. 'You know a lot of people like that?'

'Some.'

'What happened to them?'

'You'll have to talk to them yourself.'

'That bad?' Torj pressed, fists clenching at his sides. Perhaps he should have addressed the damn scars sooner.

Your body wasn't built to hold magic like this...

Hardim shrugged. 'As I said, you'll have to speak with them.' He drew a crumpled square of parchment from his pocket. 'Here are their details.'

Reluctantly, Torj took it with a mumbled thanks, looking up in time to see Wren emerging from the gnarled trees. Her apron and skirts were covered in mud, one of her gloves was ruined, and she had smudges of dirt smeared across one cheek. Blood had dried in the corner of her mouth, but for the first time since Torj had seen her after the war, her eyes were bright with something other than fury.

He followed her dutifully from the forest to the infirmary, where she and her teammates were checked over. Rage coursed through him as he overheard the diagnoses. Poisoned with something called daphne, Wren had been bleeding internally.

Do not interfere. Do not interfere. He reminded himself that he only cared because if he failed his task, he could kiss the posting abroad goodbye yet again.

When they left the infirmary, Torj said nothing as Wren turned down Odessa's offer for a shared meal in the halls, though he did suppress a laugh when she promptly told the scowling man called Zavier to 'eat shit and die.'

On their way back to their rooms, alone at last, he turned to her. 'Are you alright?'

'Yes.'

'You should eat something.'

'You should mind your own business.'

Irritation prickled at him. 'And you should do as you're told for once in your life.'

'And make things nice and cushy for the likes of you?' she scoffed. 'I don't think so.'

'When have you *ever* made things easy for me?' he bit back.

When they reached her quarters, she motioned to the door. 'Can you get your unnecessary security sweep over with so I can do my work in peace? In case you didn't realize, there's a form of weaponized alchemy that needs a cure . . .'

'And I suppose you'll be the one to discover it?'

'Yes,' she said simply.

He unlocked the door, ready to keep verbally sparring with her, but when he entered, the state of the room beyond shocked the words right out of his mouth.

'You've been here one night!' he exclaimed, gesturing to the den of chaos her once clean and tidy chamber had become. He couldn't believe what he was seeing as Wren lit the lanterns. The space was cluttered with potted plants and crawling vines; bundles of dried herbs were strung up around the room; half-empty teacups were strewn about the workbench, along with an hourglass holding loose sheets of parchment in place. Quills and inkpots were everywhere, as well as a scratched-up magnifying glass and several sketches of strange-looking leaves.

Bewildered, Torj carried out his usual checks: the locks, the window latch, under the bed. He searched the bathing chamber and his own rooms for any sign of disturbance.

'Anything out of place to you?' he asked Wren, scanning her quarters again.

'Only the massive Bear Slayer taking up all the space.'

'Would you rather a *small* bodyguard?' he retorted.

'I'd rather none.'

'Well, that's too fucking bad.'

'Are you done here?' Wren asked, folding her arms over her chest. 'I have work to do.'

'You still haven't eaten.'

'What's it to you?'

A growl of frustration nearly escaped him. This woman – Furies help him. 'Suppose you die of starvation; they'll say I didn't do my job properly.'

'Sounds like a "you" problem to me,' she replied, motioning to the door. 'Leave me be, unless you'd like to stay for a cup of tea?'

On the far windowsill was the teapot she called the Ladies' Luncheon, the one she'd used to poison the former Guild Master.

'I'll pass, thanks,' he said dryly.

'Smartest choice you've made all day.'

For a brief second, Torj considered arguing, but when it came to Elwren Embervale, he knew to choose his battles wisely. Shaking his head, he at last retreated to his room.

With Wren, it was all about the long game, and it had only just begun.

CHAPTER 26

Wren

'For a mild purgative, root of rhubarb may prove most effective when combined with a pinch of powdered senna'

– The Green Apothecary: A Guide to Medicinal Plants

'How do you kill a man before he dies?'

The clear, commanding voice rang out across the dimly lit dungeon, penetrating the chatter. As a middle-aged man entered the room, the torches flickered in the wall sconces, casting shadows that danced across the rows of dusty shelves overflowing with exotic ingredients and mysterious vials.

Tall and lean, the Master of Warfare took centre stage, demanding respect with his regal posture alone. His roughened skin hinted at a lifetime of alchemical experiments, his face a web of scarred tissue. He wore pristine, crisp clothing of a fine make, and as he gestured, several rings gleamed on his long fingers.

'Welcome, novices,' he said. 'I am Master Landis Crawford. In this crucible of shadows, you will learn the alchemy of demise: the delicate dance of toxins and the fine art of turning nature's bounty into kisses of death. What you master within these walls may just shape the destiny of the realms around you.'

Silence fell over the cohort, and Wren looked around, unsure what to make of the master's grand words.

He gave them all a flat stare. 'Warfare isn't a mystical art. It is a cold, calculated discipline, not to be trifled with. All paths lead to the underworld, novices. You'd do well to remember that.' He motioned to the shelves either side of their desks, laden with ingredients and utensils. 'Today you are required to concoct a toxin that will kill a man precisely three days before he dies.'

Wren sat up straighter. *This* was what she had lived and breathed for the last five years.

'It can take any form, but it must be undetectable to the victim,' Master Crawford continued. 'Powder, liquid, I don't care, so long as it is effective. By the end of our two hours together, you will administer your toxin to a rat assigned to you.'

'Rats, sir?' someone called out.

'Would you prefer I ask you to test it on yourself?' Master Crawford said, deadpan. 'We will get to that, I assure you.'

No one answered.

Wren herself didn't care for rats; she had seen too many of the filthy rodents scurrying through the camps during the shadow war to feel much sympathy for them. Just the thought made her skin crawl.

'What are you waiting for?' Master Crawford called impatiently.

Wren didn't rush to the shelves like everyone else, and to her surprise, nor did Zavier. The pair of them made their own notes and consulted their books, and when the rush was over, both warily approached the ingredients and tools.

Wren had planned on adapting the poison she'd used on one of her first marks after the war, only to realize it had taken her two days to distil safely, and here, she only had two hours. She wracked her brain for poisons she'd previously worked with, ingredients she could predict based on a variety of environmental factors.

Surveying the vials and jars before her, she made quick work of her decisions. She would have preferred to work with fresh ingredients, but she didn't want to waste time crossing the grounds to the greenhouses. It was the foxglove she reached for first, its bell-shaped purple flowers in stark contrast to the yellowed parchment it had been dried on, and then the delicate white petals of hemlock. In the crook of her elbow, she hung a small basket wherein she placed the blooms, along with oil and a bushel of fool's parsley. She glanced at the array of mushrooms – the death cap, the dead man's fingers, and the false morel, dismissing each in turn as too fast-acting.

Returning to her workspace, she unloaded her ingredients. There was no time for maceration, and a poultice would not work given the test subject. Whatever she created would have to be ingested, and the effect would have to unfold slowly . . .

The rest of the world fell away, and for a brief period, she could almost pretend she was back in her cottage in Delmira, grinding her ingredients and passing them through a cheesecloth. She wrung out each liquid separately, and heated them one by one above a small burner, her mind sifting through the experiments she had performed both under the tutelage of Farissa at Thezmarr and in the years after.

You've more than earned the title of the Poisoner . . . What's your ledger at now? Seven? Eight?

She scowled as the Bear Slayer's words came back to her. The Warsword had always had an infuriating understanding of the monster that prowled beneath her skin, of her dark potential. With two warrior sisters, she had often been overlooked as the intellectual one, the quiet one with her potions and books. Torj Elderbrock had seen beyond that, throughout the war and in the years after. He had seen the very best and the very worst of her, and she hated him for it—

'Shit!' she hissed, seeing too late that she'd overheated the hemlock extract. She'd have to start again.

Glancing across at Zavier, who was brewing something in a small vessel over a thick candle, she vowed to push Torj from her mind.

She had to focus. If she was lucky, Master Crawford might just let her test her poison on her teammate.

She had no such luck. At the end of the two hours, the Master of Warfare watched her administer three drops of her clear tonic to the rat's water supply. She only hoped she'd got the balance of foxglove and fool's parsley right.

Master Crawford addressed them all again, collecting what was left of their experiments. 'Before our next lesson, I expect you all to concoct a cure for the toxin you just created.'

There was a unified intake of breath. Wren gathered she had spotted the same problem as her peers. Not only did the master now hold her leftover supply, but had she known the flip side to the challenge, she might have chosen differently – something that might have been simpler to remedy.

Master Crawford offered a knowing, satisfied smile. 'Did you think it was going to be easy in my class? I didn't think you'd need reminding that the discipline of warfare is the most apt embodiment of our academy's motto.'

Knowledge is the victor over fate. The mind is a blade.

No, Wren decided. She would never need to be reminded of that again.

As they packed up their workstations and shouldered their satchels, the Master of Warfare looked around, smug this time. 'All paths lead to the underworld, novices,' he said. 'But let's see what road you take.'

CHAPTER 27

Torj

'Wounds inflicted by magic fracture not only flesh, but the bonds that bind hearts and souls together'

– Arcane Ailments: Understanding Magical Maladies

To Torj, Drevenor was becoming less an alchemy academy and more a nightmare. Protecting Wren against outside threats felt at odds with the horrors unfolding within the institution. Still, the strange classes meant that he could leave Cal on duty and attend to his own business.

Torj started at the top of Hardim Norlander's list of contacts – people who had suffered magical wounds, or knew someone who had. It was how he found himself on the outskirts of Highguard, the closest city to Drevenor, named for its vantage point overlooking the Broken Isles. There, in a small fishing village by the docks, Torj tethered his horse outside the local tavern, and crossed the dirt road to the local bakery, a bell ringing by his ear as he entered.

'It's not every day you see a Warsword of Thezmarr in these parts,' a croaky voice said from behind the counter.

Torj spotted a shrunken elderly man kneading a ball of dough on the bench, his apron covered in flour. 'Are you Branwell?' he asked, with another glance at Hardim's list.

'Afraid so,' Branwell replied. 'Norlander said you'd be paying a visit.'

He offered his hand. 'I'm Torj Elderbrock.'

Branwell shook it, not paying the flour and specks of dough any heed. 'You're here to talk about my boy?'

'If you're willing. Is there somewhere private we can go?'

'Don't get much more private than this bakery right here. It'll be a long while 'til first customers come through. There was a big party across the road last night. Whole town's still asleep, I imagine.'

Torj glanced out the grimy window. True enough, no one in the little village seemed to have stirred, and he'd seen no one out and about on the ride in. 'Alright then.'

'You can make yourself useful while we talk. Grab that batch of dough there and give it a good kneading. You look like you've got the arms for it.'

Slightly bewildered, Torj did what Branwell asked.

'So, you want to know how my son died,' the baker said without preamble.

Torj balked, but managed to give a nod of confirmation as he tipped the dough onto the floured surface.

Branwell seemed to steel himself. 'Alden fought in the war, you see. Under King Leiko's banner at first. He was at the battle of Notos – which I know you and your comrades oversaw.'

'We did.' Torj was suddenly grateful to have something to do with his hands, working the dough with the heel of his palm as Branwell himself was doing.

'Early in the fighting, King Leiko came out with one of his units. He was determined to fight, even against the orders of the Guild Master.'

This was news to Torj. He'd never had much of an impression of the King of Tver's character.

'Alden was in the King's Guard, you see. Close to His Majesty, close to his magic . . . When a group of shadow wraiths attacked, the king tried to fight them back with his sovereign power – fire.

Only, he lost control. He killed two of the monsters, but he also burned my son in the process.'

Torj concentrated on kneading the dough.

'His Majesty was mortified, of course. He oversaw Alden's recovery, compensated him generously. But no matter the skill of the healers he brought in from all over the midrealms, Alden's injury continued to ail him.'

'Did the wound heal physically?'

'In time, yes. Nasty scars left behind – typical of a regular burn, we were told. But the pain lingered. It ate away at him.'

'I'm sorry to hear it.'

Branwell took the dough from Torj and gave him a fresh batch to knead while he shaped the piece Torj had worked on, placing it in a tin and scoring the top with a scalpel-like blade.

'We tried to tell the healers that the wound impacted him more deeply than the scars showed. He was fine at first – recovering, but himself . . . And then a time later, he started having nightmares. Slowly, his vitality waned, leaving behind a hollow shell of a man. He told us he could still feel the fire in his scars, long after they had healed. In the end, he lived in fragmented memories. He lost himself. Eventually he took his own life.'

'Gods,' Torj murmured. 'I'm so sorry for your loss.'

Branwell glanced up, silver lining his eyes. 'Hardim said that you yourself suffered such an injury?'

Torj nodded. 'During the final battle of the war.' He didn't know why, but he felt compelled to part the collar of his shirt and show the man his scars. 'Are you saying this will . . . drive me to madness?'

'I'm no expert,' Branwell said solemnly. 'I can only tell you what happened to my son, and the man who fought beside him. They both met the same fate.'

The baker gave him a pitying look and passed him a rag to wipe his hands with. As Torj scrubbed the bits of dough lining his palms and fingers, he stared blankly at the flour-covered bench, Branwell's words slowly sinking in.

He lived in fragmented memories.
He lost himself.

He only looked up when the baker pushed a loaf of warm bread into his chest. 'Sorry I couldn't be of more help,' he said.

Torj nodded numbly, taking the offering. 'Thank you for your trouble.'

'My son was a good lad. And you . . . You're a hero of the midrealms. Neither of you deserve such an end.' Branwell hesitated. 'Maybe if more people knew about the effects of the rulers' magic, they'd understand what those midrealms renegades are on about, eh?'

Torj paused. 'Rebels?'

Branwell nodded, his eyes brightening. 'Got posters all over the village. Something about giving the midrealms back to the people.'

Torj realized he was crushing the bread in his hands. 'Right. Well, thank you for your time.'

'Good luck to you, Warsword.'

'I'll be needing as much as I can get,' Torj muttered, leaving the shop.

Branwell was right: the posters were all over town. Torj found several pinned to the noticeboard in the village square alone.

Are you tired of being downtrodden and ruled over by tyrants?
Do you want our kingdoms to be a place of peace?
Join the People's Vanguard in their fight for a better world.

Torj ripped the flyer from its pin and pocketed it. He'd have to show Audra – that was, if the Guild Master wasn't already aware of the problem. Given his current task, he had the sinking suspicion that she knew far more than she'd let on. As always.

With a heavy sigh, he returned to his tethered stallion, tucking the loaf of bread in his saddlebag. The war had ended five years ago, so why did it feel like he was still fighting? His scars prickled in response as he swung himself up into the saddle.

As Torj started back towards the academy, he felt a strange pull in his chest, as though a thread connected him to something there, and it was tugging him back to where he belonged. Perhaps the madness had already started to take hold. The notion created a pit of dread low in his gut.

As he rode through the outskirts of Highguard, he thought about his life – there was nothing like the possibility of a fracturing mind to make a man contemplate his existence. Torj doubted many people had lived as hard as he had. He saw his years in chapters, full of shadow and light. Some had ended in darkness, and others . . .

Others had started anew with thunder and lightning.

CHAPTER 28

Wren

'The path of the alchemist is one of cause and effect, where every action, no matter how small, can have far-reaching consequences'

– *Elwren Embervale's notes and observations*

AFTER SEVERAL WARNINGS regarding danger and discretion, Farissa had granted Wren a sample of the alchemy that had been used against King Leiko. Wren wanted to get to work on potential countermeasures as soon as possible, and so, with no formal class scheduled the next morning, she visited the greenhouses.

Unfortunately, Torj insisted on accompanying her.

He seemed intent on wallowing in moody silence, more so than usual. He'd barely spoken to her other than when he'd shoved an oatcake into her hands and ordered her to eat breakfast, announcing that he wasn't keen on lugging fainting alchemists to the infirmary. Annoyed, Wren had simply informed him that she wasn't a fainter. Though, she *had* eaten the oatcake.

At her side, the Warsword looked as formidable as ever, with his hammer slung across his back, his silver hair half-up, half-down, showing off the sharp line of his jaw, and his shirtsleeves rolled up to reveal tanned, muscular forearms. As Wren tried to tear her gaze away, her attention snagged on a jagged scar cleaving through the sinew there. How had she never noticed it before?

'What's the tale behind that?' she asked, thrusting her chin at the mark. 'More evidence of your legendary antics? A token of a monster slain?'

Something dark flashed across Torj's face. 'Something like that.'

'Oh?'

He glanced at her. 'I called him Father.'

Wren froze, her heart seizing. 'Your *father* did that to you?'

'Among other things.' He seemed to catch himself and shrugged. 'Not all monsters have scales and fangs, Embers.'

Wren didn't know what to say. 'I . . .'

'Don't worry about it,' he said, his voice gruff. 'It was a long time ago.'

She had stopped in her tracks at the edge of the grounds, clutching her oilskin satchel at her side, staring up at him, feeling as though someone were clenching her heart in a fist.

But the Bear Slayer shook his head. 'Forget it. There are more pressing matters at hand.' He motioned to the building.

Wren saw the vast, glass-domed structure of Drevenor's biggest greenhouse stretched out before her, bathed in the gentle glow of the morning sun. Towering trees with leaves in every shade of green reached towards the sky beyond the glass. Vibrant flowers bloomed in every corner, their petals a kaleidoscope of colours.

'You should see your face right now.' Torj's deep voice sent a shiver down her spine. She knew she likely looked like a child who had awoken to a pile of gifts on their name day, but that didn't mean she owed him a response.

She wanted to ask him about his father, about what had happened to leave him with that scar, but she knew now was not the time, and that the Warsword wouldn't want to share such private things with her. Instead, she stepped into the greenhouse, where the air was thick with the scent of earth and the sweet perfume of rare flowers. Butterflies fluttered past, their delicate wings shimmering in the golden light that streamed through the glass panes above.

Wren marvelled at the sheer variety of plants surrounding them. Herbs with silvery leaves and delicate petals, vines that twisted and turned in complex patterns, and strange, otherworldly specimens she couldn't even begin to name.

'You can wait by the door,' she told Torj.

He ignored her, following her down the first row, watching her like a hawk as she ran her fingers along the waxy surface of a giant, purple-veined leaf.

'What are we looking for, exactly?' he asked.

'*We?*'

Torj waited, and she acquiesced with a frustrated sigh.

'Inspiration.' She scanned the variety of foliage before her and made a mental list of things she ought to stock up on another time.

'For?'

Not taking her eyes off the array of plants, she moved deeper into the greenhouse. 'A counter to the alchemy used against King Leiko. It may have a natural neutralizing agent.'

'Like how the sun orchids repelled the shadow wraiths in the war?'

'Exactly,' she replied, noting how the perfume of the flowers was mingling with something richer, more masculine—

Him.

His scent was all around her, and rather than breathe it in deeply as she was tempted to do, she clicked her tongue in frustration. 'Must you be right on my heels? I'm hardly going to get attacked by a patch of day lilies.'

'You never know, Embervale,' he said, though to her relief, he yielded a step back.

When his presence wasn't so overbearing, she could actually *think*. And think she did as she wandered the rows and rows of Drevenor's finest greenhouse. After a time, the Warsword's footsteps behind her became part of the garden's natural rhythm, and she took out her notebook to scribble several ideas to try back in her workspace. It wasn't the first time she'd had an alchemical problem to solve, and when certain hulking warriors weren't breathing down her neck, it was a task she relished.

For the first time in a long while, Wren managed to lose herself in a place entirely. The experience was wistful, and as her tour continued, she marvelled at the supplies on hand. She could make some *very* interesting poisons with resources like these at her fingertips—

'Don't even think about it,' Torj's voice rumbled beside her.

Wren whipped around to face him. 'Think about what?'

Torj raised a brow. 'All the horrors you could use these plants for.'

'I wasn't—'

'You've got that gleam in your eye, Embervale. One I know all too well.'

Wren's lips pressed into a thin line. 'I do not.'

He gave a derisive snort, but it was cut short by a strangled noise of shock. 'What the fuck is that?' Torj blurted, pointing to something a few paces away.

Wren wandered over to the offending plant – a particularly grotesque tree nestled in a far corner of the greenhouse. Its trunk was gnarled and twisted, the bark a sickly grey colour that reminded her of decaying flesh. The branches, sparse and irregular, jutted out at odd angles like broken bones. Instead of leaves, the tree was adorned with fleshy, pulsating sacs that seemed to breathe with a life of their own.

She looked from the strange flora to the sheer look of disgust on the Warsword's face and found herself amused. 'You've carved out the hearts of monsters, but a tree unnerves you?'

Torj gaped at her. 'Are we looking at the same thing?' he asked, incredulous. 'That's not a tree. It's fucking *rancid* is what it is.'

'If you don't like it, you're welcome to leave.'

'Am I meant to believe you've got some sort of morbid appreciation for this thing?'

'I'm sure those . . . sacs . . . have an incredible medicinal use.'

'Do me a favour,' Torj retorted. 'If I'm sick, don't *ever* use that shit on me.'

'No promises, Bear Slayer.' Wren drew her harvesting knife from her belt and reached out—

A large hand shot out, encircling her wrist and stopping her from taking a cutting. 'Not on my watch, Embers.'

'It's a *tree*, Torj.'

'That looks fit to explode, or worse. Audra'd have my balls over a spit if I allowed you to be killed by a fucking plant.'

As much as the image pleased her, Wren tried to shake out of his grip. 'You're being unreasonable—'

'And you're being an idiot.' Still gripping her wrist, Torj consulted a pocket watch. 'And look at that - if we stay any longer, you'll be late to your first lesson.'

With a noise of exasperation, Wren finally twisted out of his hold. 'Fine.'

***

As they approached her quarters to retrieve her books, Wren's heart skipped a beat when she noticed the door slightly ajar. A chill raked down her spine, but she schooled her features into a neutral expression, not wanting to alarm Torj. He was insufferable enough as it was.

But Torj, ever observant, narrowed his eyes at the door. 'We didn't leave the door open.'

'We might have. Easy mistake to make . . .' Wren hoped she sounded more convinced than she felt.

'I don't make mistakes like that,' Torj said, drawing his hammer from the sheath across his back and pushing the door inwards. He entered with caution, surveying the place for hidden threats.

'How am I meant to tell if this place has been ransacked when its usual state is like a boulder was catapulted through it?' he muttered.

Wren peered around him. At first glance, everything seemed to be in its usual chaotic order. Her books were still fanned across her desk, and her alchemical equipment remained as she'd left it . . .

She went to her box of trinkets on the windowsill.

The wooden lid was crooked.

Sucking in a breath, she opened it and counted the keepsakes within. Ring, coin, watch, pendant, monocle, inkwell, brooch, figurine . . . They were all there. Every last one.

As she moved about the room, a sense of wrongness settled over her. It was subtle, but Wren could feel it in the air – a faint disturbance. Someone had been there, invading her personal space, touching her things . . .

Still gripping his hammer and scanning the room, Torj came to the same conclusion. 'Someone broke in. Is anything missing?'

The unease continued to grow low in Wren's gut as she surveyed her workbench and her notes. 'No,' she replied at last. 'It might be a prank . . .'

'I'm in fucking hysterics,' Torj said flatly.

Wren forced a shrug as she spotted a folded piece of parchment tucked under her scales. She was sure it hadn't been there before. Turning back to the Warsword, she resolved to retrieve it later. 'It's a thing, isn't it? Students hazing one another . . . Maybe I'll find Widow's Ash in my bedsheets or a family of spotted toads in the bathing chamber—'

'Save it, Embervale,' the Bear Slayer cut in. 'Your security just kicked up a notch.'

CHAPTER 29
Torj

'Magical afflictions as byproducts of arcane warfare linger in the scar tissue and defy conventional healing methods'

– *A History of Magically Inflicted Injuries*

His charge was not happy, and frankly, nor was he. *A precaution*, Audra had assured him.

'Precaution my arse,' he muttered as he performed his usual sweep of Wren's rooms. According to her, nothing had been taken, but she looked shaken, her gaze flitting to her desk where a bundle of papers were stacked.

'You're sure nothing's missing?' he pressed for the third time.

'*Yes*,' she replied, exasperated.

'You're lying.'

'I'm not.'

Gods, why did she have to fight him on everything? He stared her down, wondering who would crack first.

She did.

'They didn't take anything, I swear it,' she told him. 'But my notes on the sample Farissa gave me were disturbed. And . . .'

Her gaze fell to the wooden box on her windowsill.

'And?' he pressed.

'The lid wasn't on right . . . I might have left it like that myself.'

'But you don't think you did?'

Wren shook her head.

Torj strode across the room and opened the box, peering inside. His stomach lurched as his fingers closed around a familiar pendant . . . The one that boasted the family sigil of Edmund Riverton.

'Tell me these aren't what I think they are,' he murmured in disbelief, his eyes roaming over the other damning trophies concealed within.

'They're not what you think they are,' Wren replied flatly.

Eyes narrowing, Torj dropped the necklace back into the box as though burned. 'Liar.'

Wren closed the gap between them and snapped the lid shut. 'Mind your own business.'

'What don't you understand? Your business is my business now.' He sighed. 'I need you to give me your word.'

'What's the word of a liar worth, Bear Slayer?'

'Embervale,' he warned. 'I need you to promise me that you won't mark any more names off your ledger. Not while you're in my charge.'

To his frustration, she scoffed. 'Why should I do that?'

'Because,' he bit back, 'it's not just their lives at stake here. Your rooms were just broken into. A royal was attacked.'

'One royal.'

'An attack on one is an attack on all.'

'I disagree.'

Torj threw his hands up. 'For fuck's sake, Embervale!' A beat later, he gathered his composure and folded his arms over his chest. 'Both Cal and I will escort you to your classes today. He's still waiting for his lecturer to arrive, anyway. And I'll speak to the High Chancellor about getting a guard stationed outside your door, even when you're not here.'

Wren opened her mouth to argue, but he cut her off.

'It's not up for debate.'

The nagging sensation followed Torj all day as he escorted Wren across the academy. She attended various lessons and carried out several tasks that her male teammate unhappily dubbed 'novice grunt work.'

Torj marvelled from afar at how seriously she took her studies, at how she didn't hesitate to answer a question when asked. Even with his limited knowledge of alchemy, he could tell Wren was quickly becoming revered among her peers. The only one who seemed remotely in the same league was that teammate, Zavier, who ran his fingers through his thick dark hair and thought himself far too dignified for Torj's liking.

At last, when evening fell and Wren dismissed the idea of eating in the dining hall with the rest of her cohort, they returned to their rooms. Pleased to find the guard he'd requested stationed at Wren's door, Torj dutifully carried out his security checks while Wren waited, her foot bouncing impatiently.

No sooner than he'd finished was he pushed towards the adjoining door, which closed promptly behind him. A scraping noise sounded from the other side, and he was amused to learn Wren was jamming a chair under the handle of the door, as though that would somehow prevent him from getting in if he needed to.

Torj gave her an hour. An hour of privacy to work on whatever ghastly poison or experiment she intended to inflict upon the world next before he strode back into her quarters through the bathing chamber with a steaming bowl he'd ordered from the kitchens and the fresh bread Branwell had given him.

'Eat,' he commanded.

She looked up from her mortar and pestle with glassy eyes. 'Don't you ever knock? It's when you close your fist and strike it against the door.'

He slid the bowl and bread onto the bench beside her, pushing bottles of meticulously labelled potions out of the way, wondering if he was being paranoid or if he could, in fact, smell a faint tang of blood in the air. 'My fists are usually only closed when I'm hitting people.'

'Shocking.'

It didn't escape his notice that she was trying to push a piece of parchment underneath a stack of books, hiding something.

'What's that?' he demanded, reaching across her.

She batted his hand away. 'Nothing.'

'I'll be the judge of that—'

'You'll be the judge of *nothing*, Bear Slayer. You might have been assigned to protect me from bodily harm, but you have no right to my private possessions or correspondence.'

For a moment, he was blindsided by the radiance of her indignation. She'd wiped the smudges of dirt from her face, and tendrils of her bronze hair had escaped the pin spearing through the knot at the top of her head. He stared until his gaze snagged on a glimmer of silver on the workbench.

It was the set of scissors he'd given her in the lead-up to the shadow war, after she'd requested them for her fellow alchemists in a meeting. 'You kept them,' he ventured softly.

She raised an arched brow. 'You think I'd discard a perfectly good pair of secateurs?'

Torj fought the urge to tuck a loose strand of hair behind her ear. Instead, he gave her the smirk he knew enraged her to no end. 'I think you like to be reminded of me.'

Wren snorted. 'I'm not that sentimental.'

'That's right,' he replied. 'You're all sharp edges and slicing words these days, aren't you, Embervale?'

She turned back to her work. 'As opposed to you, who clobbers people with your hammer and threatens innocent students in the halls?'

'Exactly.' Torj pointed to the steaming bowl of stew. 'Eat.'

He left her once more to her tinctures and poisons.

Torj knew it was only a matter of time until she tried to slip past him. Her restlessness had been growing by the day; he could almost feel it vibrating in his own chest, tracing the line of scars there. He wondered if the break-in had only served to fuel her rebellious streak.

With one of the books Farissa had recommended for company, he waited, patiently. *Arcane Ailments: Understanding Magical Maladies* was a brick of a book, and if he hadn't potentially been going mad already, the introduction alone might have been enough to drive him to insanity. He skimmed over several passages, the words blurring together as that familiar sense of dread set in . . .

In this chapter, we explore the subtle yet profound impacts of magical injuries, shedding light on the hidden toll they exact on those unfortunate enough to fall victim to them.

Torj rubbed his sternum as he read on.

Arcane burns, whether inflicted by fire, lightning, or enchanted weapons, present unique challenges in the realm of healing. Traditional salves and remedies often fall short when confronted with the volatile nature of magical fire—

He stopped reading as he heard the unmistakable sound of the guard stationed outside Wren's door dropping to the ground. The fall had been cushioned by something, but not so well that it was silenced completely.

Wren had drugged the poor bastard, just as Torj had anticipated, and she was currently sneaking out of her rooms, just as he'd known she would.

The Embervale sisters had never been ones for the rules, but he couldn't help the anger surging through him. It had only been this morning they'd found her door ajar, her rooms rifled through. Though he'd asked around, no one had seen anything. There was no suspect. Which meant she was knowingly putting herself at risk, not to mention putting his job on the line yet again.

Thoroughly aggravated now, he left his room and followed her.

Wren had pulled a dark cloak over her shoulders and a hood up over her hair, but her belt of horrors still clinked as she moved swiftly through the slumbering campus, alerting anyone to her movements. To Torj's dismay, she didn't look back once. She didn't seem to sense him on her tail, nor did she take precautionary measures when rounding corners. Anyone could attack her. Anyone could snatch her away. She had to know what was at risk.

He stepped into place beside her. 'What did I tell you about being aware of your surroundings?'

To his surprise, she didn't jump, didn't so much as flinch.

'You knew I was following you,' he said.

Wren didn't look at him. 'You're predictable, Bear Slayer.'

'I could say the same for you. Sneaking out without your bodyguard? I basically had it timed down to the second.'

Wren gave a dark laugh, not slowing her pace. 'You think you know me?'

'Better than most.'

'I guess we'll see about that, won't we?'

Irritation flared, and he grabbed her arm, drawing her to a stop. 'This isn't a game, Embervale.'

'Who said I was playing?' Wren replied.

Gods, he wanted to shake her by the shoulders, wanted to yell that he hated this as much as she did. Were it up to him, he'd be on the other side of the damn world by now.

Footsteps sounded nearby, and without thinking, he pulled her into a nearby alcove, shielding her from view. He had her front pressed to the cold stone, his chest flush with the curve of her spine, his nose nearly grazing the bare nape of her neck as he covered her body with his.

And she let him.

Momentarily startled, he froze in place. Normally, he'd expect her to be kicking and clawing at him. But beneath him, her breathing hitched – he felt it in the shift of her torso. This close, the scent of her was utterly intoxicating. His own heart rate kicked up a notch, his cock hardening against his will, straining against his leathers despite all his frustration.

'You're protecting me from the groundskeepers now?' Wren murmured, though there was a sultriness to her voice.

Torj didn't budge. 'I'm protecting you from anyone and everyone.' He spotted a piece of gauze tied to the crook of her elbow, a dot of crimson stark against the white. 'What's that?'

'Nothing.'

'It's not nothing.'

Wren wriggled then, and all thoughts emptied from his head. She squirmed again, just enough that she must have felt the bulge of his growing erection above the swell of her backside.

She froze, her lips parting in surprise.

Torj eased back ever so slightly, deciding that to forge on was the best course of action. 'If there's somewhere you need to go, I'll take you there myself.'

'No, thank you,' she said coolly. 'I'm after a little discretion this evening.'

'I can be discreet.'

A choked laugh bubbled from her lips as she gestured vaguely to the size of him. 'Bear Slayer, there's nothing discreet about you. Now let me go. You've earned yourself a night off.'

'For fuck's sake.' The words were out of his mouth before he could stop them. 'You're killing me, Embervale.'

'Here I was thinking I was the one being pinned to a wall by a Warsword.'

'Somehow I doubt you'd be in this position if it wasn't where you wanted to be.'

Now, her body was practically humming beneath his. He could feel that storm raging within her, coaxing whatever magic lingered within him to rise to the surface.

'Are you *ever* going to listen to me, Embers?' He meant to pose it as a real question, but it came out low and gravelly, like a challenge.

Wren turned beneath him, so that they were face to face. Her cheeks were flushed, her eyes hooded, and as her eyes dipped between them, over every point of contact, she licked her lips.

'But I *have* been listening, Bear Slayer,' she replied.

'Is that so?'

Torj bit back a moan as she deliberately ground against him, his hardness undeniable now. She was no mere alchemist; she was a *vixen*, and she knew *exactly* what she was doing to him. Wren reached up, as though she meant to start unbuttoning his shirt here and now. Torj anticipated that first touch with his breath held, desire coursing through him like an electric current.

But it was her hairpin she sought, slipping it from the tumble of bronze atop her head, allowing her tresses to fall, framing her face, softening her hard expression. Her hungry gaze dropped to his mouth.

Still braced over her, Torj didn't move, teetering on the very edge of control as longing unlike anything he'd ever known surged through him. He had thought of this moment countless times. Had dreamed of it, even when he'd tried so hard to cast her from his mind . . . Wren was going to *kiss him*, after all this time—

'*You* should be aware of *your* surroundings,' she said at last, something tapping against the side of his neck, so lightly he wondered if he'd imagined it.

Until he saw Wren withdrawing her hairpin.

Spots swam in his vision and his legs buckled. 'You . . .'

Wren gave a wicked smile. 'Me.'

And everything went black.

CHAPTER 30

Wren

'Bees that feed on the nectar of oleander and rhododendrons create wild honey thick with toxins'

– *Toxic Tales: Chronicles of Lethal Elixirs*

WREN LEFT THE Bear Slayer in the shadows of the alcove, unconscious. She'd known he'd try something like this sooner or later; the overprotective brute couldn't help himself. He seemed to think he knew best about everything, which was nothing new. His overzealous notion of duty had been a point of contention between them for years.

But now, hot anger rippled through her, alongside something darker, deeper. How dare he try to overpower her? He underestimated her, just like the rest of them.

The Furies had played a cruel joke upon her when he'd been assigned as her protector. Wren didn't want or need a shadow. Especially not the lightning-kissed Warsword of Thezmarr. Not only did he remind her of the war, and all her worst moments since, but she couldn't seem to control her emotions around him – or her body, for that matter. The image of his gloriously naked torso was still seared in her memory, and it often came to the forefront of her mind when he was barking commands at her and constantly invading her privacy.

Try as she might, she couldn't shake the crackle of power thrumming at her fingertips, begging to be unleashed. In the alcove, the press of the warrior's body had unlocked something inside her, and it was now demanding to be freed from its cage.

With a huff of frustration, Wren left the academy grounds, the note she'd found beneath her scales clutched in her hand.

Poisoner.
The Happy Harpy. Old Town. Tenth bell.

She would have assumed it was a mere prank, but for later finding the vial of ingredients that had accompanied it: henbane, datura, and nightshade... The very same concoction she'd used to poison Lord Briar.

Someone at Drevenor knew who she was.

Not just the poisoner of the former Guild Master of Thezmarr, but *the Poisoner* responsible for ending the bastards who'd escaped official justice after the war.

Someone knew her secret, and Wren needed to find out who.

Checking her map and compass, she made her way towards the city. Though the shadow war had taken her across the five kingdoms of the midrealms, she'd never really *travelled*. Yes, she had been to Harenth, Delmira, Tver, Aveum, and Naarva, but only when they had either succumbed to darkness or were on the brink of destruction. She had never seen a *thriving city*, had never wandered the streets and drunk in the sights of her own accord. Growing up in Thezmarr's fortress had left little opportunity for exploring the world and all it had to offer. And after the war, her ventures involving her ledger had hardly been the time for frivolity.

But upon walking through Highguard's floral gates, Wren decided she already liked it best at night. The cobblestone streets were wide and framed by blooms – Naarva was the Kingdom of Gardens, after all. Golden light spilled from the windows of grand buildings, casting warmth across the lively marketplace beyond.

Thea had once told her about the stalls in Harenth's capital city, Hailford, and how Wren would have loved their exotic spices and apothecaries. Wren was willing to wager that Highguard was better. As she made her way down the road, she was greeted by vibrant stalls brimming with countless species of plants, whirring gadgets, and swathes of fine silken fabrics. The air was richly scented with roasting game, and the hum of cheerful chatter enveloped the surroundings, while a lone fiddle played somewhere in the distance.

It was beautiful.

Wren wished Sam and Ida were here to see it with her. They would have loved this place, though they would have been far more interested in the carts selling spiced wine and cider than the pots of rare shrubs.

A wave of grief washed over her. It had been half a decade, and still the thought of never sharing a drink with them again stole her breath away, catching her off guard when she least expected it. She knew they were dead. And yet there was no unravelling the expectation that she might see them around the next corner, grinning madly at her.

Blinking back stinging tears, Wren ventured deeper into the heart of the city, wondering what sort of meeting she was about to stumble into. But as she kept walking, the golden glow of the markets began to fade, giving way to narrow, winding alleys, where the radiance of the upper city couldn't penetrate. Down here, it was dark, and the mouth-watering aromas of the streets above were long gone. Instead, the scent of damp stone and smoke were thick in the air, and Wren stumbled over the uneven, gritty pathways.

She had never been to the Happy Harpy, so she checked her map by the feeble light of a streetlamp. She was no longer in Highguard proper, but the perimeter of the city's fourth quarter, near the place known as Old Town. Turning the piece of parchment over in her hands, unease roiled in her gut.

Poisoner.

Perhaps she was being reckless; perhaps she was a fool.

But there was only one way to know.

Wren continued to follow the map, observing the weathered facades and neglected structures of the city's underbelly. The hair on her arms stood up as the music from above was swallowed by silence and the occasional shuffle of unseen figures in the shadows.

Torj would kill me if he knew where I was now, she thought, rounding another sharp corner. The thought gave her a small measure of satisfaction.

Suddenly, the eerie quiet gave way to a cacophony of raucous laughter, bawdy tunes, and clinking glasses. The underbelly of Highguard opened up before Wren, a sprawling labyrinth of squalor and vices, a stark departure from the tapestry of golden revelry in the upper city.

The scent of cheap ale, stale smoke, and sickly perfume wafted across the alley, filling Wren's nostrils, getting stuck in her throat. Vandalized walls closed in around her and she averted her gaze from prying eyes as she forced one foot in front of the other for the final leg of the journey. Her hands stayed poised by her belt in case she needed to dispense a tincture or two.

She stopped before a pair of crimson-tinted lanterns illuminating the uneven steps leading to a pair of wrought-iron doors. A worn sign hung overhead: a bare-breasted woman with bird wings and a wild grin.

The Happy Harpy.

'You lost, love?' said a croaky voice to her left.

Wren ignored them and pushed through the doors.

The Happy Harpy was a brothel. She should have realized. But she had been so intent on getting away from Torj that she hadn't questioned the name, nor the location in Old Town.

'Shit,' she muttered to herself, surveying the tattered curtains leading to 'private' rooms. Coarse laughter spilled out into the main hall, along with an array of other sounds. There were several bars spotted about the space, as well as gambling tables that hummed with the frenetic pull of risk. The place smelled like old wine and coin, and flowed with an undercurrent of danger and debauchery.

Wren lifted her chin in defiance and headed for the bar on the far side that looked the least offensive. She had never been one to fold. Whoever had left her the note was likely watching in the wings, waiting for her to panic. If they wanted to see what she was made of, so be it. She'd fucking show them.

Wren slid onto a stool and flagged down the bartender. 'I'll have a pint of sour mead, please.'

She suspected the shocked look the man gave her was more to do with her manners than it was her general presence. Exchanging a piece of silver for a foaming tankard, Wren swivelled in her seat and surveyed the hall. Despite the smell, it felt good to be out in the world. She had no desire to play ward to the snarling Bear Slayer in the room next to hers, and here . . . here, she could be anyone.

Taking a long draught from her tankard, her eyes watering at the *sour* aspect of the sour mead, her gaze went to a group of people spilling out of one of the rooms, tangled in one another. One woman's breasts were exposed, a man cupping them and lavishing her neck with kisses as they staggered towards the bar in the centre. She arched into him as they moved, cries of pleasure on her lips. Wren couldn't tear her eyes away as another man joined them, his hands slipping down the front of the woman's skirts, right out in the open for all to see. The noise that escaped her was nothing short of carnal.

Wren took a longer drink this time.

'Lots of people come to watch,' the bartender said mildly. 'There's no shame in it.'

Wren balked. 'That's not what—' But she stopped herself. There was no need to explain herself here. Instead, she turned back to the hall, scanning for any sign as to who might have brought her here.

For a moment, she surveyed the gambling tables, watching as cards and coins slid across the smooth surfaces. Colourful curses echoed across the various games, winners beaming as they swept up their prizes, losers motioning for another round of drinks. There were dealings at the edges of the hall as well: the glint of a dagger here, the pocketing of illicit substances there. Wren drank it all in like a parched vagabond, the whole underworld before her, ripe for the taking.

It made her feel alive.

There was no ignoring the moans drifting out from the private rooms. Building cries of ecstasy and deep, guttural groans rang out; occasionally, the gamblers would cheer.

Wren felt her cheeks warm. She blamed it on the liquor and promptly ordered another tankard as she watched another woman swan into the main hall. Her hair was a mess, her lips swollen but tugged into a sated smirk.

Wren clenched her thighs together. She'd never had a man make her look or sound like that before. From what Sam and Ida, and even Thea, had said, it could be something incredible . . . It could justify those noises, that dazed expression. But that hadn't been her experience. The handful of times she'd ventured into bed with someone, it had been laced with disappointment and regret. And so she'd deemed it not worth her time, refusing to lower her standards.

Sighing, she ran her finger through the condensation on her tankard before nearly jumping out of her skin at a sudden noise. A group of men passed by, arm in arm, singing a coarse verse about a tavern wench.

A younger man from the party paused upon seeing Wren, lingering near her stool. Without thinking, she put a hand to one of the vials at her belt. One flick of a cork and he'd be covered in a concentrated dose of Widow's Ash, a fate she reserved for the most entitled of pricks.

But he didn't seem to want to intimidate her. He merely gave her a friendly grin and motioned to the seat beside her. 'That taken?'

Before she could answer, she froze, feeling the electricity before she saw him, his presence washing over her like a wave breaking on a shore.

'Yes, it's fucking taken,' a deep voice growled.

CHAPTER 31
Wren

'There are rare poisons that can be mistaken for desire. Both intoxicate, both consume. Often it is too late to discern the difference'

– *An Encyclopaedia of Deadly Plants*

THE POOR MAN blanched at the sight of the silver-haired Bear Slayer and scurried away.

The dose of valerian essence in her hairpin hadn't been high enough to keep his hulking form down for long. Wren made a mental note to increase the potency.

Torj slid onto the stool next to her and pinned her with hard, dark eyes. 'This is no place for a future queen.'

Wren downed the rest of her drink, a familiar fury rushing through her along with the liquor. 'I didn't fight in the fucking shadow war so a man could tell me where my place is.'

The Warsword blinked at her, stunned. And then, to her surprise, the corner of his mouth twitched. 'Fair enough, Embers.'

She expected him to haul her away from the den of vices, but instead, Torj raised a hand to the bartender, who nodded eagerly. Wren supposed it wasn't every day he could boast that he'd served a legend of Thezmarr.

'Another for you, miss?' he asked, nodding to her empty pint.

Wren thrust her chin at Torj. 'He's buying.'

'You've got a pair on you tonight, don't you?' Torj said, his voice low.

'Always,' Wren quipped, realizing the liquor had already loosened her tongue. With the Bear Slayer beside her, she was all the more aware of the vibrating energy of the hall, and the sounds echoing off its walls. 'I guess you're used to this sort of establishment,' she heard herself say.

Torj lifted his tankard to his lips and took several large gulps. 'What's it to you?'

'Nothing. Just making conversation.'

'Since when?'

Since she was two pints in, with more to go, but she didn't say so. 'What are you doing here, then?'

'You mean besides tracking down my wayward charge?' Torj raised a scarred brow. 'Not to sample the goods, if that's what you mean. I don't have to pay for it.'

'Perhaps you should. You seem hard up.'

'I'm here doing my fucking job,' he muttered.

'Oh, that's right. You're *paid* to be here.' Gods, the mead truly *had* loosened her tongue. 'How much do you charge for your services?'

He huffed a dark laugh. 'Not nearly enough coin in the world, Embervale.'

It was at that moment that a woman came sauntering up to them, draping a bare arm around Torj's shoulders, her eyes hazy with lust. 'You're him,' she murmured in a sultry tone, her fingers tracing the top of the warrior's chest. 'The lightning-kissed Bear Slayer . . .'

Wren bit back a snort, ignoring the flare of annoyance the woman's presence sparked.

Torj gave a sheepish grin. 'Guilty, ma'am.'

The woman's eyes lit up and she gestured to a group of her friends, who surged forwards, gathering around the Warsword like a gaggle of geese. They were in various states of undress and inebriation.

One of them, wearing only a corset and garters, gave Wren a nod of reverence. 'Every woman in the midrealms knows his name,' she said.

Wren rolled her eyes. 'So I've heard.'

They fawned over him, offered him everything under the sun: drinks, a pipe filled with what Wren gathered was some sort of aphrodisiac, and oddly, a full leg of honey-smoked ham. But as Torj dealt with his admirers, Wren's scalp prickled, sensing someone's gaze on her. She scanned the hall until her eyes snagged on a familiar face.

There, at one of the gambling tables, was Zavier Mortimer.

He smiled smugly and raised his goblet in a silent toast.

'I'll be back in a minute,' Wren muttered in Torj's direction, getting down from her stool, her fist closing around one of her more dangerous vials as she made her way over to her teammate. 'Is this your idea of a joke?' she demanded when she reached him.

Zavier scooped up his winnings and excused himself from the card game. 'Truth be told, I thought you might see the sign and go running in the opposite direction . . .'

'I fought in a war. A brothel doesn't scare me.'

'I can see that now,' he replied. 'I just wanted to make sure you weren't some precious princess.'

Wren snorted. 'I'm no princess.'

'Apparently not,' he allowed. 'What do you think the midrealms would do if it found out the heir of Delmira had taken justice into her own hands not just once, but several times in the last five years? That she's been killing off their nobles one by one?'

Wren tensed, but said nothing, the vial of ingredients flashing in her mind.

'Your little box of trophies was rather damning . . .' There was a note of amusement in his tone. 'You're not even going to deny it, are you?'

'Why should I? What I want to know is how you found out.'

'Let's just say there's a higher power at work here.'

'Let's not.'

Zavier just gave her a maddening grin. 'I think we will. It looks like I'm holding all the cards, Elwren.'

'Not for long,' she countered, her nape prickling again. Wren didn't have to look around to know that Torj was watching their exchange. She studied her teammate. 'What do you want, Zavier? To hold my crimes over my head? For what?'

'I told you: I want to see what you're made of. To see if we've got a slim chance or none of winning the Gauntlet. To see if you're ready for what's coming . . .' For a moment, he looked serious.

Wren wished she'd brought her drink with her. 'And?'

Zavier seemed to snap back to himself. 'You're not completely hopeless.'

'What an outstanding commendation,' she said dryly. 'Are you putting Dessa to the same test?'

'Dessa's too nice. You're not.'

'You've got that right, at least.'

'*Nice* won't win us a place as adepts.' He drained the rest of his drink. 'I'm off for a refill. Good to know you're not made of glass – such a shame when pretty things break. See you tomorrow, Poisoner.'

Wren watched Zavier go, more unsure than ever if he was an ally or a threat. Only time would tell.

'What did he want?' Torj said at her side, having extricated himself from the swooning ladies.

Wren didn't take her eyes off her teammate. 'He left me the note.'

'What note?'

She sighed, reluctantly facing her bodyguard. 'The one that told me to come to this place.'

A muscle feathered in Torj's jaw. 'You're telling me that after your rooms were broken into, you found some piece of parchment with random instructions and your first thought was to follow them? Without telling me?'

'He knew who I was.' She paused before clarifying. 'What I *do*.'

Torj tensed at her side. He'd made no secret of the fact that he didn't agree with her secret vocation. But now, his face was unreadable, his voice hard as iron as he asked, 'Did he threaten you?'

'No.'

Torj scrutinized her, as though searching for a lie. The last thing she needed was the Bear Slayer going on a hammer-wielding rampage over her teammate.

'I swear it,' she said, before adding, 'I know coming here was stupid.'

'That's one word for it.' His shoulders dropped and he led them back to their seats at the bar. 'You admitting you made a mistake?'

'A momentary lapse in judgement.'

'Sounds like a mistake to me.' Torj signalled for another round of drinks.

Wren hated being wrong, and more than that, she hated that he was right. Nothing catastrophic had happened, but she had put herself in a vulnerable situation nonetheless.

Torj seemed to sense that she was berating herself. 'You're forgetting that people messed with Thea, too. No one wanted her to be a Warsword—'

'I'm not my sister.' It was a phrase Wren found herself repeating, and she was fucking sick of it.

'No,' Torj said. 'But you share the same strength, the same stubbornness, the same rebellious streak.'

'So what?'

'So don't let little pricks like him beat that down.'

'Oh?' she challenged. 'And what about big ones?' As soon as the words left her mouth she wanted to fold in on herself and cover her reddening face with her hands.

Amusement gleamed in Torj's eyes. 'You wouldn't know what to do with one.'

The seductive edge to his words made her toes curl in her boots, but pride prevailed. 'You'd like to think that, wouldn't you?'

'You have no idea what I like to think of, Embers.'

A pulse of desire shot straight to her core, and she couldn't stop her gaze from dropping to his mouth.

His nostrils flared, as though he'd read her thoughts.

Wren felt another pulse – this time, her magic thrumming beneath her skin, as though waking beneath his attention. She crossed her legs and cleared her throat, buying herself a moment by taking a sip of her drink.

Torj was watching Zavier gamble from across the hall. 'We have to watch out for him.'

'For once, I agree,' Wren replied.

Torj eyed her warily. 'With that knowledge about you, he's dangerous.'

'So am I.'

'A lesson I'm constantly learning,' the Warsword allowed, touching the spot on his neck where she'd pricked him with her hairpin.

Zavier looked over to them again, this time making a show of his hand of cards, a reminder of the power he held over her. Wren felt the warrior tense beside her.

'Shall I kill him?' the Bear Slayer asked.

'I can kill him myself, with more pain and suffering.'

'I don't doubt it.'

Wren tore her attention away from her prick of a teammate. 'I won't let anything stand in my way. Least of all him.'

Torj nodded. 'Good. You want something, Embers . . . you take it.' He finished his drink and got to his feet. 'We're leaving.'

'And if I fancy another?'

'We're still leaving.'

Wren acquiesced. She'd won all the battles she was going to tonight. Tomorrow was another day.

Outside didn't seem as grim somehow with the Warsword at her side – that was, until the screech of wheels on cobbles pierced the air.

Wren had no time to think before Torj had her pressed up against a hard stone wall, his hammer poised to strike as his body shielded her completely. Blood roared in her ears as fear shot through her, along with the rush of something else as his thigh came between hers, heat and tension pouring from his towering build. A solid wall of muscle enveloped her, a barrier between her and the threat beyond.

A carriage careened past them, sparks flying off the axles of its wheels, the driver's arms flailing to get control of the reins as he rattled down the alley with a shout.

Wren could feel Torj's heart hammering against hers, his breath hot on her neck. Even as the sound of the carriage faded into the distance, they did not move. Wren found herself breathless, her breasts rising with every breath she tried to catch, pressing against the plane of Torj's sculpted chest. The contact was addictive, and just for a moment, she wanted to feel him *everywhere*.

He was still braced over her when he asked, 'Are you alright?'

For a second, Wren didn't answer, knowing that as soon as she did, the heat of him would leave her cold and empty. The press of his body was all that was keeping her upright on her traitorous, buckling legs.

'Embers?' he said roughly, peering down at her, his lips now so close to hers.

The nickname she hated sparked another rush of arousal and she bit back a whimper as he shifted slightly, her undergarments growing damp with need. The cords of muscle in his thigh grazed the sensitive skin between her own, the hard lines of his body rubbing against her.

'I'm fine,' she managed, fighting down the storm raging beneath her skin, causing her nipples to tighten and her back to arch ever so slightly. She felt him in her veins, in the magic that surged to the surface of her being—

'You're sure?'

Want threatened to consume her, to make her act rashly. But she forced those impulses deep down. 'Yes,' she replied, stripping her voice of anything remotely heated. 'Nothing happened.'

'Right,' he said, at last pushing off the wall, freeing her. 'Nothing happened.'

CHAPTER 32

Torj

'In the business of protecting a charge of noble birth, there is no place for attraction'

— *Mastering the Craft of Close Protection*

LIKE *FUCK* NOTHING happened.

Hours later, he could still feel the imprint of her curves against his body, still had the rock-hard cock and aching balls to prove it.

Upon their return to the academy, he'd done yet another thorough sweep of her rooms and then made his excuses, not that he needed any. Wren couldn't wait to get rid of him, and he wasn't sure he could be around for a second longer without succumbing to his baser desires.

She drove him mad.

The challenge in her eyes. The sharp edge to her words and their stark contrast to the softness of her body. Gods, he was so fucked. He was meant to be her bodyguard, her protector. To be anything else was forbidden. But all he could think of was peeling away her gown and tracing every dip and hollow, of sliding deep inside her.

The thought alone nearly had a moan escaping his lips.

'Get it together,' he muttered to himself, pacing the confines of his room like a caged beast. The instinct roared within him, to protect, to fuck, to make her his. He pushed the hair out of his eyes with a curse. This wasn't him. This was some wild animal taking over his senses.

She's your charge. She's your principal, he chanted inwardly, before reminding himself of the hundred other reasons why he couldn't stand her.

'You're a Warsword. I'm the woman who poisoned your former Guild Master. Our paths don't align.'

'Just stay away from me, Torj. Far away.'

'The offer of your post beyond the midrealms is rescinded. Immediately.'

'If I never see her again, it will be too soon.'

The scars across his chest pulsed and he rubbed at the marred flesh, hoping to alleviate some of the tension there. It was as though it were tethered directly to her, and the harder he fought it, the tauter that tether became, the tighter it drew them together. He could almost feel her moving about the room next door, could sense the restless energy of her flitting from mortar and pestle to the dried herbs hanging over the window. He could certainly picture her: the sway of her hips, the flush staining her cheeks—

'*Fuck.*' He needed to take his mind off her. Practically throwing himself down into the hard wooden chair at the small desk, he turned to the book Farissa had ordered from the archives: *A History of Magically Inflicted Injuries*. If that didn't kill his raging erection, nothing would.

Finding his place marked by the ribbon he'd left, he forced his eyes to the dense lines of text and began to read.

To wield magic is to walk along a precipice, for every incantation spoken and every spell cast exacts its toll. The practitioner of the arcane arts must reckon with the consequences of their actions, lest they be consumed by the very power they seek to command. For in the pursuit of mastery, one risks becoming ensnared by the dark tendrils of their own creation.

Torj rubbed his temples. This didn't describe Wren, not even close. Perhaps it was what had happened to King Artos in the early days before the war, but . . .

He shook his head and skipped ahead to a more relevant-sounding chapter.

Some wounds inflicted by magic defy the touch of conventional healing. They linger long after lacerations have closed, withstanding the passage of time and the ministrations of healers. The injured party is condemned to bear the burden of their affliction, sometimes overshadowed by a spectre of unending suffering.

'Sounds about right,' Torj muttered to himself, turning the page. Every word he read seemed to confirm Branwell's tale about his son.

Madness lurks at the threshold of those wounded by magic, its tendrils creeping into the recesses of the mind. Reality becomes a fractured mosaic, wherein visions of terror and delusion intertwine with fleeting moments of lucidity. The injured party is condemned to wander the maze of their own shattered psyche, lost in a realm of nightmares.

An hour passed, then another, and Torj struggled to take the information in, let alone find any answers amid all the gloom. Despite what she was now, Wren had *saved* him, not damned him. How could scars born of something so good and pure result in the corruption of reality? Of his soul? Yes, he had nightmares and flashbacks, but he was a Warsword of the midrealms; he had fought in countless battles. Kissing that edge of darkness was a consequence of war, nothing more.

He heard the door to the bathing chamber open and close, water splashing into the tub. Wren was in there, naked and wet, mere feet away from him. The thought had him facing the same problem he'd started reading to deter in the first place. It was too much to bear.

Running his fingers through his hair with an aggravated sigh, he looked down at the bulge tenting the front of his leathers. Doomed magical wound or not, there was only one way to fix this.

With trembling fingers, Torj fumbled with his buttons, stifling a moan of relief as he freed his cock from the confines of his leathers. Taking his length in his hand, he squeezed, moisture already beading at his tip.

This wasn't about pleasure, he told himself. This was a practical solution to an irritating problem. Quick, simple and efficient, that was all it had to be. Once he sorted out this urge, he could return to the books and figure out everything else. He could do his damn job.

He shuddered at the first stroke down his length, recalling the glimpse of Wren's body he'd seen beneath her shift on their first night here, how her nipples had hardened beneath the thin fabric as she'd surveyed him right back, desire simmering in her gaze.

Pure, unadulterated longing surged through him as he gripped himself harder, circling the crown of his cock with his thumb before pumping up and down. Against all reason, against all the thoughts screaming *not her, not her*, he imagined her hands on him, her tongue tracing down his torso, her smart mouth opening for him . . . He imagined her as she was, naked in that tub, her hand slipping between her legs, his name on her lips.

'Torj . . .' she moaned.

Torj jerked in his seat, his erection hard as granite in his hand.

'Torj . . .'

He *wasn't* imagining it.

Wren was wet and naked mere feet away, moaning *his* name.

His breathing hitched, and a current of power coursed through him: a ball of heat in his chest, spreading right down to his toes.

'Wren . . .' he murmured, stroking his shaft again and again, picturing what she might be doing to herself behind that door to elicit such sounds. As his touch moved over his cock in long, practised slides, pressure began to build, coiling tight within him as he climbed towards the peak of release.

He worked his hand, over and over, losing himself in the spiral of sensation. Gods, what he'd do to have her. Gods, how he'd worship her body with his.

Torj imagined pushing into the tight heat of her, imagined the feel of her clamping around him—

He lost control completely.

He climaxed with a muffled cry, collapsing over himself, panting.

But despite the evidence of what he'd just done, the want for her did not abate.

The storm raging in his chest only intensified, and wound or not, the lightning within his web of scars sparked anew.

CHAPTER 33
Wren

'In the art of poisoncraft, the adept alchemist wields tools of destruction, shaping fates with a single drop'

– *Alchemy's Dark Side:*
The Study of Malevolent Substances

Wren blamed the drink. And the sex-fuelled environment of the hall.

It was a physical response, nothing more. Entirely natural, entirely healthy, and . . . Well, she wasn't blind. She knew what the Bear Slayer looked like. All six-foot-five of him with his stupidly broad chest and dishevelled silver hair. She knew what he looked like, alright; she just couldn't stand him. Not what he reminded her of, not how he'd invaded her life again, and not how he made her feel.

She'd known there was no way she'd get to sleep in the agitated state she'd been in, so she'd opted for a relaxing bath to ease the tension. If only she'd been able to stop things there. But she'd been so tightly wound, so on edge, that she'd given in. She'd pleasured herself in the tub, yet again imagining the Warsword's body crushing hers, her legs wrapped around him . . . Afterwards, not nearly satisfied, she'd fallen into a fitful sleep, and morning light had crept through her window all too soon.

As dawn broke across the academy, Wren set about her tasks, checking the shallow glass dishes of her blood she'd prepared the night before. She was more determined than ever to learn more about the alchemy that had been used in the attack on King Leiko. Her former mentor's words came back to her: *'We have never seen this alchemy before . . . But it reminded me of you . . . Of your work during the war.'*

Wren eased a drop of liquid into the sample of her blood and watched the crimson part around the solution, just as her magic had recoiled in the presence of the sword Farissa had shown her back at Thezmarr.

It reminded her of the war, too. Of the sun orchids of Naarva and how they'd been a natural deterrent to the shadow wraiths, as Torj had mentioned in the greenhouse.

She would need more blood samples. And more of the strange alchemy to experiment with.

With a fine needle, she bled herself from her other arm this time, glancing at the adjoining door. When she was done, she divided the blood between more shallow dishes, making a note to cover them. She had the distinct suspicion that what she was doing would be frowned upon, to say the least. But who better to investigate? Who better to experiment with the alchemy that had targeted a ruler? Farissa had said so herself: *'The midrealms need you, Elwren. Drevenor needs you.'*

Pressing a scrap of linen to her bleeding arm, she paced the room, hoping the movement would dislodge some vital piece of information. She lost herself in the rhythm of her thoughts for a time, almost forgetting where she was.

Her skin prickled, and instinct propelled her to place a large tray over her samples, covering them from sight.

Wren didn't hear the adjoining door open, but she sensed Torj before he uttered a word. Her magic awoke in his presence, sparking in recognition. She hated it, the connection forged between them in the wake of that fateful battle. It had been foretold . . . *Gold will turn to silver in a blaze of iron and embers, giving rise to ancient power long forgotten.*

Wren had gone over the words time and time again, trying to decipher their true meaning. Torj's hair had turned from gold to silver. The battle itself had been a whirlwind of iron and embers. And the power? The Bear Slayer had wielded her magic as if it were his own . . . The prophecy had come to pass, just as predicted. So why were their fates still so entangled?

There had been no choice, only the instinct that she'd acted upon, but in doing so, she had scarred him and changed him for life. More so, she hated how every time he entered her rooms, no matter how furious she felt, there was also the absence of emptiness, of that palpable loneliness she'd carried with her for so long.

And there he was, waiting with his hands clasped in front of him, his expression unreadable. He had known that she was up and about, ready to leave for morning meal, as though he'd been listening to her every move.

Gods, had he heard her last night? The thought sent a hot flush from her neck to the tips of her ears.

'Have you thought more about those self-defence lessons?' he asked, leaning against the door frame as she buckled her belt of tools and potions over her apron and gown.

'To keep me safe from rogue carriages?'

He gave her a flat look. 'To keep you safe, full stop.'

Wren shook her head and made for the door. In truth, those lessons from her childhood in Thezmarr were hazy, to say the least. She had trained with Thea, Sam and Ida in their game called Dancing Alchemists, in which they'd thrown knives at each other's feet and developed quick reflexes . . . but were it to come down to hand-to-hand combat, she was no warrior. She still remembered Thea when she was younger, so keen to split her knuckles on faces, to swing a sword. Wren's thirst for violence was different, darker – the subtle prick of a poisoned pin to Thea's slashing and slicing. But she was just as angry, just as lethal. If not more so.

For the first time since her arrival, Wren attended first meal at the dining hall. She regretted it instantly. Amid the long tables lined with platters and baskets of bread, Kipp waved her over with a grin, motioning to the seat he'd saved her.

'Heard you went to a brothel last night!' he said by way of greeting, pushing a fresh pot of tea in front of her.

She balked. 'Where'd you hear that?'

'Oh, you know me, I have my sources. Though I'll admit, I'm hurt you didn't invite me.'

Wren snorted. 'Since when do you ever need an invitation to go anywhere?'

'Fair point,' he allowed. 'But if you were that lonely, you should have said. I'd have been more than happy—'

The Bear Slayer cleared his throat pointedly as he slid onto the bench at Wren's other side, his plate piled ridiculously high with food.

Kipp put his hands up in mock surrender. 'A joke, a joke, I assure you, Warsword. But then . . . perhaps you were lonely too?'

'You'll stop talking if you know what's good for you, Snowden,' Torj muttered, digging into his breakfast.

Wren shook her head at the pair of them and reached for the tea.

Kipp watched her pour. 'Figured I'd make that, given your reputation.'

Rolling her eyes, she brought the steaming cup to her nose and inhaled appreciatively: rose petals, marigold, and cornflowers. She moaned as she took a much needed sip.

Beside her, she felt the Bear Slayer tense, his eyes on her like a brand.

'What?' she asked, turning in time to see a muscle flex in his neck, heat rolling off him in waves.

'Nothing,' he replied around a mouthful of bread, averting his gaze.

Someone waving from further down the table caught her attention. 'Wren!' Dessa called. 'We've got healing with Farissa this morning. Wasn't she your mentor at Thezmarr?'

Wren cringed. She could have done without her teammate shouting about her across the breakfast table. But somehow, Dessa mistook her silence for enthusiasm and picked up her plate and cup, shuffling down the bench to join Wren.

'Isn't that right?' she pressed, tearing into a piece of toast. 'You were her apprentice, weren't you?'

'Yes,' Wren said, if only to shut her up. It was too early in the morning for this much enthusiasm.

'I've heard wonderful things about her,' Dessa gushed. 'She's a Master Alchemist of Healing, isn't she?'

'She is. Specialized in women's health,' Wren muttered.

'Fascinating,' her teammate replied, looking around at the others at the table, her eyes falling to the hulking frame that was Torj Elderbrock at Wren's side. 'You're the Bear Slayer,' she breathed, eyes growing wide. 'I've heard stories about you too—'

A hand was thrust out in the middle of the table. 'No doubt you've heard about me as well, then,' Kipp said, flashing her a grin. 'Kipp Snowden.'

Dessa's brow furrowed. 'Uh . . . no, sorry, I don't think I have . . . ?'

Completely unabashed, Kipp winked. 'The history books are still being written, then.'

'Furies save us,' Torj groaned, pinching the bridge of his nose.

Dessa turned back to Wren. 'Did you see that the first points have been awarded in the foyer?'

Wren's head snapped up. 'No.'

'They're according to our teams.'

'And?' Wren pressed, fighting back the urge to sprint to the foyer and see the black garnet stones for herself.

'We have eight,' Dessa told her. 'One of the other teams has thirteen. We're sitting squarely in the middle of the cohort.'

Wren tensed. 'That's going to change.'

A shadow fell across the table, and Wren glanced up to see Zavier darkening their breakfast.

'Enjoy your little midnight stroll last night, Elwren?' he asked, looking all too pleased with himself.

'What do you want?' she said bluntly, reluctantly placing her empty cup back in its saucer.

He gave the group a cursory glance, full of disdain. 'If you lot are done yammering, we've been given instructions for this morning's task.'

'Dessa said we have Healing.'

'We do. But it's not on academy grounds.' Then he turned on his heel and stalked off.

'Charisma in spades, that one,' Kipp declared.

※

Dessa chatted all the way to the stables, while Torj practically wrestled Wren's bulging oilskin satchel from her.

'You'll break your back lugging this thing around,' he said, heaving it over his shoulder. 'What have you got in here, anyway? Dead bodies cut up into little pieces?'

She'd put up a fight, but in truth, the bag's strap *had* been cutting savagely into her skin. 'That can be arranged,' she replied sweetly.

No, it was not her poison victims, but supplies for the infirmary they were visiting. With Farissa as her mentor back at Thezmarr, Wren had fallen into the habit of stocking up on a range of remedies that were often needed in the spur of the moment with so many warriors in their midst. She had also become the unofficial supplier of the contraceptive tonic for the women of the fortress – which she herself took religiously – along with a range of other tinctures and cures, things she knew a place of healing was always in need of.

There were no bounds to the suffering of women, and thanks to Farissa's tutelage, Wren knew better than most the practical application of alchemy in such a setting. Torj need not know that the bag he carried was bursting with pregnancy preventatives, herbs for menstrual pain, mood-stabilizing powders, pain relief capsules, and a number of other treatments. She might have been known for her poisons, but Wren was well versed in healing too. As Hardim had said, could you have one without the other?

As they moved across the grounds, Torj stuck to her side like a burr. He scanned the grounds as though he expected them to be attacked at any moment, his body rigid with tension.

'Do you think we should wait for Zavier?' Dessa was saying, looking around hopefully.

'No,' Wren replied, trying to keep the scorn from her voice. He'd set her up last night, and to what end, she still didn't know.

'Wait here,' Torj told them, disappearing into the stables.

Within, Wren could hear him interrogating the stable hands, his voice low and menacing as he demanded to know who had saddled her horse. With some reluctance, she realized she couldn't blame him for thinking someone might have tampered with her tack if they'd been bold enough to search her rooms.

'Your Bear Slayer is a tad intense, isn't he?' Dessa observed mildly, craning her neck to get a look inside.

'A pain in my arse is more like it,' Wren retorted, feeling sympathetic for the poor bastard currently taking the brunt of Torj's questioning. 'And he's not mine.'

The sound of hooves echoed across the cobbles, and the warrior emerged with his own Tverrian stallion in tow, Wren's satchel stuffed into the saddlebag. A panicked-looking stable hand passed the reins of a mare to Dessa.

'Where's my horse?' Wren said, frowning.

'You're looking at it.' Torj gestured to the enormous warhorse at his side.

Wren blinked. 'You mean there's only one? For both of us?'

'That's exactly what I mean.' The Bear Slayer pinned her with a triumphant stare. 'Did you think there'd be no consequences for your little stunt last night?'

CHAPTER 34

Torj

'In the wake of magical wounds, reality itself stands vulnerable to corruption'

— *Alchemy of Afflictions*

'I'M NOT SHARING a saddle with you,' Wren declared, her nostrils flaring, her outrage palpable.

'Wanna bet?' In one effortless motion, he circled her waist with his hands and lifted her up onto the stallion's back, fast enough that she didn't have time to kick him. The feel of her seared into his palms and the fresh memory of her moaning his name rushed back to him with a pulse of longing.

He shut those thoughts down, hard, and swung himself up behind her, sucking in a breath as he cradled her backside between his thighs. Trying to ignore the warmth of her body, he reached around to take the reins, guiding his stallion, Tucker, towards the gates and glancing back to make sure Wren's teammate, Dessa, was close behind. The redhead looked beyond uncomfortable in the saddle, but Torj had shared words with the stable hand to ensure her mare had a gentle temperament.

'This is fucking humiliating,' Wren muttered.

'You should have thought about that last night.'

'Like you'd be behaving any differently now, you brute.'

'You say the sweetest things, Embervale.'

'You haven't heard anything yet.'

He urged Tucker onwards. The sooner they got to Farissa's lesson, the better. Wren's fidgeting in the saddle was doing nothing to quell the heated notions swirling in Torj's mind, nor was the motion of the ride rocking him against her backside helping the growing hardness in his leathers.

Gods, whose idea was this again?

'Stop moving,' he ground out, feeling her tense before him.

'I'm trying to get comfortable.'

'This isn't a fucking day bed, Embervale.'

'You should have thought of that before you insisted I ride with you.' She wriggled again, this time, her curves rubbing directly over him.

Torj ground his teeth, trying to will away his growing erection. It was all he could do not to slip his hand around her waist and drag her back onto his cock. Instead, he turned his attention to the trail leading out of the academy grounds and guided them towards the city, where a large infirmary lay.

To his immense frustration, Farissa had changed the location of her lesson at the last minute, disregarding all his security protocols. The Master Alchemist had argued that spur-of-the-moment changes of plans could be good for security, given that they could catch any attackers unawares. Torj agreed, to some extent; he just didn't like that he'd not been consulted. Whether he liked it or not, though, Wren was his responsibility, and he meant to keep her safe at whatever cost.

He knew the place they were going. It was where his friends Talemir and Drue Starling had based themselves after the shadow war. Both famous warriors in their own right, they had spent much of their time there, helping the wounded, while so much of the midrealms was being rebuilt.

'We should go to the Mortar and Pestle tavern on the way back,'

Dessa was saying enthusiastically. 'Your friend Kristopher said it's a great spot.'

Wren snorted. 'I'm sure he did.'

'Absolutely not,' Torj told them.

Dessa cast a forlorn look in his direction. 'You're no fun.'

'I'm not paid to be fun. I'm paid to keep the future Queen of Delmira alive.'

He could practically hear Wren's eyes rolling in her head. 'So far you're not doing a great job,' she said. 'I'm dying of suffocation.'

Dessa laughed good-naturedly. 'Was he your bodyguard during the war as well?' she asked Wren.

Though Torj wasn't sure how, he felt the cold wash over her.

'Actually,' he heard himself say, 'it was Embervale who had my back in battle.'

Dessa's mouth fell open. '*Really?*'

'He's exaggerating,' Wren muttered.

'Not even a little,' Torj argued, enjoying the rise he was getting out of her. 'I'd be dead without her.' That much was true.

'That's incredible, Wren,' Dessa said sincerely. 'I'd love to hear about it one day.'

Wren elbowed him in the stomach. 'He's full of shit.' Torj grunted in pain, and a huff of satisfied laughter escaped her. 'Oops.'

Dessa continued to natter away, commenting on the architecture of the city, the fashions of its people, the luck they were having with the weather. She was a sweet woman, and Torj found himself hoping that Wren would warm to her eventually. He knew how lonely she had been after she'd lost her closest friends—

Tucker's ears flattened, and Torj felt his stallion tense beneath him. Before he could react, the horse let out a shrill neigh and reared up on his hind legs, his front hooves slicing through the air.

Wren let out a cry of surprise, her body pitching forwards. Instinctively, Torj's arm shot out, wrapping tightly around her slender waist and pulling her back against him. Wren's hand grasped his, her fingers cold. Torj's heart skipped a beat at the unexpected contact and the jolt of electricity that ran through him.

'It's alright,' he told her gently as he tightened his grip on the reins with his other hand, his thighs clenching around the stallion's sides as he brought the animal back under control. Dessa's startled shriek from behind them hadn't helped matters.

As the stallion's hooves returned to the ground, Wren seemed to realize what she had done. She wrenched her hand away, and Torj could sense her embarrassment in the way she shifted awkwardly in the saddle.

He did the gentlemanly thing and pretended it hadn't happened. He busied himself with scanning their surroundings, trying to determine what had spooked his mount. Tucker wasn't usually a skittish horse, but Torj could see nothing out of the ordinary. The road around them was quiet, the only sound the gentle rustling of leaves in the breeze.

Torj turned his focus back to Wren. 'You know,' he ventured, so only she could hear, 'you could be making this a lot easier between us.' He was vaguely hoping to offer some sort of truce, something that meant she might actually talk to him like a human being.

'And why would I want to make things easier for you?'

So much for that.

'Because right now, I want to throttle you more than I want to protect you.'

'I'd like to see you try, Bear Slayer. Remind me, how did that work out for you?'

'You tell me.' He drew her closer to him, so that her back was completely flush with his chest, so that the loose knot of her hair brushed against his stubble. He let his words kiss the shell of her ear, well aware that he was playing with fire. 'You were the one moaning my name last night.'

He heard the little gasp of shock that escaped her, felt her whole body go rigid in the saddle. The way Tucker surged forwards beneath them told Torj that she'd clenched her thighs together.

The poisoner hadn't been expecting that.

A beat later, Wren spoke. 'I wasn't the only one, was I?' She inched backwards and pressed herself against the hard, throbbing length of him. 'And it doesn't *feel* like you want to throttle me now, Warsword.'

Torj bit down a moan as the friction triggered a rush of short-lived pleasure, his face growing hot.

'You . . . *vixen*.' The words rushed from his lips breathlessly.

Wren gave a dark laugh. 'Challenge me to a game, Bear Slayer, and you'd best prepare to lose.'

CHAPTER 35

Wren

'The powdered florets of lavender can be made into a tea or oil for treating an array of anxieties'

– The Green Apothecary: A Guide to Medicinal Plants

AT LAST THEY entered the city, and Wren had never been gladder to see an infirmary in all her life. For all her bravado, she wasn't sure she could stand another second trapped in the saddle with Torj, molten desire pulsing between her legs. With the scent of him wrapped around her and the hard wall of muscle – among other things – behind her, she couldn't think, couldn't breathe.

Which was fucking ridiculous. Not only had she spent the last two years cursing him for sabotaging her work and interfering with her ledger, but he was currently driving her to insanity at *Drevenor*, for Furies' sake. Not to mention he was a *Warsword* of the midrealms. That was Thea's thing. Not hers.

Wren took a deep breath and gathered herself. It was a minor physical attraction, that was all. It could be stamped out if she tried hard enough.

'Wow.' Dessa whistled, swaying in her own saddle on the horse beside them. 'They're really staring at you.'

Panic seizing her by the throat, Wren scanned their surroundings. It was instantly apparent that Dessa wasn't addressing her, but rather the Bear Slayer, who had drawn their stallion to a halt and jumped down. Just like everywhere else they'd been, people gawked at him. He was the silver-haired warrior who'd closed a portal to a world of nightmares, who had saved them in the shadow war. Word about him had spread like wildfire.

And now, people were staring as Torj reached for her, offering his hand to help her down.

Wren batted him away. 'I can get down on my own.'

Torj shrugged. 'Suit yourself.'

Of course, she had vastly overestimated the height of the warhorse. The drop to the ground jarred her knees painfully. But she said nothing, not even as a glimmer of amusement sparked in the warrior's deep-blue gaze.

At least he had the good sense not to comment.

Wren turned her attention to the building before them, the time-worn stones of the hospice bathed in the soft glow of the morning sun. Statues of strange, menacing creatures were perched at the bases of arched windows, as though surveying the world below and guarding the inhabitants of the infirmary against harm. The stone figures and the building itself bore the scars of countless years and seasons.

The wooden doors adorned with wrought iron fixtures flew open, and Farissa greeted them, wearing an apron smeared with blood.

'Don't just stand there,' she ordered. 'The other teams have already been assigned their wards. Zavier's waiting for you.'

'How is everyone already here?' Wren said, climbing the stairs. 'We're not late.'

'If you're not early, you're late.'

That was the military influence of Thezmarr coming through, a sentiment Wren had never bought into. Why set a time at all if one meant something else entirely?

'You changed the schedule,' Torj pointed out from behind Wren and Dessa, having handed their horses off to an attendant.

'Still annoyed about that, Elderbrock? I'd have thought Warswords were more adaptable.'

Wren had to suppress a smile at that. The crease between Torj's dark brows deepened, but Farissa was already leading them at a charge through the ground floor of the hospice.

'You'll be in the women's wing today,' she told them.

Wren glanced back at the giant of a man behind her. 'Is that the best idea given the present company?' she asked her former mentor. From some of the previous work they'd done together, she knew that often women didn't like a male presence.

'It has been cleared,' Farissa threw over her shoulder. 'In any case, for the most part, you'll be mixing salves and following instructions in a workshop at the back, not administering medicines. Wren, tell me, how are your experiments faring?'

Taken aback by having this addressed in front of the others, Wren hesitated, brow furrowing. 'It's early.'

'But you're making progress?' Farissa pressed.

'A little. I need more samples of the substance to work with. I also haven't exactly got an endless supply of royal blood to test on . . .'

Farissa pursed her lips. 'I'll see what I can do.'

Wren shot her a dubious look.

'Keep working,' Farissa told her. 'The resources of the academy are at your disposal.'

Wren could feel Torj and Dessa's curious eyes on her, but she said no more, simply following Farissa through the labyrinth of the infirmary, trying to set her mind to whatever task lay ahead.

Farissa had been a Master Alchemist since long before Wren was born, and though it wasn't common knowledge, at least not outside of Thezmarr, her specialty was women's health and welfare. Which was why Wren wasn't overly surprised when they were taken through a closed-off section of the hospice; she had visited places like it before.

They entered a large room with a few dozen beds lining the walls, curtains drawn around some of them. It was quiet here, despite the squalling of a handful of infants; a quiet that ran like a deep, dark river through the halls. She met the vacant gazes of the women, some shadowed with bruising, some cradling broken arms . . .

At the back of the room, Zavier was waiting. Wren expected some sort of barb from him about their supposed tardiness, but he was strangely silent. As was Torj, she noticed – the warrior appeared oddly reverent as she took her satchel from him and handed it to Farissa.

'I thought you might need some additional supplies.'

Farissa nodded, taking the bag. 'Always. Thank you.' She motioned to Zavier. 'He knows what to do. Follow his directions.'

Wren wanted to argue. Zavier was giving the instructions? Hadn't *she* been Farissa's apprentice in Thezmarr for years? Didn't *she* have seniority in this setting? But even now, with their relationship still rocky, she respected the Master Alchemist too much to argue. Though she didn't want to admit it, if Farissa had made the choice to put Zavier in the lead, she had done so for a reason.

Wren turned to him. 'Well?'

To her surprise, her teammate shared the details respectfully before returning to the task at hand, leaving a decent distance between himself and the two women alchemists.

Wren and Dessa set to work on a range of herbal remedies that Wren was already familiar with: concoctions to stave off infection, poultices to pack wounds with, and brews to subdue pain during childbirth. It was meticulous work, and Wren lost herself in it. The air grew heavy with the familiar fragrance of herbs – evening primrose for skin conditions, tea tree oil for cleansing cuts. Wren was sure to label the tea tree clearly, for if ingested, it could be poisonous.

She handed Dessa several stalks of dried lavender to tie. 'These are good for a calming effect, particularly if a patient is distressed.'

'In what way?' Dessa asked.

'Perhaps they've woken from a night terror, or experienced a traumatic event. Perhaps they've endured hallucinations . . . Essential oils, tea made from lavender – it can help.'

In a mortar and pestle, Wren ground down turmeric into a bright yellow powder.

'What's that for?' her teammate asked, sniffing the highly fragrant spice.

'Mainly treating inflammation. Rare and highly sought after, of course.'

Dessa nodded enthusiastically. 'Of course.'

Wren got the sense that Dessa didn't have a natural affinity for medicinal alchemy, which prompted her to ask, 'What are you hoping to specialize in?'

'Oh, that's easy. Design,' she replied. 'I've always loved creating things.'

Wren found herself pleasantly surprised. 'Are you working on anything at the moment?'

Dessa nodded eagerly. 'I have several ongoing projects. I've always been fascinated by the history of the Stone of Knowledge and how it pertains to memory.'

Wren's brows shot up. 'Really?'

'I'm working on something in my spare time . . . I can show you sometime, if you like.'

Wren's instinct was to decline the offer. She wasn't at Drevenor to make friends, but . . . the ache in her chest said otherwise. 'That sounds fun.'

The red-headed beauty beamed. 'What about you? What do you hope to specialize in?'

Wren opened her mouth, but faltered. In truth, she had assumed she'd delve deeper into warfare, into poisons, but now . . . There was so much to learn, so many different avenues one could take. 'I'm not sure yet,' she replied truthfully.

'That's alright,' Dessa told her kindly. 'Plenty of time for that.'

For a while, Wren almost forgot where she was. It could have been Sam and Ida chattering away at her side, telling her of their latest antics with one of the porters or cook's assistants. She knew there was no hope of filling the void those women had left in her life, the ones she'd grown up with, who had known her better than anyone else. But perhaps . . . perhaps she was too young to cut herself off from the world entirely.

She turned away from Dessa, spotting Torj at the perimeter of the room, where a small group of women had approached him.

Every woman in the midrealms knows his name . . .

There was certainly no denying that now. But as Wren watched the scene unfold from afar, she knew it was different to the others she'd seen in their travels. Torj's discomfort was clear as day in the muscle that twitched his jaw, in the subtle clenching and unclenching of his fists . . . and in the erratic heartbeat that she could somehow sense from across the way, the relentless pounding that had her lightning crackling beneath her skin. However unnerved the Bear Slayer might have been, he gave the women kind smiles and gently shook his head at their offerings of biscuits and tea.

As the group dispersed, Wren found herself at her bodyguard's side. 'Do you know someone who lives here?' she asked quietly.

'Not here,' he said, voice hoarse. 'A place like it. A lifetime ago.'

He moved away, his countenance hard as iron as he returned to his duties, watching the ward like a hawk.

In turn, Wren watched him, noting the strained set of his shoulders and the measured weight of his steps. As she went back to her place at the workbench and took up her mortar and pestle again, she wondered who he'd known who had stayed in a women's infirmary, and why.

'Shit,' Dessa exclaimed, shaking her finger as she placed a lid over a small ramekin, smoke wafting from its sides over a thick candle. 'Burnt myself,' she told Wren sheepishly. 'Damn, got the end of my hair too—'

But Wren had smelled it before the words had left Dessa's lips.

She knew the acrid aroma all too well. Burnt hair. It was the smell that had permeated every battlefield during the war, the smell that clung to the shadow wraiths and reapers that had nearly torn the midrealms in two.

She drew a ragged breath, her hands growing clammy as the scent filled her nostrils and the claws of panic latched into her chest. All-too-familiar images started to flash before her. Wren clutched the sides of the table, but it did nothing to ground her, not as horror after horror invaded her vision.

Sam and Ida's heads on spikes.

Shadows lashing at Anya, sending her flying across the battlefield to her death.

Torj leaping from that wall, hurtling towards that terrifying maw of darkness.

That talon of evil carving down her own throat, the metallic tang of blood tangling with the reapers' stench, the air thick with it.

She was going to be sick. Everything was spinning and she was right back there in the shadow-drenched world of nightmares. The screaming, the gore, the terror – it was amplifying all around her, and she couldn't stop the war raging.

Electricity took hold of her – a current, a song of lightning, calling out to her in the dark.

CHAPTER 36
Wren

'The greatest discoveries often
come at the greatest cost'

— *Elwren Embervale's notes and observations*

A GENTLE MURMUR rumbled by her ear. Deep, soothing whispers vibrated down into her chest – words of comfort, of safety. The sound of home.

The harsh scent of burnt hair was gone, and instead, Wren breathed in black cedar and oakmoss. Her body was no longer cold and clammy, but dry and warm.

When she opened her eyes, she was in the Bear Slayer's arms.

The last thing she remembered was the unadulterated fear that had engulfed her in the women's ward. She didn't know where they were now, only that it was somewhere enclosed and quiet. Somewhere shielded, secure.

Wren tried to exhale, but couldn't find the air in her lungs. She was still trembling; her legs were weak beneath her.

'I've got you.' Torj's voice was soft, but firm and solid in a world where reality was still hazy. She clung to it desperately. 'I've got you, Embers,' he murmured again into her hair.

As the sharp edge of her panic ebbed, Wren tasted rain on her tongue, felt the demand of a storm raging within, tethered to the man holding her.

'Look at me,' he commanded.

And she did, her eyes meeting the dark sea blue of his.

'We survived it,' he told her. 'You and me. Together.'

Wren didn't ask how he knew what had happened to her in the ward. She couldn't stop the broken sob that escaped her. 'But I shouldn't have.' The words flew out of her, raw and unfiltered, the dark truth she'd carried since that battle. 'It should have been me. Why did I live when Sam, Ida and Anya all died?'

Torj's chest expanded against her as he took a steadying breath. 'There is no rhyme or reason to why people are taken from us. No greater meaning, no justice. I have long ago stopped trying to find those things in death . . .' A gentle touch brushed her hair away from her face. 'You deserve to live, Wren. You have as much right to life as anyone else does.'

'But—'

A finger pressed gently against her lips. 'Fight me on almost anything, Embers. But not that. That's not up for debate.'

Wren found the air she needed, and a part of her fractured as she released it in a long, trembling exhale.

Then, she saw him, as though for the first time.

Achingly beautiful. A lock of silver falling into his eyes, his strong brows and chiselled jaw tight with concern for her. The faint lines around his eyes crinkled as he studied her – she couldn't remember the last time he'd laughed with her, not properly. The thought devastated her all over again.

'Whatever you're thinking,' he murmured, 'don't.'

She locked eyes with him. 'How do you know what I'm thinking?'

'I don't know,' he said, reaching for her hand. He drew it up to the broad plane of his chest and placed her palm over where she knew those lightning-shaped scars marked his inked skin. 'But I feel it. Here.'

She felt his heart pounding beneath her touch, felt the prickle of magic in her fingertips as they connected with him. 'I did that to you . . .'

'You did it *for* me. Without you, I wouldn't be here.'

Another breath shuddered out of her, and with it went the pain. All that spiralling agony left her, her body sagging into his arms. But in its place was something else. Something that burned hotter than wildfire, raged with more force than any storm.

Desire.

Every point of contact between their bodies lit Wren ablaze, that heat turning molten and surging through her. She leaned into his touch, into the carved perfection of his war-honed body, feeling him in her very bones, in her blood.

The scent of him drove her wild, as intoxicating as any drug. Even with all the years apart, she'd never forgotten it.

She lifted her chin, peering up to find him watching her.

There was so little distance between them. She could close it with a push up onto her toes.

Torj's gaze turned hungry, as though he could indeed feel every thought of hers in his chest. Her hand still rested there, his heart hammering beneath it as he surveyed her, and she surveyed him right back.

'You look like you're going to kiss me,' she said, her body calling out for his touch.

'You look like you'd enjoy it,' he replied, his fingers entwining with hers.

His words were more than an observation; they were a promise. And she felt the truth of them pulse between her thighs, felt the slickness that gathered there. If he could have that effect with a simple turn of phrase, what could he do with—

'Elwren?' Farissa's voice cut through the haze of lust. 'Wren?'

It was only when the door swung inwards, revealing her worried-looking mentor, that Wren realized they were in the prayer room.

To her surprise, Farissa didn't look shocked to see her in the Bear Slayer's arms. Had Torj carried her from the ward? Embarrassment threatened to rise to the surface, but she shoved it down.

'Are you alright?' Farissa asked, assessing her as the colour returned to her face.

'I am now,' she replied, peeling away from Torj with a grateful glance.

Farissa was the only person who knew the full extent of her flashbacks and other difficulties since the war. The worry in her expression did not abate. 'Perhaps this isn't the place for either of you right now.'

Wren flinched. 'But my studies – my team—'

'Are fine with it. It was Zavier who alerted me to your episode. He suggested you might need a break.'

Wren clenched her jaw. 'Did he?'

'A very observant young man. A good ally to have, Elwren. But that's neither here nor there. Go back to Drevenor. Get some rest. Fight another day tomorrow.'

Farissa left no room for argument. She gave Torj a quick but meaningful look before she headed back to the ward.

'What did she mean?' Wren asked. 'When she said this isn't the place for *either* of us?'

'She knows I'm not a fan of infirmaries,' Torj replied cryptically, leading her towards the exit.

Though she sensed there was more to the story, Wren didn't press. Perhaps there would come a day where he'd share his tale with her openly, and maybe, just maybe, she'd do the same.

Outside, they stood at the foot of the stairs while an attendant went to fetch Torj's warhorse. It felt as though something had shifted between them, and despite herself, Wren felt compelled to say something – what, she didn't know. But the Warsword had been there for her in a way she hadn't known she needed, in a way that she'd never let someone before. She hadn't had to ask, and he hadn't drawn attention to it after, either.

You deserve to live, Wren. You have as much right to life as anyone else does.

She opened and closed her mouth several times before she said the only thing she could. 'Thank you.'

He glanced down at her in surprise. 'For what?'

'For everything—'

Her words were cut off as something barrelled into her. She went flying across the stairs, the collision sparking stars in her vision as she hit the stone, hard.

CHAPTER 37

Wren

'The seeds of the common valley apple contain substantial amounts of the poison cyanide'

– The Poisoner's Handbook

'WREN! TAKE COVER!' Torj yelled, brandishing his war hammer and throwing himself between her and their attacker. There was a pleading note to his order, but Warsword or not, Wren wasn't going to let him weather the storm of violence alone.

She scrambled to her feet, her hands flying to the vials at her belt. She wrenched them free as she would any weapon. *Knowledge is the victor over fate. The mind is a blade.*

Wren let her potions fly.

A loud bang sounded, and smoke filled the air, disorientating a handful of masked men who were surging not just for Torj, but for her.

Though the shadow war had left its scars on Wren, freezing in the face of danger was not one of them. She threw another bottle, a concentrated dose of Widow's Ash blanketing a pair of assailants heading right for her. They collapsed in seconds, shrieking in pain as boils formed across their exposed skin, bursting with the slightest contact.

Her magic sang in her veins, begging to be unleashed, but she hesitated. It had been so long since she'd wielded it, so long since she'd had complete control—

'Who are these people?' she cried, ducking as a small blade hurtled for her.

'No idea. Get back inside!' Torj swung his hammer into the face of another attacker. The man's skull caved instantly, his blood spraying the cobbles.

There were a dozen or so, but they moved too fast for Wren to count. Within moments, three were already mangled heaps of bloody pulp, courtesy of the hammer-wielding Bear Slayer in the heart of the fray. He moved like a war god, cutting down men as though they were nothing.

At the sight of him, Wren's lightning crackled again, deep in her chest, and her hands fell away from the potions at her belt. The current surged through her, a living force to be reckoned with as it gathered at her fingertips. It had been five years since she'd wielded storm magic from the deepest, darkest part of herself. The memory threatened to consume her: the roar of thunder, the searing pain—

But Torj was here, and he was whole, battling by her side once more. She wouldn't leave him to fight alone.

Wren's jaw set in grim determination as, at long last, she let the storm build within her like a vortex. Vibrant power arced across her fingertips, tendrils of blue-white energy coiling around her forearms.

When she released the first bolt, it exploded from her palm in a blinding flash. The air crackled as the blazing lightning struck her charging attacker in the chest, not in the arm as she had intended. Nevertheless, his body went rigid, limbs flailing, before he crashed to the cobblestones, a smouldering husk of what he'd been moments before. The man's scream died on his lips as her lightning burned him from the inside out.

Wren had only meant to hinder him, not strike him down. She'd thought they might take him alive for questioning – but that didn't matter now.

The scent of burnt hair and charred flesh filled the air once more and she staggered as it filled her nostrils, trying to drag her into another round of nightmarish flashbacks. But she clung to her magic, like a tether to this world, to Torj, who was fighting three more of the assailants.

He was a vision, wielding his war hammer like an extension of himself. For someone so big, he moved with a predatory grace that struck fear into the hearts of all who faced him. It was a dance of death, a whirlwind of Furies-given power, and he held nothing back.

Thunder clapped overhead. Gathering herself once again, Wren channelled the storm in a rush of wind that swept up around them, the sky opening up above.

She drew the chaos up from within, holding her unruly power in the palm of her hand, ready to unleash it upon the remaining attackers. She struck one so hard his mask was burned right off his face, and another went flying onto the road, a bolt hitting him square in the chest.

In front of the hospice was bedlam. Common folk fled the scene, screaming, while healers and fellow alchemists had emerged to see what the commotion was about, finding themselves in the heart of the battle that had spilled out across the street.

Wren threw another crackling ball of power, narrowly missing an onlooker and knocking one of Torj's attackers from where he'd raised his blade at the Warsword's back. She surged forwards, ready to end more of them, ready to release her wrath upon them all—

Wren staggered suddenly, feeling something cold and hard clamp around her wrists.

Manacles.

Nausea hit her like a blow, and she had to inhale long and hard to keep from vomiting on the cobbles. Her feet were slipping out from under her as someone dragged her by the manacles' chains, hauling her away from the fighting. Vision blurring, she reached for her storm magic – only to find it completely snuffed out. There was not a spark of lightning to call into being, no taste of rain on her tongue; only a sickening emptiness in her gut, and the cold lick of panic up her spine.

If she couldn't use magic . . . Wren reached for her belt, only for her hands to be jerked forwards in the painful irons, causing her to stumble over the stone—

'I don't think so,' her captor snarled.

Vision still blurred, Wren lashed out as best she could, shoving, kicking, twisting her body, thrashing like a wild animal. But the manacles around her wrists . . . They were not made of iron alone. Something was sinking into her skin, not only suppressing her storm magic, but clouding her senses as well.

The sounds of the fighting grew softer as she was dragged away. Where were they taking her? She had to escape, had to get back to Torj—

The world around her was a haze of bleeding colours and muffled sounds, indistinct shapes surging across her field of vision, the terror now thick in her throat. And yet, she still fought, hitting out blindly until her fists connected with something soft.

Her captor grunted, then struck her across the face.

The blow was like fire over her cheek, and she thought her eyes might pop out of her skull as she staggered, falling to her knees on the cobbles, face throbbing.

Her chains jerked again—

Something wet and hot hit her like a slap, then ran down her neck, seeping into her gown.

She knew from the metallic scent that it was blood.

And that it was not her own.

'*Wren.*' Torj was suddenly there, his voice like a balm over her panic. She felt his hands on the manacles, heard the sound of a key being fitted to a lock.

A ragged gasp escaped her as the irons fell away from her wrists. Power rushed back through her and her hands shot out.

Torj clasped them in his own. 'Easy, Embers . . .'

His fingers threaded through hers and squeezed, grounding her as her senses came back to her in an overwhelming wave. The air was thick with the scent of blood, and as Torj came into focus, she realized the Bear Slayer was covered in it, just as she was. Around them, all their masked attackers were dead, pulverized by Torj's hammer and her lightning.

'Gods . . .' Wren muttered as she watched the rivers of crimson running between the cobbles. She spotted a body that seemed untouched, but for the white spittle that had foamed at the edge of the man's mouth, his eyes wide. He'd poisoned himself, she realized, rather than be taken alive for questioning.

'What the fuck just happened?' she asked, searching the Bear Slayer's face for answers. 'Who are these men?'

'Later,' Torj said quietly, helping her to her feet. 'Let's get you out of here first.'

'Wait.' She reached for the manacles, an eerie sensation crawling across her skin. Taking them in her hands, she felt their strangeness instantly, along with something more concerning: *familiarity*.

'We need to leave,' Torj urged, surveying the gathered crowd, his mouth set in a hard line. He put an arm around her and guided her between the corpses to his horse, who was waiting loyally, abandoned by the stable hand.

Wren's mind was racing, the fresh memory of her own helplessness leaving a bitter taste on her tongue as she ran her fingers along the rough chains.

She glanced up at Torj. 'Alright,' she said.

'Alright what?'

'I'll learn self-defence.'

A beat later, Torj's expression softened. 'I'm sorry it took something like this for you to—'

But Wren shook her head. 'It wasn't the men,' she told him, raising the irons. 'It's these.'

'What about them?' he asked, brows furrowed.

'It was me,' she murmured. 'I made them.'

CHAPTER 38

Torj

'Even the most skilled wielders of magic are not immune to the unforeseen ripple of consequence'

– A History of Magically Inflicted Injuries

EVEN BACK AT the academy, in the safety of Wren's rooms, Torj's heart was still pounding. The glint of a blade, the whoosh of an arrow as it flew past Wren, missing her by a hair's breadth – it was all too close for comfort.

He hadn't felt fear like that in five years. Icy terror had gripped his heart as Wren's life hung in the balance. Nothing else had mattered. Only her.

Torj shook his head, trying to clear his thoughts. He was her bodyguard, sworn to protect her. Of course her safety mattered to him. But this feeling, this intensity – it was something else, something he couldn't quite define. All he knew was that the thought of any harm coming to Wren filled him with a dread more chilling than the winter storms in Aveum.

Wren was tending to a small cut on her arm, the strange manacles she had brought with them on the workbench before her. They hadn't spoken on the ride back to the academy, both reeling from the encounter with the masked men, but her words echoed in his mind.

I made them . . .

Torj peered over her shoulder at the offending pair of irons. 'What do you mean, you *made* them?' he said at last.

Wren started wiping the blood from her face with a wet rag. 'Well, I *designed* them. Years ago . . . When we all thought Wilder was a traitor, and Thea needed something to contain him once she captured him.'

Torj ran his fingers through his hair and grimaced, finding it matted with blood, too. In the year leading up to the shadow war, his fellow Warsword, Wilder Hawthorne, had been accused of treason, and Wren's sister had been ordered to hunt him down and bring him to justice.

'I treated the chains with a unique form of alchemy,' Wren continued, dropping the blood-stained rag on the bench, not taking her eyes off the irons. 'Alchemy I had previously used to suppress Thea's storm magic.'

'Why would you do that?' Torj asked, goosebumps rushing across his skin.

Wren paused a moment before answering. 'Perhaps it was wrong, but when we were growing up, I discovered my magic long before my sister's started manifesting. I knew what it meant: that we weren't just orphans, we were royals – the heirs to Delmira – and that the second someone discovered our heritage, we would be in danger. I also knew that Thea wasn't ready to face those truths. So . . . I treated the stone she wore around her neck day and night, with a subtle concoction I'd tested on myself. Enough to suppress her magic, but not make her ill . . . Then later, when we suspected Wilder wasn't who he said he was, I revisited the formula. I made it stronger, harsher, added elements to quell a Warsword's Furies-given strength . . .'

'And these are the same chains?' Torj lifted them from the table, turning them over in his hands.

'Almost,' Wren replied hoarsely, taking them from him. 'Where I amplified the properties that dull strength, whoever created these did so to quell sovereign magic. From what I can tell, they took my design and my methods and tweaked them to suit their own purposes . . . To capture rulers of the midrealms. It's the same sort of alchemy that was used on the blade in the attempt on King Leiko's life.'

Unease coiled in Torj's gut. 'You're sure?'

'Yes.'

He swore. 'And now they've used your own weapon against you.'

'So it would seem.' Wren dropped the soiled rag on her workbench and sighed. 'Why would they attack me?'

'Whether you wear a crown or not, you're the heir to the Delmirian throne,' Torj said slowly. Why had Audra not told him that there was something larger at play? That his guarding of Wren was no mere precaution, but a response to a larger fear for all royals of the midrealms? He unclenched his jaw, rubbing the aching muscles there.

'But my kingdom has nothing,' Wren countered. 'And I wield no political power. I'm just an alchemist.'

'You've never been just an alchemist, Embers.' Torj stared at the manacles. 'You have to hand them over to the academy. And I have to talk to Audra, immediately.'

'I know.'

Wren was tense, shadows flickering in her eyes as she scanned the irons. She was covered in dried blood the colour of rust, her gown and apron ruined. A bruise was blooming around her right eye where that bastard had struck her. Torj had ended him too quickly.

'You should get cleaned up,' he said.

She didn't look away from the manacles. 'So should you.'

Torj sighed. 'I have to report to the High Chancellor and send word to Thezmarr. Cal's on his way to take over for me.'

He held out his hands for the manacles. Wren reluctantly handed them over.

'They'll want to speak to you about the specifics,' he told her. 'About what you used to treat these.'

Wren nodded, looking forlorn. 'I . . . I don't know what would have happened if you hadn't been there. Thank you.'

'Are you sure you're feeling alright? Should I call for a healer? That's two expressions of gratitude in a single day . . .'

Wren huffed a dark laugh. 'Don't get used to it.'

'Wouldn't dream of it, Embervale.'

A faint smile tugged at her lips, just as a knock sounded at the door.

'That'll be Cal,' Torj said, taking in the exhaustion lining her face. 'Get cleaned up,' he told her again.

Wren started towards the bathing chamber, but stopped and turned back to him. 'When do we start self-defence lessons?'

A fresh wave of guilt washed over him, turning his guts to lead. He'd nearly thrown all manner of duty and mission to the wind and kissed her then and there in the prayer room. Holding her like that . . . It had been both joy and torment, reawakening a yearning he had tried to stamp out long ago. The scent of her, the soft feel of her in his arms – it had fractured whatever walls he'd built around himself in her absence. He'd been so rattled by the experience that he'd been caught off guard with the attack. He should have smelled it coming a mile away, but she'd nearly been taken.

All because he'd been so wrapped up in her.

Then there was the matter of the wound that festered in the scars above his heart. Everything he had read so far spelled doom: an altered reality, an altered self . . . Was he changing? Was he himself putting Wren in danger?

Torj cleared his throat, trying to force down the memory of her pressed against him. 'Tomorrow,' he answered her at last. He'd make sure of it.

Compelled as he felt to be her sole protector, it was time he taught her how to defend herself.

CHAPTER 39

Wren

*'The body tires before the mind. Keep it strong.
Learn to protect it'*

– *Drevenor Academy Handbook*

THE FOLLOWING DAY, it was Cal rather than the Bear Slayer who escorted Wren to the dining hall. As soon as she crossed the threshold, an eerie quiet fell across the cohort, every gaze latching onto her from around the tables. Word about yesterday's conflict had clearly spread.

Her face burning, Wren drew back her shoulders and made for her usual seat, trying to ignore the eyes boring holes into her back as she moved between the benches. She had spent over an hour soaking in the tub the night before, yet she could still feel the slide of blood on her skin and the itch of where it had dried. Her hands felt dirty, no matter how many times she scrubbed beneath her nails. The attention on her had her skin crawling all over again.

At the clearing of a throat, she looked up to find the High Chancellor positioning himself at the centre of the dais, his expression sombre.

'Alchemists of Drevenor,' he called, and Wren was relieved to feel the stares leave her at last as she slipped into her seat opposite Dessa and Zavier. 'As no doubt many of you will have heard, there was a vile attack outside the infirmary in Highguard yesterday. As such, we have suspended all official lessons outside of the academy grounds for the time being. While you are still permitted to visit the city to retrieve supplies, you will need to inform an academy master of your intentions to do so, and you must do so accompanied by your team. You will also notice an increase in security and a new class added to your schedules today. An investigation into the incident is underway. For now, we ask that you remain vigilant, that you take your place here at Drevenor more seriously than ever.'

Whispers broke out across the hall once more, but Wren looked up to find Zavier and Dessa watching her. Dessa's brows were knitted together with concern, while Zavier's sharp features resembled something more akin to curiosity.

'Are you alright?' Dessa asked, reaching across to fill Wren's empty cup with steaming tea, her eyes falling to the cut on Wren's arm.

'Nothing more than a scratch or two,' Wren told her, giving her a grateful smile as she lifted the tea to her lips.

Zavier hadn't stopped studying her either. 'Did you see who it was?'

'They were wearing masks.'

'None were left alive?' he pressed.

Wren's eyes narrowed. 'No. They took precautions so that didn't happen.'

Zavier's brows shot up. 'That was organized of them.'

'That's not what I'd call it,' Wren muttered, her lightning crackling at her fingertips at the memory.

'And before the attack?' Zavier said. 'What happened to you? One minute you were fine in the ward, and the next your Warsword was practically carrying you away.'

'We thought you'd fainted,' Dessa added.

'Headache,' Wren lied.

Dessa winced. 'Oh, you poor thing. Are you feeling better now? You look a little pale . . .'

Zavier shook his head, clearly not buying it. 'If there's something we should know as your teammates, tell us.'

'There's nothing to tell—'

A shadow cast across the table, and Wren looked up to see the High Chancellor staring down at her. 'I'd like a moment of your time, Miss Embervale. Please come with me.'

Cal made to rise from his seat beside her.

'Your presence won't be required, Warsword Whitlock,' the High Chancellor dismissed him.

Cal's brow furrowed. 'I'm—'

'It's fine, Cal,' Wren told him, getting to her feet to follow Remington Belcourt and his billowing robes from the hall.

She found herself in a small classroom, the door clicking closed behind her and the High Chancellor. They didn't sit; instead, Master Belcourt turned to her, his grey-streaked black hair cascading to his collarbones, framing his line-etched face as he fixed her with his piercing eyes.

'Warsword Elderbrock made his report last night,' he said without preamble. 'He explained about the manacles, and your contribution to their design.'

Wren swallowed hard. 'I had no idea they would be used in this way.'

'Nor do most creators envision their work being used for evil when they're deep in the throes of innovation. But there is danger in invention, risk in all design. You will come to learn that here at Drevenor.'

Wren nodded. She already had. 'What now, High Chancellor?'

'Now, I need to know who else knows of these designs. Is there anyone you shared the alchemy with? Anyone who might have passed the knowledge on?'

Wren rubbed her temples as they started to ache. 'It was more than five years ago . . . At the time, the only Master Alchemist I knew was Farissa.' She fought back the sudden burn of tears. 'I had two friends who helped me with the details of the design. But they were killed in the war.'

The High Chancellor paused before reaching out and placing a hand on her shoulder. 'And would they have told anyone, Elwren? Before their deaths?'

Wren's heart seized as a wave of panic crashed against her. For a moment, all she could do was close her eyes and let herself breathe. In through the nose. Out through the mouth.

When she opened her eyes, Master Belcourt was still waiting.

'You mean, if they were interrogated?' Wren asked, her voice hoarse.

'Yes.'

'I know their final days were full of pain and suffering. But that's all I know. I can't tell you who they spoke with or what they said under duress. Nor would I hold them accountable for anything under those horrific circumstances.' The words came out harsher than she intended.

'So it's possible,' the High Chancellor murmured.

'It's also possible that my work was discovered more recently,' Wren countered.

'Are you sure you haven't told anyone else? About your work at Thezmarr or here? Have you been keeping our secrets, Elwren? I hope you're not underestimating the seriousness of this situation. Your own design was—'

A sharp knock sounded at the door, and Wren had never been gladder to see Zavier as the door swung inwards.

'I've been sent to fetch Wren, sir,' he said, as though he were oblivious to the tension permeating the room. 'The additional lesson starts shortly.'

The High Chancellor's nostrils flared, but he glanced at his pocket watch. 'So it does. You're dismissed, then, Elwren.'

Wren followed Zavier from the room, forcing herself to walk at a normal pace, to keep her breathing steady.

'You're shaking,' he murmured, giving her a sideways glance.

'It's nothing.' Wren stuffed her hands into her apron pockets. 'Who sent you?'

Zavier shook his head. 'No one. You were gone a while. It didn't feel right.'

Wren looked at him in surprise. 'Thanks.'

'What are teammates for?' Zavier replied with a wry grin.

'You mean your sole purpose isn't to drive me to madness?'

'Not quite.' He led her back to the hall and gathered his things. 'I wasn't joking about the additional lesson. We're due at the gymnasium in ten minutes.'

Wren blinked. 'There's a gymnasium?'

'See you there, Poisoner,' Zavier said before heading out.

Cal was waiting for her, looking worried, but it was Kipp who Wren's gaze fell upon. He was now seated next to Dessa, his arm around her shoulders, whispering into her ear. Dessa let out an obscene giggle.

'There's no stopping him, is there?' Wren muttered.

''Fraid not,' Cal offered with a sympathetic grimace. 'Is everything alright?'

Wren looked around for the familiar towering figure. Instead of answering Cal, she asked, 'Where's Torj?'

Her friend shrugged, getting to his feet. 'Warsword business.'

'So he's allowed to know every detail about me, invade my private space, and follow me like a shadow, but all I get as to his whereabouts is *Warsword business*?' she retorted, snatching up a piece of toast. With all the interruptions, she hadn't had a chance to eat.

'Pretty much,' Cal said. 'Why'd you wanna know, anyway?'

'Forget it,' Wren mumbled around her food, shouldering her satchel. 'When does this special lecturer arrive? The one who *specially* requested you?'

'Next week,' Cal replied proudly.

'How exciting for you, Callahan,' Kipp injected from across the table. 'You must have impressed someone high and mighty.'

Wren gave Kipp a warning look. 'Don't tease him.'

He threw his hands up. 'Who said I was teasing? It's no small feat, becoming a Warsword of the midrealms.'

Cal's eyes narrowed suspiciously.

Wren elbowed him. 'Let's go. I'm supposed to arrive early for every lesson.'

'Any idea what this next one's about?' Cal asked.

'Apparently, our protection.'

CHAPTER 40

Wren

'In the grand tapestry of alchemy, each thread woven has the potential to unravel the work of others'

— *Drevenor Academy Handbook*

WHEN THEY ENTERED the gymnasium, most of Wren's cohort was already there, as was an alchemist she hadn't seen before. She was younger than their other teachers, wearing tight leggings and a vest that clung to every curve and muscle of her toned body. She watched them with eagle eyes, her stance like a blade balancing on its point as she scrutinized each novice before she spoke.

'My name is Olsen Oakes. You may call me Oakes. I'm not a Master Alchemist, but I am a seasoned expert who has been called here today under special circumstances.' She crossed her arms over her chest, her sculpted biceps shifting impressively. 'Alchemists have never been mere scholars. Our work often calls for risking our lives. Here at Drevenor, we have always lived by the following mantra: *train the body, tame the mind, transcend limitations.* However, yesterday's attack on the infirmary has called for action to be taken. Should anyone wish to change into more practical clothing for physical activity, you'll find a range of trousers and tunics by the changing rooms over there. Be ready within the next fifteen minutes.'

Looking down at her skirts, Wren left Cal to guard the door and went with Dessa and a few other female alchemists to change. She couldn't help but be amused at the flaw in the guild's guard assignment as she looked around at her peers. She knew better than most that the women around her were just as deadly as any assassin on the streets – more so, even. They didn't need masked assailants armed with blades. They could inflict death with a kiss of fine powder, or a drop of perfume on a swathe of fabric. Oddly, the thought cheered Wren up – until she registered the topic of conversation among the others as skirts were removed and leggings were tugged on.

'Haven't you seen the way he moves? Like the stories of those teerah panthers from Tver . . . All predatory and powerful . . .'

Wren cast a glance in the woman's direction. She was lacing up a shirt and smirking at her friend.

'I heard he beds at least five women a night, to take the edge off,' another chimed in.

'I heard he has the strength of a hundred men,' Dessa added enthusiastically.

'And who in the midrealms are we talking of?' Wren demanded, tugging on her own pair of trousers.

'Callahan the Flaming Arrow, of course,' Dessa replied, shaking her head as though Wren had asked her what colour the sky was.

'Cal?' Wren couldn't help it; she burst out laughing. 'Beds five women a night?'

The first woman nodded in all seriousness. 'He's got quite the appetite, apparently.'

'Good gods,' Wren muttered, thoroughly amused.

'Well,' Dessa said, quietly enough so that only Wren could hear, 'you can't expect them to swoon over your silver-haired Bear Slayer for ever. Everyone knows he's off limits.'

'What?' Wren blurted.

But Dessa just smiled and headed for the door, leaving Wren to hang her skirts up in a spare locker.

Still reeling, she caught a glimpse of herself in one of the nearby mirrors. The leggings were tighter than she liked, making her feel a little uneasy. But she'd opted to keep her own shirt and bodice on, along with her belt of tools and tinctures. She wasn't stupid enough to leave it unattended in a locker.

'Hurry up,' Cal's voice carried through the changing room from outside, and Wren hurried back into the gymnasium, where Oakes was waiting.

'I want to impress upon you the importance of today's lesson, in light of what happened yesterday. That is why I have sought help from the very best,' Oakes told them. 'Someone who has fought all manner of monsters, who has emerged victorious from battle countless times . . .'

Wren's nape prickled as her teacher spoke again.

'I have asked one of our resident Warswords to assist me in today's class.'

Wren hated the heat that crept up her neck, the way her chaotic magic thrummed insistently in her chest, as none other than Torj Elderbrock entered the gymnasium.

CHAPTER 41

Wren

'Very few poisoners die old in their beds'

— *The Poisoner's Handbook*

He'd told her himself that their lessons would start today. Wren just hadn't realized he meant with her entire cohort.

Torj's deep-sea eyes found her instantly. They roamed over her face and trailed down, lingering on her form-fitting bodice and leggings, heat blazing in his dark gaze.

'We'll start by warming up,' Oakes declared. 'Five laps around the gymnasium. Go.'

Leaving Cal at the perimeter, Wren surged into action with the rest, feeling ridiculous. This was certainly not what she'd had in mind when she'd learned she would be studying at Drevenor. She felt more like a shieldbearer in training than an alchemist. By the end of the second lap, she was sweating, and by the fifth, she was cursing herself for not staying in better shape. After the war, when she'd moved to her ramshackle cottage in Delmira, she'd gone on walks through the forest every day, sometimes venturing to the barren lands beyond. But she'd never exercised like this, and now, she knew she was in for a rude awakening.

Thankfully, she was not the only one whose fitness needed

improvement. Dessa's cheeks were bright red, her hair damp with perspiration, while several others were hunched over their knees, dry retching. Wren decided then and there that she would endeavour to channel Thea in her quest for a higher level of endurance, and Anya in her steadfast resolve.

Train the body, tame the mind, transcend limitations.

'Another two laps,' their teacher called, looking utterly unsympathetic.

Wren bit back a groan and did as she was told, joining the others at a run around the outskirts of the gymnasium. One lap, then two, and Wren suffered through them both. If only Thea and Anya could see her now . . . A disgrace to the Embervale name.

'Alright,' Oakes said. 'Let's stop there before someone passes out.'

Wren made the mistake of meeting Zavier's eye. To her disdain, he hadn't even broken a sweat. She certainly couldn't have him win this.

'Warsword Elderbrock.' Oakes motioned for him to take her place. 'Care to shed some light on what we're doing here today?'

The Bear Slayer was all business as he came to stand before the cohort, his movements measured, the embodiment of discipline and strength. Wren observed his striking, powerful figure: unattainable and godlike, bordering on terrifying. By the looks of some of her peers, he'd crossed that threshold.

'I have always known alchemy as an art far more physical than the world perceives,' he said, his husky voice capturing the attention of every novice. 'In the shadow war, I saw many alchemists fight alongside the great warriors of Thezmarr. Though we are no longer at war, in life, you will be at risk. That is the burden of knowledge.'

Wren sucked in a breath as his eyes met hers all too briefly.

'Today, Oakes, Warsword Whitlock and I will be showing you the basics of self-defence. You will not leave this hall until you've mastered all three moves: the groin kick, the palm heel strike, and the elbow strike. These are the fundamentals. I want you to remember the following: *understand the surroundings. Come to grips with your limitations. Find a solution.* Remember to stick to the basics – remain light on your feet so you can pivot, don't talk back to your instructor, and don't sabotage your fellow alchemists. There will be time enough for that during your Gauntlet trials. When it gets tough, and it will, I want you to recognize the power of combining your alchemy knowledge *with* combat prowess. Many of you are already far more deadly than a trained warrior . . .' He glanced at Wren. 'Imagine that ability multiplying tenfold if you knew how to guard your flank, if you knew how to twist out of an attacker's grasp.'

Wren knew he wasn't saying it to embarrass her, but she was well aware that had she taken up his initial offer of lessons, she might not have found herself in those irons yesterday, helpless, her powers hindered.

I'll never be helpless again, she vowed to herself.

Torj wasted no time taking them through the initial manoeuvres of the three basics, demonstrating on Cal at the front of the gymnasium. Wren had to admire the way the pair of them moved and the sheer control they had over their bodies, both holding back their true strength as they broke each motion down into a slower version.

'Pair up,' Oakes shouted, and Wren watched in dismay as Zavier commandeered Dessa, and those others whose names she had learned – Selene Tinsley, Alarik Wingate, Gideon Sutten, Kyros Sorrell, Blythe Rookford and even Jasper Greaves – all managed to find partners among the cohort, leaving her solo. This had never happened to her back at Thezmarr. It had always been her, Thea, Ida and Sam for as long as she could remember, and even on the rare occasion where they'd been an odd number, no one ever actively avoided her.

'You're with me, Embervale.' Torj's deep voice vibrated across the space between them.

She stared. 'You can't be serious.'

'I'm always serious.'

She scoffed. 'You really want me to spar with *you*?'

'Unless you'd rather someone else's hands all over you?' he murmured darkly.

'That's—'

'Stabilize yourself as best you can,' he cut her off, crowding her with his enormous frame. 'Let's try a groin kick.'

'You're game,' she retorted.

'You'd have to actually land that foot for me to be worried,' he told her. 'Lift your dominant leg   that's it.'

Wren followed his directions, holding her balance.

'Now you begin to drive your knee upwards. Exactly. Extend the dominant leg. Drive your hips forwards.' Torj's warm hands closed around her leg and positioned her knee. 'Now I'm in trouble—'

'Aren't you always?' The words slipped from Wren's mouth.

A ghost of a smile played at Torj's mouth, but he ignored her comment. 'From here, you lean back slightly – don't lose your stability – then you kick as hard as you can.'

Wren did as he bid, and the Warsword jumped back with a hiss. 'You're a fast learner, Embers. Either that or you like the idea of burying your foot in my nether regions.'

'Why can't it be both?' she said sweetly.

At her words, he overpowered her, closing his arms around her and gripping her firmly. 'You got too cocky. Now I've got the upper hand, you can't extend your leg in the same way. What do you do?'

'Use my knee.'

'Show me.'

Wren checked her stance, ensuring that she wasn't at risk of falling over, before thrusting her knee towards the Bear Slayer's groin.

He blocked her easily, but he was smiling now. 'You've got it,' he said, a note of pride in his words. 'You always aim for the sensitive areas . . . to start, anyway.'

'Thea did always tell me to aim for the soft parts.'

He fixed her with a stare. 'Believe me, there's nothing *soft* about me, Embers. And unlike your previous attackers, I've seen what you're capable of. I don't want your lightning – or alchemy, for that matter – anywhere near those parts. Now, show me your palm heel strike. And make it count.'

Wren positioned herself in front of Torj, lifted her right hand, and flexed her wrist, jabbing up towards his nose.

'Good,' he told her, batting her hand away. 'You could also go for my throat.' His fingers closed gently around her wrist as he directed her palm heel strike beneath his chin. 'You have to make sure you retreat as soon as you strike. Pull that arm back as quickly as you can. It'll help shove your attacker's head up and back.'

Wren practised the motion in real time. 'Like this?'

'Exactly like that. It'll make your attacker stagger back, giving you the room to escape.'

'With those manacles on, I wouldn't have been much use anyway,' she said quietly, remembering the muting of her senses, the blurring of her vision.

'They might not have got them on you in the first place,' Torj replied. 'But it's never that simple. We can only speculate on what might have happened. The important thing is what *did* happen. You got out. You're safe.'

Wren nodded. 'I heard you made your report?'

'I did.'

'What did Audra say?'

'I can't tell you that, Embervale.'

'What about the High Chancellor?'

'I can't tell you that either.'

Wren made a noise of frustration. 'Of course you can't.' Letting her irritation get the better of her, she struck out, throwing herself through the motions of another blow to Torj's nose. 'You don't think I have a right to know? The High Chancellor came to me this morning,' she ventured through gritted teeth.

'And?'

She didn't know why she'd said it, given how much the experience had rattled her. 'I'll show you mine if you show me yours.'

Ignoring her comment, Torj not only blocked her by closing his hand over her fist, but spun her around so that she was trapped with her back against his chest, his huge frame enveloping her. She couldn't move a muscle.

'These are defensive moves, not attack techniques. If you want to know how to fight, we can work on that.' His words vibrated against her, waking the storm that slumbered within. She felt it yawn wide in her chest, drawing her closer to him.

'Alright,' she managed.

The Warsword tensed at her back, surprised. 'Alright?'

'I don't like repeating myself, Bear Slayer.'

'Then that can be arranged. But for now . . .' He shifted around her, his grip tightening so that she could feel every ridge of muscle behind her. 'If your attacker is in close range like this and you can't get momentum to punch or kick, I want you to use your elbows.'

Wren tried to slam her elbow back into his stomach, but she was instantly off-kilter, her feet slipping out from underneath her. He was like a fucking brick wall.

'You need to lock your stance before you do that,' he told her, his hands drifting down. He placed a flat palm against her stomach, and his other hand gripped her thigh. 'You need a strong core and strong legs to ensure you don't go tipping over like that, to maintain the force behind your blow.'

Every strategic thought emptied from Wren's head as the heat of Torj's touch seeped through her clothes and set her ablaze. She could feel the imprint of each finger around her thigh, and imagined him spreading her open beneath him. His grip tightened as though he could read her thoughts, his touch so close to where desire now pooled between her legs. A current ran between them, full of fire.

Cheeks flaming, she could sense her cohort's eyes on them, but Torj didn't release her. She felt the bob of his throat at her shoulder and the slight shift in his stance so that his lower half wasn't flush with her backside.

'From here, bend your arm at the elbow, shift your weight forwards, brace yourself, and ram your elbow back. In this position, aim for the belly, the ribs, the groin . . .'

Ignoring her racing heart, Wren did as he bid, landing her elbow in his side.

Torj cleared his throat. 'Good,' he said, voice rough. 'Very good. Hopefully that would be enough to cause your attacker to loosen their hold, enough for you to escape. Or douse them in your choice of poison.'

Wren smiled at that.

But the smile didn't last long, because the Bear Slayer broke away from her fully and turned to the rest of the cohort. 'Five more laps of the gymnasium,' he barked.

No one bothered to suppress their groans this time.

By the end of their training, anyone who had previously swooned over the Warsword was cursing him. And back in the changing rooms, drenched in sweat, the women alchemists were more vocal still.

'What a bastard.'

'Sadist.'

'Prick.'

Dessa nodded sagely. 'Nice shoulders, though.'

Wren had to laugh.

CHAPTER 42

Torj

'Phantom sensations, such as pain or tingling, are a perplexing phenomenon in the realm of magical injuries. They can continue to affect the afflicted long after the physical wounds have healed and often arise from severed magical connections'

– *A Study of Accidental Curses*

IT HAD BEEN a mistake, sparring with her. The lightning in his chest thrummed with renewed madness, and nothing would quell it. His thoughts were a tangled mess. He'd spent so long resenting the beautiful alchemist, but when it boiled down to it, Torj couldn't stand the thought of someone else being so close to her, touching her. He told himself that if *anyone* was going to teach Wren how to defend herself, who better than a Warsword of the midrealms? Who better than *him*?

The thought of her getting hurt set his teeth on edge and made his fists clench to the point of drawing blood from his palms. Which was exactly how Wren found him waiting outside the changing rooms. She surveyed him from head to toe, her hand pressing against her sternum absentmindedly.

'What's wrong?' she asked. She had washed and changed back into her skirts, the damp hair at her nape curling slightly, her cheeks still flushed with the exertion of exercise. Her eyes were bright, though they narrowed in concern as she studied him.

'Nothing,' he said quickly, pushing a canteen into her hands. 'Drink. You need plenty of water after so much physical activity.'

Frowning, Wren lifted the canteen to her lips and took a sip.

'Drink it all,' he told her.

'I'm not—'

He silenced her with a stare. 'You also need to eat something before your next class.'

'Kitchens are closed,' she replied.

Torj had known she'd have an answer for everything, so he handed over the pastry he'd saved for her.

'You made this?'

'No, I just swiped it from the breakfast spread,' he told her, motioning for her to keep moving. 'But I don't mind cooking, when time allows.'

Wren studied the sugar-dusted scroll. 'Should I check it for poison?'

'That's usually my question.' Torj raised a hand to Cal across the gymnasium, dismissing him. He knew his fellow Warsword wanted to map out the north building for when his special guest lecturer arrived. Torj turned back to Wren, who hadn't taken so much as a bite. 'Just eat. You're wasting away.'

'Hardly.' But she took a bite and moaned, melted butter coating her lips. 'I didn't know you liked to cook.'

Torj had to refrain from adjusting himself, suddenly hard at the sound that had escaped her wicked mouth. 'There's a lot you don't know about me.'

'Oh?'

'My grandmother taught me a few basic recipes. And usually if I'm in a unit, it's me who's cooking on the road.' He didn't know why he had offered up that kernel of information so freely, especially about Grams. It had been a long time since he'd spoken of her.

'I remember,' Wren said quietly. 'It was always you preparing the meals during the war . . .'

They fell into step with one another as they left the gymnasium and crossed the grounds towards one of the conservatories.

'You need to stock up on supplies between lessons, yes?' Torj asked, nodding at the circular building in the distance.

Wren nodded. 'Is she still alive? Your grandmother?' she asked.

It was as though an invisible hand had reached in and squeezed his heart, causing his mind to reel with memories. Each recollection was both precious and painful, like pressing on a bruise.

'No one knows,' he replied, catching the hoarseness in his voice. 'She went missing a long time ago, presumed dead. I searched for her for years, but never found anything.'

'I'm sorry,' Wren said gently. 'What happened . . . ?'

A hollow ache pulsed behind Torj's eyes, a heaviness settling in the pit of his stomach. 'A lot of things happened.'

Wren nodded, as though this was answer enough. 'What was she like?'

'She was a formidable woman from Tver. Ran a shelter like the one we went to yesterday.'

'You're from Tver?'

'All these years and you don't know where I'm from?' he teased, trying to turn the conversation to lighter subjects. 'Yes, originally.' He stopped himself there, knowing where all questions would eventually lead. He didn't share those earlier years of his life with anyone. Instead, he turned the queries back to her. 'And you? What did you make of your homeland these past five years?'

Wren's hand drifted to the belt around her waist, where a dozen or more vials and tools clinked together. 'It was quiet.'

'I'd expect as much, given that no one has settled in that kingdom in decades.'

Wren seemed suddenly distant, gazing across the grounds as they walked. 'I could see it,' she said quietly. 'What it once was, what it could have been . . . were it not for the stain of the shadow war across its plains.'

'You wish you could make it different?'

'I wish a lot of things were different. But wishing doesn't make it so . . .'

Her words reminded him of a conversation he'd had with Wilder long ago, during the war.

'Not going to deny it?' Wilder pressed, clearly hoping to rile him.

But Torj shook his head. He had watched Wilder and Thea together with a pang of envy: the familiar touches and the private smiles, the way they always sought each other out in a room full of people. 'Why should I? Why shouldn't I want what you have?'

Wilder looked thoughtful at that. 'You shouldn't deny it,' he said. 'You deserve what you want, brother.'

'If only wanting made it so, eh?'

'If only,' Wilder agreed.

Torj came back to himself, his chest tight from the memory. It had been a long time since he'd been so candid with someone, a long time since he'd been so honest about what he wanted.

But he was a Warsword of the midrealms. His job wasn't to want, but to serve, to protect. And once his job was done, he would be on the first ship out of here, to the lands far beyond.

He glanced at Wren, who was finishing off the pastry and licking the butter from her fingers. A fraction of the tension he carried with him ebbed away. At least she was eating.

When they reached the conservatory, Torj gave a low whistle, impressed. There was no need for torches or candles here. The glass walls and ceiling ensured an abundance of light flooded the interior, revealing sturdy wooden shelves lining the walls, each one filled with a myriad of jars, bottles and containers of various sizes and shapes.

Wren let out a breath beside him, apparently equally awed. In the centre of the room, several large worktables stood, their surfaces marked with the stains and scars of countless experiments. Burners, alembics and other apparatus were carefully arranged on the tables, ready for use. The air was filled with a complex blend of aromas, ranging from the sweet scent of dried flowers to the acrid tang of sulphur and other chemicals.

As they entered, they passed a large chalkboard that dominated the wall, covered in complex formulas, equations and hastily scribbled notes. There were other alchemists here, scribes and researchers too, but they hardly glanced up from their own projects, utterly absorbed in the work at hand.

Wren was beaming. 'This is . . .' But she trailed off, apparently unable to find the right words. Torj had to fight back a smile.

She instantly made herself at home at one of the worktables, removing her toolbelt and assessing the contents that needed to be restocked. She flitted about the conservatory, taking jars from the shelves and examining potted plants, humming quietly to herself. Torj watched her, begrudgingly admiring her work ethic, her passion.

Returning to the table, she scribbled in a notebook as she sifted through several glass dropper bottles, small hessian bags of bulbs, and an assortment of dried leaves held in place by sheets of parchment.

'If you're just going to stand there, you may as well make yourself useful,' Wren said, tossing him a small pouch. 'Count those seeds.'

Torj caught the pouch and blinked at her. 'You want me to count seeds?'

'You *can* count, can't you?' she replied, a teasing note in her voice.

He sat down beside her. 'One of my many talents, Embers.'

The tips of Wren's ears flushed pink, and she seemed to be concentrating awfully hard on shredding the bark she had between her hands.

Torj set about counting the seeds, realizing halfway through that he had no idea what they were and if they were poisonous. He hoped Wren might warn him if skin contact was ill-advised, but with their turbulent history, he wasn't sure he could count on it.

He stole a glance at her. Her already messy bun had loosened, bronze locks escaping to fall across her face and curl at the nape of her neck. She was biting her lip as she worked, her brow furrowed in intense concentration. The sudden urge to reach out and tuck her hair behind her ear hit him.

He started, his knee hitting the underside of the worktable.

Wren peered up at him, a single brow arched. 'You lost count, didn't you?'

Torj looked down at the tiny brown seeds and groaned.

'Thought it was one of your many talents. Doesn't bode well for the rest, does it?'

'Don't you worry about the rest,' Torj replied in a low voice.

Wren refixed her attention on the stalks she was slicing, but there was no missing the way she caught her bottom lip between her teeth again, biting hard.

Smiling to himself, Torj started his recount.

CHAPTER 43

Wren

'The master poisoner is a shadow, moving unseen and unheard, leaving only death in their wake'

— *The Poisoner's Handbook*

THE HIGH CHANCELLOR had not been overstating Drevenor's increased security measures. More guards had been stationed beneath the wrought iron entrance and along the fence line, with several more posted throughout the main building itself. Their presence left a blemish on an otherwise crisp and beautiful day.

That afternoon, Wren sat at a workbench with Dessa and Zavier at her sides, their parchment, ink and quills already laid out. The foundry was the closest thing to an actual classroom she'd been to in the academy. So far it had been eerie forests full of deadly flora, an infirmary, a dungeon and a gymnasium, but here . . . This reminded Wren of Thezmarr, of the good old days where she, Sam and Ida had worked side by side at Farissa's instruction, often hindered by Thea's attempts to help.

The vast chamber was bathed in the glow of countless torches hanging from the vaulted ceiling, illuminating the banners draped down the stone walls, depicting alchemical symbols and blueprints for various inventions. Their entire cohort was seated at the rows of polished wooden benches, watching the front of the room, tense with anticipation.

They didn't have to wait long. Master Nyella Mercer swept into the chamber, her violet dress billowing after her, her robes belted over the top. Her curly grey hair was cropped short, and large gold earrings swung from her lobes.

'Novices,' she began, her voice projecting to the far reaches of the room. 'The realm of alchemical design is where many of our other core disciplines converge. It is within these walls that we will take lifelore, medicine and warfare to new heights. Here, we will thread them through our inventions and innovations. Design is where we delve deep into the creativity and precision of the alchemical arts . . .'

Wren sat up a little straighter. Her first few lessons at Drevenor had shown her as much. Given her most recent vocation, she had assumed that her affinity would lie with warfare, but the truth was that she had passion and experience within each of the four pillars. And design . . . She had come to love design a lifetime ago, back at Thezmarr. The Ladies' Luncheon teapot had been one of her first creations, and during the war she had also invented a range of exploding alchemical weapons – devices that blew up upon impact, showering the enemy with sun orchid essence, a bloom that was toxic to wraiths and reapers and all manner of darkness. And of course, there were the manacles that had been used against her in this very kingdom.

Wren shook the thought from her head as Master Alchemist Nyella continued with her introduction. 'As you settle in here, you will learn that there are many overlaps in our arts. As our High Chancellor warned you during your welcome, secrecy is paramount, and it is particularly crucial to the study of design, for in the wrong hands, brilliant work can have devastating consequences.

'Design at Drevenor involves a delicate dance between discretion and recognition. You may discover that some creations born here are meant to remain hidden, safeguarded by ancient laws, while others may find their way to the marketplaces of the midrealms and beyond, where collectors and scholars seek the extraordinary. For the extraordinary is what we do here, novices. I will settle for nothing less.'

The room buzzed with excitement and curiosity as Master Nyella motioned to something draped in silken fabric on the bench before her.

'Today, we focus on a single magical artefact, imbued with ancient alchemy. You have already witnessed its power . . .'

Wren's blood ran cold as she recalled the horrific scene in the Evermere Forest where the former student had been stripped of his memories. She felt queasy, and beside her, Dessa had turned pale.

Master Nyella gestured to the concealed object. 'Well, gather around – you can't very well see from your seats.'

Wren followed Dessa and Zavier to the front, where their teacher pulled the fabric away from the artefact with a flourish.

'A memory weave,' she declared.

Wren stared. Again, she noted how it looked like a small tapestry, its threads shimmering.

'A memory weave is spun from the essence of lost thoughts, or thoughts forcefully taken from a person,' Master Nyella explained.

A young woman Wren knew as Blythe finished pinning her hair atop her head in an unruly knot, its gold-and-bronze shade quite similar to Wren's own. 'How is that possible? Only the rulers of the midrealms possess magic, and—'

The Master of Design held up her hand. 'Blythe is right, of course. But what she fails to grasp is the power of alchemy when combined with other magical objects. A memory weave does not hail from the midrealms. It was a gift sent to us from faraway lands long before the war, and we have studied its properties.'

'How does it work?' someone else called out.

Wren's palms grew clammy. She hoped Master Nyella wouldn't interpret that as a request to see another demonstration.

'Should we wish it to store your memories, you would be required to take a tonic that softens the recesses of your mind. Under the influence of this concoction, you would enter a state of paralysis, and a Master Alchemist would be able to select which memories to retract. They need to be bound to something, hence the threads you see in the artefact here.'

'All of those contain someone's memories?' Dessa asked in an awed voice.

'Many people's memories, in fact,' Master Nyella told them. 'This object has been in the academy's possession since long before I was a student here.'

Slowly, Wren put her hand up. 'Did the current masters vote to keep this artefact active when reopening the academy after the war? Has it always been used as a punishment?'

'It is not punishment for punishment's sake, Elwren,' Master Nyella replied, 'but for the protection of this institution, and thus, the midrealms themselves. The knowledge that flows through these halls can be deadly in the wrong hands. It must be guarded at all costs.'

'And what does the broader world make of such a device?' Wren pressed.

'The only knowledge of this artefact is within these walls. And so it must remain.'

Wren forced herself to swallow her objections. The pledge of secrecy she'd made in the Evermere Forest came back to her:

I will delve into the dark abyss of knowledge and guard the secrets entrusted to me.

With my body as a shield, my mind as a blade, I will not hesitate to sacrifice.

'You are to sketch the design of this artefact, both what you see and what you suspect might contribute to its workings.'

Wren was equal parts fascinated and horrified by the object, and judging by the expressions of her peers, she wasn't the only one. No doubt Bertram's screams were still echoing in all their minds.

They spent the next few hours sketching and researching the design elements for the strange device. Wren knew there was little chance her work even came close to understanding the intricate workings of the magical object. And for the first time, she wasn't sure she wanted to understand.

When the lesson was over, Dessa turned to her with a look of dire desperation. 'I don't know about you, but I could really use some fun . . .'

Wren huffed a tired laugh and surprised herself with her answer. 'What did you have in mind?'

CHAPTER 44

Wren

'The scales of alchemy are delicate,
and a single misstep can upset the balance,
unleashing forces beyond our control'

– *Arcane Alchemy: Unveiling the Mysteries of Matter*

Dessa invited Wren and Zavier back to her dormitory, an invitation Zavier promptly declined. Wren, however, went with her, insisting that Cal remain guarding the door from the outside.

Dessa's room was simple, and though she shared with three others, none of them were there. She reached under her bed and pulled out a bottle of wine with a grin. The action reminded Wren so much of Sam and Ida that it hurt, but for the first time, there was also a tentative spark of joy.

Dessa tossed several cushions onto the plush rug on the floor and settled herself there before pouring Wren a generous mug of wine.

Wren took it gratefully and seated herself on one of the pillows. 'How do you find the dormitories?' she asked, looking around at the charts pinned to the walls and the overflowing trunks.

'They're alright,' Dessa replied, filling her own mug. 'It's a bit odd to put us in with people who are on different teams. There can be a bit of rivalry.'

'Somehow that doesn't surprise me.' Wren took a sip of her wine. 'This is good.'

'The perks of being an alchemist, isn't it? Perfecting the fermentation process.'

Wren snorted. 'You sound like Kipp.'

'Well . . . I have been spending a bit of time with him.'

'Have you now?'

An ache bloomed in Wren's chest as Dessa gave a coy smile that reminded her of Anya. 'I'll share if you do.'

'I've got nothing to share.' Wren's cheeks heated, though she told herself it was from the wine.

'Another time, then,' Dessa said. 'I actually wanted your thoughts on something . . .' She reached for a large notebook and opened it, pushing it towards Wren. 'I've been thinking about it since we saw that awful demonstration, but today's design lesson prompted me . . .'

Wren surveyed the spread, seeing different sketches for something like the memory weave object they'd spent the last few hours drawing. Dessa had filled pages upon pages with rough plans, accompanied by precise handwriting.

'My father suffers from a condition,' Dessa told her. 'He's losing his memories. At first, I thought he was just being forgetful, but the healers say it's a disease. One that slowly destroys memory and mental function. Some days he doesn't even recognize me.'

'I'm so sorry,' Wren said. She couldn't imagine what it would be like to watch someone progressively forget their loved ones.

Dessa continued, 'I was wondering if it might be possible to alter the design of the memory weave so that someone might be able to store and access memories of a different nature. So, rather than losing memories to a disease, you could store them for when you need them.'

Wren stared at her teammate's sketches. 'You should talk to Master Nyella,' she said. 'Though you'd have to address the issue with the tonic . . .'

Dessa nodded. 'The pain? Definitely. Part of me suspects that it could be addressed relatively easily, but the masters haven't done so because it adds an additional layer of suffering to the punishment.'

'I suspected the same,' Wren agreed, looking up to find Dessa watching her, eyes bright with hope. 'It's a good idea. It's nice to see talent used for good for a change.'

Dessa smiled, reaching across to refill her mug. 'From what I hear, you did plenty of that in the war.'

Wren's blood ran cold. Dessa was wrong. Everything Wren had created, both during the war and since, had only caused destruction. When was the last time she had created anything of note that had healed? That had improved something in the world? Was that not what Farissa had been telling her for years? *You took what you'd learned about preserving life and made it about revenge. About death.*

Wren forced herself to swallow the lump in her throat. 'I don't like talking about the war, Dessa.'

'So I've gathered,' she replied. 'But when you need to . . . I'll be here.'

'Why?' Wren asked.

Dessa shrugged. 'That's what friends do. Besides, how else will I get all the Warsword gossip?'

Wren snorted. 'Sounds like you already have a source for that.'

Dessa's clear peal of laughter made Wren smile. And she realized it felt good, this easy camaraderie. Dangerous, but good.

CHAPTER 45

Wren

'The ripples of our discoveries can touch shores we never intended to reach'

— *Elwren Embervale's notes and observations*

'Have you been to the archives yet?' Wren asked her new friend.

Dessa shook her head. 'Not yet. Do you want to go?'

Wren found herself draining her mug and nodding.

It was still Cal waiting for them outside the dormitory. 'Where's your Bear Slayer?' Dessa whispered, as Cal stepped into place just behind them.

'He's not *my* Bear Slayer,' Wren hissed. The self-defence lessons of that morning felt far away, like a distant recollection of the past. So much had happened in a matter of hours, and yet, she could remember the press of his body against hers, his scent wrapping around her like a drug. There was something taut between them, something that was bound to snap at any moment, and it was going to drive her to the point of insanity if she wasn't careful.

Dessa grinned. 'Nobody believes that for a second. Are you saying you haven't noticed the way he looks at you?'

'You mean like he wants to throttle me?'

'If throttle means "fuck senseless", then yes.'

An incredibly undignified sound escaped Wren. 'What?'

Dessa shrugged. 'I'm just saying.'

'Well, don't. He's my *bodyguard*. He's meant to watch me.'

Another wicked smile flashed across Dessa's face. 'It's not the watching itself I'm commenting on, it's *how* he's watching.'

'Shush.' Wren elbowed her, mindful of Cal behind them.

'Just saying,' Dessa repeated with a wink.

A pang of grief hit Wren as she realized something about her new friend. 'You . . . you remind me of my sister,' she admitted, glancing Dessa's way.

Dessa's brows shot up. 'The Warsword?'

Wren shook her head. 'My other sister, Anya. She died during the war . . . But before that, she teased me about Torj as well. She was always looking to get a rise out of me.'

Her friend's features softened. 'I'm sorry.'

'Don't be,' Wren told her. 'It would do me well to remember the good times, not just the bad.'

'You don't want me to stop teasing you, then?'

Wren gave a thoughtful smile. 'Anya certainly wouldn't.'

They passed through the foyer, noting that the black garnets in their team's vessel had increased by six. Climbing the stairs with Cal and Dessa, Wren set her sights on the archives once more. She had been wanting to get to the ancient library since she'd arrived, knowing that the shelves there contained texts she'd only ever dreamed of reading. Thezmarr's library had always been limited, favouring military histories and war strategy texts. During the war, she had seen the library at the University of Naarva, but it was nothing compared to the enormous space that yawned open before her now.

It was larger than any building she'd ever seen: a sprawling, hallowed hall, rich with the scent of leather and parchment, glowing with the flicker of candlelight. The towering wooden shelves were endless, stretching all the way up to the vaulted ceiling and the far reaches of the hall. Ladders on wheels lined the rows of shelving that housed thousands upon thousands of heavy volumes.

Dessa let out a low whistle. 'Well . . . this is something.'

'It's beautiful, isn't it?' Wren replied in a whisper, unable to contain her awe. She could hear the hushed murmurs of the scholars in the study nooks, and she breathed in the scent of fresh ink, the taste of discovery light on her tongue.

Knowledge is the victor over fate.

'We should look up the previous Gauntlets,' she told Dessa.

Her teammate nodded enthusiastically. 'Anything that might help us prepare for the trials. Shall we start in the history section?'

'Sounds good.' Wren kept her voice low, conscious of the quiet that seemed to swallow up the archives. The wooden floor creaked underfoot as they moved through the entrance, Wren trying to drink it all in at once. She had never been in a single place that held so much knowledge.

They reached the start of the history section and were instantly overwhelmed. Books towered above them beyond sight; the rows beyond were countless.

'I think we'll need to ask someone another time . . .' Wren ventured.

Relief washed over Dessa's face. 'Definitely.'

Cal trailed behind them as Wren and Dessa moved between the shelves, both craning their necks to get a glimpse at the forbidden masters' section that Zavier had mentioned a while back. The section was marked by heavy iron doors, an enormous lock, and two academy librarians stationed either side. Novices weren't permitted. Adepts and sages could only enter with written permission from one of the masters themselves.

Reluctantly, Wren and Dessa continued on.

Moonlight streamed through the stained-glass windows, casting a spectrum of coloured light dancing across the spines of the ancient tomes. There was no way they could peruse the entire library in an evening – it was far too vast, with far too many offshoots and different wings. But that didn't stop them from giving it a damn good try.

'Do they have anything like this where you're from?' Dessa murmured, running her fingers along the leather spines.

'No,' Wren replied. 'You?'

Dessa shook her head. 'My home was destroyed in the war, but even before . . . there was nothing like this.'

Wren's heart ached for her. She had been so caught up in her own grief that she'd forgotten she wasn't the only one who'd suffered losses. 'I'm sorry about your home.'

Dessa gave her a sad smile. 'We're here now, aren't we?'

'We are.' Wren surprised herself by reaching out and squeezing her friend's hand.

Dessa squeezed it back.

For the first time in a long while, as Wren wandered the rows of books, the restlessness crawling beneath her skin quietened, as did the memories that so often rose to the surface. She lost herself in the rhythm of Dessa's quiet stories, in the scratch of a nib on parchment, in the diligent restacking of the leather volumes by the reverent scribes pushing trolleys.

It was only when her power gave a surge of recognition that she faltered, coming to a halt between the stacks, a hand resting over her heart. She knew she was out of practice, that all those years of little use had made her control rusty, but . . .

'Are you alright?' Dessa asked, noticing the shift in her.

Wren frowned. 'Yes, I just . . .' She looked around, suddenly filled with the sensation, the knowledge, that she had to follow that pull within her, that surge of power. 'I'll be back in a minute.'

Wren ducked between the shelves, searching – for what, she didn't know. All she knew was that it was here somewhere, and she had to find it. Perhaps it was a volume on the Gauntlet, or something that would give her a clue as to the origins of the alchemy used against Leiko. Whatever it was, it belonged to her—

She skidded to a stop so abruptly that Cal bumped into her back.

'What is it, Wren?' he whispered, his voice laced with concern.

Wren peered between the stacks, her heart racing.

There, tucked away in one of the study nooks, was Torj Elderbrock. The Warsword was poring over several open books, his lantern burning low.

Cal made a noise of discomfort. 'I don't think we should be spying—'

'Shhh,' she cut him off.

Of all the places she thought she might find the Bear Slayer, the academy archives was not one of them. He was hunched over yellowed pages, his brow furrowed, a lock of silver hair falling into his eyes.

So strange, that her magic had led her here. She couldn't seem to escape him, no matter how hard she tried. It was as though they were drawn together, over and over again.

But for once, he didn't seem to sense her. Torj was utterly absorbed in whatever it was he was reading, rubbing the scars on his chest absentmindedly.

From afar, shielded by the bookshelf, she admired him. His powerful build, the way his lips moved as he read the text in front of him, the surprisingly straight line of his nose—

'If you're done gawking at him,' Cal hissed, irritated.

'I'm not—'

Cal scoffed. 'Please. Mind you don't slip in your drool on the way out.'

Wren bit back a laugh. 'Alright then, Flaming Arrow. Lead the way.'

As they found Dessa and made their way out of the archives, with Wren a few books lighter than she would have liked, the back of her neck prickled.

She whirled around, only to find the aisle behind them completely empty.

'Problem?' Cal asked, instantly scanning their surroundings, alert and at the ready.

'No problem,' Wren told him, turning back, ignoring the strange sensation that someone was watching her. 'Let's just get back to my rooms. I have work to do.'

'I thought you'd never ask,' Cal quipped.

They left the archives and headed back to the residence halls, dropping Dessa off at her room. Dessa gave Wren a hug goodbye – a brief embrace that surprised Wren, but that she returned, her chest warming.

When it was just her and Cal, she offered him a sly grin as they turned another corner. 'I heard the most salacious rumours in the changing rooms today . . .'

The Flaming Arrow looked bewildered. 'About what?'

'Oh, you know, about a hero of Thezmarr who has to bed five women a night just to keep the edge off.'

Cal snorted. 'I wouldn't believe everything you hear about the Bear Slayer.'

'Oh, it wasn't about him.'

'Aren't alchemists meant to be clever? They know Kipp's not a Warsword, don't they? Just a menace to society, among other things.'

'Wasn't about Kipp, either,' Wren told him.

Realization dawned on Cal's face. 'Oh, for Furies' sake,' he muttered, flushing deeply. 'That was one time. And it was only two women! I think . . .'

'So it's true?' Wren laughed. 'Kipp finally corrupted you, Callahan!'

'No, I—'

But Cal's protest was cut off by a scream.

CHAPTER 46

Torj

'The unintended aftermath of an injury can be just as devastating as an intended effect'

– Magical Transference

THE BOOKS IN the masters' section of the archives had proven far more detailed than those Torj had tried before. He lost track of time, completely absorbed in the text Farissa had recommended on magical wounds. His lightning scars prickled as he read about injuries that never healed, and lesions that were cursed, slowly taking hold of their victim and poisoning from the initial site outwards . . . The tome went into great depth about several case studies throughout history wherein a magic wielder – a royal of the midrealms – had inflicted their magic upon a subject, resulting in a life-altering wound.

He ran his fingers through his hair as he started on a paragraph about power transference. According to the author, in dire situations, power *could* be transferred from a royal-blooded magic wielder to another host . . . but how those hosts processed magic they were not built for was another thing entirely. Depending on the amount of exposure to raw power, the consequences could range from mild to extreme.

Torj rubbed his chest again, glancing at the letter from Audra he'd read four times already, lying open by the book.

I expect a report by the end of the week, she demanded. *We need to know if this wound has compromised your abilities. We need to know the extent of the damage immediately. Do not share this information with anyone. Not even Elwren. Especially not Elwren.*

The blunt, efficient orders were no less than he expected from Thezmarr's Guild Master. He didn't like the urgency of her commands, but he understood the discretion she required. While Farissa had encouraged him to share his troubles with Wren, Torj agreed with Audra. He didn't want Wren knowing that in saving him, she had potentially doomed him. No matter how much she resented him, he knew she would punish herself if she thought she'd caused him harm.

Midway through turning to the next page, Torj froze. The intoxicating scent of spring rain and jasmine washed over him in a tantalizing wave.

But Wren wasn't here. Or if she had been, she wasn't any more...

At the thought of her name, something jerked in his chest, and suddenly he found himself on his feet. A tug from within led him through the shelves, and he noticed that for the first time, the archives were completely empty. The scholars who had occupied the other study nooks had vanished, and all their books lay strewn about, unattended, as though they had all left in a hurry.

Panic bloomed like a poisonous flower in his gut, and he found himself running towards the exit.

Something was wrong.

He broke into a sprint, his hammer at the ready as he charged through the corridors and spotted a crowd gathered at the far end.

No, no, no... Not again.

Fear was acrid on his tongue, and he shoved past the students and teachers.

In his presence, they stepped back, making room to reveal a body crumpled on the stone floor.

A simple linen gown, an apron tied at the back...

I promised I'd protect you. I vowed to shield you from harm.

Torj wasn't breathing, not as his gaze rose to the mass of bronze pinned in a messy bun. He had faced death many times throughout his years of fighting, but this? This was something he could not comprehend.

She was his to protect. His—

Hands trembling, ready to tear the world apart, Torj reached for the familiar slim shoulders. It was the cruellest thing, willing time to slow, to stop entirely, only for it to speed up, his heart hammering against his ribs as he turned her over.

A strangled sound escaped him.

She had a similar build, a similar complexion.

But it wasn't her.

This poor dead woman wasn't Wren Embervale.

He didn't register leaving the body and the crowd in the hallway, only the air whipping at his cheeks as he ran through the residences, navigating the twists and turns by muscle memory, his thoughts only of her, of the panic that still raged like a black storm in his chest.

Cal was stationed outside her door, and Torj shoved past him without a word, bursting into Wren's rooms.

'She's—' was all Cal managed behind him as he shut the door in his fellow Warword's face and scanned the chamber wildly. Chest heaving, he saw her, dropping his hammer to the ground with a heavy thud.

She stood where she always did, at her workbench, several books lying open on the chaotic surface, her hands busy with ingredients, her hair swept up off her neck into that poison-tipped pin. A breath shuddered out of him as she met his eyes.

In two strides he was in front of her, a vial clattering to the bench as he skimmed her body with his hands. 'Are you hurt?'

'Torj, no, I—'

But her assurances did nothing to convince him. He scrutinized her from head to toe for injuries, for any sign of harm, something inside him raging like an inferno.

'I thought you were dead,' he said, breathlessly. 'I thought that was you lying there in that hallway. I thought I'd failed you, like I failed—'

'Torj . . . I'm fine,' Wren told him, flushing as she glanced down at his hands on her.

Torj did the only thing he could think of to expel all that pent-up energy coursing through him. He rounded on her. 'You were out in the halls when you shouldn't have been. You were meant to be in your rooms. I told Cal to keep you—'

'Cal is not my keeper,' she hissed back. 'And nor are you, for that matter.'

'That's *exactly* what I am. It's my job to keep you safe,' he snarled.

'I went to the archives,' Wren snapped back. 'To a fucking *library*. If you're so damn concerned about my safety, why weren't *you* there with me?' She jabbed him in the chest with her finger.

'That's none of your concern.'

'*None of my concern?*' Wren blazed on. 'I can't deal with this. You demand to know *everything* about me, have access to *everything* I do, and yet I ask you a simple question and it's *none of my concern?*'

'This isn't a two-way street, Embervale,' he bit back. 'I'm your bodyguard. You're my principal.'

'So you keep fucking saying.'

Anger flared brighter. 'What is *that* supposed to mean?'

A cry of frustration escaped Wren, her chest heaving. 'I can't stand you.'

'You think I can stand *you*?'

As the fragile truce between them went up in a blaze, Wren was radiant in her fury. By the looks of things, she wanted to throttle him, and the feeling was fucking mutual. Whatever moment of understanding they had shared in the infirmary was eclipsed by his anger. A second ago he had thought she was dead, and now, here she was, her breaths coming fast, her breasts rising and falling, her cheeks tipped with pink as she yelled back at him. He could feel the heat of her, and in a moment of insanity, his eyes fell to her mouth. Emotions crashed through him, hard: guilt, pure terror and rage, a blow with the strength of the gods themselves.

Torj didn't think. He moved on instinct alone, pulling her towards him. Wren peered up at him and touched her palm to his still pounding heart. It was the weight of a sparrow, nothing more, and yet, it was almost enough to bring him to his knees.

Hardly breathing, he let his head dip, and her pupils dilated.

'Embers . . .' he warned, his anger giving way to a need that turned molten. The warmth of her hand over his chest only amplified the roiling storm beneath his scars, but it was not alone. Wren's storm thrummed alongside the magic in him.

Fury, power and want entwined as he warred with himself. *Heir. Ward. Poisoner. Off limits.*

But it was a force bigger than him, bigger than them both.

And he was helpless against it.

'Fuck it,' he muttered.

He speared his fingers through her silken hair, and kissed her.

She gasped as his lips met hers. Nothing had ever felt so good, so right. Her mouth was lush and warm, and she tasted like all manner of temptation. Wren shifted in his hold, pressing herself against him entirely. A tight coil of desire unfurled within him, and he had to hold himself in check, had to wait for her to make the choice, to deepen the kiss.

A desperate groan escaped him as Wren's lips parted beneath his.

At long last, Torj took what he'd been yearning for so long.

Potion bottles and tools clattered as he pushed Wren up against the workbench, kissing her with the force of the storm that raged within. A claiming. A declaration without words. He kissed her hard and deep, his need morphing into fervour.

The kiss spoke for him, fierce and passionate, unyielding. The end of one thing, and the beginning of something new.

His mouth moved over hers in the way that he'd imagined countless times. She kissed him back, her tongue brushing against his, her fingernails digging into his arms as though she'd never let go. He crushed her to him, feeling the swell of her breasts and the heat of her body soaking into his.

When she whimpered, his knees buckled. That *sound*.

He lost himself in her, in her taste, in the way her body responded beneath his, pulling him closer, demanding more. He would give her everything. There had never been any question of that.

He was like granite against her softness, and he moaned low in his throat as she ground against him. His hands traced down her sides, following every dip and hollow with reverence until he cupped the curve of her backside and lifted her.

More books and potions, and a mortar and pestle, went tumbling from the workbench as Torj slid Wren onto it, never breaking their kiss, his breathing ragged as she wrapped her legs around him.

Gods, the taste of her, the feel of her melting into him – the magic coursing through them both, connecting them so thoroughly that Torj couldn't imagine the intensity of being inside her.

'Gods,' Wren gasped against his lips, her cheeks flushed, her breasts rising at the top of her bodice. She followed his gaze, her own hooded. 'Touch me.'

His mouth was on her again in an instant. His hand circled the delicate column of her throat, feeling her pulse flutter wildly beneath her skin before he let it trail across her collarbone and down, cupping her breast.

Her moan nearly undid him then and there. He had never dared to hope that he'd be the one to coax those noises from her, and now here she was, writhing beneath his touch, arching into him as though she couldn't get enough.

Nor could he. He could feel her life's blood in his own veins, in the marrow of his bones. Whatever the tether was between them, it went taut – a cord of lightning from one to the other.

He was completely overwhelmed by her, completely rattled, and completely and utterly addicted. The scars marring his flesh didn't feel like an old injury, not as her hands found their way under his shirt and traced the fire in his skin. They felt like a source of strength, of power. They felt like *Wren*.

You're mine, he wanted to say. He wanted to claim her in every way imaginable. He wanted to follow the instinct roaring within him.

But he couldn't.

She would never be his. Not truly.

And at that realization, he broke away.

CHAPTER 47

Wren

'Subtlety is a far deadlier weapon than a blade or brute force. Turn a target's body against them and the war is won without ever drawing a sword'

– *Elwren Embervale's notes and observations*

ALL-CONSUMING. SOUL-DESTROYING. MIND-ALTERING. His kiss had set Wren on fire.

At last. At fucking last.

A blinding force of passion had coursed through every part of her, desire thrumming across her skin like a fever. She had never felt so alive, so desperate for another person in all her life.

And then he had doused the flames.

'There are a thousand reasons why I shouldn't have done that . . .' Torj said, pulling away from her, trying to catch his breath.

Wren was still perched on the workbench, her thighs open, her chest heaving. She knew she must have looked thoroughly ravished. Flushing furiously, she jumped down and smoothed her skirts. The damp ache still pulsed between her legs, and her nipples were hard and sensitive against the fabric of her bodice. 'Then why did you?'

Torj's expression was pained. 'I . . .' He cleared his throat and straightened his clothes, adjusting himself in his leathers. 'I'm sorry. I made a mistake. It can't happen again.'

It was like a bucket of icy water had been tipped over Wren's head, with the icy wrath to match.

'Get out.'

'Embers—'

'*Don't* call me that.'

A woman had died tonight, and what was Wren doing? Kissing her damn bodyguard, who apparently thought kissing her was a *mistake*.

It was all she could do not to physically shove him through the adjoining door. 'Get out,' she repeated, voice cold and brutal.

He at least had the sense to listen. She slammed the door after him and jammed her chair underneath the handle in a fit of rage. Giving the same treatment to the shared bathing room door, she looked around wildly, wanting to break something, wanting to expel the rage that seemed to dance with her magic so dangerously.

She glanced at the main door, where outside she knew Cal was standing guard. He'd be easier to slip past than the brute on the other side of the wall, but she calmed herself, listened to her own voice of reason.

A woman had been killed.

Cal had whisked her away from the scene within seconds, blocking the body from view and hurrying her back to her room. There, she'd tried to distract herself with her experiments until the Bear Slayer had all but kicked in the door.

Wren pressed her fingers to her bruised lips, the taste of him still on her tongue, the echo of his touch still dancing across her skin. *There are a thousand reasons why I shouldn't have done that . . .*

'Bastard,' she muttered, though the anger she felt was just as much for herself. She'd been stupid, had allowed herself to get caught up in the moment, caught up in *him*.

A light knock sounded at her door.

'Yes?' Wren called tentatively.

To her surprise, it was Farissa who entered.

'How goes the work?' her former mentor asked softly, eyeing the messy bench.

'Good, I think . . .' Wren shifted on her feet. 'I dedicate what little time I have left to it, but I need—'

Farissa reached for the satchel slung over her shoulder and produced a metal flask. 'You didn't get this from me.'

'What—' But as Wren unscrewed the lid, a metallic scent hit her nostrils. 'Blood?' she asked in disbelief. '*Royal* blood? Where did you—'

'Audra procured it for you at my insistence.'

'Whose—'

'I don't know,' Farissa told her. 'All I know is that when I asked, this is what I was given.'

Wren took a deep breath. Her work could continue; she could create more controlled tests, trial more reactions . . . 'Thank you.'

Farissa nodded. 'I want to hear more about your experiments when you're ready. For now, I have to . . .' She gestured to the door, to the commotion they could still hear in the halls.

'I'll send for you,' Wren offered quietly. 'When I have something solid.'

Farissa stared at her for a moment, her gaze flitting to the scar at Wren's throat before meeting her eyes again. 'You do that.'

When her old mentor had left, Wren paced the room. She was under no illusion that sleep was anything but beyond her now. The woman's death, the flask of royal blood on her table, and most of all . . . the heat of Torj's mouth on hers. Her mind raced, her heart pounded against her sternum, and her hands itched to move . . .

And so, Wren did what she did best.

She worked.

She couldn't bring herself to meet the Warsword's eyes the next day – not as he opened her door for her, not as he escorted her through the corridors. Wren could still feel the imprint of his hands on her, making the lightning beneath her skin sing. And she could still feel the flush of her cheeks as he told her it was a mistake.

But the memory of their kiss was soon swallowed up by the presence of Guardians from Thezmarr, stationed at every entrance throughout the academy. An alchemist had died, and Drevenor had answered in kind.

Everywhere Wren looked, she saw a warrior presence, and a militant efficiency seemed to hum throughout the building. Morning meal had been sent directly to students' rooms, and so Torj was escorting her straight to the poisons dungeon.

When Wren slid into her seat next to Dessa and Zavier, their expressions were sombre as they listened to the surrounding buzz of speculations and theories.

'Do we know how she died?' Dessa asked in a hushed whisper.

'Strangled,' Jasper Greaves declared.

'No. Someone slit her throat,' someone else argued.

'Horseshit,' Selene chimed in. 'She was poisoned.'

'*She* had a name,' Zavier said quietly. 'Blythe Rookford.'

'Poor Blythe,' Dessa sighed. 'What will happen to her team?'

'Who cares about her team?' Zavier muttered, clearly agitated. 'What about *her*? Her family?' Then he glanced at Wren, lowering his voice even more. 'You notice anything about her, Poisoner?'

'What do you mean?' Wren asked.

'You're saying you never noticed the likeness you shared with Blythe?'

Wren tried not to flinch as an image of the woman's bronze topknot flashed in her mind's eye. 'I never really gave it much thought . . .' Truth be told, she hadn't known Blythe at all. Since arriving at Drevenor, she had focused solely on her own team, her own ambitions.

'Oh, your hair colour was basically identical,' Dessa nodded.

'Not to mention you had the same unfortunate taste in clothing,' Zavier added.

'What are you suggesting?' Wren hissed at him.

'That perhaps she wasn't the true target . . . ?' Zavier replied with a raised brow.

Their conversation was cut short by the arrival of the Warfare Master.

'Novices.' Master Crawford's voice was as sharp as ever. 'As many of you have already heard, one of our own, Blythe Rookford, was found dead last night under troubling circumstances. Today, we mourn not only the loss of a student, but also a friend, a classmate, and a member of our tight-knit community here at Drevenor. In this time of grief and uncertainty, it is important that we come together. Together, we will weather this storm and emerge stronger, wiser and more united than before.'

To Wren's surprise, Master Nyella entered the dungeon after him. They were in stark contrast with one another – the pressed, precise attire of the Master of Warfare against the flamboyant colours of the Master of Design.

'We decided to set a task together today,' Master Nyella explained. 'One that incorporates both warfare and design . . . Given that it was a combination of these that infiltrated our halls last night and resulted in the death of one of our own.'

Silence fell across the dungeon as Master Crawford clasped his hands together and addressed the cohort. 'The brief is this. We want you to imagine that a ruler has sought our help to eliminate a target in their kingdom. Someone who has posed a threat to the peace and safety of their lands for years; an assassin in their own right.'

The hair on Wren's nape stood up. For the first time, she saw her alter ego as the Poisoner from Torj's perspective. The mark Master Crawford was describing could have easily been her before she came to Drevenor. But what Wren had done as the Poisoner was different. She had helped rid the midrealms of its rot. She pushed her feelings of discomfort aside as Master Crawford continued.

'This person is incredibly paranoid. They will not ingest anything without a cupbearer or food taster. They are known to be incredibly violent, with a proclivity for crossbows, and they are as cruel as they are cautious. We want you to present a proposal on how to deal with such a target.'

'The team who impresses us the most will receive thirty points,' Master Nyella added.

Inspiration was already sparking in Wren's mind. Two of her passions had come together in this task and she'd be damned if she didn't give it her all. She turned to Dessa and Zavier. 'I have an idea.'

Dessa grinned. 'Me too.'

'Let's hear them, then,' Zavier said.

The trio gathered around their table and talked in hushed whispers. Wren didn't quite know when things had changed between them, but they had, for the better. The looming Gauntlet had brought them together, and the strength of three minds rather than one was instantly apparent to Wren. With Dessa's talent for design, Zavier's natural affinity with lifelore and her own experiences during the war, they found themselves in sync for the first time, and Wren, who'd initially hated the thought of a team, was suddenly grateful for their insights, their innovation.

An hour later, their cohort presented their concepts to the masters.

Wren watched the other teams' proposals, her heart pounding with anticipation. The first team suggested using advanced alchemical smoke diffusions to incapacitate the target's guards during a staged diversion.

While clever, Wren noted the plan's vulnerability in its lack of adaptability should the diversion go awry, and the likelihood of trace evidence with a broader method of dispersion. The crease between Master Crawford's brows deepened, while Master Nyella pursed her lips and said nothing.

The second team proposed developing a slow-acting alchemical compound that could accumulate in the target's body over time, introduced through various environmental factors. Wren recognized the ingenuity, but also the inherent difficulty in controlling the dosage and preventing collateral exposure.

The third team's proposal showed some promise, recommending the use of disguises and personality-altering potions to infiltrate the target's inner circle. They suggested creating a 'miracle cure' for a fabricated illness to appeal to the target's health paranoia. But Wren knew the time required for such a plan made it less than ideal for a quick resolution, not to mention the risks if the alchemical effects were to wear off unexpectedly.

She exchanged glances with Zavier and Dessa as they stood to deliver their concept.

'Our design is a crossbow wherein the trigger holds the poison,' Wren told them, holding up their sketches. 'When the mark fires the weapon, a mechanism activates a tiny prick – so slight it can't be felt over the recoil of the crossbow. It would spring from the trigger and inject the deadly toxin into the pad of his finger.'

'And how do you propose to get this crossbow in the hands of a mark?' Master Crawford asked bluntly.

'A number of ways,' Dessa replied. 'Modify an existing crossbow he owns, pose it as a gift from someone he trusts, or introduce it as a new product on the market – create demand, speculation and intrigue around it. The latest weapon that every crossbow-loving enthusiast simply must have.'

'And the poison itself? What would you use?' the Master of Warfare pressed.

Zavier spoke next. 'It depends on the details of the brief, but generally I'd opt for a dose of the death cap mushroom. No purgative can save a victim from it, as the poison is in the bloodstream, particularly with this pinprick method.'

'And the symptoms of such a poisoning?'

'At first, the victim experiences a deep feeling of unease,' Zavier continued. 'Then a while later, violent stomach cramps that improve after a day or two . . . Then death from kidney or liver failure within the week.'

An awed silence followed.

'Can a novice obtain this poison?' Master Nyella asked quietly.

'Yes,' Wren answered. She had asked Zavier that very same question. 'It grows in the Evermere Forest beneath the birch and spruce trees. It has a red cap and white warts.'

The two masters exchanged looks, and Wren didn't know if they should be troubled or proud.

The answer came moments later. 'Elwren, Zavier, Odessa,' Master Nyella said. 'See to it that you collect several specimens of the mushroom during your next lifelore lesson. And check the garnet leaderboard at the end of the week.'

CHAPTER 48

Wren

'We are all connected by the web of cause and effect, and the actions of one alchemist can have repercussions that echo through the ages'

– *Arcane Alchemy: Unveiling the Mysteries of Matter*

Every day, the Bear Slayer was waiting outside for her, like he always did when he wasn't away on 'Warsword business'. He escorted her to her lessons in silence. He escorted her to the dining hall in silence. And he escorted her to her rooms in silence.

Wren wanted to yell at him. Yell and scream at him, then tear his clothes off and finish what they'd started in her room. But she did no such thing. Instead, she shut him out of her chambers, and returned to her work.

She had successfully poisoned several rats in her warfare lessons, and successfully cured them of the various toxins she'd created. All the while, Master Crawford threatened to make them test their potions on one another. Their work for the medicine discipline had been contained to academy grounds after the attack on Wren's life at the infirmary, while lifelore was just as dangerous as it had ever been as they graduated to capturing venomous snakes.

The days and weeks blurred together as Wren fell into the steady rhythm of the academy, and for a time, it was as though that fiery kiss she'd shared with the Warsword was a distant dream that called out to her in her weaker moments. But Drevenor's added security brought with it a familiar sense of foreboding, the very same that had followed Wren in the lead-up to the shadow war. There was no ignoring its presence, no pretending that the rumours from the outside world hadn't started to circulate in the academy itself.

'What do you make of the so-called "People's Vanguard"?' Zavier asked her during another lifelore lesson, where they'd been directed to a nest of vipers and told to retrieve their venom.

'No more than I've heard whispered in the corridors,' she replied, carefully reaching into the vipers' nest with a long stick.

Zavier frowned. 'Seems like an oversight to me.'

'What do you mean?'

A viper emerged from the nest, and Zavier trapped its head beneath a pole while Wren put a cloth-covered jar to its fangs, watching the venom drip down into the glass vessel.

'It's a group protesting the power of the rulers . . . Being an heir yourself, I thought it might be something they keep you informed about.'

Unease squirmed in Wren's gut as she removed the jar from the creature's fangs. 'How do you know about them?'

'I listen,' Zavier said, releasing the viper. 'There's talk among the guards, among the staff. Perhaps it's time you asked . . . If I were you, I'd want to know.'

Zavier's words haunted Wren. No one – not Thea, not Torj, not even Kipp – had mentioned anything to her. But the attack outside the infirmary, Blythe Rookford's death, and the increase in academy security caused a familiar pit of dread to yawn wide within her. It grew by the day, telling her that something was coming.

But Drevenor was relentless. Lessons that were not lessons, tests that were brimming with sabotage, and the constant loom of the Gauntlet ahead left little mental energy for anything other than work.

After several more self-defence lessons with the Bear Slayer, Wren and Dessa created a fitness regime of their own, having grown tired of always being the last to finish their laps in class. The crisp mornings running at Dessa's side offered Wren a brief respite from the darkness that seemed to be latching its talons into the academy, and even with her surly bodyguard shadowing them every time, Wren began to truly enjoy Dessa's company and her relentless optimism. It forced Wren to get out of her own head, and though Dessa could never replace Sam or Ida, she offered Wren that same balm of female companionship that she so sorely missed in the wake of her friends' deaths.

Dessa soon had the skill of running and talking mastered. Unfortunately for Wren, the main topic of conversation was Kipp.

'He's honestly not like anyone else I've ever been with,' Dessa was saying, as Wren tried not to cringe at the thought of Kipp in that context. 'Honestly, Wren, he's so attentive. Always makes sure I'm pleased before he . . . Well, you know. It's so rare, isn't it?'

Wren thought back to the moans of ecstasy she'd heard in the pleasure dens, to the noises she'd heard from her own sister's tent in the war camps . . . and then she thought of *him*, of the sounds the Bear Slayer had dragged from her throat with no more than a kiss.

'Must we talk about this?' she muttered.

'You're right. We're always talking about me,' Dessa said with a note of apology. 'Let's talk about you. Things are still frosty between you and the—'

'Dessa!' Wren hissed, increasing her pace and trying to put more distance between them and the Warsword trailing them.

'Sorry, sorry!' Dessa replied with a sheepish grin. 'Still . . . don't hold out on me, Wren, I've told you all my secrets!'

'They're not secrets if you gush about them to the first person you see in the morning.'

Dessa laughed good-naturedly.

'I've got nothing to tell you,' Wren admitted.

'What about from before? Was there someone in the war? Someone back at Thezmarr?'

The *someone in the war* was the same someone who ran behind them just now, all six-foot-five of him, clad in warrior's armour and battering enemy forces with that iron hammer. And before?

'There were boys, back at Thezmarr . . .' Wren admitted at a whisper, mindful of being overheard by the great brute in their wake. 'But they were nothing. Less than nothing.'

Dessa frowned. 'What do you mean?'

'Truthfully? I have never understood the fuss. The boys I've been with have been underwhelming at best. I've never . . .'

'Never what?'

Wren forced the words from her mouth. 'Never been . . . *pleased* by one, as you said, before they . . .'

A horrified noise escaped Dessa. 'Oh, Wren.'

'It's not that bad!'

'No, it's a *disaster*. Furies know that some men just need a bit more training than others, some guidance . . . But to have such bad luck? It's a travesty, Wren.'

'I was always told it was my fault,' Wren admitted quietly.

'Well, that's just not true.' Dessa stopped at the water fountain they favoured and took a long drink before wiping her mouth with the back of her hand. 'Can you get there yourself?'

Wren refused to be embarrassed. There was no shame in it. She would have spoken openly about this with Sam, and Ida. As she'd grown closer with Anya during the last few months of the war, they too, had talked freely about such things. 'Yes,' she replied.

'Then you just haven't been with the right man, my friend,' Dessa said with a wink, followed by a pointed glance behind them.

'Furies save me, will you stop that?'

But Dessa simply laughed, and after a time, Wren found herself smiling as well.

Wren had started studying with Dessa and Zavier in her rooms. The Gauntlet was fast approaching, and they remained in second place on the black garnet leaderboard. Zavier was still a smug prick, but Wren didn't mind so much when he was using that to benefit the team. Together, the trio complemented one another's skillsets, and for that, Wren was grateful.

A dark mood had settled over Drevenor, and it was Kipp, of course, who sought to alleviate it. He barged into Wren's room one evening and surveyed the team's scattered books and contraptions, then threw himself down on Wren's bed dramatically.

'You work too hard,' he told them.

Wren scoffed. 'And you don't work enough.'

'I work plenty, just not to the point of broken exhaustion.'

Bleary-eyed, Zavier looked up from his book. 'And what is it that you do here again, Kristopher?'

'Ahh, all in good time. You know that I'm most effective when I work behind the curtain, so to speak. For now, we're going out.'

'Out?' Wren snorted. 'Has this been approved by—'

'No approval needed.'

'Somehow I don't think that's how it works,' Wren said, with a glance at the adjoining door. She hadn't heard a peep from the Bear Slayer since he'd silently checked her rooms hours earlier. It would serve him right if she decided to go out and not inform him.

'We're not leaving the academy grounds,' Kipp insisted. 'Surely you've heard by now? There's a tavern on campus.'

Wren shook her head in mock disbelief. 'Of course there is . . .'

'Come on, Your Most Royal Highness—'

'Kipp, calling me anything to do with the Delmirian throne is a sure-fire way to convince me *not* to do what you want. You call yourself a strategist?'

He answered with a grin. 'Come on. We'll be escorted by Callahan the Flaming Arrow, the Warsword who beds three women a night—'

'I heard it was five,' Dessa chimed in.

That only encouraged Kipp. 'Callahan, killer of monsters, the warrior with the strength of a hundred men! What could be safer? Or more thrilling?'

'I can fucking hear you, you prick,' came Cal's voice from the other side of the door.

Wren's interest was piqued. That could only mean that Torj was not in his rooms, nor was he guarding her, for a change.

'We must strike while the iron's hot!' Kipp declared, throwing her door open.

'What does that even mean?' Cal said, rolling his eyes.

'I think he means we should get going while the drinks are cold and the morals are loose,' Wren suggested.

Kipp slung a long arm around her shoulders. 'And that, oh royal one, is why we're friends.'

Wren looked to Zavier and Dessa. 'You in?'

Zavier got to his feet, stretching and cracking his back. 'Now you mention it, I do have a thirst.'

'That's the spirit,' Kipp declared. 'Dessa?'

The pretty redhead was already gathering her things.

At last, Wren gave Kipp a gentle shove out the door as she took her cloak from its hook and checked her belt for full supplies of all her tinctures and powders.

'There'll be no cups of tea for anyone tonight, Elwren,' Kipp warned with mock sternness. 'You need to *make* some friends. Not scare them off.'

Wren smiled sweetly. 'We'll see about that, Kristopher.'

CHAPTER 49

Torj

'The relationship between bodyguard and charge is built upon the sanctity of boundaries. Romantic entanglements sow seeds of distraction, diverting attention from the primary mission of protection'

– The Protector's Manual

TORJ HADN'T STOPPED thinking about their kiss. Wren's breathless moans, the softness of her lips, and the way her body had reacted to his touch were all seared permanently into his mind. He knew if he'd stayed with her a moment longer, she would have got a lot more than she bargained for. In all his life, no woman had consumed him so thoroughly.

It was these thoughts he tried to push away in the middle of this endless meeting. In the High Chancellor's large private study, a council had assembled to assess the current threat. Tensions were high in the wake of the murder that had tarnished Drevenor's halls, and it had not gone unnoticed that the poor woman, Blythe, had possessed a startling resemblance to the heir of Delmira.

Audra had travelled from Thezmarr and was looking as irritated as ever, flanked by two of her women warriors. Farissa was in the chair to their right, along with the rest of the academy's masters.

Torj had asked after Wilder and Thea, for Wren's sake more than his own, but they were sequestered away, guarding the Queen of Aveum in an undisclosed location.

'Has any more information come to light on the murder of Blythe Rookford?' the Guild Master asked, folding her arms over her chest.

Farissa's expression was grim as she answered. 'A delayed type of poison. I'm still investigating, but for all we know, the crime could have been committed up to a week ago, in any number of locations.'

'But we believe the true target was Elwren Embervale?' Hardim Norlander asked.

Farissa dipped her head in confirmation. 'There were traces of the same unknown alchemy found on Blythe's body. With no royal blood, the substance had no effect on her, but the poison had already done its job.'

'It's a clumsy mistake for the enemy to make, confusing the two . . .' Audra pointed out.

'Perhaps,' Farissa allowed. 'But for much of the past five years, Wren has been hidden away in Delmira. For all intents and purposes, a general description of her would match that of poor Blythe.'

Torj suppressed a shudder, remembering the terror that had raced through him in those moments when he'd first seen the body in the hall.

'I trust Drevenor has it in hand,' Audra said brusquely, before continuing, 'There has been another assassination attempt. This time on the regent of Harenth.'

Torj's stomach bottomed out. 'Attempt?'

Audra nodded. 'One of my newer Warswords was on guard. She managed to stop the assailants.'

'What do you know so far?' the High Chancellor asked.

'That they'd rather take their own lives than risk capture,' Audra replied ominously.

'Then they're connected to those who attacked Wren outside the infirmary in Highguard,' Torj said. 'Those who didn't perish by my hand or Wren's storm magic ingested a poisoned pill. I'm told it contained a lethal dose of what the alchemists call cyanide.'

Audra nodded. 'Indeed. Their weapons were imbued with the same alchemy used in the attack on King Leiko as well. We can no longer deny that these events are all connected.'

'You suspected this from the start,' Torj observed. 'Or you wouldn't have had me guard Wren in the first place, nor would you have assigned a Warsword guard to the other royals.'

'Suspected? Yes. But I wasn't sure until now. Which brings me to these . . .'

Audra gestured to the array of posters littering the table. The same posters Torj had found in the fishing village the day he'd spoken with Branwell about his magically wounded son.

'*Join the People's Vanguard in their fight for a better world,*' Audra scoffed. She balled one up in her hand and threw it into the hearth, where it was quickly swallowed by flames.

'Similar propaganda to this has been reported in Tver, Harenth, and Aveum,' Torj told her. Reports from his sources had been coming in by raven all week, all sharing the same information about the posters.

'I have received the same reports, Elderbrock. And we have reason to believe that these are the people responsible for the attacks.'

'What reason?' the High Chancellor demanded. 'You make it sound as though there will be an uprising . . .'

Audra sighed. 'The feeling of dissent among the common folk has been spreading for some time,' she told the council. 'The most vocal are those who blame the rulers and their predecessors for all the bad that has come to the midrealms. Magic, in the hands of an elite few, is an imbalance in power. The late King Artos was a prime example of that, and this new group is using him to their full advantage to gain followers.' She motioned to the posters. 'It seems that they want their name out there, ready to claim responsibility when the time arises . . . We need one of these bastards alive for questioning.'

'There is little to be done to avoid them taking matters into their own hands in such a way,' Master Crawford said. 'It is a common practice in war where a party takes prisoners with the intent to interrogate or torture.'

Torj knew that well enough. It had been Wren herself who had handed him a pill of a similar nature before the final battle for Thezmarr. The enemy had had plans to capture Warswords and magic wielders and make monsters of them with shadow magic. Wilder had suggested the tactic, should things go badly, and Wren had executed the request. Thankfully none of them had ever had to take such measures.

'Do the common folk have any knowledge about the threat posed against their rulers?' Torj asked.

'Not yet,' Audra replied. 'Though word will spread that they now have Warsword guards. I fear this will only fuel these rebels and their argument. A Warsword's true purpose is to protect the midrealms *as a realm*, not powerful individuals . . .'

'It's a fair point,' Master Crawford said wryly.

'Point or not, they are breaking the laws of the midrealms,' Audra snapped. 'No one is above those laws, and they will be dealt with accordingly.'

'Are you calling us back to Thezmarr?' Torj asked, his heart rate spiking.

Audra shook her head. 'No. Your place is by the Delmirian heir's side. She is to be kept safe at all costs.'

Something about Audra's tone told Torj that the Guild Master wasn't telling him all there was to know, but when he opened his mouth to ask more, she silenced him with a look.

On and on the meeting went, the conversation going in circles when all Torj wanted to do was go back to Wren and make sure Cal was taking his duties seriously. He had the sneaking suspicion that the younger Warsword might be struggling with the blurred line between friendship and duty – not that Torj himself could talk. He'd *kissed* Wren, for Furies' sake, and he'd wanted to do a lot more than that.

He couldn't cross that line again. *Wouldn't.* Wren was off limits. Bodyguard and ward.

That was all.

At long last, the meeting was called to a close, but as he made to leave, Audra gripped him by the arm, her hold surprisingly strong for a woman of her age. Together, they left the High Chancellor's study and walked the hallway towards the archives.

'What of our other investigation?' she asked in a low whisper. 'Farissa tells me you've been researching.'

Torj speared his fingers through his hair with a resigned sigh. 'The Master of Lifelore gave me a list of contacts. So far, I've spoken with three of them who all share similar stories regarding magical injuries. Increasing phantom sensations, nightmares, an altered state of reality . . .'

'What became of them?'

'All dead. Two driven to the point of taking their own lives.'

They walked for a time in silence before Audra spoke again. 'And you? What of your symptoms?'

It felt wrong to talk about this with Audra and not Wren. Though they hadn't spoken properly since their kiss, he knew on a bone-deep level that this was something she'd want to know, that she deserved to know. Audra's orders aside, he didn't want to hurt her; he didn't want her to feel responsible for whatever fate awaited him. In his mind, she'd saved him – saved the whole damn midrealms, for that matter.

'Elderbrock?' Audra prompted. 'Your symptoms? And don't even think about holding anything back.'

Clenching his fists at his sides, he took his time to reply. 'I feel . . . *drawn* to Wren. Like there is some lingering ghost of a connection between us from that bolt of lightning.'

'It's getting worse?'

He sucked in a breath and stopped himself from touching his scars. Sometimes he could feel Wren's heartbeat echo against his.

'Define worse,' he said.

'You tell me, Bear Slayer. It's your wound.'

Torj ground his teeth. He didn't want to talk about this. Not with Audra, not with anyone. 'There is no consistency to it. Some days whatever magic remains inside me is more intense. Other times I barely notice it but for a tingle.'

Audra's brow furrowed, and he didn't like how interested she looked.

'When is it most intense?' she asked.

When Wren's mouth is on mine. When I hear her moan my name. When her fingernails are trailing down my chest. His cheeks flushed with heat. 'When Wren's near,' he said instead. 'And when I think she's in danger.'

Audra made a thoughtful noise at the back of her throat. 'I wonder . . .'

'Wonder what?'

'If by allowing you to wield her magic, some sort of loyalty was created between you—'

'I've always been loyal to Wren, shared magic or not.'

'I don't doubt that, Warsword,' Audra replied. 'But perhaps it's something worth exploring. Do you have other contacts to speak with?'

'Yes,' Torj said reluctantly. 'More books to read, too.'

'Good. Perhaps make a point of asking if there was any sort of bond between magic wielder and wounded after the fact – if there was some profound sense of allegiance, more so than prior to the injury.'

'You don't ask much, do you?' he said between gritted teeth.

'I ask what is required,' the Guild Master answered. 'Nothing more.'

Torj motioned to the fork in the corridor. 'I'm this way. Duty calls.'

Audra pinned him with her penetrating stare. 'Protect her, Elderbrock.'

'I intend to.'

'Even if it's from you,' she pressed. 'Even if it's from herself.'

Torj sucked in a trembling breath, irrational anger roiling within him. 'I don't need you to tell me how to do my job, Audra.'

'Don't you?' she countered, a brow raised.

'I vowed to guard her, to shield her from harm, to *protect her with my life* if need be. I would never—'

'I know, Elderbrock,' the Guild Master allowed. 'You're a good man.'

A good man? I'm not so sure any more.

Shaking his head, Torj left Audra at the entrance to the archives and turned back to the residence halls, picturing Wren's face.

He clutched his chest as he crossed the corridors. His scar was prickling, the sensation stirring up something darker within: a nameless hunger that plagued him more and more, a hollowness that he could not fill.

He needed to see her.

As soon as he clapped eyes on her, he'd leave her be. He'd stand guard at the door, he'd . . . He didn't know. He just needed to see her.

But when he turned the corner into their hall, Cal was not stationed outside her door. And when he knocked, there was no answer from within.

A wave of unease washed over him as he unlocked the door and peered into the empty room beyond. The lanterns burned low, but the golden glow was enough to illuminate something that did not belong on Wren's workbench.

A yellow handkerchief, with a fox embroidered in the corner.

'Fucking Kipp,' Torj muttered, snatching it up, the lightning beneath his skin echoing his frustration.

He scanned the utter chaos of the room once more. Everything was so *Wren*. A potion bubbling away on a burner, the dried bushels of lavender strung across the window, the pile of scrolls on the workbench, the skull of some animal he didn't recognize . . . Her scent lingered in the air, and that nameless hunger gnawed at him still.

He surged for the door. He'd find her and take his place at her side. Where he belonged.

CHAPTER 50
Wren

'Liquor is a poison'

— *Someone wise*

THE MORTAR AND Pestle sat on the fringes of the eastern grounds: an oddly shaped building that stood out like a sore thumb, smoke drifting in plumes from its crooked chimney into the cool night air. Surprising no one, Kipp threw the doors open like he owned the place and strode inside, greeted by a dozen shouts or offers of drinks before the doors had even swung closed behind him.

Given the current tensions at Drevenor, the tavern was louder than Wren expected, and fuller – as though every alchemist, scribe and scholar had decided that tonight was the night to forget the pressures of the academy and the darkness looming at its edges, and drink to excess. The lively chatter of students and professors engaged in animated discussions filled the air, along with the faint notes of a piano coming from the far corner.

It seemed strange, disrespectful even, that they were all here when Blythe Rookford's body had only just been put to a pyre. But Wren had seen first hand how life went on in the wake of death. There was no stopping the rolling wheels of time, or the need to move on. With a pang of remorse for the dead alchemist, Wren steeled herself and continued to take in her surroundings.

A mixture of tall and low tables were dotted around the tavern, all of them occupied, though Wren knew Kipp had a way of making things work in his favour. The heady aroma of bubbling stew and foaming ale mingled with the comforting scent of the fire burning in the hearth. It cast a warm glow on the bar, which appeared to be crafted from repurposed laboratory benches.

'Nice, huh?' Kipp called over the noise.

Wren's boots kept sticking to the floor, but she nodded. 'It's no Laughing Fox, but it'll do.'

'You just earned yourself a pint!'

As it turned out, Kipp didn't even need to approach the bartender; one of the tavern girls had seen him and was already bringing over a tray full of foaming tankards.

'This way, Mister Snowden,' she said with a warm smile. 'Saved you a table.'

'Have I mentioned that the service here is impeccable?' Kipp said, grinning broadly.

Wren exchanged a look of disbelief with Cal. They should have been well acquainted with the Son of the Fox's notoriety by now, but it seemed to know no bounds.

As they moved through the tavern, Wren saw various patrons, clad in academic robes and adorned with curious trinkets, clinking glasses over tomes from the archives and design sketches that took up entire tables.

When they sat down, she had to laugh at the eclectic food menu that featured concoctions inspired by alchemical experiments, offering patrons a taste of the arcane. 'If you were in some of our classes, you wouldn't be so keen on mushroom pie,' she told Cal.

He pushed the menu back in disgust and drank deeply from his tankard instead.

'That's the spirit,' Kipp said, clapping him heartily on the back before pulling out a chair for Dessa with a flourish.

Shaking his head, Zavier took the seat to Dessa's right.

Kipp addressed Cal next. 'Callahan, tell us, when are you taking on your prestigious guarding duty?' He made a vague motion to Wren. 'Not that our friend here isn't an equally prestigious assignment.'

Wren took a deep drink of her ale, savouring the crisp taste on her tongue and enjoying how it eased the tension she carried in her shoulders.

'Not that it's any of *your* business,' Cal was saying. 'But I start next week. The professor is due to arrive from abroad and start then.'

'What was his name again?' Kipp asked. 'Perhaps one of Her Queenliness' teammates has heard of him.'

Cal gave an irritated sigh. 'Professor Vulpine.'

Wren looked to Dessa and Zavier. 'Any idea who he is? Or what subject he's taking?'

Dessa shrugged. 'No idea.'

'Hopefully something that doesn't put our lives in peril for a change,' Zavier said, rubbing his thumb over two puncture marks where a snake had bitten him a few days earlier.

'Enough talk of work, anyway,' Kipp said, signalling the bartender for another round. 'We came here to have fun, did we not?'

'Do you do anything else?' Cal muttered into his drink.

'Not if I can help it, Flaming Arrow. Life is short, and you've gotta die from something.'

Dessa appeared positively smitten with Kipp. Zavier, on the other hand, just seemed vaguely amused. Wren had to admit, there was a certain charm about the strategist; there always had been, even when he'd been dubbed no more than a 'useless' shield-bearer at Thezmarr. Kristopher Snowden had only been biding his time, it seemed.

'I have a game,' he said with a wink. 'It's called *I have never*.'

Cal groaned. 'Not this again, Kipp—'

'You *love* it.'

'I don't know how to play,' Dessa said.

Nor did Wren, though she knew Kipp well enough by now to anticipate the explanation he was already launching into.

'It's simple – we each take turns going around the group with a statement. For example: I have never got a tattoo of a laughing fox on my arse.'

A laugh bubbled out of Wren as Cal's face went bright red.

Kipp's eyes sparkled. 'And since our renowned Flaming Arrow has indeed got a tattoo of a laughing fox on his behind, he has to drink. As would anyone in the group who has actually done the thing stated.'

Dessa was staring open-mouthed at Cal. 'You don't actually . . . ? Surely there would be rumours? After all, your—'

'I keep my clothes on,' Cal muttered before downing his drink and half of Kipp's.

Dessa and Wren burst out laughing. Even Zavier gave a bark of amusement, while Kipp clapped his hands.

'Excellent. Dessa, you start.'

Dessa looked around at them thoughtfully. 'I have never been to Thezmarr.'

Wren, Cal and Kipp all took a drink.

'A little boring, Dessa, but a solid strategic opener. You'll get better.' Kipp took another swig. 'I have never vomited in my closet thinking it was the bathroom basin.'

Cal let out a noise of protest before he reluctantly raised his tankard again. 'You can't just target me—'

'I can and I will, Callahan. That's the beauty of the game.'

'Fine. I have never had a sex-related injury,' Cal shot back.

Kipp laughed and drank his fill. 'Don't remind me.'

Wren refrained from asking Kipp exactly how he'd injured himself – she wasn't sure she wanted the mental image. To her utter disbelief, Zavier took a drink as well.

'Never have I tried smoking brugmansia pollen hoping to see a mountain drake in my visions,' Wren offered.

Kipp elbowed her. 'I can't believe you'd use that against me.'

She simply grinned and watched him finish his drink.

As they played, each statement becoming more ridiculous and targeted than the last, the tavern around them grew more rowdy. The drinks flowed freely, the music grew louder, and Wren felt lighter than she had in a long time.

Which was the only reason that when Dessa declared, 'Never have I kissed a Warsword,' Wren drank deeply, while Cal and Kipp whistled.

'I knew it,' Zavier said with a smirk.

Kipp, whose words were slurred, slung an arm around Cal. 'Didn't you try to kiss Thea once?'

This was news to Wren. She gaped at her friend.

Cal swayed in his seat. 'She wasn't a Warsword then. And I didn't try to kiss her. I only suggested . . .' He shook his head. 'So Wren's the only one to kiss one by the looks—'

Kipp clasped Cal's face in his hands and planted a wet kiss smack bang on his lips, before chugging his ale and calling for another.

Wiping his mouth with the back of his hand in disgust, Cal gave his friend a look of disbelief. 'What the fuck was that?'

'What?' Kipp grinned. 'I was thirsty.'

Cal spat on the ground and then drank again. 'You fucking prick.'

Wren nearly fell off her seat, she was laughing so hard. That, and she also had no idea how many pints she'd had. But gods, it felt good to laugh – to be in such ridiculous company and forget, if only for a few hours.

But all good things came to an end, eventually. And end they did as a large shadow cast across their table, and the Bear Slayer lifted his fellow Warsword up by his collar.

'You call this taking your duty seriously?' he growled, fire flashing in those deep-sea eyes. 'You couldn't even tie your damn laces, let alone protect a future queen.'

Torj's gaze slid to Wren, but she was just drunk enough that she lifted her chin in defiance. 'I suppose you're going to throw me over your shoulder and drag me back to the academy?'

Dropping Cal, Torj lowered himself into a chair. 'Not this time, Embervale. I need a fucking drink.'

CHAPTER 51

Wren

'Liquor, the concoction that whispers sweet nothings in your ear, only to leave you with a spinning head and a tongue tied in knots'

— *Elwren Embervale's notes and observations*

THE MOOD SHIFTED instantly, and Wren, feeling brazen with liquid courage swirling in her stomach, leaned in to address the Warsword. 'So now you're drinking with us? I thought you were enjoying giving me the silent treatment.'

The bartender brought over Torj's drink personally, lifting three fingers to his left shoulder in the midrealms' salute to their protectors.

'I assure you,' Torj muttered, taking the tankard with a nod of thanks, 'there's been no enjoyment.'

Wren glanced around, making sure the others were occupied with their own conversations, at last letting her fury bubble over. '*You* kissed *me*.'

'That was a mistake.'

It didn't sting any less hearing it a second time, but Wren narrowed her eyes. 'Good,' she said. 'I'm glad we agree. Now you can get over yourself and start acting like a human being again.'

Torj huffed a pained laugh. 'Simple as that, eh?'

'Some of us prefer not to behave like children, Elderbrock. Some of us have more important things to worry about.'

Leaning back in the chair that was too small for him, he studied her thoughtfully and nodded. 'The dead woman was meant to be you.'

'Of course it was. Even *you* thought she was me from a distance.'

A shudder seemed to run through the Warsword before he spoke. 'An easy mistake given the similarities. They know by now that they got the wrong woman, though. You're still in danger. Which is why outings like this are a *terrible* idea.'

'Am I meant to stay locked away like a prisoner for the duration of my time here? Am I meant to be punished for the actions of others?'

'I never said it was fair.'

'Well, look at that. We agree on something for once.'

The warrior chuckled. 'Don't get used to it.'

'I wouldn't dare.'

There was a sudden thud as someone placed a decanter of amber liquid in the centre of their table.

'Kipp,' Cal warned. 'We've had enough—'

But Kipp was on a mission, pouring everyone a glass of what Wren realized was the horrific throat-burning liquor called fire extract.

'Callahan, it's high time we heard the story of how the Bear Slayer earned his name. I've waited *years* for this.' He fell back into his seat, glass in hand, and looked to Torj expectantly.

Wren expected Torj to tell the strategist to fuck off, but instead, he downed the fiery liquid in a single shot and poured himself another with a grimace. He ran his hands through his hair, that rogue lock falling back into his eyes as he surveyed his audience with apprehension. But even Wren couldn't help the curiosity burning within. She too wished to learn how the infamous Warsword had earned his name, and so she leaned in with the others, ready to hear the tale.

Torj shook his head, as though he couldn't believe where he'd found himself. 'I was sent to the mountains to the north-west of Tver,' he began, reaching for the fire extract again. 'It's mostly dense forest up that way, small villages scattered throughout. There had been reports sent to Thezmarr about savage deaths at the hands of monsters, and the Guild Master sent me to investigate.' Torj's voice was deep and husky, and his eyes reflected the dancing flames in the nearby hearth. 'When I arrived, I was taken on a tour by a local elder, shown the spots where entire villages had once stood, now completely destroyed. I saw the mass graves of those who had been attacked. And the empty faces of those who had been left behind . . . The elder told me it was bears, which at the time seemed ridiculous. Bears are vicious, but they couldn't have done what I saw. Still, the elder was insistent. Told me to wait and see for myself if I didn't believe him.'

Wren studied the lines of the Warsword's face, and the shift of his body as he paused to take a breath.

'I stayed in one of the outer villages for three nights, and nothing happened. It was fucking cold out there – nothing like Aveum, but enough that you never quite feel your toes. But bears or not, I couldn't report back to Thezmarr with nothing. *Something* had ruined those villages and killed those people, and it was my duty to put an end to it.

'On the fourth night, every hut within miles trembled as a creature roared in the distance. I told the elder to gather the men and have them form a wall of protection around the women and children. It didn't take long for the creatures to sniff us out . . . They held the shape of bears, no doubt, but there was something far more sinister about them.'

'Shadow magic,' Wren heard herself whisper.

Torj bowed his head in confirmation. 'The same sort of warped magic used in the war. The midrealms was festering, even all those years ago, though we didn't realize it. The creatures might have been bears once, but were now something else entirely. They were so much larger, with misshapen jaws, enlarged fangs and claws . . . Monsters, in every respect of the word.'

'What did you do?' Kipp pressed.

'What do you think? I took them on myself. Two cursed bears in the heart of the northern forests, with my hammer and my sword.'

'You killed them?' Dessa gaped. 'Single-handedly?'

'I'm a Warsword,' Torj said, as though this explained the feat alone. 'I carved out their hearts as I would any monster of darkness.'

'Who did it? Who cursed the bears like that?' Dessa asked, wide-eyed.

'A mage from one of the villages,' Torj replied. 'Though we didn't discover that until later. I heard whispers in the wind, tales from survivors. I tracked him across Tver easily enough. Like many power-hungry fools, he sought chaos, and he found it by twisting something natural into something monstrous with bottled darkness from beyond the Veil. He didn't live to do so again. He met the same fate as those cursed bears, at the iron head of my hammer.'

Quiet fell.

Wren had seen Torj fight a million times, and she knew how much poetry was in the violence he inflicted when it was owed. But the image of him wielding his war hammer against two shadow-cursed bears was something else, and she understood now why the legend had followed him ever since.

'A toast,' Kipp declared, getting to his feet and tapping his fork on the side of his tankard so the entire tavern quietened.

'Gods,' Cal groaned, putting his head in his hands.

'Tonight, my fellow drinkers and thinkers, we are in the presence of a legend of Thezmarr!' He swayed slightly. 'To Torj Elderbrock, lightning-blessed war hero, the Bear Slayer of Tver—'

He was silenced by Torj's large hand clapping down on his shoulder, forcing him back into his seat. 'I'm never telling you a story again,' the Bear Slayer muttered.

Kipp simply offered a lopsided grin and tipped back the rest of his drink. 'Perhaps we should play *I have never* again.'

'Not a chance,' Torj replied, though Wren saw the faint tug of a smile.

The drinks and conversations continued to flow, and laughter echoed through the Mortar and Pestle. Wren had no notion of the time, only the vague inclination that it was only a matter of hours until she was expected back in the poisons dungeon—

Her thoughts were interrupted by a beautiful woman approaching their table, making a beeline for Torj.

'So you're the lightning-kissed Bear Slayer,' she murmured, trailing her fingers across his shoulder.

'Obviously,' Kipp snorted into his drink.

But Wren's skin prickled, particularly as the woman brazenly seated herself in the Warsword's lap.

'I've always wanted to meet a Warsword,' the woman purred. 'I'm Soraya.'

Wren's fingernails were digging into her palms.

'Now you've met one, Soraya,' Torj replied, moving to shift his admirer from his lap.

'But I'd like to get better acquainted.' Soraya was insistent; she draped her arms around his neck, practically pushing her breasts into his face.

Torj turned away. 'I'm afraid we're not staying.'

But she stroked her hand down the corded muscle of his arm. 'Oh, don't be like that. The fun's only just getting started.'

Wren's chest was burning. She watched as Torj tried to politely remove the woman from his lap. In the end, he lifted her bodily and placed her back on the ground.

'We're leaving,' he muttered to Wren and Cal, starting towards the door.

Soraya blocked his path. 'Come now . . .' She lay a seductive hand on Torj's chest. 'I wanted to—'

'He said no.' Wren's voice was sharp with venom, and she reached for her hairpin, releasing it from her locks and twirling it between her fingers.

Soraya blinked at her, as though she hadn't even noticed Wren was there.

She'll come to regret that, Wren thought, closing the small gap between them, her hairpin poised for damage, lightning singing in her veins. She could feel Torj's eyes on her like a brand, but her gaze didn't leave Soraya's.

'I didn't realize the Bear Slayer was spoken for,' the woman ventured.

'He spoke for himself,' Wren ground out. 'You just didn't listen.'

Soraya opened her mouth to reply—

'I can't *believe* you made us stay out so late,' Kipp slurred, staggering into the group, slinging his arms around Cal and Wren's necks. 'Gods, we're going to feel like *death* tomorrow.' He gave Wren's hairpin a pointed look. 'And what did I tell you about poisoning people tonight?'

CHAPTER 52
Torj

'A bodyguard's watch is unending'

– *Vigilance and Valour: Tactical Training for Professional Bodyguards*

TORJ HAD FELT her rage rolling off her in the tavern, had felt all her emotions toiling in his own heart. Jealousy at that woman's hands on him; anger at him being touched without his consent . . . and yet, before tonight, she'd hardly spoken to him since their kiss.

She was a storm of contradictions. There was a wildness to her that he knew would never be tamed, and it was dangerous.

But as soon as the cool early morning air hit Wren, so did the liquor.

She stumbled, her vials rattling as he caught her, setting her upright only to have her lean too far right and stumble again. She hadn't returned her hairpin to her bun, so her bronze hair flowed freely to her shoulders, sticking to her lips as she laughed at herself. The ominous mood from the tavern had vanished, and in its place was a Wren he hadn't seen in a long time: carefree and smiling.

Cal, Kipp, Zavier and Dessa staggered a few yards ahead, arm in arm, while Torj held Wren protectively close to his side, trying not to marvel at her warmth.

'You know, I can walk by myself,' she told him, gently pushing him away.

'That's debatable.'

She had the gall to look offended. 'You think you know everything.'

He had to bite back a laugh at that. Instead, he released her. 'By all means, Embervale. Let's see you walk.'

'See?' she declared as she took a single stride forwards, and promptly tripped over her feet into the dew-soaked grass.

She craned her neck to look up at him from the ground.

'Torj?'

'Embers?'

'I don't think I can walk by myself.'

A chuckle bubbled from his lips. 'You don't say.' He offered her his hand. 'Want some help?'

Her palm brushed his as she accepted his assistance, and he helped her to her feet. She lost her footing again, sending her crashing straight into his chest.

For a moment, he didn't move. And nor did she, resting flush against him.

'I didn't like her touching you,' she admitted in a whisper.

He had to remind himself to breathe, that the living storm of a woman in his arms was off limits. That without the liquor, there was no way in a million years she'd ever make such a confession.

'You're drunk, Embers,' he said gently.

'Blame Kipp,' she replied.

'Trust me, I always do.'

Wren sighed and broke away from him, starting back towards the residence halls. He didn't let her get far without him at her side; she was liable to fall over again.

'Wren?' he heard himself say, catching her as she did just that.

'What?'

'I didn't like her touching me either.'

She smiled openly then, and he revelled in it.

In the foyer of the main building, Wren lingered, gazing up at the glass cylinders that held stones of black garnet. She pressed a palm to the shiny surface of one, her lips moving as she counted.

'We won,' she breathed, eyes wide. 'Our idea in design . . . It won us the thirty points.'

Torj watched the joy wash over her face, warming at the sight. 'Congratulations,' he said quietly. 'Though I can't say I'm surprised. Your ideas have changed lives, Wren.'

She blinked at him, her mouth slightly parted. 'You mean that?'

'Am I not living proof?'

It took far longer than it should have to get Wren back to her room, and he knew there was little chance of her attending first meal at this rate, only an hour or so away. He doubted Dessa was faring much better. Kipp was just as likely to continue the party in his rooms as he was to quit while he was ahead.

'Keys?' he asked Wren as they turned into their hallway.

'Like you don't have one,' she mumbled.

Torj huffed a laugh and reached for his own. 'Thought you'd appreciate the pretence of privacy.'

'I don't.'

He glanced at her to find her already looking at him, her lower lip caught between her teeth. Gods, the Furies were testing him tonight.

It had been days since he had overheard her discussion with Odessa about sex. He'd nearly fallen over himself as she'd told her friend how she hadn't ever experienced a climax at the hands of a man . . . He still couldn't get it out of his head. How could he, when he was at her side nearly every waking minute? When he'd heard first hand the sounds she made when she experienced desire, pleasure? Knowing what she tasted like, how she writhed beneath his touch, was pure torture . . . Worshiping her would be a privilege, an honour. And it drove him mad that he couldn't be the man to do it.

He tore his eyes away from her. This woman had set him alight, and there was no snuffing out the fire now, as hard as he might try.

At last, when they reached her door, he fitted his key to the lock and opened it for them. Torj entered the room first to do his usual security sweep, checking everything with honed efficiency. Deeming the space safe and untouched, he went back to Wren, who was slumped against the wall outside.

'Come on, Embers.'

But it was like her limbs were now refusing to cooperate, and in the end, fed up with her futile attempts at walking like a newborn foal, he scooped her up in his arms and carried her to her bed.

She nestled against him with a sigh. 'You didn't want me,' she murmured, eyes closed. 'It's alright. I don't blame you . . . Nobody wants a broken thing.'

'You're not broken,' he told her hoarsely as he pulled back the sheets and laid her down in her bed. 'Not even close, Embers.'

Her wild hair spilled across the pillow as she curled up on her side, her nose tipped pink from the cold night air and the liquor. With gentle fingers, Torj removed her belt of potions and sharp tools, lest she roll over and somehow poison herself in her sleep.

'There's something wrong with me,' she breathed, blinking up at him with bleary eyes. 'Like all the rest said.'

Torj's heart broke, then, at just how much pain Wren carried with her. He shook his head sadly and sat on the edge of her bed, pulling the blankets up around her. 'Only a fool would look at you and see anything less than perfection.'

Wren's lashes fluttered against the tops of her cheeks, and he made to leave.

Her small hand gripped his forearm. 'Stay,' she whispered. 'Please.'

Torj hesitated, just for a moment, heart hammering, before he lowered himself back onto the edge of the bed. 'I've got you,' he told her, covering her hand with his. 'Sleep now.'

It was the only time she'd ever listened to him. Wren's breathing evened out, slow and steady as she drifted into a deep slumber.

He sat at her bedside, studying how she tucked her hands beneath the pillow and curled her feet under her, her face softening in sleep.

'I'm sorry,' he murmured, pressing a tender kiss to her temple and running his fingers through her hair. 'For everything.'

And then the Bear Slayer watched over her until dawn bled through the stained-glass windows.

CHAPTER 53

Torj

'In the study of the alchemy of afflictions, one must be prepared to delve into the darkest corners of the arcane arts, and their own mind'

Alchemy of Afflictions

WHEN DAYLIGHT HAD well and truly washed across the sky, Torj slipped from Wren's room to find Cal waiting by the door with his head hung in shame.

'You look like shit,' Torj said, surveying his fellow Warsword's messy hair and the dark circles beneath his eyes.

'I know,' Cal replied sombrely. 'I fucked up.'

'You did.' Torj was furious with his former apprentice. He thought he'd taught the Flaming Arrow better than that. 'You abandoned your orders, your duty to the midrealms last night.'

'I know. I'm sorry.'

'What good is sorry if she had been attacked, or taken?' Torj snapped. 'What good is sorry if she was—'

'*I know*,' Cal cut in. 'Believe me. I know how bad this is.'

'You don't,' Torj snapped. 'I would have briefed you last night if you hadn't been so inebriated. There's a real threat to the rulers of the midrealms. Audra confirmed it. Multiple attempts on royals' lives. A group called the People's Vanguard is taking responsibility.'

'Shit . . .' Cal muttered.

Torj sighed. 'Sometimes it's easy to forget who she is. I know she's your friend, but she's also the future Queen of Delmira, Cal. She needs to be kept *safe*.'

'She doesn't *want* to be queen. Same as Thea.'

'What she wants isn't our business. Our business is the orders that come from Thezmarr. The Guild Master orders us to protect Delmira's heir, that's what we do. Do you hear me?'

Cal's throat bobbed. 'Are you going to report me to Audra?'

'Do I look like a rat to you?'

'No.'

'Don't let this happen again,' Torj warned him. 'You don't want that guilt, that blood on your hands if something happens to her, believe me.'

Cal searched his face. 'Did you let someone down?' he asked. 'In the past, I mean?'

Torj's patience ran out then and there. 'Go and clean yourself up, Whitlock. You're no good to anyone in your current state. I'll take her to morning classes.'

'I—'

'Know when to quit, Cal.' Torj gave him a stern look. 'We keep her safe. No matter what.'

Cal gave a reverent nod. 'We keep her safe,' he repeated, touching three fingers to his shoulder.

Torj watched his former apprentice walk off, hoping he'd learned his lesson.

A groan sounded from within Wren's rooms. Torj was inside in an instant, just in time to see Wren bolt to the bathing chamber and slam the door behind her.

He waited precisely a second before striding in, finding her on the cool floor with her head in a bucket.

'Go away,' she moaned.

He couldn't help but laugh. 'Here,' he said, filling a cup with water and offering it to her.

With an unsteady hand, she took it from him and brought it to her lips, drinking deeply. 'I never used to feel this shit after drinking with Sam and Ida,' she muttered.

'It gets harder to bounce back when you're older,' Torj told her, wetting a towel and wringing it out, pressing the damp, cool fabric to the nape of her neck.

She sighed, closing her eyes as though she were enjoying the sensation. 'You'd know.'

'I'm an expert,' he agreed.

Wren gave a tired laugh and lurched to her feet. 'False alarm,' she said. 'I'm not going to hurl my guts up today.'

'Charming.'

'But I do need to get ready for class . . .' She motioned to the wooden tub. 'May I?'

'I strongly advise it; you smell like a tavern floor.'

'Now who's being charming?'

'Just telling it like it is, Embers.'

The nickname seemed to spark something in her memory, her brow furrowing. 'Did we talk last night?' she asked.

Torj froze on the way to his room. 'About what?'

'I don't know . . .' Wren sounded distant, like she was combing her mind for clues. 'Something important?'

He met her gaze, seeing the panic flaring in those willow-green irises. 'Nothing,' he told her. 'Nothing important at all.'

※

Torj knew he should be continuing his own investigations into magical wounds, but with Cal as hungover as a sailor after shore leave, he refused to leave Wren inadequately guarded. Which was how he found himself beside her workbench during her healing workshop as she finely sliced an ugly green plant.

In quiet awe, he watched her work. Regardless of her heritage, he had always known she was bound for greatness, that she would become someone the historians wrote about in their books. But now, he realized he was watching that unfold in real time, that history was here, in the making. For a moment, that fact weighed heavily on him, the responsibility for her safety all the more paramount.

As Wren added her cuttings to a small cauldron on her workbench, a potent smell snatched Torj from his thoughts. It wafted from the boiling liquid, catching him off guard: bitter and eye-watering, and *very* familiar.

He gripped the edge of the bench to steady himself, his heart kicking into its fighting rate.

Wren looked up sharply, as though she had sensed the change coming over him. Her gaze dipped to where his knuckles were nearly splitting as part of the workbench splintered beneath his grasp. He had to get a hold on himself.

'What is that?' he asked, struggling to keep his voice even as he nodded to the potion she was brewing.

'It's the foundation for a balm we use for bruises,' she replied. 'Though there's hours of work ahead before it remotely resembles that.' Wren gave him a funny look before adding a thimble of fine pale-pink powder to the mix. 'It's for the infirmary. We'll be sending it there next week.'

Torj simply nodded, the scent of the balm still sharp in his nose. 'My mother used to use something similar,' he said quietly.

Slowly, Wren turned to face him, sliding the jar she was holding onto the workbench. 'Your mother?'

Torj came back to himself, scanning the busy laboratory. 'Here probably isn't the best place.' He cursed himself for saying anything at all, for inviting questions.

Wren was watching him closely. 'I'm done here anyway,' she declared. 'And this stuffy room is doing *nothing* for my pounding head.' She wiped her hands on her apron and strode out the door, giving Torj no choice but to follow her.

Wren led them out into the academy grounds, where she and Dessa usually did their morning runs. The air was brisk, on the cusp of winter, but Wren breathed it in appreciatively before turning to him as they walked.

'Tell me about her,' she said simply.

Torj surveyed the woman beside him. She had the world believing she was all sharp edges and words like blades, but . . . he saw her. There was kindness beneath the hard exterior, the same kindness she offered him now.

His words came out quiet and slow, as though cautious to be spoken aloud for the first time. 'My mother is the reason I knew what that section of the infirmary was for. She's the reason I knew what that potion was you were brewing back there. She's the reason I . . .' He could feel every knot in his shoulders draw tight. 'My father wasn't a good man.'

Wren's eyes flitted to his forearm, where his shirtsleeve hid his scar.

'Not all monsters have scales and fangs, Embers,' he'd told her.

Now, her eyes met his, full of understanding. They didn't waver, didn't falter under the ugly truth of his words.

'I don't know when it started, exactly, or if he'd always been like that and my mother was good at hiding it when I was younger. But he hit her – badly, constantly. The smallest thing would set him off, and he'd be throwing her across the room, slapping her across the face, punching her in the gut . . .'

The familiar swell of anger rose up in Torj as he spoke, flashes of the past coming back to him, along with the spike of panic he'd felt as a little boy, watching the violence unfold from his hiding spot beneath the bed.

'When I was about six, I tried to stop him. Which earned me a place in the local infirmary for a week. My mother insisted that I live with my grandmother after that.' He drew a trembling breath. 'When I visited home, it was terrifying. Constantly walking on eggshells, waiting for one false move to trigger a tidal wave . . . But my mother wouldn't leave him. For all the bruises and broken bones, for all the times she could barely walk, she stayed.'

They walked in silence for a moment, and he knew Wren was giving him the time to find the words that came next.

'I was terrified he was going to kill her. I'd seen him at the height of his rages. He was a monster. Even at ten years old, I knew it would only take one strike at the wrong angle to end it all, one too many knocks to the head . . .'

'Torj . . .' Wren murmured, her hand reaching for his arm.

He didn't pull away; instead, he let her touch ground him. 'I was right, in the end,' he said hoarsely. 'He killed her. Hit her over the head with a lantern, and she bled out on the floor.'

Wren's hand tightened on his arm. 'Were you there?'

Torj shook his head. 'I found her.'

'Gods,' Wren murmured. 'I'm so sorry.'

'I couldn't save her.' The confession fell from his lips, raw and broken.

Wren turned to him, her hand gripping his jaw firmly and forcing his gaze down to hers. 'You were only a child yourself – what could you have done?'

'Nothing. Not then,' he conceded. 'But when I was fifteen, I found him.'

'You killed him?'

'Yes.'

Wren didn't balk at the violence of his words, her grip still firm, not letting him balk from it either. 'Good,' she said.

'I beat him with the same lantern he'd killed my mother with. When I went back to my grandmother's house, she took one look at me and told me to pack my bags.'

'She kicked you out?'

'She said that she'd been waiting for the day I closed that chapter. That the next was waiting for me at Thezmarr. That all my anger, and all my strength, would be put to better use at the fortress.'

Wren's fingers were moving now, tracing the line of his jaw in a featherlight touch, her stormy eyes bright. 'You couldn't save your mother, so now you try to save everyone else,' she whispered. 'But who's saving you, Torj?'

You did, he wanted to say. *You saved me*. But he let the words fade on his tongue.

CHAPTER 54

Wren

*'The art of poisoning is often attributed to womenfolk.
A weapon for the weak against the strong.
Or so they believe'*

– Elwren Embervale's notes and observations

FOR THE LONGEST time, Wren hadn't wanted to understand Torj, but now she did. His protective streak, his need to save people, his grief . . . It all made sense. And now, after sharing the deepest, darkest part of his past with her, he was pulling his arm from her grasp and turning back towards the residence halls.

'We should get you back inside,' he said, his voice stripped of all the emotion that had been there moments before.

In silence, she followed him to her rooms and waited for him to go through his checks, understanding his regimented nature so much more clearly now. He gave her a nod to tell her it was clear, then went into his own adjoining room, closing the door softly behind him.

Wren stared at the door, her heart aching for the Warsword. Looking down, she found her hand rubbing her sternum, in the same place where Torj's chest was marked with lightning scars. She could feel his turmoil in her own body, deep inside herself, as though it were her own pain. And it was. What hurt him, hurt her.

The realization had her surging for the adjoining door. Without knocking, she threw it open.

The Bear Slayer stood braced against the windowsill, the muscles of his back taut with tension, straining against the fabric of his shirt.

'Don't,' he growled.

'Don't what?'

He remained at the window, staring out onto the grounds below. 'Pity me.'

'I don't.'

'You're telling me that if I turn around now, I won't see it on your face?'

'Only you can know what you see, Torj,' she said.

The Warsword's broad shoulders rose and fell with the deep breath he took before he slowly turned to face her. Wren didn't know what to say, or what he needed, only that *she* needed to be here with him. She took a step towards him, and another, slowly closing the distance between them.

His deep-sea eyes met hers, his muscles bunching as he tensed, taking in the sight of her.

'Well?' she prompted, surveying the length of his war-honed body before meeting his stare once more. 'What do you see?'

Torj's gaze darkened. 'The calm before the storm.'

As if in answer, her power surged inside her – at his words, at the heat in his eyes, at the energy that seemed to roll off him in waves, so intense that Wren could hardly bear it.

'And you?' Torj asked, moving closer. 'What do you see?'

Her breath whistled between her teeth as she inhaled sharply under the searing brand of his stare, the masculine scent of him wrapping around her, toying with her senses. They were face to face now, merely inches apart. Wren looked up at his handsome face, taking in the lines around his eyes, the scar through his brow.

'The man behind the armour,' she said quietly. 'The man behind the legend.'

'Is that so? Discovered I'm human after all, have you?'

If Wren pushed herself up onto her tip-toes, and fisted the fabric of his shirt to pull him down to her . . . She wet her lips. 'Don't worry. I won't tell anyone.'

'I'd appreciate it. I'm meant to be infallible.'

Gods, she wanted to touch him, wanted to run her hands up the corded muscle of his arms and across the tattooed planes of his chest. She didn't. 'No one is infallible. So I'm constantly told.'

Torj's throat bobbed. 'You'd do well to remember it. You're hard enough to guard.'

'I've been a model principal.'

'Sure.' Torj snorted at that. 'It's been a real walk in the park, Embers.'

She could feel the heat radiating from his body, the pull of that cord growing tauter between them.

'Have you got enough of my secrets for one night?' he asked.

'That depends. Is there anything else I should know?'

'Perhaps . . . Though if I tell you, I might have to kill you.' The words came out in a growl.

'How intriguing,' she managed.

He huffed a laugh that had her toes curling in her boots. 'It's a little-known fact that I, Torj Elderbrock, have a sweet tooth.'

A laugh bubbled out of Wren and she revelled in the brightness gleaming in his eyes. 'A sweet tooth?'

Torj gave a hum of agreement. 'A particular proclivity for salted caramel, to be precise.'

She placed a hand over her heart, ignoring the way it pounded beneath her palm. 'You have my word. I'll keep your secrets. I especially won't tell anyone that my big bad bodyguard likes confectionery . . .'

Torj pushed a loose strand of hair behind her ear, his fingers trailing down to linger at the column of her throat. 'I like a lot of things I shouldn't.'

Wren's breath caught, and she was sure he could feel her pulse racing under that featherlight touch as his words went straight to her core. A fierce longing took hold of her, swelling in her chest, dampening her undergarments.

That bond of lightning amplified and tightened, and Wren stared up into his smouldering gaze. The need for him was all-consuming.

She almost whimpered as he removed his trembling hand and stepped back. Cold swept in between them, but it did nothing to douse the inferno of want that tore through Wren. Every sensation was coiled all too tight inside her. She couldn't look at him again, not without crushing her mouth to his and begging him to touch her.

'Good talk,' she mumbled, before she fled.

With the door closed behind her, she exhaled shakily. What *was* that? How did he have such a spell over her? Her breasts heaved against her constricting bodice, and she was all too aware of how sensitive her nipples were against the rough fabric, of how her hands were already drifting to her skirts. She needed to get rid of the incessant ache between her legs, the desperate sensation that emptied all other thoughts from her head.

This was insanity, she realized. The Bear Slayer had driven her to the point of madness. And yet, she cupped her breast and squeezed, imagining it was his rough hand closing over her curves, his fingers diving beneath the material to pinch her hard nipples.

Gods, it wasn't enough. It wasn't nearly enough.

Biting back a moan, she let her hands explore her body, the act feeling entirely forbidden with the Warsword on the other side of the wall. They had done this before, though, hadn't they? She'd heard him groan her name as he found his release, as he had heard her. What was one more time? What difference did it make, as long as that wall remained between them?

A gasp escaped her lips as she freed her breasts from her bodice, the cool air teasing her naked skin, tugging her nipples into tighter points. She imagined the Bear Slayer's mouth on them, his teeth grazing the sensitive skin.

She was too hot, her skirts too heavy. With a muffled cry of urgency, she stripped away her outer layers, leaving them in a pile at her feet, more cool air kissing her exposed flesh as she braced herself against her workbench. Her hand traced up her bare thigh, her shift bunching up beneath her touch as her fingers met the slickness there.

'*Gods*,' she murmured, unable to hold off any longer—

The adjoining door opened.

Torj's powerful body darkened the doorway. He no longer wore a shirt, the muscles of his bare tattooed chest tensing as he leaned against the frame, his eyes full of fire as they landed where her hand was nestled between her legs.

'Don't stop,' he rasped, voice rough with need. 'Don't you dare stop.'

Wren wasn't sure she could, even if she'd wanted to.

His stare emboldened her, added more fuel to the fire coursing through her. With her breasts already bare, she lifted the hem of her shift.

At last, the deep moan she'd been biting back broke from her lips, and she started to touch herself in earnest.

CHAPTER 55

Torj

'A bodyguard's focus must remain undivided.
His business is the safety of his charge, nothing more'

– *Mastering the Craft of Close Protection*

HE HAD NEVER seen anything more erotic than Wren in that scrap of fabric. His cock pulsed relentlessly, straining painfully against his leathers as he drank her in. Her breasts were exposed and flushed, perfect nipples hard as the hem of her shift rose, revealing more of her thighs, and that sacred place between them.

He didn't dare breathe, not while Wren spread her legs, her fingers rubbing decadent circles over her core. Her eyes didn't leave his, not once, as she worked herself, her breaths coming hard and fast.

'I want you to show me.' Her voice was low and demanding.

'Show you?'

One of her hands drifted up to capture her nipple between her fingers. And her request? It nearly ruined him.

'Show me what you do when you moan my name at night.'

'Furies save me,' he muttered, his eyes glued to her, mouth dry at the sight. 'Only this,' he said. 'We'll allow ourselves this. Just this once.'

'Just once,' she agreed breathlessly, still playing with her clit.

Was she going to slide a finger inside herself? Would her knees buckle beneath her as she found her release in front of him? He didn't dare cross into her room, the line between them clear. Instead, he stayed leaning against the door frame, needing the support, not sure he'd manage to stay upright for this. His hands shook as they went to the laces of his leathers, the bulge there undeniable.

Wren licked her lips as he worked the ties loose, and at last freed his cock, the tip already beading with moisture.

He heard her sharp inhale as he wrapped his hand around the thick base and glided it over his shaft in one unhurried stroke. Her heated stare alone made him want to explode, the urge unfurling, threatening to crest with every pump of his hand.

A distant voice at the back of his mind told him this was ridiculous, standing there touching themselves in front of one another. But another voice goaded him, told him that it was fine, that there was still a line between them they weren't crossing, that they could do this one thing to ease the want, the lust—

Torj moaned as he fucked his hand and Wren's finger slid from her clit to her entrance, disappearing inside her. Gods, there had never been a more glorious sight.

'Put your foot on the chair,' he ordered hoarsely, jerking his chin to the stool at her side.

He expected her to deny him, but her leg was already lifting, baring more of her to him. She spread herself wide for him, showing him the wetness coating her finger as it slid in and out of her.

'I'm pretending this is your cock,' she told him, whimpering as she increased the pace and added another digit.

He matched the stroke of his hand to what he saw before him, imagining the wet heat of her clamped around him. 'How does it feel?'

'Tight,' she moaned. 'And so good. Like I could break apart at any second.'

'It'd be a lot tighter with my cock driving into you.' He squeezed the thickness of his shaft for emphasis.

'I know.'

It was intoxicating, watching her play with herself without being able to touch her. An excruciating form of torture, but he couldn't stop. Couldn't stop stroking his cock, couldn't tear his eyes away from the bounce of her full breasts as she fingered herself with one hand, and rubbed her clit with the other.

'That's it, Embers . . .' he murmured, pleasure building at the base of his spine, gathering in his balls as he worked his shaft. 'Show me exactly what you like.'

How they were both still standing, he didn't know – nor did he care, because the view of Wren spread out for him with one leg perched on the stool was to die for. He could see her desire glistening across her skin, could hear the subtle wet sound as she pushed her fingers into that slick heat over and over.

She bit her lip, her eyes glazed over with lust, trained on the motions of his hand, up and down over his length, pausing when it got too much to squeeze the damp tip.

Wren let out a strained cry, and he knew she must be close.

Gods, he didn't want it to be over. This small taste of her would drive him to madness, knowing that he'd never have it, have her, again. But Torj was also on the precipice of no return, his own climax edging towards detonation.

He drank in the sight of her flushed body and met her gaze. 'Let me see how you fall apart, Embers.'

His words were like a match to kindling. Wren's head tipped back in ecstasy, and he watched as her release barrelled through her, her knees buckling just as he'd imagined, another moan spilling from her mouth.

Beautiful. Perfect.

Everything.

At last, he let himself go over the edge, his own orgasm like a storm of her making, rattling him to the very fibre of his being, lighting that spark that lived inside his chest where Wren had marked him for ever.

Torj came with a shout, spilling his release into his hand, his eyes not leaving Wren as each burst rolled through him, until he was spent.

CHAPTER 56

Wren

'Poisons can promise oblivion, a symphony of suffering and a delayed end. From the venom of the arachne to brews from beyond the Veil, the poisoner's art knows no bounds. Let the adept alchemist embrace the darkness within, for in the shadows lies the true path to mastery'

– Alchemy Unbound

AFTER ALL THAT time in close quarters, after sharing a magical connection for so long, they had finally hit a breaking point. They'd well and truly broken, and now they'd find a new normal. That was what Wren told herself as she watched Torj disappear into their shared bathing chamber and shut the door behind him.

It was out of their system.

Wren cleaned herself up with a bowl of water and a cloth before readying herself for bed. She tidied her workspace where she'd knocked over several instruments, wondering if he knew the effect he'd had on her: a blinding, overwhelming need to have him. So powerful that even now, she wasn't sated. It had been *his* hands she wanted on her, his cock between her legs . . . But he'd braced himself against the door frame, a clear boundary drawn between them, a barrier he would not cross. She'd seen the turmoil lining his face as he warred with himself, had felt it tightening in her own chest. The scars he wore, the scars she had cursed him with, linked them somehow. She was no fool. There was a physical tether between them, beyond attraction; a connection forged in violence and desperation that bound them together all this time later.

Water splashed within the bathing room, bringing Wren back to herself as Torj also washed away the evidence of what they'd done.

Sliding beneath the bedsheets, her cheeks heated at the fresh memory of his eyes on her nakedness. Wren chastised herself, rolling onto her side with a huff of frustration, but she was already craving that thrill again.

༄

The next morning, a loud knock at her door made Wren jump.

'Wren!' Dessa called. 'Are you in there?'

She surveyed herself quickly in the nearby mirror before flinging the door open. 'What is it?'

Her friend gave her a strange look. 'We said we'd walk to the warfare class together . . . ?'

'We did?' Wren had no recollection of that conversation. She already had enough escorts everywhere.

'Oh,' Dessa said with a sheepish grin. 'It was at the Mortar and Pestle . . . I'm surprised I remembered myself, now that I think of it.'

Wren laughed. 'No wonder I have no memory of it. Let me get my bag.'

Torj chose that moment to re-enter her rooms. Larger than life, he made the space seem so small.

How does he do it? she wondered. He looked as fierce and unruffled as ever, as though nothing had happened between them. His silver hair was swept back in a half bun, his hammer was strapped to his broad shoulders, and he scanned the room for danger.

Always a bodyguard.

Her bodyguard.

Lightning sang beneath her skin, and his eyes flicked to her, as though he could hear its call—

'Wren?' Dessa prompted from the door, glancing between Warsword and poisoner.

'Coming,' Wren replied, snatching up her oilskin satchel and checking the supplies at her belt.

As they walked, Torj shadowed them, and only with her last remaining shred of willpower did Wren keep herself from looking back.

❦

The dungeon was dimly lit as always, and Master Crawford was waiting impatiently at the front. Wren took a seat at the back, as she usually did, Dessa claiming the seat to her left, Zavier to her right.

'All paths lead to the underworld, novices. Especially those walked by latecomers and dawdlers.' Master Crawford cleared his throat. 'The subject of warfare is often associated with large-scale battle and mass bloodshed, but in truth, war starts long before forces clash on a field. Like poisoning, it can be cold, meticulous, and deliberate. Strip away the passion, and at its core, it is a crime that must be planned.'

In the front row, someone coughed.

'Over the centuries we have proven ourselves to be a race of greed and malice, not content with the poisons gifted by nature herself. We have always sought to amplify the worst, to make artificial horrors of our own . . . As Master Norlander would ask, "*Are we not the poison in this realm?*"'

The coughing continued, and Selene muttered her apologies, covering her mouth with her sleeve, trying to muffle the sound.

Master Crawford continued without paying her any heed. 'To that question, I'd answer *yes*. But we are not here to reflect on humanity's morals or lack thereof. We are here because at the heart of warfare, an alchemist must make themselves apt at the art of murder . . .'

Wren sat up a little straighter.

Master Crawford brought a large box from the supply cupboard and slid it onto the desk at the front. 'These rats have been poisoned,' he stated bluntly. 'Each team has twenty minutes to identify and cure the toxin. Your time starts now.'

Zavier rushed forwards to retrieve their rat, while Wren dashed to the supplies to snatch up a number of common purgatives and antidotes, and Dessa pulled out her copy of *Elixirs and Toxins: A Comprehensive Guide*.

The trio crowded around their workbench as Zavier placed the rodent before them. Its body still rose and fell with laboured breaths, but the creature was unconscious.

'No bleeding that I can see,' Dessa observed, baring the rat's teeth with the tip of her quill.

'Don't be putting that in your mouth after,' Zavier said, grimacing at the sight. Dessa waved it in his face in response, causing him to rear back in disgust.

'Enough,' Wren snapped. 'What else do you see? Its claws are curled . . .'

Zavier nodded. 'Tail too. There are any number of poisons that would cause contracture like that . . .'

Wren sighed. 'I know. The fact that it's affecting its brain doesn't narrow things down for us . . .'

'What about this discoloration here?' Dessa asked, pointing to the rodent's claws. 'See the yellowing?'

'Good catch,' Zavier said. 'Could mean the poison is attacking the liver?'

Wren's heart leapt. 'I think you might be right. Look at this bald patch here – it's been losing its fur . . .'

Together, they pored over their books, and tried several purgatives to no avail. Around them, their peers weren't having much more luck, with one rat already dead.

Nearby, Selene's cough turned violent and ragged, and Wren spotted her trembling fingers reaching for a flask on her desk.

The hair on Wren's nape stood up as a feeling of unease washed over her. She recalled Master Crawford's words from their first lesson. *Would you prefer I ask you to test it on yourself? . . . For we will get to that, I assure you.*

'You've poisoned her . . .' Wren didn't even register getting to her feet, but suddenly she was standing in front of Selene, pulling her hands away from her face, trying to survey the symptoms beyond the cough.

'Have I?' Master Crawford said simply.

Almost instantly, Zavier was at Wren's side, taking Selene's pulse at her wrist while she coughed. But Wren looked to Selene's teammates, Alarik and Gideon – both were pale, perspiration beading at their brows.

'It's not Selene,' she murmured. 'It's these two. They're the ones who've been poisoned.'

Zavier balked. 'But Selene—'

'Is having an allergic reaction to the chrysanthemums.' Wren pointed to the out-of-place vase of flowers on Master Crawford's desk. 'Alarik and Gideon, however, are suffering from acute poisoning.' She grasped Alarik's face in her hands and studied his eyes. 'Blurred vision?' she asked, noting his unfocused gaze.

He managed to nod.

'Same for you?' she asked Gideon.

'Yes,' he rasped, blinking slowly, as though he couldn't quite see her.

The rest of the class had gathered around, but she ignored them while she took both young men's pulses. Their heartbeats were rapid – too rapid.

'We need calabar bean and the fruit of the manchineel tree—'

'Identify the poison first, Elwren,' Master Crawford chided, as though two of his students were not rapidly deteriorating before his very eyes.

Wren's own heart rate spiked. Did he mean for them to die?

'Belladonna,' she said.

'Also known as?' Master Crawford prompted.

She was already surging for the supply cupboard. 'Deadly nightshade. Atropa belladonna. Poison berry.'

Wren rifled through the potion bottles and samples on the shelves, looking for anything that might help – some sort of extract containing the ingredients she'd mentioned. She snatched up a vial labelled *Essence of Calabar* and darted back to her peers, who had clearly started to hallucinate, their eyes wide, their bodies flinching at phantom touches. She tipped half the vial into Alarik's mouth and brought the rest to Gideon's lips.

Stepping back, she scrutinized them. It could take anywhere between five and fifteen minutes for the antidote to take effect, if she had, in fact, diagnosed the poisoning correctly. With some degree of shock, she registered that she hadn't consulted any of her classmates, or even looked to Crawford for reassurance. If she was wrong, there was a very real chance that she could have hastened Alarik and Gideon's demises—

'Well, that was rather anticlimactic,' Master Crawford announced dryly, as both young men blinked slowly.

Wren loosed a breath, watching as both seemed to come back to themselves.

'I'll have to try harder next time,' the Master of Warfare said. 'Elwren correctly identified both the misdirect and the poison itself. The rest of you are to write essays on the effects of belladonna and its antidotes. Four pieces of parchment. On my desk by the start of our next lesson. Now . . . Has anyone cured their poisoned rat?' Master Crawford scanned the cohort with a look of sour disappointment. 'No? Pity. That will be another four pieces of parchment on identifying the symptoms of strychnos seed poisoning.'

Disbelief seemed to have shocked the cohort into silence as they gathered their belongings and made for the door. Both Alarik and Gideon tried to catch Wren's eye, but she busied herself at the back of the room with her satchel, unsure how she felt about it all. The lesson was a brutal reminder that the Gauntlet grew closer by the day, the moment of reckoning. The academy was alive with learning and ambition, there was no doubt about that, but it was also cold, and calculated.

Knowledge is the victor over fate. The mind is a blade.

Zavier and Dessa gave Wren a distracted farewell as they debated the origin of strychnos seeds, and Wren suddenly found herself alone with Master Crawford, whose voice made her start.

'You've used belladonna before, I take it?'

'It grew in the Bloodwoods back at Thezmarr,' Wren answered carefully. 'Every now and then, someone would ingest it accidentally, thinking it was—'

'That's not what I meant.' Master Crawford's eyes narrowed. 'You've used it intentionally. You've seen its effects first hand.'

Wren debated trying to deny the facts, but she knew they were written all over her face. 'I have,' she said finally.

Master Crawford simply nodded. 'Very few poisoners die old in their beds, Elwren.'

'And all paths lead to the underworld,' she recited back.

'Exactly. Well, the Gauntlet will show us what you're made of, won't it?'

Wren held his gaze, unflinching. 'I suppose it will, Master Crawford.'

CHAPTER 57

*W*ren

'I have gazed into the abyss of the most lethal potions, and I fear that the abyss has stared back at me'

— *Elwren Embervale's notes and observations*

WHEN WREN LEFT the dungeon, her nose was still filled with the scent of belladonna, her stomach still churning with unease.

But all was forgotten as her eyes found Torj, waiting for her.

Her breath caught as she drank in those strong brows and square, chiselled jaw, and that stray lock of silver that tumbled over his forehead. His eyes met hers, piercing, the colour of a violent sea.

She wanted to tell him that what they'd shared hadn't been enough for her. That after all these years of turmoil, she wasn't sure she could stand another moment pretending she didn't want him, pretending he hadn't crowded her mind for half a decade.

Something must have shown on her face, because Torj gave her a questioning look.

'I don't want to go back to my rooms,' she told him instead, her hand brushing the secateurs secured to her belt. She turned on her heel towards the doors.

'Where are we going then, Embervale?' the Warsword asked.

'To the gardens.'

The gardens were well beyond the academy buildings, where they drank in the full force of the sun's rays, far enough away that the towers and spires cast no shadows. Bordered by a handful of greenhouses on the perimeter, with wrought iron gates adorned with ivy vines marking the entrance, the lands beyond unfolded like a tapestry of colour and scent.

Wren breathed in deeply, appreciatively, as she led Torj through the entrance, picking up a basket on the way. They were greeted by an endless sea of sprawling garden beds, a verdant expanse of vibrant blooms and richly aromatic herbs. To her left, towering sunflowers stood tall, their golden faces turned towards the sun, while to her right, clusters of purple coneflowers swayed gently in the breeze, their quaint petals a testament to the artistry of nature and alchemy alike.

Wren sighed contentedly, drinking in the sight. 'Beautiful,' she murmured.

She heard Torj's intake of breath beside her. 'Yes.'

But when she glanced at him, he wasn't looking at the flowers. He was looking at her.

Along the winding pathways, borders of fragrant rosemary and delicate lemon balm delineated the garden's various sections, their aromatic foliage mingling with the sweet perfume of lavender and jasmine. The lavender was something else. Great bushes of the bright purple heads reached up to Wren's chest, dancing in the crisp breeze that rippled through the gardens. Wren ran her fingertips across it, mindful not to disturb the bees flitting about the blooms. She could feel Torj's eyes on her, but she ignored the attention, wanting – needing – to ground herself in the nature around her.

Patches of scarlet beebalm and crimson hibiscus punctuated the landscape, drawing the eye with their fiery allure, and in the centre of the garden, a tranquil pond reflected the sky above, its surface adorned with lily pads and water irises in hues of emerald and sapphire. With the handle of her basket resting in the crook of her elbow, Wren navigated the garden's winding paths and breathed deep, feeling a sense of reverence for the natural world, each one of the blooms before her a testament to the boundless magic that lay at their feet.

'These are pretty,' Torj ventured, reaching down to cup a cluster of dainty white blooms in his large palm.

'It's feverfew,' Wren told him. 'Part of the daisy family . . . We use it to treat fevers and headaches, among other things.'

'And those?' He pointed to the rows of calendula officinalis basking in the sun's rays, the petals a vibrant burnt orange hue.

'Commonly known as marigold,' Wren said. 'Another from the daisy family. We dry the petals to use in ointments for burns and bruises.'

'I'm surprised we're not going straight for the poisons today, Embers.' He said it with a teasing note, but Wren sighed, closing her eyes and tipping her head back to the sky, savouring the warmth of the sun on her face.

'Perhaps I need a break from pain and death, Warsword.'

Her attention snagged on the fields further in the distance, close to the University of Naarva, where the crops of sun orchids bloomed. She let her eyes linger there for a moment, remembering harvesting the flowers for their use in the war.

To her surprise, the Warsword nodded, scanning the same field before turning to her. 'Where do we start?'

'We?'

Torj arched his scarred brow. 'I'm not just a pretty face, Embers. Put me to work.'

Wren shifted on her feet, the intensity of his gaze heating her blood. 'Alright then, Warsword. We start with the lavender.'

She led him to the giant bushes and knelt down in the dirt. Torj followed suit, his arm brushing against her shoulder as he lowered himself to the ground beside her. His scent mingled with that of the lavender, and Wren had to stop herself from closing her eyes and inhaling deeply. Instead, she offered him her secateurs.

His fingertips grazed hers as he accepted the tool. 'You don't need them?'

'I'll use this.' She showed him her harvesting knife, a small scythe-like instrument she'd borrowed from Dessa. 'Use your thumb and middle finger,' she explained, demonstrating. 'You encircle a small bunch of stems, just above the leaves there . . . Make a clean cut – you don't want to bruise or damage anything – and make sure you don't crush the flowers. We can take about half the height. Just don't cut into the woody part – it might not recover then.'

Torj watched her closely, listening carefully before gathering the lavender in his calloused fingers. 'Like this?'

Wren bit back a smile. Without thinking, she wrapped her hand around his, an electric current rushing through her as she did. Ignoring the sensation, she positioned his grip around the bunch of stems. 'There.'

Nodding to himself, Torj used the secateurs to make the cut, while Wren handed him a short length of twine to bind the bundle together.

'How many cuttings do we need?'

'About twenty or so.'

'Then what are we waiting for?'

They gathered the cuttings together, Wren stealing glances all the while at the fierce warrior kneeling among the flowers. His movements were considered, gentle, and he often looked to her for guidance and reassurance, as though concerned he'd make a mistake or disappoint her.

A lump formed in Wren's throat during those stolen glances, as her basket began to fill with their bounty of blooms. Gods, he was beautiful, beautiful beyond reason.

And he had no idea.

When the sun began to dip behind the horizon and the rose-gold glow of dusk drenched the sky, Wren got to her feet, dusting her skirts off at the knees and settling the basket in the crook of her elbow once more. 'We should head back.'

Torj stood, but lingered for a moment, regret lining his handsome face. 'You're probably right.'

'I thought you'd be all about getting back to the halls before dark.'

'I should be, but . . .' He took a breath and surveyed the gardens. 'This was . . . nice.'

The clouds above seemed to ignite in the fading light, a canvas of coral and tangerine, while the towering sunflowers swayed, beckoning them back to the gates.

'It was,' Wren said quietly.

Torj's eyes were on her again, full of warmth and longing. 'Here.' He reached out, gently taking the basket from her. 'Allow me.'

Heat unfurled in Wren's chest as the warrior hooked the wicker handle over his own arm and started towards the gates. For a moment, all she could do was watch him, his huge frame navigating the winding path, his iron war hammer gleaming across his back, his silver hair shining in the last of the sun's rays, the basket brimming with flowers swaying at his side.

Wren found herself biting her lip, where she could taste the beginnings of a storm. And as Torj reached the garden gates, she absentmindedly rubbed at her sternum, where, beneath flesh and bone, thunder gathered.

CHAPTER 58

Wren

'Let the seeker of forbidden lore tread carefully'

– Arcane Alchemy: Unveiling the Mysteries of Matter

TIME EBBED AND flowed like the streams that cut through Drevenor's grounds. Wren's days were punctuated with the masters' teachings and scare tactics, training, and the more menial tasks appointed to novices of the academy. Peaceful hours in the gardens became a thing of the past, and instead she laboured over her studies with Zavier and Dessa, both in her rooms and in the poisons dungeon.

As the Gauntlet drew nearer, the Master Alchemists became colder and harder towards them. Wren figured it was because they knew not all of the novices would be returning to study in these halls. She understood. It was hard to get attached.

The glass cylinders in the foyer grew fuller with pieces of black garnet, and Wren's team was in close second place behind Selene Tinsley, Alarik Wingate, and Gideon Sutten. Not even their near-death experience had slowed their influx of points.

Wren pushed herself harder than ever before. She ran drills with Dessa every morning, and was no longer last in the fitness classes. Begrudgingly, she admitted that the exercise helped. She felt stronger, her head was clearer, and she was able to keep her magic in check far more easily.

'You've improved a great deal,' Torj told her in the privacy of his rooms, where he was teaching her more complex manoeuvres of self-defence. In the dimly lit confines of his chambers, the air was thick with anticipation as he took Wren's hand, guiding her stance with a searing touch. She ignored it, as she ignored the fact that he wasn't wearing a shirt. 'Remember: understand the surroundings. Come to grips with your limitations. Find a solution.' Torj tapped her ribs, where she'd left herself vulnerable.

Wren clicked her tongue in frustration. 'Why am I *still* leaving my left side exposed? Why am I failing to—'

'You're still learning,' Torj said gently. 'You're too hard on yourself.'

'If I want to be the best, that's how it goes.'

'Everyone has to make mistakes in order to learn,' he replied, shifting behind her and placing his hands on her hips.

Wren stifled her sharp inhale at the sudden contact, at the sheer brand of his touch.

'You have to trust your body.' His voice was low, resonating with authority. 'You've got strength. You just need to follow your instincts.'

Her breath caught as Torj's hands lingered on her, his touch igniting a spark she couldn't deny no matter how hard she tried. With each step, their bodies brushed, sending shivers down her spine and conjuring memories of him stroking himself in her rooms.

'Where'd you go just now?' he murmured. 'You're not concentrating.'

'It's a little difficult,' she ground out, wiping the perspiration from her brow.

'I know it's hard, but you'll get there. You just need to focus—'

'That might be easier if you put a damn shirt on.' The words were out of her mouth before she could stop them.

Torj blinked at her. 'What?'

'You heard me, Warsword.' But her voice betrayed the pounding of her heart. Their eyes locked, a silent understanding passing between them as they danced on that same line they had been skirting for weeks, somewhere in the shared space of unspoken desires.

Slowly, a grin spread across the Warsword's face. 'You're saying you can't concentrate because . . .' He gestured to the muscular expanse of his chest, amusement gleaming in his eyes.

'Well, it's not *helping*,' Wren bit out, her cheeks flaming. 'Don't let it go to your head.'

'Would I ever?' Torj teased, though she noted he didn't reach for his shirt as requested. 'Come on, Embers. Try again.'

As the lesson progressed, the air crackled with tension, their bodies moving in sync, each touch lingering a fraction longer than necessary. Torj's hands traced the curve of Wren's waist, sending her pulse racing, as she fought to focus on the techniques he imparted. Was he *trying* to drive her mad? She drove her elbow back, hitting his side.

'You're a quick learner, you know,' Torj murmured.

That bond between them tugged at the centre of Wren's chest.

'Not as quick as Thea,' she answered.

Torj's hands dropped. 'You compare yourself to her a lot, don't you?'

'Doesn't everyone?'

'I don't,' he said. 'You've always been your own woman to me. And certainly not one I'd want to cross . . .'

Wren's cheeks flushed. She dropped her head to hide the emotion welling in her eyes, but her attention snagged on the network of scars marring the inked flesh across Torj's chest.

'We all have our own battles to face,' he told her quietly.

'We do,' she agreed.

A hushed sense of intimacy washed over them as Wren's fingertips delicately traced the web of scarring, her touch featherlight yet laden with grief. She had done this to him, marked that perfect skin with her own ugly violence. The ridges beneath her touch told the story of the battle they'd waged and the wounds he had endured, each line a testament to the price of survival. A kaleidoscope of emotions flooded her heart – a mingling of desire and sorrow, and a river of unspoken words.

The ever-present storm in Wren's chest awoke, searching for the remnant they shared from the final stand at Thezmarr, the one that had fused them together amid the darkness.

Torj stared down at her as she touched him, and in the soft glow of flickering candlelight, their breaths intertwined, a quiet song of longing and regret echoing in the air. In the silent language of touch, Wren felt the weight of Torj's past, *their* past, his scars not just of flesh but of heart, too. She could feel his beating in time to her own, as though it *were* her own.

'Torj . . .' she murmured, at last allowing herself to look up at him, his name a tangled knot of yearning and frustration.

A broken breath shuddered out of him and he pulled away. 'We can't.'

CHAPTER 59
Torj

'A bodyguard stands as a steadfast shield against chaos. He must remain resolute. Distraction is the death of duty'

— *Mastering the Craft of Close Protection*

Torj knew he had royally fucked things up with Wren, because she hadn't spoken to him for three days. Three excruciatingly long days. It was a feat, considering how much time they spent together. He'd escorted her to every class, every novice errand to the city and back, and she hadn't so much as told him to piss off.

It was his own fault, he knew. He kept letting her get close, get under his skin until his resolve was on the verge of shattering, and then he'd reel back as though burned. And he'd done it one too many times. The only comfort he found was that Wilder wasn't here to give him shit about it – the knowing glances from Cal and Kipp were more than enough, and Torj had half a mind to throw them both on a ship back to Thezmarr.

Now, he sat beside Wren in a packed supply cart full of barrels and ceramic jugs as it rattled back down the road from the city. The cart, its timber weathered and its wheels worn, trundled along the winding dirt road with a rhythmic cadence while the road cut through tranquil forests and dew-kissed meadows, but Wren's silence was louder than any crack of thunder she might inflict upon him – especially now, as she was pressed so tightly against him. After collecting specimens and ingredients from several apothecaries at Master Norlander's instruction, Zavier had insisted that riding in someone called Roderick's cart would be faster than re-saddling six horses at the stables. They had left them in Highguard to be re-shoed, which was how the Warsword found himself beside Wren, Dessa, Zavier, Cal and Kipp, with hardly any room to hold his hammer.

Oblivious to any tension, Dessa was chatting with Zavier. 'Going to the city and back seems a bit excessive,' she was saying. 'I thought we weren't supposed to leave the grounds?'

'For official lessons, no,' Zavier replied dryly. 'But to pick up supplies for the masters? Apparently, that's worth the risk.'

Cal made a disgruntled noise. 'Believe me, you're not the only one unhappy about it.'

'I still can't believe it's taken until now for you to tell us about Roderick and his cart route,' Wren muttered. 'Decided to be a team player after all, have you?'

Annoyance laced her words, and Torj was keenly aware it was less to do with Zavier's actions and more with his own presence beside her.

But Zavier snorted. 'If I want to be the best, I have to compete against the best. Unfortunately, that means getting your sorry arse through the Gauntlet alongside me first.'

'I suppose I should be flattered.'

'I suppose so.'

'You're lucky I told you at all,' Zavier quipped.

The man driving the cart piped up. 'I told him to introduce me to his friends weeks ago.'

'If I had any, I would have, Rod.'

As the alchemists chatted, Torj tried to focus on the road, on the icy breeze whispering through the trees, increasingly bare as winter well and truly set in. But the warmth of Wren's side against his was enough to drive him to distraction, and not for the first time, he cursed himself and all the stupid decisions he'd made leading up to this moment. All he wanted to do was drag her away from the others and press his lips to hers, eliciting those breathless whimpers from her, and all she clearly wanted to do was kill him.

He lost track of the conversations. Instead, he breathed in the scent of pine, watching the sun cast dancing shadows before them.

I'm sorry, he wanted to tell Wren. But Audra's words came back to him.

Fraternizing with the wards is strictly forbidden.

He'd fraternized, alright. Now it was purely a matter of degree, and willpower – which faltered every time he caught the poisoner's eye.

He opened his mouth to say something to her – what, he didn't know. He just couldn't stand the silence, the rage rolling off her in waves—

All at once, the quiet of the road shattered like glass.

Around two dozen men, their masks obscured by dark hoods, emerged from the dense undergrowth on all sides, brandishing swords and spears, arrows nocked and ready. Roderick's horses reared in panic, and the older man struggled to get them under control. Torj made a grab for the reins, to wrangle the poor beasts back into submission, but they were terrified, and as the ambushers closed in, a masked man sliced through the lead ropes and reins, freeing the horses.

The creatures bolted, leaving the cart and their master behind, dust billowing in their wake.

The enemy moved with trained precision, quickly encircling the group and cutting off any easy escape routes. Torj had his war hammer in his hand, scanning the blur of movement around them for an opening to get Wren through.

Also on his feet, Cal had his arrows nocked and ready to fly. 'Torj?' he asked.

'Loose,' Torj shouted, leaping from the cart and ploughing into the unit of attackers with a powerful swing of his hammer.

Cal's arrows went flying. Dessa screamed. It was not a scream of fear, but of rage as she snatched up Roderick's riding crop and unleashed a series of blows on a man grabbing at her ankles.

Beside her, Wren's hands were at her belt, distributing potions between her fellow alchemists. They sent them hurtling into the attacking force; cries of agony followed. But enemy arrows fired back, whistling through the air. One grazed Torj's arm, slicing through leather and flesh. He barely registered the burn of it, already swinging his hammer to cave in the archer's skull with a sickening crunch.

Another scream sounded. Torj whipped around in time to see Dessa reaching for Roderick, who was being dragged from the cart.

Wren flung a small knife in his direction. There was a startled cry as the blade found its mark in the assailant's neck. But a wave of attackers tipped the cart, sending Wren and her friends airborne before they hit the ground hard, skidding across the road. Without the advantage of the high ground, they clambered to their feet amid the ambush, reaching for whatever weapons they had or could steal.

From there, the conflict descended into utter chaos. Torj lost sight of Wren as three attackers converged on him at once. He took a glancing blow to the ribs before his hammer smashed through a jaw and then an exposed throat, arterial blood spraying.

He pummelled his hammer into the next attacker who dared to charge him. The impact ricocheted up his arm as the sickening crack of bone breaking beneath iron sounded. He cut his way toward Wren, whose bronze hair glinted in the sun amid the swarm of bodies. Desperation clawed at him, roaring at him to reach her side, to protect her—

An arrow punched into his shoulder. He barely felt it, wild with bloodlust and single-minded purpose.

He reached Wren just as a trio of black-garbed figures did, blades flashing. Torj roared and launched himself bodily at them, hammer crushing flesh and bone. He positioned himself in front of Wren, shielding her, an immovable wall of bloodied iron. She was his to protect, his to guard.

'Torj, get down!' Wren's voice was pure command.

He ducked without hesitation, lightning spearing over his head to blast a lunging swordsman into oblivion. Wren stepped up beside him, hands alive with crackling energy, thunder booming overhead as storm clouds swirled into being at her call. She was magnificent, a queen of chaos, wreathed in lightning and fury.

He swung his hammer again, while Cal and Zavier continued to meet the onslaught head-on. Zavier brandished an elegant sword that Torj hadn't seen before. Out of arrows, Cal unsheathed his own Naarvian steel blade, and together, the pair's shouts punctuated the flash of steel. Dessa and Kipp used the upturned cart as a wall against the onslaught, throwing more of Wren's potions from behind it, while beside them, Roderick hurled a series of empty glass jars at the attackers.

Heat blasted alongside Torj as a bolt of brilliant white light carved through the air. Whatever lingered in his scar recognized its likeness, a strange sensation rising in his chest.

The enemy was closing in like a pack of hungry wolves who had scented blood in the wind, none of them deterred by the powerful storm whipping up around them.

'Wren, take cover with the others,' Torj shouted, eyeing up a duo who were making straight for her.

'You take cover,' Wren bit back, directing a bolt of magic to an attacker on his left. Out of practice, she missed, but struck again, determined as ever, hitting her target this time.

Torj whirled his hammer, carving a path through the main group of assailants, his movements a practised symphony of wrath and iron.

Wren fought alongside him, refusing to hide.

'Gods, woman. Do you ever listen?' he muttered, dodging another blow and delivering a bone-shattering strike of his own.

'Do *you*?' Wren replied, tipping her head to the gathering clouds. Wind tore through the trees, thunder rumbling around them, and at her call, the sky opened up.

Attackers fell before them like stalks of wheat beneath a scythe. Torj couldn't look away, not even as he kept swinging his hammer, not even as a word formed on Wren's lips, her eyes widening in horror—

Three men attempted to take him down at once, leaping upon his right side and wrangling his arm away from his body. Something cold and hard closed around his wrist.

Despite the men latched to his arm, he lifted it, realizing what they'd done.

A manacle had been clamped in place there.

All at once, it was as if he'd been plunged underwater, half his strength and senses muffled, nausea twisting his gut. He staggered, struggling to breathe past the vice crushing his chest.

The Furies-given strength in his whole right side had been snuffed out like a candle.

It was a good thing his dominant hand was the left.

With a furious shout, he tore the first man off him, pulling his arm from its socket in the process. The scream that followed was near deafening. A moment later, he sent the second attacker hurtling through the trees, and had the third by the throat, squeezing the life out of him—

'Torj!'

His name sounded distant, muted beneath the roaring in his ears. He surged back towards her, half of his strength still dulled. A bellow of primal rage escaped him and he lashed out as he saw a streak of silver slice through the air. A spear, heading for Wren.

It whistled as it flew straight for her heart.

There was no time.

All Torj could do was throw himself in front of it.

He dived into its path, blocking Wren with his body. White-hot agony punched through his side, a gleaming point piercing through armour and flesh to grate against bone. He felt his blood gushing out, but still he fought, running on pure adrenaline and desperation.

He would not let them take her. Wren was his to protect, his to shield, *his*.

He fought. And fought. And fought.

Until darkness crashed over him like a wave, dragging him down into its cold embrace. He couldn't see, could barely hear, and all he could smell was thick smoke.

For a brief moment, he tasted the end, felt the underworld yawn open in greeting beneath him. He had faced death many times before, but this . . . this was the first time he wasn't ready. There was something – *someone* – he didn't want to leave behind.

Torj clawed to stay in the heart of the battle, shouting as the clash of metal echoed in the distance.

The last thing he saw was a blinding flash of lightning. The last thing he heard was Wren screaming his name.

CHAPTER 60

Torj

'When uncertainty creeps into the heart of the guardian, the walls of defence crumble'

– *The Guardian's Handbook:*
Principles and Practices of Personal Protection

TORJ WOKE IN a blur of confusion, struggling to take in his surroundings. He reached for his hammer. Which wasn't there. Nor was his sword. Or his dagger.

Flailing, his head spinning, he realized that he wasn't on the battlefield, or on his horse. He was in a bed, and not his own. It smelled of spring rain and jasmine, of a life he coveted and would never have.

Wren's bed. He was in Wren's bed. His large frame took up the entirety of the mattress, but someone had taken great care to ensure his comfort: pillows beneath his head, blankets tucked around his body.

Torj tried to sit up, the details still fuzzy, still unable to comprehend exactly what was happening, but a small, firm hand pressed him back down into the sheets.

'Easy,' a familiar voice murmured, as something damp and cool pressed against his brow. It felt good. His skin was hot beneath it, but the heat ebbed away beneath the compress.

But he reared up again. It wasn't his job to lie idle while someone nursed him—

'No you don't,' Wren commanded. 'You're not going anywhere.'

At long last, Torj blinked the room back into focus and spotted the beautiful poisoner at his bedside. 'Embers,' he croaked, trying again to rise.

'Move a single muscle from this bed, Bear Slayer, and I'll pour a sleeping draught down your throat.'

Torj stilled.

'Better,' Wren said.

'What happened?' he managed, scanning her from head to toe for any signs of injury. But Wren stared back at him, unharmed, her eyes brimming with that same resilience and determination he always saw there.

'You took on a group of them,' she said slowly. 'You tore them apart. Ripped limbs from bodies, even with your strength halved . . . It was a bloodbath. And when Cal saw what you were doing, he joined you. I've never seen anything like it.'

Torj's breath rattled out of him. 'I don't really remember . . . What happened after?'

'What always happens,' she replied. 'You Warswords took charge without so much as a thought, and a storm wielder had to swoop in and finish the job.'

'We were still outnumbered . . . ?'

'Not against lightning, Bear Slayer,' she replied. 'Though I'll admit . . . I don't have the control I once did. I'm . . . out of practice.'

He swallowed painfully before he asked, 'But they're all dead?'

'Or wishing they were, yes. I finished it.'

'Oh.'

'Sounds familiar?'

'More than I care to admit.'

Wren held a canteen to his lips. 'Drink.'

He didn't dare disobey. Cool, fresh water hit his lips, and he made an undignified noise as it washed over his parched tongue. When he'd finished drinking, Wren gently took the canteen away and watched him closely.

'What about Cal? Kipp? Your teammates? What about the cart driver?'

'All safe. All unharmed. Zavier sent up a smoke signal while you were still fighting. Drevenor sent guards to retrieve us, and Dessa sedated the injured attackers and anyone trying to escape, so they were easy to take into custody. None of us were seriously injured. No one except for you . . .'

'How bad?' he asked slowly.

'Bad enough to bring you here. You took an arrow to the shoulder, a spear to your side – a spear meant for me . . .'

At her words, the memory came crashing down on him, filling him with that same desperate need to protect. He hardly remembered tearing the enemy apart with his bare hands, but whoever they were, they had deserved what they got.

'Farissa's been to see you, of course,' Wren continued. 'Can't have a novice treating a legendary Warsword. But she's assured me that I'm more than qualified to tend to you.'

'I'm not worried about that.'

'Well, you should be. I wounded you once before—'

He pressed a finger to her lips, silencing her. 'All you have ever done, Wren Embervale, is save me. You can argue with me, tell me off all you like, give me the silent treatment, but that? I won't hear you say that again.'

She narrowed her eyes, and he thought for a second that she would fight back. Instead, she pulled away, tending to something at her workbench.

'It's certainly not the first time you've patched me up, anyway,' he said lightly. He waited for her to glance his way before he gestured to the small, neat scar between his pectoral and shoulder. 'The Furies were smiling down on me the day we met as well.'

'I have no idea what you're talking about,' Wren replied, busying herself with stirring something.

The logical part of his mind knew she just wanted a rise out of him, that there was no way she'd forgotten that afternoon. He'd felt that pull towards her from the moment he'd clapped eyes on her. And he remembered it like it was yesterday – the dirt staining her apron, the orders that brooked no argument, the leaf in her hair . . .

Now, Wren thrust a cup at him. 'Drink this. It should bring down your temperature.'

'Feverfew?' he asked, remembering their time in the gardens that he cherished so dearly.

'You'd make a good alchemist,' she said, pushing the steaming cup towards him.

He took a sip of the tea, not surprised that it tasted like dirt. 'No, I wouldn't.'

Wren huffed a laugh. 'No, you wouldn't.'

Torj winced as he shifted, realizing that he was injured worse than he thought. A sharp pain seared his side. It must be a deep wound. He vaguely remembered a blade hitting bone . . .

'How . . . ?' he murmured.

'You mean how did they get past your Warsword prowess to hurt you so badly?' Wren offered.

Torj grimaced. 'Without wanting to sound arrogant . . . Yes.'

'They used the manacles on you. Or tried to, at least. Same ones as they used on me. Considering I originally designed them to subdue a Warsword, it's not surprising that they were effective against you. They only managed to get one on, which was how you were able to keep fighting, but it's worrying . . . Audra agrees that it means at some point they produced more of them. The pair I created during the war was a sample model. It appears they moved past that phase of development . . .'

He couldn't think of the irons now. All that mattered was the woman standing before him. 'You . . . Are you—'

'Perfectly fine.'

He loosed a painful breath. 'I failed you. I—'

'I won't hear it, Torj.' Her voice was sharp as a blade, hard as iron. 'You did your duty. You almost lost your life in doing so. If you torture yourself over this, I'll stab you myself.'

Torj met her gaze and was astounded by the woman staring back at him, a warrior in her own right, a force to be reckoned with.

Something must have shown in his expression, because Wren nodded to herself and handed him something else, something small and round and golden.

'More terrible-tasting alchemy?' he asked.

'Actually, it's salted caramel.'

Torj stared at her. 'Who are you and what have you done with Wren Embervale?'

'Shut up and eat your sweets, Warsword.'

He wisely did as he was told.

Torj hadn't been wounded this badly since long before the war. Not since he'd fought those cursed bears in Tver and one of them had got a deep slice across his middle that had festered on his way back to Thezmarr. He realized all too quickly that being bed-bound didn't suit him, especially with Wren by his side day and night, administering tonics and tinctures.

'When were you going to tell me about the People's Vanguard?' she asked a few days later as she mixed something at her workbench.

Torj grimaced, trying to sit up. 'Soon.'

Wren raised a brow. 'Not even mildly convincing, Bear Slayer.'

'Who told you?' he asked, his voice rough.

'Audra briefed me yesterday. The attack on the road wasn't an isolated incident; they coordinated assassination attempts all over the midrealms. They came after Thea while she was guarding Queen Reyna in Aveum. But Reyna had a vision – saw it coming and was able to warn them. King Leiko's Warsword guard managed to get him to safety and slay the attackers. They caught the assailants before they even made it into the palace at Harenth.'

'Gods . . .'

'Everyone is fine,' Wren told him. 'More than fine, actually. Between our efforts here and Thea's in Aveum, as well as those of your Warsword comrades in Tver and Harenth, the threat has been subdued. Audra has more people in custody than she knows what to do with.'

'They're being interrogated, I assume?'

'Naturally. By all accounts so far, it looks as though we thwarted their efforts. There's talk of pulling back the additional security measures as early as next week.'

'So soon?'

Wren nodded. 'The rulers and the various councils are wary of spreading resources too thin and don't want to be seen prioritizing the wellbeing of the rulers over the common folk – which was half of what the rebels were campaigning against. Kipp was able to reverse engineer a lot of their strategies . . . If they weren't caught in the act, they've been hunted down and imprisoned based on that information.'

Wren brought a dish of rancid-looking paste over to him, along with a bowl of steaming salted water. Seating herself on the edge of the bed, she drew back the covers carefully. 'As such, you may not be stuck as my guard for much longer . . .'

Torj faltered. Months ago, he would have done anything to hear those words, to be relieved of his position by her maddening side. Now, unease gripped him, and he found himself wanting to argue.

Instead, he hissed in pain as she began to remove the bandages at his side. 'Well, that's a relief . . .'

'For both of us, I'm sure.'

He glanced down at his wound. Covered in the crusted paste she'd applied yesterday, it looked particularly gruesome. It hurt like a bitch, too.

'I'm going to have to clean it and reapply this,' Wren said apologetically.

'Go ahead. I've had worse—'

She swept a warm rag across the injury and Torj had to bite the inside of his cheek to stop a stream of curses from spilling out. But Wren's touch was gentle and efficient, the practised hands of someone who had done this kind of work time and time again. Dipping the linen back in the water, she cleared the old paste from the wound and inspected it, pressing her fingertips lightly to the skin around it.

'Well, it's not infected,' she said with a note of satisfaction. 'I was worried the solution they treat their blades with might act as some sort of delayed poison, but that doesn't seem to be the case. This is just a regular flesh wound.'

'What good news,' Torj muttered with a wince as she finished her poking.

A smile tugged at her mouth. 'Don't be ungrateful. This could have been much worse.'

Torj watched as strands of bronze hair escaped her bun and fell across her eyes. Gods, she was breathtaking. She needed no cosmetics, no fancy gown or jewels. She was perfect in her own skin, doing the thing she loved.

'I am . . .' His voice was hoarse.

Wren looked up, brow furrowed.

'Grateful.' Torj swallowed. 'I am grateful, you know.'

Wren's expression softened as she applied the fresh paste across the wound, the cool glide of it across his skin instantly soothing the pain and irritation.

'I know,' she replied, wiping her hands clean on another scrap of fabric.

'Were you scared?' he asked. 'During the attack?'

Wren's hands stilled. 'I was scared for you.'

'Not *of* me?'

'Why would I be scared of you?'

Taking a deep breath, Torj gathered himself. He had never spoken the next words aloud before. 'When I fight . . . I have to go to a dark place inside myself. Become something more animal than man . . .'

Understanding filled Wren's eyes, but Torj told her anyway.

'What I become in the heat of battle . . . It reminds me of my father. Sometimes I worry that the same blood flows through my veins. That I have the same violence, the same potential to become what he was. That I could be a monster.'

Wren's hand covered his. 'You're not.'

'How can you know?'

Torj's heart stuttered as Wren brought his palm to her chest. Even through the fabric of her shirt and bodice, the touch sent a jolt through him. He could feel *himself* there.

'I can feel it,' she said. Her gaze was fierce upon him, a storm within waiting to break, ready to fight him, should the need arise. 'Through whatever curse links us, I can feel what you are. And you are no monster, Torj Elderbrock.'

CHAPTER 61
Wren

'Fear in itself is a poison'

— *Elwren Embervale's notes and observations*

WREN THOUGHT SHE had known fear. The shadow war had taught her plenty. She had known it in the moments before realizing her dearest friends were dead, in seeing her eldest sister struck with darkness across the battlefield, in seeing an arachne fang protruding from Kipp's chest . . . Worse still had been seeing Torj suspended in the air over that vortex of darkness, not knowing if she could save him. The fear in those moments had run bone-deep; she could taste the bitterness of them even now.

But seeing Torj speared in her place on the road . . .

She had never known terror like it.

A terror that had her storm nearly bring down the sky.

She would never forget it for as long as she lived. Her heart ached even now as she watched the healing Warsword sleep.

Wren had barely left her room for days, missing lessons and tasks assigned by the masters, and for once, she didn't care. Her place was at Torj's side. The Warsword had thrown himself in front of a spear meant for her. She would see to his recovery herself, or she had no business being at the academy at all. She could manage her workload from here.

She could no longer recall how many times she had counted his breaths in his sleep, how many times she had pressed the back of her hand to his brow to check for fever. Sometimes, she simply stared, watching his unfairly long lashes flutter against the tops of his cheeks as he dreamed. When he had tossed and turned and his shirt had fallen open, she looked upon the web of lightning-shaped scars there, at her mark carved into his flesh. It took all manner of self-restraint not to trace them with her fingers, not to be overcome by guilt.

In the past, she hadn't known him – not well. But Furies, had she wanted to. Now, she knew small, intimate things. Like that the Warsword murmured in his sleep. A handful of phrases that sank hard into her chest: *I'll save you. I'll protect you. I'll always protect you.*

With a sigh, she sat back in the chair at his side, thumbing through the book in her lap without actually reading it, her attention constantly drifting back to the warrior in her bed. To her great surprise, the Bear Slayer had been a model patient, except for when she'd tried to help him in the bathing chamber.

'I refuse to let the first time you touch me be for a fucking sponge bath, Embers,' he had growled.

Wren had quietly backed away, giving him his privacy, but not without repeating his words in her mind. *The first time you touch me . . .*

'That's a dangerous look,' he said to her now, rubbing the sleep from his eyes.

She raised a brow. 'What look?'

'The one that was just written all over your face. Kingdoms fall over looks like that.'

'My kingdom's already fallen,' Wren scoffed.

With a wince, Torj pulled himself into a sitting position. Wren was instantly on her feet, arranging the pillows behind him to give him more support.

'Stop fussing,' he told her gruffly, but his words were warm, as though he actually *liked* her fussing.

'Stop complaining,' she quipped, sitting back in her chair.

'No horrible potion for me to force down this morning?' he asked, eyes twinkling.

'Not yet,' she replied. 'It's brewing—'

The door burst open, and Wren found herself shoved back.

Torj had leapt from the bed and thrown himself in front of her, wearing nothing but a pair of undershorts and a tattered shirt. He shielded her bodily, scanning the room wildly, no doubt for his hammer.

'I'm in love,' Kipp declared, flinging the door closed behind him and dragging another chair up to the bedside.

Sagging with relief, Wren slapped Torj's arm. 'If you've ripped your stitches, I'll not be impressed.'

Torj groaned before rounding on Kipp. 'What the fuck are you thinking, bursting in like that? If I wasn't half drugged to the moon I might have killed you.'

Kipp's brows shot up. 'Drugged to the moon? That sounds fun.' He turned to Wren. 'I'll have what he's having.'

Wren ducked out from behind the towering Warsword and gently pushed him back towards the bed, noting that the bandage at his side was stained with fresh blood.

'Sorry,' he muttered.

'You will be,' she replied, waiting until he was lying down once more to inspect the wound.

'Didn't anyone hear me?' Kipp said impatiently. 'I said: I'm in love.'

The door opened a fraction and Cal's voice drifted in. 'It wasn't all that long ago you were insisting that you and Wren would end up together.'

Wren whipped around to face her friend. 'What?'

Kipp waved her off as though it were a minor detail. 'Ancient history, Your Queenliness. Long before I knew you were spoken for—'

He stopped abruptly and gave Torj a wary glance. 'I mean, before I knew you were such a formidable killer. I'd never survive you. And I like surviving.'

Wren's eyes narrowed before she turned back to Torj and carefully peeled the dressing away from his injury. 'Who is it this time, then?'

'Dessa.'

'Naturally,' Cal said from where he now leaned against the doorjamb.

'Shouldn't you be guarding out there?' Torj called.

He shook his head. 'There are two other burly Guardians from Thezmarr here. Don't you worry, Bear Slayer. Besides, the guild has formally declared that the threat is over. They captured the leader last night.'

'If you're going to stand there, just come in and shut the door,' Wren told him.

Cal did as she bid. Torj gave her an incredulous look, but she ignored him. He'd torn three of his stitches in his leap to defend her, but the bleeding had slowed, and she decided against restitching them.

'So, you're in love, Kipp. What's the problem?' she asked.

Kipp sighed dramatically. 'Only the world against us. She's an alchemist, I'm a – strategist. A Guardian of Thezmarr. We're too different.'

'Really?' Torj scoffed. 'You're like two peas in a pod to me. Neither of you know when to shut up, for a start.'

'You wound me, Bear Slayer.'

'Nothing wounds you,' Cal added from where he had perched himself on her workbench. 'Not even a fucking arachne fang to the heart.'

'I assure you, that hurt plenty.'

'And yet here you are. Living to annoy us all for another day.'

'I'm not sure I appreciate this line of conversation,' Kipp commented. 'I come to you with a problem, and this is what I get? Where's the sympathy? The support?'

'You'll no doubt find plenty down at the Mortar and Pestle,' Wren said. 'But this isn't a tearoom for gossip. This is a makeshift infirmary, in case you haven't noticed.'

Kipp looked alarmed, his eyes latching onto Torj. 'Don't tell me you've drunk any tea *she's* given you?'

A rough laugh escaped Torj. 'Every drop, Snowden. Guess that makes me invincible now.'

'Or an idiot,' Kipp retorted.

'Kipp.' Wren crossed her arms over her chest. 'If you've just come here to be a menace, kindly piss off. Torj needs rest.'

Kipp gave a mock gasp. 'Such filth from a princess' mouth. Unbelievable. It wasn't all that long ago you were wishing *he'd* piss off. How times have changed, eh?'

She rolled her eyes. 'I'm sure *Odessa* would love to hear all about it.'

Kipp shook his head and got to his feet. 'After all these years of friendship, you turn me away during my time of need.'

'I still don't see the problem,' Wren replied. 'But you'll figure it out, being the strategist you are and all that.'

'*Love* is the problem!' Kipp insisted. 'But I know when I'm not wanted—'

'Finally,' Torj muttered. Wren had to bite down a laugh at Kipp's wildly offended expression.

When Cal at last managed to escort Kipp out of the rooms, Wren shook her head, unable to stop the smile of disbelief breaking across her face. 'Where did we even find him?'

'I'm surprised it wasn't at the bottom of a wine barrel somewhere,' Torj replied, a smile softening his features.

Warmth bloomed in Wren's chest. 'Truth be told, I'm not sure what I'd do without him . . .'

'Maybe you should tell him that one day.'

'Maybe . . . Though I'd never hear the end of it.'

'True.'

Wren shifted in her seat, smoothing out her apron. 'Do you think he's really in love with Dessa?'

Torj snorted. 'Kipp's in love every other week.'

'So that's a no?'

The Warsword shrugged. 'I suppose it's not for me to say. The Son of the Fox knows his own heart. When it's not located in his liver.'

Quiet settled between them for a moment, the air shifting with tension as the words formed on Wren's tongue: 'And you?'

Heat flared in Torj's eyes, in stark contrast to their deep-sea hue. 'What about me?'

'Have you ever been in love?'

'Every man thinks he's been in love at one point or another in life.'

A swell of envy swept through her, leaving a bitter taste in her mouth.

'But I don't think so,' he continued, voice low. 'Not truly, not deeply. Not since—'

'It's alright,' she cut him off, suddenly realizing she didn't actually *want* to know the answer. She had heard the stories. She had seen how people looked at him . . . She just didn't know why she cared. Torj was older, well-travelled, worldly . . . He likely had more experience in his little finger than she'd had in her whole life. And experience . . . That was good, wasn't it?

'How many women have you been with?' she heard herself ask.

He raised that scarred brow of his. 'Rather personal question there, Embers . . .'

Heat stained her cheeks. 'A great many, then.'

'Do you want me to lie?' he asked gently.

'Never.'

The fire in his gaze was akin to the desire that had once blazed there in these very rooms, where they'd watched each other find release in a haze of desperation and longing.

'Then I'll say this,' he told her. 'There have been many, yes.'

Wren's ribs squeezed tight, her heartbeat quickening.

'But it's not about the fleeting moments that came before, or the number of lovers who've warmed a bed.'

'Then what is it about?' she managed.

Torj reached out and brushed a gentle thumb over her lower lip, and her breath caught in her throat.

'It's about the person who's holding your hand at the end. The person you can't let go of, no matter how hard you might have tried.'

CHAPTER 62

Torj

'A bodyguard's lapse in judgement, however fleeting, can be the catalyst for calamity'

– The Protector's Manual: A Practical Guide for Safeguarding Nobility and Royalty

Thanks to Wren, Torj recovered far quicker than he had from any other wound. Her constant care meant he was back on his feet weeks earlier than he might have been otherwise, and back in the training ring much sooner as well. She watched him like a hawk, warning him not to push himself too hard too soon, and though he'd never admit it out loud, her concern for him touched him deeply.

'Does your recovery mean you'll be off on your secret Warsword excursions again before long?' she asked casually one afternoon, flipping through an enormous tome.

'Probably,' Torj replied, suppressing a grimace. He'd barely thought of his secondary mission since his injury, but at its mention, he instantly dreaded having to make another report to Audra. He liked the idea of doing more field research even less.

'Care to tell me where you've been going?' Wren pressed, a single brow raised.

'It would go against my orders,' he said roughly.

He was no stranger to bending the rules when it suited him, but this? The truth would only hurt Wren. He knew she would blame herself for whatever fate awaited him, and he refused to subject her to such anguish, not after everything she had done for him.

She made a dissatisfied noise, turning back to her book. 'I suppose things will go back to normal now the perpetrators of the royal attacks have been captured . . .'

'So it seems,' Torj allowed. 'Security has certainly lessened.'

'And what will you do after this bodyguard duty ends?' Wren closed her book and turned to labour over her experiments, taking notes on shallow dishes of strange substances. Torj had been horrified to learn that she'd been using *her own blood* in her investigation into the unknown alchemy. But it explained the dots of crimson that often peppered her shirtsleeves at the crook of her elbow.

He cleared his throat. 'I'm to be posted abroad.'

'Oh.' Wren didn't look up from where she was using a dropper to add pale pink liquid to one of her samples. 'How far abroad?'

'Beyond the boundaries of where the Veil used to be,' he replied, unable to stop himself from pacing across the room. 'There are many places we haven't yet explored. Places with different kinds of magic, different creatures . . . I've been wanting to go since—'

He cut himself off. *Since before you sabotaged my chances by killing Edmund Riverton,* was what he was going to say, but it somehow didn't feel right now. The anger that had boiled so hotly in the wake of that event was gone. He did not resent being here, being her guard. In fact . . . he rather liked it.

'Since?' Wren prompted.

'Since the war,' he said instead.

She nodded to herself, still not meeting his gaze. 'Then I'm happy for you. That you'll get to go where you've always wanted. Another adventure to your name . . .'

What he wanted was to tell her that life had been full of adventure with her at his side, that he needed nothing more, wanted nothing more. But she wouldn't look at him.

'It's the life of a Warsword,' he told her.

Wren's quill scratched against parchment as she scrawled something furiously across the page. 'So it is.'

Torj returned to his usual duties of escorting Wren to her classes and assignments tasked by the masters. He knew she had given up a lot of time and opportunities to look after him in those first few weeks after his injury, and so he tried to help her in any way he could: bringing her food when she'd forgotten to stop for a break; leaving his restricted books open for her to read, knowing that she didn't have clearance for the masters' section of the archives. Sometimes he'd find her asleep at her workbench, and he'd carry her to bed and drape the blankets over her. In those quiet breaths of hers between waking and sleep, he'd allow himself a moment to drink her in, to imagine another life, where things might have been different between them.

He dreaded the missive from Audra telling him he was no longer needed as the poisoner's guard, but it didn't come. The post abroad he had wanted so badly now felt like an ambition belonging to someone else.

As the Gauntlet drew closer, and Wren's efforts intensified, Torj found that the storm magic lingering inside him did the same. He felt her passion and her fury beneath his scars like it was a part of him, and there was no greater privilege than to watch her come into her own as she surpassed every expectation put upon her shoulders.

Something had shifted between bodyguard and ward – something minute to the outside eye, but undeniable to Torj himself. He'd never told anyone about his past before, not Wilder or Talemir, not Cal or Kipp. He had long since suspected that Farissa knew, as she'd known his grandmother years before, but he'd talked to no one about it. Until Wren. When she wasn't scowling or sniping at his overprotective nature, she was easy to talk to. There was no judgement, no pressure, only a quiet thoughtfulness that made him *want* to talk to her, *want* to share things he'd buried deep down.

It was so much more than just words. Months had passed and he still thought daily about what she'd told Dessa on their run. That no man had brought her to orgasm. It was one of *many* things he wanted to share with her.

'What are you thinking?' she asked from her workbench, having paused to survey him.

He was sitting on the edge of her bed, cleaning his weapons while she worked. His hands stilled over the runes on his hammer.

'Nothing,' he said, clearing his throat. 'Why?'

Wren chewed her lower lip. 'You had a look . . .'

'Oh?'

Her hand drifted to her chest. 'And I felt . . . something.'

'Did you now, Embers?' He let the teasing note linger and waited for her to object to the nickname.

She didn't. Instead, she picked up a small blue vial and brought it to him. 'Here.'

'What's this?' he asked.

'It's a cleaning aid,' she told him. 'I made it for you – for your war hammer.' She knelt at his side, and all the thoughts emptied out of Torj's head.

Wren was on her knees. He couldn't count how many times he'd imagined her exactly like that.

Cursing himself and his filthy mind, he exhaled a tight breath and looked at her, trying not to stare at her pretty mouth and the dusting of freckles across her nose.

She uncorked the vial and took the rag he'd been using from his hand. Only decades of training enabled him to remain still, ignoring the jolt of electricity that passed between them as his fingers brushed hers.

Applying a generous amount of the concoction to the fabric, Wren swiped it across the weapon's iron head, and he watched with fascination as the grime and dried blood fizzled away into nothing, leaving his war hammer looking freshly forged.

'That's incredible,' he murmured, tracing the now clear runes with his thumb. 'Thank you.'

Pink stained Wren's cheeks. 'It was nothing.'

'No,' he told her. 'It wasn't.'

'We were asked to combine our knowledge of design and warfare. I thought something like this might be useful . . .' She tossed the vial to him as she got to her feet, and he caught it between his fingers.

'Well . . . Thank you for thinking of me,' he said, finding his voice hoarse.

'I do, you know,' she ventured. 'Think of you.'

Gods, his chest ached, and it took all his self-restraint not to go to her. 'And I you.'

She nodded stiffly, and they both returned to their work.

Preparations for the Gauntlet were well underway, and every team was pushing themselves to breaking point. The tension in the air was palpable. As the days passed, Wren became more private about her work, and Torj knew she was keeping things from him. They still talked, but sometimes when he entered her rooms, he could smell the metallic tang of blood, could taste the lightning singeing the air. But there was no trace of either – just potions and her usual chaos.

When Wren was immersed in her studies and experiments, Torj continued his research on magical injuries, often from his place on the end of her bed. *Royal Magic and Its Consequences. Accidental Curses and Life-Altering Events. The Thesaurus of Magical Connections.*

Each was blander and more uninformative than the last. Whenever Wren asked what he was reading, he'd wave one of the bodyguard textbooks at her. He'd taken to fitting their dust jackets around his true reading material, hoping that the titles alone would be enough to lose her interest.

Sitting on Wren's bed now, he tossed another book aside with a frustrated sigh and glanced up at the alchemist. Her hair was a mess, her sleeves rolled up to the elbows, and something purple stained her hands and was splattered across the front of her apron.

He traced the outline of his scars while he watched her. She was a vision, as always.

'I've been meaning to ask you,' he heard himself say, already regretting the words spilling from his traitorous mouth.

'Ask me what?' she said without turning around.

'What you asked me weeks ago . . . Have you ever been in love?'

He saw her hands still over her crucible, but she still didn't turn around. 'I have known the deep, enduring love of friendship, of sisterhood . . . But no, I've never been in love.'

'That makes two of us, then.'

'I thought you had,' she replied quietly. 'You told me not since . . .'

What he'd been about to say was *not since you*. 'You misunderstood,' was all he told her now.

'I see.'

He shifted uncomfortably. 'So, no romantic interests for you, then?'

'I've been with men, if that's what you're asking, Bear Slayer . . . But found them to be disappointing, shallow, and underwhelming at best. Thea thinks I became closed off after the war, but truthfully . . . it was happening long before then. She just wasn't around as much to see it.'

'And now?' Torj ventured slowly.

To his surprise, Wren laughed, a beautiful, melodic sound that he'd sell his soul to be the source of.

'Now there's a certain bodyguard who has issues with boundaries,' she said. 'So it's been harder to keep my walls up.'

A smile broke across his face at that, and Wren looked at him, smiling back.

'For what it's worth,' he told her, 'you deserve more. You deserve everything.' He stopped himself before he said something he shouldn't. Before he told her that if she was his, he'd never let her go.

He heard her sharp intake of breath, and her hands went to the ties of her apron. She undid the laces and lifted the fabric over her head, turning to him. 'You truly believe that?'

He felt his throat bob as he swallowed the lump that had formed there. 'You know I do.'

She stood in the centre of the room, her fingers still stained purple, a smudge of colour on her cheek as well. But there was nothing but thunder in her stare as she pinned him with it. 'And yet you refuse to give me what I want.'

Slowly, Torj stood, heart hammering. 'And what is it that you want, Embers?'

'I want to know what it's like,' she murmured as he took a step towards her. 'What it can be like . . . with someone like you.'

'Wren . . .' Her name shuddered out of him, a plea. 'We can't. I'm your bodyguard . . .' The words caused him physical pain as he forced them out. All the while, his steps betrayed him, closing the gap between them.

'Not here. Not inside these walls,' she said. 'Right now, it's just you and me. Torj and Wren. I know what I want. And I think you want it too.'

There was no hiding the bulge in his leathers, the rise and fall of his chest, and deeper still, the torrent of blazing magic coursing down the bond between them.

'What I want isn't a factor,' he ground out. His whole body was rigid with tension, with wavering restraint as he warred with himself, and Wren's gaze tracked the bunching of his muscles.

He couldn't breathe. Not with her so close, not with her scent wrapped around him like an intoxicating spell, not with the words she'd spoken swinging between them like a pendulum. He wanted to fall to his knees before her, to worship her.

'Tell me you don't want me, Bear Slayer,' she said, taking another step towards him.

The rules, the barriers – none of them mattered. All that mattered was the piece of her that had already burrowed itself deep in his heart.

'I'll never tell you that,' he murmured, before he lunged for her.

CHAPTER 63

Torj

'The line between the afflicted and the afflicter becomes blurred, raising profound questions about the nature of magical responsibility and culpability'

– *Magical Transference*

Torj crushed his body to hers, his mouth to hers. The kiss was searing and brutal, the culmination of months of denial. *Years.*

She tasted just as he remembered, just as he'd dreamed of every night. He traced her lips with his and moaned as she opened for him, allowing his tongue to sweep inside and brush against hers.

The noise that escaped her had his knees buckling, and as her body melded to his, he savoured every point of contact, every curve pressed against him, every burst of connection between them. He was drunk on her, and she was somehow in his blood, making him feverish, sending rushes of lightning coursing through him, the heat of her sending him into some kind of madness.

She kissed him back with matched ferocity, as though everything he felt, she felt as well.

Longing like he'd never known swept through him, and he cupped the back of her head, holding her in place as he claimed her mouth again with another deep, frenzied kiss. Her mouth moved with his, her tongue matching his stroke for stroke, her fingers raking down his chest as though she meant to tear his shirt open. It was enough to drive him completely and utterly wild. Gods, he wanted her – but first . . . first he wanted her falling apart at the seams for him.

He wanted to be the first man who undid her.

The *only* man.

He trailed his hands from the back of her neck down her body, tracing her curves ever so lightly, teasing her so she was arching into his touch. And then he spun her around, so that her back was pressed against his chest.

'Arms up around my neck, Embers.' The words came out as a rough demand, but he held his leash of control tightly as Wren obeyed, her arms shifting up around him.

He kissed the sensitive spot on her neck, and she pressed her backside against his rock-hard length, causing him to hiss through his teeth. Gods, she could make him come in his leathers just from that.

Gritting his teeth, he focused on her writhing body. It was entirely too clothed. His hands went to the laces at the front of her bodice. He'd been dying to cup her breasts and he was granted that wish as they spilled from the fabric. He groaned appreciatively as his hands closed over their soft fullness, her nipples hardening into his callused palms.

'Furies save me,' he muttered. 'You feel incredible.'

'Don't stop,' she gasped, bucking against him as he rolled a nipple beneath his thumb.

'The gods themselves couldn't hold me back now, Embers . . .' He squeezed her breast in one hand while the other bunched up the fabric of her skirts. 'I have dreamed about this for so long,' he told her, trying to steady his breathing as his hand grazed the soft skin of her bare thigh.

'So have I . . .' she panted, as his hand climbed higher still.

'What did you dream of?' he whispered, pinching her nipple again, eliciting a cry of rapture from her.

'Of you,' she managed. 'I dreamed of you, of your hands on me, of your mouth . . . and your cock . . . Seeing you touch yourself that day . . . I—'

She moaned as Torj dragged his finger through the wetness at her centre.

It was exactly how he'd imagined. Soft and slick, perfect.

He drew a featherlight line through her arousal and her nails dug into the back of his neck as she bowed off him. His cock was about to burst through his leathers, but he ignored the insistent pulse of it. This was about Wren, about worshiping her so thoroughly his name would be on her tongue for days to come. For ever, if he had his way.

He caught a glimpse of them in the mirror, the sight making him groan. There was something so filthy about having her like this, skirts bunched around her thighs, her bodice undone, breasts bare.

'Look at you,' he said, directing her stare to her flushed reflection. 'Gods, you're beautiful.'

'Torj . . .' she pleaded, her cheeks tipped pink at the sight of them together.

Slowly, torturously, he began to circle her clit in earnest, and she rocked against him, demanding more. He built pressure and speed as though he had all the time in the world, revelling in every cry that escaped her at his touch.

Wren spread her legs wide, not seeming to care that she was completely exposed, that he could see the sheen of her arousal in the mirror, or that his gaze flitted all over her body as she moved with him.

Torj took her to the edge, and then eased a finger inside her.

She was as tight and wet as he'd imagined, clenching around the single digit. The thought of sliding his cock into her had him groaning into the crook of her neck, where he bit down on the soft flesh there, just as he added a second finger.

Wren moaned, and he lifted his other hand from her breast to cover her mouth, muffling her sounds.

'That's it, Embers . . .' he coaxed her, moving his fingers rhythmically in and out of her, rubbing her clit with the heel of his hand as he did. 'Take what you need.'

She ground back against him.

'Not that,' he said, a chuckle on his lips.

Wren made a stifled noise of protest.

'Not yet,' he clarified, driving his fingers into her again, feeling her bite into his palm to keep from screaming. 'You don't get my cock yet, Embers. Because when I fuck you . . . We're going to need all. Damn. Night.'

CHAPTER 64

Wren

'The alchemist of war engineers tinctures of destruction with meticulous precision'

— *Transformative Arts of Alchemy*

TORJ'S FILTHY WORDS were punctuated by the deliberate thrust of his thick fingers inside her, and Wren lost all control. The pleasure that had been building and building within blossomed into something that hurtled into her, a tempest breaking upon the shores.

Shattering into a million pieces, she broke away from the hand over her mouth and moaned loudly as it hit, her legs giving out beneath her, her arms slipping from around Torj's neck.

He caught her.

'That's it,' he murmured, his fingers still moving, still circling the most sensitive part of her until she was shaking. What had he done to her? She was a molten mess.

She caught a glimpse of herself in the mirror on the other side of the room. He'd called her a vixen before, and now she looked the part. Half her hair had escaped her bun; her breasts were exposed, nipples hard, and her skirts were still hiked up around her thighs. Her cheeks flushed at the sight, but he took her chin between his fingers and forced her to look at him.

'You're fucking perfect,' he said, his voice strained with want. 'Even better than in my dreams.'

She could still feel him between her legs, under her skin, in her magic. From the weight of his stare alone, she knew he could feel her too. The thing coursing between them was alive, heat surging through the strange tether she had forged on that fateful day at Thezmarr.

There was a dark glimmer to Torj's sea-blue eyes, and he dipped his head to hers, kissing her soundly. She had expected him to pull away the moment her climax faded, but this kiss was just as intense, just as claiming as those that had come before. He wasn't taking it back . . .

She moaned into his mouth, the need for him already blooming back to life, her hands gripping fistfuls of his shirt, dragging him closer. She knew it was wrong, knew that there were a thousand reasons why she shouldn't have asked for it . . . but the thing between them was palpable, a force so powerful, pulling them together in a way that she just couldn't understand. Nor did she care to, not with his mouth on hers and his fingers tracing down her spine.

All of a sudden, she knew what Ida, Sam, and Thea had talked about all those years before. How it could *be* with a man . . . Though, not just any man for her. *This* man.

Her hands moved south to where that irresistible bulge tented his leathers, when a knock sounded at the door.

At least Torj had the good sense to gently guide her into the bathing room, closing the door once she was inside, giving her the privacy to fix herself up before whoever was at the door spotted her. She recognized Cal's muffled voice as she adjusted her skirts and re-laced her bodice. Releasing her hair from its pin, she combed out the knots with her fingers before sweeping it back up into a neater bun. There was nothing she could do about her swollen, bruised lips, or the red mark Torj had left on the side of her neck. She flushed at the sight of it, brushing her fingers along the subtle teeth indents there.

He had truly claimed her. And she'd liked it. She'd liked it *a lot*.

A soft knock sounded, and the door swung inwards without another moment's warning. Torj entered the bathing chamber, his gaze heating as he spotted the mark on her neck.

He reached for her without hesitation and drew her body to his, leaning down to kiss her fiercely. For a moment they were lost in one another again, before Torj pulled away with a frustrated noise.

'Cal's just brought word. I've got orders from Thezmarr. He's here to relieve me.'

Wren's stomach dropped. 'You're leaving?'

'Not for long,' he assured her, tucking her hair behind her ear and kissing her again. 'They couldn't keep me away with a hundred Warswords.'

Wren scanned his face, waiting for the familiar shift in him. 'You don't regret . . . ?' She glanced down, and though most of the evidence of what they'd just done was gone, she knew from the heat in his stare that he was picturing it all over again.

His eyes were like a brand. 'My only regret is waiting so long. And not being able to finish what I started.' He kissed her hard and deep, creating a whirlpool within that had her hands shooting to the buttons of his leathers, but he broke away reluctantly once more. 'There's no going back now, Embers.'

'Is that so?'

He huffed a laugh as he reached for the door. 'Not a fucking chance.'

CHAPTER 65

Torj

'Magical debris can be left inside a wound,
causing it to fester'

– *Arcane Ailments: Understanding Magical Maladies*

Leaving Wren felt like leaving a piece of himself behind. The warmth of her touch still lingered on his skin, the taste of her still coated his lips . . . Torj tried to focus on the road ahead as he travelled to a cottage on the outskirts of the Broken Isles. Audra was right: he needed to do this, needed answers. But his mind kept drifting to the poisoner – *his* poisoner. Duty might be pulling him forwards, but his heart strained to turn back.

He had crossed that threshold now, stepping into uncharted territory. Whatever the cost, he would make Wren his. This promise to himself, this vision of a future with her, became the bedrock of his resolve. He'd complete his task, each step bringing him closer not just to his mission's end, but to Wren.

Soon he sat in a tattered armchair before a small, crackling fire, a mug of fire extract cupped between his palms.

'I've never met a Warsword before,' the middle-aged woman sitting beside him said.

'We're not that special,' he muttered, taking a sip of his drink.

'The world begs to differ, Bear Slayer. Even I have heard tales of your glory in these isolated parts.'

'Perhaps they've been exaggerated.'

'Perhaps. Though from the look of you, I doubt it,' she replied. 'Are you going to tell me why you're here?'

'Ma'am, I—'

'Call me Lillian.'

'Lillian,' Torj echoed back. 'Master Hardim Norlander gave me your details in regard to some research I'm doing.'

'Research? I thought Warswords of Thezmarr were all about slaying monsters and hunting down villains.'

'I can multitask.'

'I'm yet to meet a man who can, but go on. What is this research you speak of?'

Torj took another sip of fire extract, relishing the burn of the liquor down his throat as he mulled over his next words. 'Magical injuries. Wounds inflicted by a magic wielder.'

'I have suffered no such injury, Bear Slayer.'

Torj blinked. 'But Hardim—'

'Hardim has a big mouth.' Lillian sighed heavily. 'It was not I who was injured. It was me who did the injuring.'

Torj stared at her. 'Only royals wield magic.'

'I am second cousin to the late King Artos. A fraction of the Harenth royal empath magic flows in my veins,' she explained grimly. 'Naturally, after everything came to light about his role in the war, I had to go into hiding.'

'And you . . .' Torj still couldn't quite believe it. 'You hurt someone with magic? How? What happened?'

'I didn't mean to,' Lillian said. 'I want you to know that.'

'I understand. Tell me.'

'It was a long time ago now,' she began, her voice laced with regret. 'My childhood friend, Maxus, had been injured in the first shadow assault on Naarva. The royal family had fled, and its kingdom was in ruins, trying to rally a force together to fight off the wraiths. They had no chance, of course – we know that now – but Maxus . . .' Lillian topped up both their mugs with more fire extract and took a long draught. 'He was hurt in the fighting. And he was in so much pain. I couldn't bear to see him in such agony, so . . . I tried to take it away.'

'With your empath magic?'

'With what little power I had, yes. But you see . . . I don't think I've ever fully understood how it worked. Still don't. It's not a simple matter of giving or taking from someone with magic. There is a cost.'

'What do you mean?'

'By trying to take Maxus' pain, I had to take it on myself, and give him something of me. It was as though we somehow swapped pieces of ourselves in that moment.'

As if in answer, Torj's web of scars prickled. 'It was painful?'

'For me, yes. But we both healed. It wasn't until later that I realized something wasn't right.' Lillian swallowed down more drink. 'The original wound in Maxus changed over time . . . It changed him, changed us. I had always cared deeply for him. We had grown up together, but . . .'

'What?'

'We grew close. Very close, in the year or so after the incident. We had a connection like nothing else I've ever known, but he became obsessed with the scar the wound had left. He said he could feel it all the time. For months and months, all he could talk about was feeling a vibration there. Most people thought he was mad.'

'Was he?' Torj asked.

'I honestly don't know.'

Torj suppressed the urge to rub at his own scar. 'And where is he now?'

Lillian closed her eyes, as though bracing herself for what came next. 'I'll show you.'

'Show me?'

But the woman was already moving through the cottage, motioning for him to follow her down a dimly lit corridor.

He did as she bid, subtly wiping the sweat from his palms on his thighs as he walked.

Lillian put a finger to her lips as she gently pushed open a door.

A small room was illuminated by a handful of candles, revealing a man lying on a bed. His arms were strapped to his sides, and he writhed among the blankets, his eyes wide and panicked.

Lillian's expression was sombre as she turned back to Torj. 'He tried to carve out his own heart.'

CHAPTER 66

Wren

'From the smallest seed to the mightiest oak,
every part of a plant holds a secret waiting
to be discovered'

*— From Root to Petal:
Understanding Plants and Their Properties*

INSTEAD OF WRAPPED in the Warsword's arms, Wren spent the evening with her experiments, coaxing blood from her arm and mixing it with more of the nauseating substance that had coated the enemy's blades.

'What have you used as your control variable?' Farissa asked later that night, having answered Wren's summons to her room. The older woman peered over her shoulder at the sample dishes, her worn expression brighter in the face of a potential discovery.

Wren was equally impassioned, forgetting the tension between them. 'Oddly, the powdered leaves of a plant I brought from Delmira . . . I've found no mention of it in *From Root to Petal* or *The Green Apothecary*, but it seems to be an excellent binding agent. It helps balance out—'

'From Delmira?' Farissa cut in.

Wren nodded. 'Strange, isn't it? For the most part, the lands are ruined, but every now and then—'

'Every now and then, something is more resilient . . .'

'Exactly.'

Farissa smiled. 'You're onto something here,' she said. 'I'm sure of it.'

But the contents of Wren's stomach were curdling. 'I hope so,' she replied. 'I haven't forgotten what they did to Blythe – that it was meant to be me. Torj told me that traces of this alchemy were found on her body. The rebels need to be stopped before more innocents become collateral.'

'That wasn't your fault,' Farissa soothed.

'She's dead all the same,' Wren said, using a dropper to add her blood to one of the shallow dishes. 'Who else is working on an antidote?'

'Myself and the other masters,' Farissa replied. 'And one or two other promising adepts.'

'So, no one I know?'

Farissa shook her head. 'Just keep at it . . . You're on the verge of something here.'

Wren didn't argue as her former mentor left her quarters. A counter to the weaponized alchemy was within her grasp, and she would not stop until she had it.

੶

The next day, Cal refused to tell her where Torj had been summoned to. If she heard the term 'Warsword business' one more time, she'd throttle him. It was only the fact that neither he nor Kipp seemed all that concerned that kept her amiable. That was, until the pair started to interrogate her about the mark on her neck.

'Someone's been busy,' Kipp remarked with a wiggle of his brows on the way to the dining hall that morning.

'Piss off, Kristopher.' But Wren couldn't stop the blush staining her cheeks. She was still flustered, the unfinished business with Torj occupying her mind incessantly. There had been a smouldering intensity in his eyes as he'd left, one she was desperate to see unfold between them. For the first time in a long while, her thoughts were not of her studies and the upcoming Gauntlet, but of the silver-haired Bear Slayer and what he had done between her legs.

'Oh, come on,' Kipp whined. 'I tell you all my secrets.'

'I wish you wouldn't,' Wren muttered.

'Seconded,' Cal added, though Wren didn't miss the way his eyes flitted to her neck.

She had fleetingly considered making up some cosmetics to cover it. Back at Thezmarr, she had done just that both for Ida and Sam when they'd needed to mask their romantic antics, and for Thea, when she had cuts and bruises from her secret training to hide from Audra. But when it had come to mixing the powders this morning, Wren had run her fingers over the mark instead, and had decided that she wouldn't hide it – hide *him* – from the world.

Naturally, she regretted that choice now.

As they passed the points tally in the foyer, Wren was frustrated to see that her team was still in second place, with Jasper Greaves's team closing in behind them; several shiny new black garnets had been added to their vessel. She meant to address it with her teammates over the breakfast table, but when she entered the dining hall, she was greeted by hushed whispers as quiet blanketed the tables. A quick scan of the room told her the silence was not for her. The High Chancellor had taken to the podium at the front of the hall and raised his hands to capture their attention.

'Today marks two weeks exactly until our novices face the Gauntlet,' he declared. 'With the leaderboard as it currently stands, it can be anyone's game. The team with the most points will receive a ninety-second head start for the challenge. The following teams will then enter in ninety-second intervals in the order of the leaderboard.'

Ninety seconds. A lot could happen in ninety seconds . . . It could mean the difference between life and death.

'These next two weeks are crucial to your advantage in the Gauntlet. Do not waste them. Do not grow complacent. Knowledge is the victor over fate, and the mind is a blade. Be ready, novices. These challenges will be the fight of your lives.'

The High Chancellor stepped down from the podium and joined the other masters.

Dessa was particularly overexcited, and wanted to delve into every single possibility and outcome of the upcoming event. That was how Wren found herself next to Zavier, both of them sitting in silence, needing the reprieve from their teammate's constant chatter. To Wren's relief, Zavier said nothing about the mark on her neck, nor did he so much as look up as Kipp alluded to it again.

A little further down the table, a heated debate had unfolded, and Wren found herself listening.

'It's horseshit,' Kyros said. 'Previous cohorts were never expected to fit a year of study into six months. You can't rush knowledge and experience.'

Zavier huffed a laugh. 'Scared, Sorrell?'

'More like realistic,' Kyros answered, his eyes narrowing. 'The only reason we're working at this pace is because of the fucking royals.'

Wren's cup of tea froze midway to her lips as several gazes slid to her.

Zavier leaned back in his chair. 'You mean because of those so-called loyalists who attacked the rulers unprovoked?'

Wren almost did a double take. She forced herself to take a sip of tea and set her rattling cup back down on the table. But Zavier's words only seemed to fuel the fire, and Kyros' nostrils flared.

'That group had a point. Everything bad that has ever happened in the damn midrealms is because of the rulers.' He counted on his fingers. 'The fall of Delmira and how its lands rot around it. The fall of Naarva to the shadow wraiths. The destruction of Thezmarr. And now the Warswords are being used to protect the very people who bring the conflict to our doorsteps. At least the Naarvian royals had the courtesy to run off and die in a hole somewhere—'

Two things happened at once.

Lightning shot from Wren's fingertips, up towards the ceiling beams, causing several people to startle.

And a pair of salt and pepper shakers went flying.

Kyros sneered at Wren. 'See? You can't even keep it under control.'

Wren's lightning winked out just as quickly as it had bloomed to life, but the storm surging through her was not her concern. She stared at the salt and pepper, now rolling down the length of the table. Her nape prickled. Her power had not done that.

Ignoring Kyros' jeering, she slowly looked around, a strange sensation crawling across her skin. She'd felt it before, during the war. In Queen Reyna's presence. In the presence of King Leiko, and of the late King Artos and Princess Jasira.

Royal magic.

Panic threatened to swallow her whole as the feeling brought her memories to the surface. She focused on her breathing and recalled Olsen Oakes' words: *train the body, tame the mind, transcend limitations.*

'Who knew you were so political, Sorrell?' Kipp addressed Kyros dryly.

Zavier scoffed. 'Anyone can be political once issues actually start to affect them.' He looked to Wren and Dessa. 'Let's go. We've got some points to earn.'

For once, Wren didn't argue with her teammate. She got to her feet and followed him from the hall, the taste of royal magic still on her tongue.

CHAPTER 67

Wren

'From poisoned fog to the fury of arcane explosive devices, a battlefield can become a canvas upon which the alchemist paints their masterpiece of devastation'

– Alchemy Unbound

Days later, Wren was still reeling from that hint of foreign magic. As far as she knew, the rulers of Aveum, Tver, and Harenth were all a thousand leagues or more from Drevenor, as were any magic-blooded relatives they might have. Had she imagined it? Had it been her own power after all?

Not even the ongoing success of her private experiments could tear her mind away from the strange sensation that had crept over her. By nightfall on the third day since, she still hadn't let it go, and so, with Cal on her heels, she went to see Farissa.

Leaving Cal outside to guard the door, Wren entered her former mentor's chambers. They were almost as messy as hers, with every surface covered in books and potions and instruments. Wren distantly wondered if she'd learned her chaotic habits from the Master Alchemist herself.

Farissa was seated beneath the window, scribbling on a piece of parchment with a feathered quill. 'What is it, Elwren?'

Their relationship had been fraught since the war, and Wren still hadn't forgiven Farissa for interfering with her Drevenor applications for all these years. And yet . . . the Master Alchemist had known her since she was an infant. It had been Farissa whom Wren had confided in long before the rest about her heritage, her storm magic . . .

'Elwren?' Farissa prompted, brows knitting together in concern.

'Something happened,' Wren replied, approaching the desk and shifting a pile of books to the floor so she could sit. As soon as she did, the words came tumbling out, explaining what had happened in the dining hall. She finished, 'I could have sworn . . .'

'Sworn what?'

Wren rubbed her temples. 'That I felt the presence of royal magic.'

Farissa stared at her.

'It's ridiculous, I know. Queen Reyna is in Aveum, King Leiko in Tver, and Queen Regent Liora in Harenth . . . You said Thea is somewhere else, and Anya is dead. None of the royals have children wandering about the academy, I'm assuming?'

'You assume correctly. None of the rulers have been blessed with heirs yet – it's a point of contention throughout the midrealms. But the shadow war left its scars upon everyone.'

'So there are no other royal-blooded folk in existence?' Wren pressed.

Farissa shrugged. 'Can we be certain? No, of course not. It was only before the war that we discovered you and your sisters. But is it *likely* that if such a person exists, they were in the dining hall of Drevenor Academy with you? I think not.'

'I know it's not *likely*,' Wren replied between gritted teeth. 'What do you suggest, then?'

Farissa sighed, looking suddenly weary. 'I suggest you put it from your mind and focus on the upcoming Gauntlet.'

'That's it?'

'You said so yourself: you might have imagined it.'

'But . . .'

'Elwren. With or without the accolades of being a student here, you have been an alchemist your whole life. The Gauntlet will determine how far you go in that endeavour. Do not stray from the path now.'

'I'm—'

'Go and find your teammates. It is their help you need; it is in *them* you must trust.'

Wren stared at Farissa, unsure if she was looking at the same alchemist who had practically raised her all those years.

Only when Wren reached the door did her former mentor speak again. 'Knowledge is the victor over fate,' she said. 'The mind is a blade.'

Begrudgingly, Wren took Farissa's advice and met with Zavier and Dessa in the archives. The trio sat in one of the private study rooms, dozens of books splayed out before them as they tried to find accounts of the previous Gauntlets.

Zavier sat with a scowl on his face as he massaged his temples, while Dessa held her head in her hands, looking bleary-eyed. 'We're not going to find anything,' she said for the third time.

'Not if you keep complaining as opposed to reading,' Zavier muttered.

'We've been at it for hours,' Dessa moaned.

'She's right.' Wren leaned back in her chair. 'Anything worth our while would be in the masters' section. We know that.'

'Then why didn't you use your connections to gain access?' Zavier retorted.

'My connections?' Wren laughed. 'What are you talking about?'

Zavier started counting on his fingers. 'You know all the Warswords personally. You know all the rulers. You're a fucking heir of Delmira – surely there are strings you could pull? Not to mention, you used to be the apprentice of Farissa Tremaine herself.

You can be damn sure the other teams will be leveraging anything they've got for an advantage. Why aren't we?'

Wren frowned. 'Is that how you want to win?'

'Winning is winning,' Zavier said. 'Doing whatever it takes to pass the Gauntlet is winning.' As he spoke, Wren noticed the unkemptness of his sable hair, the dark circles beneath his eyes.

'I want to win as much as you,' she told him. 'But you're tired...'

'We're all fucking tired, Wren,' he sighed. 'So why—'

Ever the peacekeeper, Dessa put her hands up. 'Zavier, please...'

But Wren pinned him with a hard stare. 'Why aren't I using my "connections"?' She gave a sardonic laugh. 'Warswords know fuck all about alchemy. Until recently, most wouldn't have been aware of this academy's existence. The rulers? What do you expect them to do, write me a fucking note? And Farissa? Farissa and I haven't been on good terms since the war. She was the one who kept me from attending Drevenor for the last five years. So no, I don't have any fucking connections to leverage. What about you? What are *you* bringing to the table?'

Zavier stared at her for a moment before a broken chuckle escaped him. 'Jeez, Wren, why didn't you just say so?'

She rolled her eyes. 'You're a pain in my arse, Zavier.'

'The feeling's mutual,' he replied, though there was no bite to his words. He rubbed his temples again. 'You're right. We're tired. Let's call it a day and start fresh tomorrow.'

'Thank the Furies,' Dessa said, already on her feet.

'You two go ahead. I'm going to stay a while,' Wren told them.

Zavier gathered his books. 'Suit yourself.'

When her teammates had left, Wren told Cal, who was waiting outside the private room, that she wanted to peruse the shelves, and he followed her dutifully.

Nothing could dull the awe Wren felt every time she wandered the archives. The sheer volume of books, the history, the smell of parchment and leather... The small room at Thezmarr full of military histories was nothing in comparison. She forgot about Cal trailing after her and immersed herself in the rows and rows of titles, imagining the alchemist she might have been with resources like these at her fingertips from the very beginning. Perhaps she would not have become the Poisoner, but something else entirely.

A tome with a red spine caught her eye on a higher shelf, just out of reach. She strained on her tip-toes to reach it – only for a large hand to stretch above hers and pull the book from its place.

'Is this what you wanted?' a familiar husky voice said.

CHAPTER 68

Wren

'Only in the fires of adversity
can true greatness be forged'

– *Drevenor Academy Handbook*

THE BEAR SLAYER took the volume from the shelf and offered it to her.

'You're back,' she managed, pulse hammering in her throat as she stared up at him. He wore his usual white tunic, black leather vest and shoulder armour, his war hammer strapped behind him.

A lock of silver hair fell across his forehead, and he pushed it from his brow. 'I told you I would be.'

Wren couldn't remember what to do with her hands, other than to reach out and touch him. So she drew the book he'd given her tightly to her chest and glanced down the aisle of shelves. 'Where's Cal?'

'Dismissed,' Torj said simply. He hadn't taken his eyes off her.

'And where have you been?' she managed.

'It doesn't matter . . . I'm back where I belong now,' he told her, stepping closer and drinking in the sight of her. 'Why? Did you miss me, Embers?'

'I . . .'

Torj braced himself either side of her, caging her in against the bookshelf, the intoxicating scent of him wrapping around her. 'Because I missed you . . .'

'Did you now?' she said lightly. Gods, her body came alive in his presence, calling out for his touch, his kiss . . .

Torj's eyes darkened, his gaze dropping to her mouth. 'Shall I show you how much?'

Wren's breathing hitched. 'Here?' The archives were empty, but there was nothing to hide behind. 'We'll get caught.'

Torj dipped his head, brushing his lips against hers so lightly she wondered if she'd imagined it. 'Not if you're quiet.'

Wren dropped the book she was holding. The thud echoed down the aisle.

A dark laugh bubbled from Torj as one hand encircled her waist, the heat of his palm searing through her clothes. 'You'll have to do better than that . . .'

Wren surged for him, entwining her arms around the back of his neck and dragging his mouth to hers.

Her lips scorched his in a kiss that set fire to all her senses. He tasted like dark promises and desire incarnate, and she was starved for him. She nipped at his lower lip, and his mouth opened for her, allowing her to deepen the kiss, for her tongue to explore him. She pulled him closer and demanded more, heat swelling between her thighs as he answered every stroke of her tongue with his own.

Pressing against him, she marvelled at how he was braced over her – a mighty silver-haired god whose body responded to her like the storms answered her call. She released his hair and let her hands trace the steel of his shoulder armour, then drop to his chest and the rippling abdomen below, feeling the shift of those muscles beneath her fingers. Her hands went lower still, until they brushed the hardness between his legs—

'Fuck,' he groaned as she palmed him through his leathers.

'What happened to being quiet?' she murmured, white-hot need making her shift, seeking friction. She was wound so tight, every shallow breath reminding her of how she ached to be touched.

'We'll see who struggles more,' Torj growled in her ear.

And then he dropped to his knees.

Her eyes must have gone wide, because he had the audacity to give her a wicked grin, his hands sliding beneath her skirts, dragging the fabric with them.

'You can't—'

'Tell me to stop.'

Cool air kissed the tops of her thighs, and suddenly she was exposed. He pushed her skirt layers into her belt, tucking them there so they didn't fall back down.

She could feel the whisper of Torj's breath against her skin, and her knees quaked as his hands explored more of her, gently thumbing the juncture of her hip and thigh before kissing the same spot with reverence. Want was growing slick between her legs, and with him being so close, he'd see it soon enough . . . His hands mapped the curve of her hips, her backside, her abdomen, as though he meant to memorize the shape of her by touch alone.

No man had ever knelt before her like this. No man had ever trailed soft kisses to her inner thighs and—

He parted her gently and dragged his tongue up her centre.

Wren's hands shot to the shelves on either side of her, gripping hard, her heart pounding.

A molten line of ecstasy.

An otherworldly sensation.

She bit her lip hard to keep from moaning, her head tipping back, hitting the shelf behind her, as Torj's tongue swept across her again.

Heat bloomed in her chest and flushed her face.

This was insanity.

A low, rumbling sound of need came from the Warsword between her legs as he lavished her with long, luxurious strokes of his wicked tongue. His stubble grazed her sensitive skin, causing delicious pinpricks of pain as he worked her with a gentle rhythm, as though he were trying to suspend time, as though it didn't matter that they were out in the open.

The pressure building within her was unbearable, and she wanted nothing more than to arch her hips towards his face and ride his tongue. He seemed to sense her need heightening, for he shifted his thumb to her clit and rubbed light circles around it.

Wren gasped, the added sensation almost too much – or not enough. Her mind was in pieces, pure bliss soaking through her bones.

Torj's mouth moved over the most intimate part of her, his shoulders trembling in what she could only imagine was restraint. Wren was shaking too as the storm gathered in her body, threatening to break. Her hands gripped his hair now, and he moaned against her heat, all the while focused on her and her alone.

Knees quaking, she clung to him, wanting desperately to come apart on his tongue, and at the same time, wanting to feel him deep inside her.

Sucking on her clit now, Torj slid two fingers inside her, as though reading her mind, understanding that she needed to be filled—

Wren cried out, knocking a book from the shelf as she jerked beneath him, his fingers finding a spot inside her that caused stars to burst across her vision. The pressure within built and built, her orgasm unravelling with full force until all she could do was surrender.

'Torj . . .' she whispered, before it hit.

Books cascaded from the shelves around her as wanton pleasure rushed through her: liquid fire in her veins, lightning in her chest. She could do nothing but give in, nothing but ride the wave of it into oblivion.

CHAPTER 69

Torj

'The lasting impact of magical injuries is a study wherein scholars have only scratched the surface'

– *Alchemy of Afflictions*

THIS WOMAN. TORJ sent his thanks up to the Furies for her. Gods, the taste of her, the shudder of her release under his touch . . . He was done for, well and truly done for.

With her, he could forget it all – his father, the war, the wound in his chest threatening to send him mad. None of it mattered when he was with Wren.

Still on his knees, he looked up at her, at the fire he saw in her stormy gaze, at the gasp still on her lips. A queen he'd gladly bow to. A queen he'd serve.

'You're addictive,' he told her, untucking her skirts from her belt and letting them fall about her legs. 'I could taste you a thousand times and it would never be enough.'

Wren's eyes were dark, her face flushed as she pulled him to his feet, breathless. 'Let's get out of here.'

'Where to, Embers?'

'Your room. Now.'

He laughed, but her hand was already in his, pulling him towards the exit. Who was he to argue?

They took the halls at a run, laughter spilling from their lips. Torj had never felt so light, so free. He stole glances at the beautiful woman running alongside him, her hair coming loose from her bun, a wide grin on her face.

'Do you think people heard me?' she asked.

'I hope so.'

'What? Why?'

'So everyone knows you're mine.'

'Just like that?' she said, fighting to catch her breath.

'Just like that, Embers,' he told her recklessly as they reached the door to his room. 'No games. No secrets. You're what has been missing all my life. And I intend to keep you. Consequences be damned.'

Wren reached into his pocket, pulling out his key and fitting it to the lock. In seconds, she was dragging him across the threshold, slamming the door closed behind them.

'Good,' she said fiercely.

He laughed at that, joy spilling through his chest. 'You're it for me. I've just been waiting for you to catch up.'

She kissed him then, hot and demanding, fierce and claiming, shoving him against the wall. His words seemed to unleash something in her, her hands clawing desperately at the buttons of his shirt.

'Take it off,' she panted, gesturing not only to his shirt, but his armour and leathers as well. 'Take it all off. I want to see you.'

'Far be it from me to disobey a princess's orders . . .'

He reached for his shoulder armour, unbuckling each piece and tossing them to the floor carelessly, before dragging the back of his shirt over his head. The fabric fluttered to the floor.

'And the rest,' Wren told him.

'As you command,' he said, kicking his boots off, his hands already moving to do her bidding. Her stare was like fire on his skin as he pushed his leathers down, his hard length springing free as he slid the material past his thighs and down his calves.

Wren stared at him, and Torj let her, enjoying the flare of her nostrils, the way her tongue darted from her mouth to wet her lips. His cock pulsed with need at the sight. He wanted to say something clever, something to spark that fire inside her, but . . . what he saw in her eyes silenced him. There was something so raw, so beautiful there, as though she were committing every scar, every faint line to memory.

She reached for him, like a bloom turning towards the sun, her fingertips tracing his storm magic scars first, following the jagged lightning bolts across his naked flesh.

Torj could hear her shallow breaths as she mapped his tattoo next, her nails trailing the whorls of ink across the expanse of his chest, down his abdomen. He swore he could feel the flicker of electricity in their wake.

He didn't move, didn't break the spell she was weaving across them both – not even as her gaze dropped to his cock, thick and hard between his legs. He'd been hard for days, thinking of her. And now? He was hanging onto his self-control by a thread.

And then she wrapped her hand around him.

'*Fuck* . . .' The word came out shocked and guttural, and he nearly bucked into her touch then and there. Her grip was warm and firm, and it took every ounce of willpower not to thrust—

'I haven't done this many times before,' she said slowly.

He blinked. 'Done what?'

Wren took a breath. 'This.'

She lowered herself to her knees.

'Wren,' he panted. 'You don't have to—'

He stumbled over his words as Wren licked him from base to crown, and his knees threatened to give way.

'*Holy shit* . . .' he moaned.

She licked him again, pausing at the top to curl her tongue around the tip. Gods, he was going to lose it. No better than a teenager, no control . . .

'Wren,' he bit out as her hand worked the base of his shaft. 'You don't have to do this. It's not a quid pro quo situation, I—'

She pulled away and stared up at him. 'I appreciate the clarification,' she said. 'But I want to suck your cock, Bear Slayer. Be a good Warsword and let me, will you?'

He was speechless. Completely lost for words.

Which seemed to satisfy Wren, because she licked the length of him again, and then swallowed him down.

A carnal moan escaped Torj then, and his fingers shot into her silken hair, gripping it at the roots. 'Furies fucking save me, *Wren* . . .'

She hummed around him, the sound sending vibrations right to his balls, and he had to fight every possessive urge that rose up to the surface, screaming at him to take her then and there. Instead, he watched her, mesmerized by the way her lips stretched around him, at how her hand pumped him at the base. He was too big for her, he realized, and it pleased him more than it should have.

Her other hand grabbed his arse, drawing him closer to her, encouraging him to move with her. And he did. At her encouragement, he fucked her mouth with long, deep strokes, gripping her by the hair.

Ripples pulsed through his whole body, and he clenched, trying to hold back the desperate urge to come. It felt too good. Too intoxicating.

And then he hit the back of her throat.

He nearly lost all semblance of control.

Wren spluttered for a moment before she caught herself, and he tried to pull away instantly. But she was having none of it. She took him deep again and again, in a luscious glide over his cock that had his eyes rolling back in his head. There was a storm gathering around them, the energy palpable as passion blurred his senses and tethered him completely and utterly to Wren.

A princess was on her knees for him.

His whole body shook with the effort of restraint. Her tongue flicked over the crown of him, and as though she could sense him holding back, she hollowed her cheeks and sucked harder.

A desperate sound slipped from Torj's lips as he neared breaking point. But he wanted to give her the choice. 'Wren . . . I'm going to—'

In answer, she doubled her efforts.

And he lost control.

'Wren,' he half-shouted, curling over her as his climax hit. He came with a moan, spilling into her mouth with slow, deliberate thrusts. Wren moved with him, dragging out the last ripples of pleasure and swallowing his release.

The orgasm was so intense that he thought he might have blacked out for a moment. When he blinked the room back into focus, Wren was staring up at him, swiping a thumb across her lower lip.

'You . . .' was all he could manage as he looked upon the storm wielder in wonder.

She smiled, getting to her feet. 'Me.'

Her gaze mapped him again, and shock registered on her face. He glanced down and gasped.

Tiny bolts of lightning were dancing across his chest.

'What the fuck . . .' he muttered. 'How . . . ?'

Magic rumbled beneath that web of scars, and Torj flinched at the strange sensation, struggling to comprehend what was happening and how the fuck it was possible. It didn't hurt. The whisper of a storm skittered along his skin, uninhibited and yet familiar.

Wren trailed her fingers through the electrical current. 'You look good in lightning . . .'

Torj surged for her, bringing her face to his. He didn't care that she tasted of him; he kissed her deeply, picking her up in his arms and carrying her to the bed, the sound of her laughter hitting something deep in his chest.

'Wait!' she cried out as he went to throw her on the bed. 'My belt.'

More laughter as he set her down again and helped her out of her belt of horrors.

'I'm suddenly very aware of how naked I am, and how clothed you are,' he ventured, carefully placing the contraption on his desk.

'Hmm . . .' Wren said, surveying him appreciatively, his cock already hardening again beneath her stare. 'I like it.'

She didn't move to undress further, though, and he didn't mention it. He didn't want to pressure her. So, he got onto the bed, still nude, and held out his arms.

'Come here.'

Biting her lip, Wren did as he bid, the mattress dipping beneath her weight as she climbed up beside him, her skirts brushing over his bare legs. She paused, reaching for something on the windowsill.

She twirled the bushel of dried purple florets between her fingers. 'What's this?'

Heat crept up Torj's neck as he closed his hand over hers. 'The lavender, from the gardens . . .'

Her brows shot up, her eyes meeting his. 'You kept it?'

Torj swallowed the lump in his throat. 'I did.'

Biting her lower lip, Wren gently placed the flowers back on the windowsill before she leaned down and kissed him, slowly, thoroughly.

He didn't know how it had happened. He had a Princess of Delmira, a future queen, in his bed, and this time, he couldn't push her away, couldn't let her go. It felt right, having Elwren Embervale in his arms.

She toyed with a lock of his silver hair, curling it around her fingers, and for the first time, he felt self-conscious. 'Not quite as golden as it once was, is it?'

The golden-haired Bear Slayer . . . That was what they'd called him before the war, his hair once a mane befitting a lion. Now it was the silver of an old man's.

A strange expression crossed Wren's face, but she gripped him by the chin and forced his gaze to hers. 'You're beautiful.'

CHAPTER 70

Wren

'The greatest alchemy of all
is the alchemy of the heart'

– Arcane Alchemy: Unveiling the Mysteries of Matter

WREN NEVER THOUGHT she'd live to see the day when Torj Elderbrock, Warsword of Thezmarr, blushed. But here he was, the tips of his cheeks tinged with pink.

'Beautiful?' he said, blinking at her.

She kissed him again, long and deep, cupping his face in her hands, pouring everything she had into him. 'More than you could ever know.'

How many times had she watched him in awe? How many times had she forced down her desire for him? How often had she admired him from afar?

Years, she admitted to herself. She had wanted him for *years*.

And now she had him.

But it couldn't be like this, could it? The Poisoner and the Warsword? The heir and the soldier? Ward and bodyguard? He had said no games, no secrets – but that wasn't their reality, was it?

'I should go,' she said quietly.

Torj drew a blanket up around his waist, his hand curling around her wrist. 'Stay.'

'But . . .'

'Do you want to?' he asked plainly. 'Stay, I mean?'

She didn't understand the swell of emotion rising up in her then, didn't know why tears suddenly pricked at her eyes. 'Yes,' she whispered.

'Then stay. Forget the rest.'

'It's that easy?'

Gently, he pushed her onto her back and propped himself up on his elbow, dipping his head to brush a kiss across her lips. 'It is tonight, Embers. I'm not letting you go.'

He traced the line of her jaw with his thumb and her shoulders hitched.

'Are you going to fuck me?' she asked.

A slow, wicked smile spread across his face. 'When you're ready.'

'You don't think I am?'

'Only you can tell me that.' He trailed his hands down her bodice. 'But your current state of dress tells me that perhaps not quite yet, hmm?'

She didn't know why she was still dressed when there was a gloriously naked warrior beside her, especially when he'd seen nearly every inch of her anyway . . . He'd had his tongue between her legs, for Furies' sake. And yet something stopped her. She was no virgin, but . . .

'You don't have to explain,' he said, as though he could read her thoughts. 'You never have to explain to me. It's your choice. Always.'

'And you still want me to stay?'

He looked at her as though she were mad. 'I have wanted you in my bed for as long as I can remember, Embers.'

And so, in his bed she stayed.

Wren woke to the warm weight of Torj Elderbrock hugging her to his bare chest, which rose and fell evenly, the Warsword still deep in sleep. He was everywhere, his golden tattooed skin in stark contrast to the pale sheets tangled around them. For a moment, she simply let herself be, drinking in the feel of him, inhaling his scent. In the brief pocket of time between dream and waking, she could pretend that there was no Gauntlet, no attacks against royals, no threats beyond the one to her heart . . .

For that was exactly what the man beside her was: a threat to the very thing she had built a fortress around in the years since the war. She had been so lost, so broken . . . He had offered her a piece of himself back then, a piece that she had refused out of fear, out of guilt. And now? That fear lingered, as did her secrets, her brokenness.

Yet he looked at her as though she were something precious, something worthy . . .

'You watching me sleep, Embers?' he murmured, voice thick with drowsiness.

She smiled into his warm skin. 'Maybe.'

He drew her closer still, pressing a kiss to the top of her hair. 'I like waking up with you,' he told her, his words raw, as though he didn't quite believe he was doing exactly that.

Outside, dawn was spilling across the grounds, and reluctantly, Wren pulled away from him. 'We've got that guest lecture this morning. I told Cal I'd go with him to greet Professor Vulpine. Make a good impression, give him a warm welcome . . .'

'Callahan the Flaming Arrow can surely handle that on his own.' Torj hauled her back to him so that she landed flush against his chest.

Wren bit back another smile. 'I promised.'

'You need to be more discerning when dishing those out.'

'I'll keep that in mind.' She savoured his warmth for a moment longer. 'Then it's a full day of alchemy, I'm afraid.'

Torj groaned. 'I swear they work you harder here than the shield-bearers at Thezmarr.'

'Don't let Audra hear you say that,' Wren laughed.

'I don't have a death wish.'

'Glad to hear it, Bear Slayer. Now, will you let me up?'

'If I have to . . .'

Wren's heart stuttered. She had always known Torj was a good man, but this sweeter side . . . She had never seen it, not like this, not for her. He seemed physically pained by the thought of her leaving his bed. Warmth bloomed in her chest at that.

She peeled herself away from him and headed for their shared bathing chamber. Closing the door behind her, she couldn't help the grin that tugged at her lips, especially when she caught her reflection in the mirror. Her hair was a mess, her clothes wrinkled beyond fixing, and something had changed . . . She scanned her face, but nothing was different. And yet she felt it: a shift in herself, a wall coming down, a shield being dropped. It wasn't as terrifying as she thought. Not when she remembered the weight of those arms around her, or the look of reverence in those sea-blue eyes.

Still smiling, Wren washed and entered her own rooms to prepare for the day. She donned a fresh linen gown and apron, and tugged on her boots. Just as she was scanning the workbench for her belt of tinctures, the adjoining door opened.

Torj padded in barefoot, wearing leathers slung low around his hips, holding her belt in his hands. He came to her without a word and fastened it around her waist, his fingers lingering ever so slightly.

'Can't have you without your weapons,' he said gruffly, stroking his thumb down her cheek. 'I'll be ready in five, Embers.'

She watched him go, that ball of power in her chest growing tight. Things had shifted between them so suddenly. When? What had been the moment? She tried to pinpoint the second she'd let herself see the Warsword for who he was . . . But the truth was that he'd been chipping away at her walls for a long time, slowly allowing her to peer out from behind the barriers, in her own time. And when she'd finally stepped out from behind the fortress she'd built? The world had been beautiful once more.

There's no going back now... His words echoed in her mind. She touched a hand to her bruised lips. Why, in the name of the Furies, would she want to go back?

When Torj was dressed in his usual warrior's garb, he escorted her to the lower levels of the building and forced an apple into her hands. 'You don't eat enough,' he told her.

'Since when?'

'Since always, Embers.'

'You're used to the appetites of Warswords and Guardians who have been training and fighting all day. I don't need as much, my activities aren't so physical—'

He raised a suggestive brow at her.

'I'm serious,' she said.

'As am I. You run every day. And the mind needs fuel just as the body does.'

Wren sighed and bit into the apple, suppressing a laugh at the satisfied look on Torj's face.

When they reached the foyer, the glass cylinders of black garnet looming over them, Cal was already there. He was pacing the marble floor beneath the shadow of the ancient tree that stood at the foyer's centre, its branches stretching up into the dome-capped ceiling.

'He's late,' he said, glancing up at Wren and Torj's arrival.

'Punctuality isn't a strong suit of a lot of these scholars.' Wren gave a sympathetic shrug. 'Give it a minute or two.'

'But . . .' Cal shook his head. 'What if something's happened? What if I've failed before my duty even—'

'I'm sure it's nothing,' Torj interjected.

Footsteps sounded and Cal whipped round, only for his shoulders to sag as he spotted Kipp, looking particularly pleased with himself.

'It's only you,' Cal muttered, turning back to the main entrance.

'Only me?' Kipp scoffed. 'You sure know how to make a friend feel special, don't you, Callahan . . . Where's this professor you're supposed to be guarding, anyway?'

'Not here,' Cal grumbled, growing steadily more restless. Kipp's grin, on the other hand, was growing wider by the second.

Wren hated to add pressure, but a glance at her pocket watch told her they couldn't delay much longer. 'We're supposed to be in the lecture theatre by now, Cal,' she said gently.

'Fuck,' he said. 'Where is he? My instructions were perfectly clear.'

Kipp gave Cal a comforting pat on the shoulder. 'Maybe he's already in the theatre. Someone probably forgot to pass on the message.'

Cal glanced around the empty foyer anxiously. 'Can't hurt to look.'

Together, the group crossed the marble floor to the entrance of the buzzing lecture theatre beyond. Torj carved a way through the crowd, making for the intricately carved wooden benches that stretched towards a raised platform at the front. Wren had no doubt that he'd chosen a particular bench due to its proximity to the exit.

When she was at last seated, she had the opportunity to survey the hall. The rows of benches lined the staggered levels that reached up the incline of the space, all the way to a wall at the back. The air was thick with the scent of parchment as students rummaged through satchels similar to hers, taking out quills and inkpots. Stained-glass windows depicting flowers and plants cast a kaleidoscope of colour across the hall.

Beside Wren, Cal was scanning the room in a panic. 'Something has happened to Professor Vulpine,' he said. 'I just know it. I've fucked this up—'

'I'm sure it'll be fine . . .' she tried to reassure him, but trailed off as the High Chancellor, Remington Belcourt, took to the stage, his robes billowing. Quiet fell across the hall, and those who hadn't already taken their seats hurried to do so.

'Today marks a special occasion as we welcome a distinguished guest lecturer to Drevenor. In the ever-changing landscape of alchemy, where the alchemist's intellect must navigate myriad possibilities and complexities, the importance of strategic thinking cannot be overstated.'

Wren craned her neck, but couldn't make out the figure standing in the wings. She elbowed Cal. 'That must be him there,' she whispered. 'He just went directly to the theatre . . .'

Cal looked put out. 'Those weren't the instructions,' he said sourly.

'Our guest lecturer comes to us with a wealth of experience, garnered through years of practical application,' the High Chancellor continued. 'Most recently, in the shadow war.'

A wave of disbelief washed over Wren. She stole a glance at Torj, who looked equally baffled.

The High Chancellor pressed on. 'His expertise in combining battle tactics with alchemy has been recognized throughout our lands and beyond. Our own Master of Warfare recommended this lecture as part of our core curriculum. So, let us delay no more, and open our minds to new horizons of understanding and innovation. Please join me in extending a warm welcome to our esteemed guest . . .'

'What the fuck?' Cal muttered beside Wren, rising out of his seat as they saw who strode out onto the stage.

The High Chancellor had already begun clapping. 'Kristopher Snowden.'

The applause was thunderous as Kipp took to the podium with a grin.

'You've got to be fucking joking.' Cal was shaking his head in disbelief. 'I'm going to kill him.'

'That might be at odds with your sworn Warsword duties,' Torj said from Wren's other side. 'But I wouldn't blame you.'

Cal looked livid. 'The fucking Son of the Fox strikes again . . . *Professor Vulpine* . . . For fuck's sake.'

One glance at Torj told Wren he was doing everything he could to maintain a straight face as he said, 'Now that I think on it, Cal . . . Pretty sure the word "vulpine" has something to do with foxes . . .'

Wren glanced from her furious friend to the menace that graced Drevenor's lectern, and couldn't help it. She burst out laughing.

Torj's shoulders were shaking beside her, and at last, a rich laugh spilled from his lips, too. Wren wished she could bottle the sound.

CHAPTER 71

Wren

'An alchemist's intellect must navigate myriad possibilities and complexities ... The importance of strategic thinking cannot be overstated'

– High Chancellor, Drevenor Academy

AFTER THE SHOCK of having *Kristopher fucking Snowden* as their guest lecturer wore off – if that was at all possible – Wren wasn't surprised to find his presentation one of the best she'd ever heard.

The cohort was enraptured by the way he shared his experiences from the war, and by the strategies he'd put into place that had helped the midrealms defeat the enemy – all artfully done without mentioning anyone by name, for which Wren was eternally grateful. Though she had been there right alongside Kipp and had always appreciated his cleverness, it was another thing entirely to learn about it from an objective perspective. Or as objective as she could manage, having lived through the battles and war councils herself.

The interplay between warfare and alchemy had never been so clear to her, and her appreciation for both her friend's mind and the discipline itself reached new heights. Though Wren pitied Cal for being the brunt of an elaborate joke, Kipp had earned his place on that stage, and she was proud of him, proud to know him.

Kipp's conclusion was met with cheers from the cohort, and the fanfare only died down once he left the lectern and disappeared into the wings of the stage. Cal made a beeline for him with a muttered curse.

From the seat beside her, Torj's muscular thigh slid against hers, and warmth flooded her body. 'Tell me I can take you back to our rooms now,' the Warsword murmured in her ear, bringing a flush to her cheeks.

Wren was more than eager for him to do exactly that, until she saw slips of parchment were being handed out. Dessa leaned across Cal's empty seat to pass her one, and reluctantly, Wren skimmed its contents. 'I have to be at the gates in fifteen minutes,' she told Torj with a sigh.

'That wasn't on the schedule,' he argued.

Wren shouldered her satchel and stood. 'It was added just now. We're to go into the city for a task.'

'I briefed them about this sort of shit,' Torj grumbled. 'It's a security hazard.' But he got to his feet and followed her from the theatre.

They walked through the grounds together, and Wren found herself wanting to slide her fingers through his – willing him to put his arm around her, like she'd seen Wilder do with Thea. But the Bear Slayer did no such thing. Instead he scanned their surroundings for any signs of a threat, a muscle twitching in his jaw as the gates came into view.

'Why meet at the gates?' he asked. 'Why not the stables?'

Wren shrugged. 'It's what the High Chancellor's instructions specified.'

The crease in Torj's brow only deepened as the master in question approached them.

'I'm afraid your services won't be required today, Warsword Elderbrock,' Belcourt said.

Torj's demeanour changed entirely. His chest expanded as he pinned the High Chancellor with a cold stare. 'What?'

'It was cleared with the Guild Master of Thezmarr.' Belcourt produced a scroll with Audra's seal. 'This is an official task for the novices, and as you can understand, we can't have one guarded by a Warsword throughout.'

'Her life has been threatened several times at this academy, as you well know,' Torj growled. 'You expect me to suddenly step aside and let her walk off into harm's way?'

'It's an order.'

'I don't take orders from scholars.'

'You take orders from the Guild Master of Thezmarr. And she orders you to stand down.' The High Chancellor opened the letter and showed the Warsword the script within. Peering over their arms, Wren could see that it was indeed Audra's hand.

But Torj's eyes narrowed. 'I refuse.'

Wren touched the warrior's arm, feeling the tension corded there. 'Torj . . .'

'If you think I'm leaving you undefended—'

'It is part of her studies, Warsword,' Belcourt said flatly. 'If she cannot participate in this task, she cannot participate in the Gauntlet, nor graduate to adept.'

Wren's heart was hammering. 'Torj, please. I am not without my own defences.'

Torj turned his back to the High Chancellor, blocking him out.

Belcourt made an insulted noise. 'You have five minutes. Elwren, if you are not at those gates by then, you can pack your bags and return to that hovel in Delmira.'

Torj's fists clenched at his sides. Wren watched the High Chancellor go, her own anger simmering just below the surface.

'Embers . . .' He said the nickname gently, but there was no mistaking the note of panic in his voice.

Was this how it was going to be between them, now that things had changed? She sucked in a breath, steeling herself. She cared for him deeply; she would no longer deny that. But did that mean that her goals, her ambitions should be compromised? Did it give him authority over her?

Wren lifted her chin in defiance. 'Do you mean to bar the way, Bear Slayer?' she asked. 'Do you truly mean to stop me?'

Understanding flared in his eyes. 'I only mean to protect you. You *have* to know that.'

'Then step aside. Knowledge is the victor over fate, and the mind is a blade,' she told him. 'I have honed my mind sharper than any sword. And the rest, you have taught me well.'

His handsome face was etched with conflict. 'Please don't ask this of me,' he murmured. 'If anything happened to you . . .'

'Please don't ask this of *me*,' she argued. 'You stand there asking me to give up the thing I have worked for my entire life. Where does it end after that? Tell me.'

Torj ran a hand through his hair. 'I—'

'I'll ask you again: do you mean to stand in my way? Or will you be the one to lift me up?'

The Warsword inhaled deeply, his knuckles turning white as he gripped the hilt of his sword. 'This is truly what you want? To become a Master Alchemist?'

'It is. You know it is.'

He seemed to brace himself. 'Then I mean to support you, Embers. Always.'

'You will be with me,' she said. 'Everything you taught me will be right here.' She touched a finger to her temple.

Torj shook his head, looking torn between shaking her by the shoulders and hauling her mouth to his. 'I don't like this.'

'You don't have to like it,' she replied, with a worried glance at the gates. 'You just have to let me go.'

'We both know I don't *let* you do anything, Embers.'

For a moment, they stared at each other. Wren's gaze dropped to his mouth. She wanted to kiss him, wanted to feel the strength of his arms as he held her, but the cohort was in view . . .

Torj's eyes slid to the gates. 'Go.'

Swallowing the emotion that had surged into her throat, Wren nodded and gave him a smile. 'I'll see you later, Warsword.'

Torj's returning smile was tight.

CHAPTER 72

Wren

'Knowledge can be both a blessing and a curse'

– Alchemy Unbound

Wren joined Dessa and Zavier at the gates.

'I'd have trouble leaving him behind too,' Dessa said with a wink and a backwards glance at the lone figure on the grounds.

'Shut up,' Wren replied, though she couldn't help the smile breaking across her lips. Dessa just laughed.

'If you two are done ogling the Warsword, we have a task to complete,' Zavier said, a haughty note to his voice.

'Which is?' Wren prompted, turning to him expectantly.

'Remember the lesson where we designed the crossbow? We've been given the details for an arbalista in—'

'A what?' Dessa cut in with a frown.

Zavier shot her an irritated look. 'An arbalista - a maker of crossbows. We've been given their address in Highguard. Master Nyella wants us to commission our design.'

Wren's heart soared. 'Really? That's—'

'Unheard of for novices? Yes, it is,' Zavier replied proudly. 'I've already collected the death cap mushrooms from the forest, but I was thinking we might do well to get something less deadly from the apothecary, so we can create a working prototype to be tested . . .'

Wren found herself smiling. 'Always two steps ahead, aren't you?'

Zavier offered a wolfish grin. 'I try.'

'Then let's get us a crossbow,' Wren said.

Roderick escorted them to the city in his new cart, recalling the events of the attack on the road. It was a version of the story Wren was unfamiliar with – one in which Roderick took on several assailants with the strength of a Warsword himself. Laughing, she listened with the others, glad that they could make light of the situation now, and that the Bear Slayer had fully recovered from his injuries.

When they reached the gates, they jumped down from the cart and waved farewell to Roderick, vibrating with excitement at the task ahead.

'You two go straight to the arbalista,' Wren told the others. 'I'll stop by the apothecary to get a sedative we can use for the demonstration.' There was also a rare kind of lavender she wished to get for a certain Warsword, though she didn't share this with the group.

Zavier handed her a scrap of parchment. 'That's the address.'

'I'll meet you there in twenty minutes,' she said, tucking it into her apron.

Dessa was practically bouncing. 'I can't believe we're actually getting this commissioned. A credit to our design portfolios as mere novices . . .'

Wren smiled, knowing how much it meant to Dessa, who was intending on pitching her altered memory weave design to Master Nyella over the next few weeks.

'It's going to be amazing,' Wren told her before she broke away from her teammates and wove through the throngs of people.

Mid-afternoon, the city was still bustling. Merchants were in no hurry to take down their colourful stalls or pack away their gleaming trinkets and wares. Latecomers were darting among them, scouring what remained of the freshly harvested vegetables and fruits. The square buzzed with the clang of metal upon stone as craftsmen continued their work, some fashioning bespoke jewellery, some working on plates of armour.

Wren headed to the apothecary, feeling a soaring sense of freedom as she breathed in the city air, the scent of freshly baked bread and hot cocoa dancing in the breeze around her. It was the first time in a long while she'd gone anywhere on her own. She had missed her autonomy greatly, and yet . . . there was an absence at her side. One day, she told herself, one day she would get to wander the markets for her own enjoyment, perhaps hand in hand with—

She shook the thought from her head, though not without a smile. There would be time for daydreaming of muscular Warswords later. Right now, she had a job to do. Chastising herself, she made a beeline for the apothecary, spotting its wooden sign swinging just a little further down the street.

The cobblestoned path grew narrower, putting her shoulder to shoulder with the other busy city folk, and she found herself jostled several times. In that moment she realized just how much Torj shielded her from the world, always putting his body between her and everyone else—

She was knocked hard, almost sent flying across the stones. Luckily, she managed to get her feet back under her just in time. But as she righted herself, there was a sharp sting at the back of her neck. Wondering if she'd been bitten by an insect, she put a hand to the spot of skin that was still tingling.

Her fingers met something cool, wrapping around some sort of fletching . . .

A dart.

Swaying, she pulled the tiny arrow from her flesh with a hiss.

But before she could reach for the poisons at her belt, a cold, wet cloth was forced over her mouth.

She struggled, aiming her elbows at her attacker's vulnerable side, stamping on his feet, just as Torj had taught her. But with her senses blurring and her magic suddenly closed off, she swayed, the material still clamped over her mouth.

A bitter taste bloomed across her tongue.

Silver boxweed, she realized distantly, before her body slumped beneath her, and her mind went blank.

CHAPTER 73
Torj

'Never underestimate the power of intention'

– Bear Slayer, Warsword of Thezmarr

A RESTLESS CURRENT stalked beneath Torj's skin. Every instinct within him had roared at the High Chancellor for separating him from Wren, and every moment since had stretched out endlessly.

Even now, as he trained with Cal in the gymnasium, his thoughts were of her. The way her voice softened when she said his name. Her scent on his clothes, and how he could still feel the brush of her lips on his skin—

Cal's fist collided with his jaw.

Torj reeled back, more startled than hurt, rubbing the dully throbbing spot in a daze.

'Shit! Look alive, Torj,' Cal said. 'I didn't actually think I'd land it—'

'About time you did,' he retorted. 'This sparring's been one-sided.'

'Like you'd know. You're a million miles away.' Cal raised his fists in invitation. 'Another round?'

Nodding, Torj took a breath, digging deep for the focus he needed. He tried to push Wren from his mind, using the scent of sweat and polished wood to ground him. His muscles tensed with anticipation as Cal gave him a confident grin from across the sparring mat.

'Ready to get your arse handed to you again?' Cal quipped, bouncing on the balls of his feet.

Torj chuckled, rolling his shoulders to loosen up. 'Don't get too cocky, Flaming Arrow. I might have to remind you who taught you everything you know.'

'Everything? That's a bit of a stretch . . .'

'We'll see about that,' Torj muttered, assuming his stance and clenching his fists, ready. They circled each other, as they had done many times before, gauging one another's movements.

Cal lunged forwards first – he always did, like he had something to prove – aiming a flurry of strikes at Torj's midsection. Huffing a laugh, Torj deftly dodged and weaved, his motions fluid and precise. He countered with a swift kick to Cal's thigh, causing the younger warrior to stagger back.

'Not bad,' he remarked. 'But you'll have to do better than that, won't you?'

Cal's brow furrowed in determination as he launched another assault, his attacks coming faster and more aggressive. Torj parried each blow with ease. It was probably unfair, given that he'd been the one to train Cal. He knew all the Flaming Arrow's moves, for they were his own, only less practised.

'You should train with Wilder or Thea on occasion. Learn different fighting styles,' he advised.

Cal nodded, blocking one of Torj's blows. 'Fighting with Zavier during the attack was interesting. He's got a very—'

He grunted as Torj struck his side.

'A very what?' Torj asked, circling his former apprentice again.

'Refined style,' Cal replied, wheezing. 'There's an elegance to his swordplay.'

'That so?'

'You were too busy getting speared to notice.'

'Don't remind me.' Torj's side was still tender.

The door to the gymnasium swung open with a loud creak. Kipp strode in, several scrolls tucked under his arm. He gave Cal a grin. 'Glad to see my protector is staying in shape.'

'You can fuck right off, Kristopher.'

'That's *Professor Vulpine* to you.' Kipp took up a place on one of the benches and unfurled a piece of parchment, but glanced up again, seeming surprised. 'Still haven't forgiven me? Honestly, I assumed it was an obvious reference, but perhaps you Warswords are a tad dimmer than I thought.'

Cal merely grunted and turned back to Torj, poised to start again.

Torj felt for the young Warsword. He knew how seriously Cal took his duties – most of the time – and he'd been humiliated. Often it seemed as though life was one big joke to Kipp, and though he brought a lot of fun with him, the more Torj thought about it, the angrier at the strategist he became, at his audacity and treatment of his closest friend. Kipp was still grinning, but the spark in Cal's eyes had dimmed.

'Fancy a round, Son of the Fox?' Torj challenged.

Kipp raised a brow in apprehension. 'Not fucking likely.'

'Then shut up and let us train.'

Kipp blinked at them, clearly taken aback. 'I—'

But Torj turned his back on him and returned his focus to Cal. 'Ready?'

A small smile tugged at Cal's mouth, and he nodded.

Their sparring continued, a dance of fists and feet across the mat. With every blow and block, the tension in Torj's body ebbed away, as did the thoughts at the forefront of his mind. His worry for Wren, his impending madness . . . For a moment, his training took over. It was a rhythm Torj could lose himself in, a song he knew by heart after decades of fighting. He didn't have to think, only move.

They forgot that Kipp was watching from the sidelines and pummelled each other relentlessly, Warsword to Warsword, Furies-given strength evenly matched. It reminded Torj of training the shieldbearers with Wilder back at Thezmarr, and oddly, he found himself missing the fortress – or what it had once been.

As the minutes stretched into hours, Torj couldn't help the swell of nostalgia that washed over him as he observed his protégé. There was still a gap between their experience that Cal was yet to bridge; Torj had years of battles and fighting monsters on him, and it showed, but the potential was there. Cal had come a long way since their first meeting, and Torj himself had helped get him there.

With a final flurry of strikes, Torj caught Cal off guard, sending him sprawling to the ground with a satisfied grunt.

'Looks like this old dog still has a few tricks up his sleeve,' he remarked, offering Cal a hand up.

Cal accepted the gesture with a grin, his eyes alight with challenge. 'Just you wait, Bear Slayer. One of these days I'll have you beat.'

Torj laughed, clapping Cal on the shoulder as they made their way off the mat. 'Not today, apprentice. Not today.'

Cal mopped the perspiration from his face with a towel, his smile fading as his gaze fell to Kipp. 'Where do you need to go?'

'I'm supposed to have a meeting with the Master of Warfare in half an hour, but we could meet for a pint at the Mortar and Pestle afterwards?' Kipp replied hopefully.

'Can't,' Cal said. 'On duty.'

The strategist's face fell. 'Oh, come on, Callahan—'

Torj raised a brow in Cal's direction. 'Doesn't sound like an apology to me.'

Cal's mouth twitched. 'No, it doesn't.'

'You're right.' Kipp leapt to his feet and picked up something cylindrical from the floor. 'I'm sorry,' he said. 'I didn't mean for it to go so far. It was stupid, even for me.'

Eyes narrowing, Cal took the offering and turned it over in his hands. 'A new quiver?'

'New and improved,' Kipp told him. 'And new arrows, too.' He pulled one from the leather. 'Wren actually gave me the idea when she was going on about the sap of bluebells . . . It's perfect for binding the fletching to the arrow, see? The arrows travel further, they're less affected by crosswind . . . You could shoot the wings off a fly with these.'

Cal thumbed the feathering experimentally. 'You made them?'

'The Flaming Arrow deserves the best,' Kipp replied.

'That's true,' Cal allowed.

'Forgiven?' Kipp pressed.

Cal considered him, glancing across at Torj before he punched Kipp on the arm and shouldered his new quiver of arrows. 'Thin ice, Professor Vulpine. Thin fucking ice.'

A wide, familiar grin broke out across the strategist's face and he winked. 'It's the only way to skate, my friend. So, Mortar and Pestle later?'

Dabbing the sweat from his neck, Torj shook his head. 'You're a pair of idiots.'

As they left the gymnasium, he realized he'd lost track of time. The hour was late. There was no commotion from the dining hall, barely anyone crossing the grounds.

Frowning, he glanced at Cal and Kipp. 'The novices aren't back yet . . .'

'Doesn't look like it,' Cal agreed.

Unease rolled through Torj's gut. 'Shouldn't they be?'

Kipp shrugged. 'Any idea what this task was?'

'No,' Torj said, his body coiling with tension. He rubbed at his sternum, his scars prickling. 'But whatever it was . . . it didn't feel right to me.'

'How do you mean?' Cal asked.

Torj swept the loose hair from his brow. 'I just . . . I don't like what this place asks of its students.'

Cal made a noise of disbelief. 'It's no worse than what Thezmarr asks of its shieldbearers.'

Torj balked. 'Isn't it?'

But Cal eyed him with keen interest. 'You're being . . .'

'What?'

'Nothing.'

'Don't hold back now,' Torj goaded. 'What am I?'

Kipp chimed in. 'Paranoid? Overprotective?'

'It's my job to be those things,' Torj argued, suppressing the urge to throttle the strategist. He had some fucking nerve.

But Cal gave him a knowing look. 'Just your job, is it?'

'Spit it out, Callahan,' Torj muttered.

Cal's expression turned surprisingly sharp. 'You think we haven't noticed what's going on with you and Wren?'

'There's nothing—'

'Save it, Bear Slayer.'

Torj had never heard his protégé use that tone, especially not with him.

Cal didn't break eye contact. 'Don't hurt her.'

'I would never.'

But Cal looked sceptical. 'She's been through a lot. Her sister died. Her best friends died. We know she's changed, but she's still our friend. She's ours to protect, too.'

The humour had vanished from Kipp's expression as he nodded in agreement.

'I know that,' Torj said quietly.

Kipp made a derisive noise. 'Do you?'

'Yes,' Torj ground out. 'I won't hurt her.'

'And why's that?' Cal pressed.

Torj swallowed the rock that had formed in his throat, and tried to speak aloud what he'd known in his heart for a long time. 'Because I . . . I . . .'

His throat closed on the words, but Cal and Kipp both seemed to understand. Kipp smiled, and Cal simply nodded.

And that was that.

The hours bled into one another, and Torj felt Wren's absence like a piece of himself was missing. Nothing would quell his unease or take the edge off his restlessness. He tried to turn his attention to his research, trawling through the seemingly endless piles of books that had been recommended to him. Had he known of the damn task Wren was attending to, he could have made better use of his time.

He stared at the list of Hardim's contacts, of which only one remained. He had half a mind not to visit them at all; he doubted he'd learn anything new. All of the Lifelore Master's associates had shared the same experience – a descent into madness, the ultimate destruction of the self. Sifting through his notes offered no reprieve from the despair, either. Every line spelled the same conclusion: his demise.

How was he meant to tell Wren? He had promised he wouldn't hurt her. Knowing this would destroy her, he couldn't bear the thought of her pain.

As if in answer to his thoughts, a sharp pang speared through the lines of his scar, and a crackle of lightning shot across his heart.

Torj could feel her, somewhere out there.

CHAPTER 74

Wren

'It is not only ingredients that transform in the crucible, but the alchemist themself'

– Alchemy Unbound

WREN WAS WOKEN with an icy bucket of water to the face. She reeled back, gasping, only to find that she was bound to a chair. Magic-muting manacles were clamped around her wrists, chains of a similar make snaking around her body and ankles.

Her mouth was dry and furry around a gag, and as she blinked the room into focus, she recalled the taste of silver boxweed on her tongue. She'd been drugged and kidnapped, and by the looks of things, was now being held hostage.

She fought the panic rising in her chest and tried to assess the situation objectively. The manacles at her wrists instantly suggested that the People's Vanguard was involved. Had the Warswords been wrong to think they had quelled an uprising before it started? Or was this another coordinated attack on the royal-blooded magic wielders? She was alive, which meant they wanted something from her . . .

Coughing around her gag, a headache already blooming behind her eyes, Wren refocused on the room. It wasn't so much a room as it was a crypt. She could tell by the damp, cool air and the lack of windows that she was beneath layers of stone and earth. Torches flickered weakly in rusted sconces, illuminating the moss-covered walls.

Her chains rattled as she shifted in the chair, craning her neck and trying to spot the exit. *Understand the surroundings. Come to grips with your limitations. Find a solution.* She could do that. Her mind was a fucking blade.

Methodically, her gaze swept across the crypt, and she noted with a pang of sickening dread that there was a wall of gruesome instruments just to the left of her: pliers, hooks, tongue locks, saws, whips, and beneath them, a cage full of rats. The door to the chamber was several feet away and looked to be reinforced with wrought iron. The scent of decay hung heavy in the air, along with the metallic tang of blood. Glancing down, Wren bit back a cry of horror to find rivers of crimson trickling between the cobbles. Who had been here before her? What had been done to them?

The rats in the cage were restless, squeaking and rocking the whole vessel. The sound made her think of the rats Master Crawford had forced them to poison during his lessons. There was a chance they would have the last laugh now . . . Panic made another attempt to squeeze her insides, and she struggled to fight it back this time. The chains binding her to the chair were tight, and she was nauseous at the press of the alchemy they'd been treated with.

Wren cursed herself. Her own fucking invention was being used against her yet again. She should have worked out how to make herself immune to her own creation by now, especially after the experience outside the infirmary. Gods, she'd been a fool, and now . . .

That was her panic talking. She had to stay calm. There had to be a way—

A key rattled in the lock from the outside. Wren snapped her head towards the door, which swung inwards, revealing two hooded figures.

True fear yawned wide inside her then. She had forced Torj to remain behind, and she had no idea where she was – if she was even still in Highguard, or how long she'd been gone. The Gauntlet advantage they might have won through their prototype was a distant dream now, one that seemed irrelevant if she was carved into pieces and fed to a bunch of rodents. Wren reminded herself to breathe, to remain calm. She had fought in battles; she had faced down shadow wraiths and won . . .

The figures approached, their faces fully covered by masks, long dark cloaks covering up any stitch of fabric or colour that might have been recognizable. Wren noted that the masks weren't quite the same as those worn by her attackers at the infirmary. Perhaps they were a different faction, or a different group of assailants altogether.

'What do you want?' she tried to say, but with the gag in her mouth, it came out a muffled garble.

One of them reached forwards, and Wren flinched as gloved fingers brushed her face to remove the gag.

She coughed and spat the taste of poison onto the stone floor. 'What do you want?' she repeated, clearly this time.

'You are Elwren Embervale, are you not?'

With their masks and her dulled senses, she wasn't sure which one of them had spoken. It didn't matter either way. There was no point in lying. Not yet.

'You know who I am.' She shook her chains. 'I wouldn't be wearing these otherwise.'

'Are you Elwren Embervale?' They spoke as though they hadn't heard her.

'Yes,' she hissed through her teeth, ignoring the blood roaring in her ears and the hammering of her heart against her sternum. 'What do you want?'

Wren's blood ran cold as the taller of the two went to the wall of instruments. A twisted combination of relief and terror surged through her as he selected a thin wooden cane.

Without warning, it whipped through the air and struck her right side. She cried out in shock as it left a sharp, burning stripe across her upper arm.

'We ask the questions here.'

Wren couldn't even see his eyes through the mask, not as he raised the cane again, ready to strike. She held her tongue, fighting down nausea.

'You are sister to Althea Embervale, the Shadow of Death?'

Wren eyed the blood spatter on the hem of the speaker's cloak. *That better not be Thea's blood*, she thought distantly.

The cane cracked across her other side and she yelped, hissing at the pain. '*Yes*. Thea is my sister. She's a Warsword of Thezmarr.'

Answer truthfully for as long as you can, she told herself. *There will no doubt be something that I won't want to tell them, and that they do not already know . . .*

She tried not to squirm as the shorter interrogator moved behind her and placed his thick hands on her shoulders. 'And you fought in the shadow war alongside her?' he murmured, his rotten breath coasting across her ear.

'Yes,' Wren replied, fighting to keep the quaver from her voice. If she could just be free of these damn irons, she could unleash her lightning upon them both. She could bring down the whole fucking crypt if she so wished.

She must have been testing them in her grip behind her back, because the man rattled the chains menacingly. 'These are on good and tight, lass. There'll be no lightning show in here today.'

Today. Had she been there all night? Or was that a promise of how long her interrogation would last? Surely someone would have reported her missing by now . . .

Breathe, she reminded herself.

'How long have you been in Naarva?' the taller man asked, tapping the cane against his gloved palm. As he did, a set of keys jangled at his hip. Keys to the crypt. Keys to her manacles . . . Keys to whatever was beyond these wretched walls. She forced her attention away.

'A few weeks,' she said, tensing in anticipation of the blow.
'Doing what?'
'Travelling—'
Strike.
Stars danced in her vision as the cane hit the side of her face this time. It broke the skin. Through the line of fire across her cheek, she could feel the trickle of blood.
'You have not been travelling.'
'I have,' she said hoarsely. 'All over the—'
Hands closed around her throat, squeezing tight, crushing her windpipe. Wren's legs kicked out, her whole body flailing against the chains as she fought with all her might to get air into her lungs.
'You're a shit liar.' That sour breath was hot on her face again.
Wren gasped and gasped, the chains rattling as she struggled.
Suddenly, she was released. She wheezed, coughing and spluttering and trying to take in as much air as she could, her heart pounding painfully. Eyes streaming, throat throbbing, she sagged in the chair, only the chains keeping her upright.
'Where's your Warsword? Not here to save you now, is he?'
Rhetorical questions. Wren's cheek was burning where she'd been struck, the dry blood already itching. Her gaze flitted quickly to the keys and back again, and she clenched her mouth shut.
'You're learning,' the man with the cane sneered. 'That's good.'
Thick fingers threaded through her hair from behind and yanked her head back.
'You're an alchemist, aren't you?'
'No.'
The cane struck her legs this time, and when she flinched, the second man pulled her hair painfully tight again. 'This is going to get so much worse. This is just a warmup for us.'
'You attend Drevenor Academy, don't you?' asked the first.
As soon as the words left his lips, realization dawned on Wren. These men weren't rebels. They weren't part of any conspiracy against the rulers or royal blood . . .

'How many greenhouses at Drevenor?'

Wren's breath rattled in her chest, her eyes going wide as the man returned the cane to its place on the wall and kicked the cage of rats towards her.

'This little talk is going to hurt either way. The question is . . . how much?' he said. 'Tell us, how many greenhouses?'

Wren didn't know if she was losing circulation to her brain, but she couldn't think what a bunch of cut-throats would want with the academy. Were they looking for a bounty to steal?

'I don't know what you're talking about.'

Her vision went white as she was struck across the face again, this time with the back of the man's hand. Her head snapped to the side with the force of it, and the man behind had to hold her chair to stop it from tumbling over.

Her chains shifted just slightly, allowing her a glimpse at the far wall.

There, amid an array of torture instruments, hung her belt of potions.

CHAPTER 75

Wren

*'An alchemist's experiments
can shape the world around them'*

– Transformative Arts of Alchemy

'Who are the masters at Drevenor?' the second man demanded, just inches from her face. 'Name them!'

Wren hated that she flinched, knowing that neither of her sisters would ever let a bastard like this see fear. She didn't know how long they'd been at it now. Her entire body ached, both from their blows and from the chains. The attacks to her ribs were particularly vicious and her breath whistled between her teeth at the pain. But every strike loosened the chains around her middle, and behind her back, she could move her hands.

So, she welcomed their violence.

It would be their downfall before the end.

Wren's mind raced through the inventory of potions, powders, and tinctures she'd stocked in her belt the day before. If she could escape the chains and get to her supplies, there were plenty of potions that could fell a man where he stood . . . She thought of the keys at the belt of one of her interrogators. Maybe - just maybe—

Her chair was suddenly dragged backwards, the scraping noise making her wince.

'Get the branding iron,' the closest one drawled. 'That'll loosen her tongue. It always does . . .'

The scrape of metal sounded. Wren thrashed against the chains.

'You hear that?' the taller one asked as he approached.

They all fell quiet, listening.

Then Wren's stomach turned to lead. In the near distance, she could hear screams. High-pitched, broken screams for mercy. She knew the sound intimately, like an old song. Flashes of Thezmarr came back to her: the fortress wrapped in shadow, onyx power lashing through the air, screams echoing in their wake—

'You see? You're all the fucking same. You all break in the end.'

Wren's breaths came hard and fast as she tried to wriggle without being noticed in her restraints. *You all break in the end . . .* Something about his words snagged, but a flurry of movements across the crypt had her heart hammering, threatening to burst through her chest.

'Last chance before we heat this beauty up,' the man warned, brandishing the poker at her. 'Let's try a new one . . . Tell us about the memory weave. What does it look like? How does it work?'

Wren struggled to swallow, fought to remain calm in the face of that white-hot piece of metal.

Behold the price of betrayal, novices . . . Hardim's words echoed in her mind, followed by those of the High Chancellor, ringing out through the fog of pain and fear: *The teachings and inner workings of this academy must remain confidential. When you take your pledge, you will make an oath of secrecy. This will be tested at some point during your time here. Do not take it lightly.*

The realization hit her as hard and fast as the blows did.

It was a test.

This had nothing to do with rulers and royal magic. This was not the work of the People's Vanguard or some other conspiracy group.

It was the test the High Chancellor had promised.

At last, she understood why she was there. Wren braced herself and tried to meet her captors' eyes, or as close as possible with their masks.

'Greenhouses. Masters. Memories. I don't know what you're talking about. I don't know what you want from me.'

The men laughed cruelly. 'That so?' one said.

'Yes.'

'Fuck the branding iron,' said the other. 'Use the rats.'

'I don't know what you're talking about. I know nothing.' Wren repeated it like a chant, unable to stop the shudder of fear washing over her as one of them went to the cage.

'They haven't been fed in a week,' the other man told her.

'I don't know what you're talking about.'

'Just imagine them burrowing into your innards, tasting that flesh—'

'I don't know what you're talking about.'

'Get her on her back. Let's see what these rats make of alchemist flesh. We can start with her feet. Work our way up—'

The world tilted, and Wren was slammed backwards onto the ground, still in her chair. She cried out in pain as her hands were nearly crushed behind her.

'I know nothing,' she sobbed. *'I know nothing.'*

The heat of a flame singed her skirts.

'What weapons do they have?' her interrogator demanded. 'What magical artefacts?'

'Vasen . . .' the one holding down her chair warned.

'No names,' Vasen snapped.

'It's time,' the other said.

'What?'

'It's *time*,' he repeated.

The heat vanished from Wren's feet. A whimper of relief escaped her, however temporary.

She was still on her back when she felt the chains loosen. She didn't dare move as they gave way around her body, falling to the cobbles in a heap. Wren slid from the chair, curling on her side on the cold stone.

'You passed,' Vasen's voice sounded from the door. 'Six hours and not a word of Drevenor's secrets . . .'

Wren coughed violently, spitting blood onto the ground, not looking up as the door swung closed. She allowed herself a minute, just one, to process what had just happened. She had been tested, tortured, and her oath of secrecy remained intact.

Steeling herself against the pain of her bruised body and aching wrists, Wren dragged herself upright. Sweat beaded at her brow and dampened the armpits of her dress, not that it mattered. She'd be burning it the second she was out of this cesspit.

Grimacing at the blood and filth on the cobbles, she pushed the last of the heavy chains away and shoved down the restraints around her legs, standing with a ragged gasp. Her wrists were rubbed raw, and blood dotted her clothes. A wave of queasiness washed over her. Breathing deeply through her nose, she staggered towards the far wall, where her belt of potions and tools still hung.

Fastening it around her waist, she clawed back a piece of herself.

Some of her supplies were missing, but she chewed a piece of dried iruseed to help her stay present, and braced herself against the wall, waiting for the alertness to take effect. As it kicked in, she shook her head, wincing at the ache that had blossomed, and surveyed the crypt one final time.

You passed. It seemed like a shallow victory in light of her injuries, in light of the terror that still simmered beneath the surface.

Taking another deep breath, Wren rolled her aching shoulders and palmed her dagger, which she found among the tools. She opened the door.

A cold voice rang out in the darkness.

'Welcome to the Gauntlet, Elwren Embervale.'

CHAPTER 76

Torj

'Over time, a bodyguard's dedication endures
as an eternal vigil, an unyielding presence
in the ever-shifting sands of fate'

— *The Guardian's Handbook:
Principles and Practices of Personal Protection*

TORJ PACED THE dining hall like a caged animal, stalking up and down the rows between the tables, fists clenched at his sides, his body wound tight with tension. He should never have let her go. Or at the very least, he should have followed. But now, as dusk began to blanket the grounds outside, he was beyond panicked. And there was nothing he could do.

If he wasn't going mad already, this was sure to do the job.

Throughout the day, he had felt spikes of terror in his chest that did not belong to him. They belonged to *Wren*. He knew it in his bones, could feel it in the lingering storm in his scars. He had gone straight to the High Chancellor, demanding to know where she was and what the tests for the day entailed. But the bastard wouldn't say a word. It took all of Torj's self-control not to start inflicting pain for answers.

The other masters gave away nothing, not as he yelled in their faces and threatened their lives. It was all he could do not to tear them limb from limb. The tension in the air was palpable, as though the masters themselves were at odds with one another. Farissa refused to tell him, citing academy law, but he didn't miss that she watched him closely, monitoring him as the hours passed.

'Sit down, Elderbrock,' she said at last. 'You're making me seasick with all that pacing.'

'I don't give a fuck.' He continued the same path, up and down, likely wearing the stone down beneath his boots. 'Where is she, Farissa?'

'She'll be here.'

She was lying, he knew it in his bones. 'You've said that all fucking day. And I know this wasn't some simple mission to get ingredients. I can *feel* it.'

She fixed him with an intense stare. 'What is it that you feel?'

He narrowed his eyes. 'Fuck. Off.'

'You feel *her*, don't you?'

'I don't want to talk about the damn curse now,' he ground out.

'But is it a curse?' Farissa ventured.

'I don't have the patience for your cryptic horseshit. Where. Is. Wren?'

Brisk footsteps sounded, and Torj turned to see both Audra and the High Chancellor approaching. It was Audra who spoke first.

'She's partaking in the Gauntlet.'

'What?'

Audra didn't balk at his thunderous expression. 'She is doing what she came here to do, Elderbrock.'

'Why wasn't I told?'

'Because no one was told. Thus is the nature of the Gauntlet,' the High Chancellor supplied. 'I suggest you retire for the evening—'

'When is it over?' Torj growled.

Belcourt gave an infuriating answer. 'When it's finished.'

Torj had half a mind to throw him through the nearest wall.

Audra's bony hand closed around his arm. As though she had read his mind, she said, 'I suggest you leave, Elderbrock. Drevenor can't afford to lose its High Chancellor just yet.'

Torj stormed from the hall, but as soon as he was alone and the fury abated, fear coiled like icy tendrils in the pit of his stomach, every beat of his heart echoing with dread.

How many hours had passed since Wren had been in his bed? Since she'd coaxed tiny lightning bolts from his skin and tilted his world for ever? Even now, he could feel that soft storm current within, heightening his pulse and amplifying his fear for her.

You're what has been missing all my life. And I intend to keep you . . . He should have said more, should have been clearer. But in the face of the Gauntlet, that didn't matter.

Elwren Embervale might have been his, but she also belonged wholly to herself. Though his whole body was tense, suppressing the urge to scour the kingdom for her, to intervene, to shield her from whatever harm she was facing in that trial, he remained bound by another vow: that he would never stand in her way.

Torj burst into his room, all but kicking the door in to face the deafening silence.

But he wasn't alone.

A familiar figure sat in his chair, twirling a dagger between his fingers.

'What are you doing here, Hawthorne?' Torj eyed his brother in arms wearily, hazarding a guess that Cal had let their fellow Warsword into his chambers.

'Traditionally, the rulers of the midrealms have always attended the graduation ceremony of the novices after the Gauntlet,' Wilder told him, still toying with his blade. 'Though I suspect they're also heavily invested in the development of our alchemists, given the threats they've faced recently . . . In any case, I'm here in an official capacity.'

'And who, exactly, are you meant to be guarding?'

'Thea's got it covered.'

'She didn't want to see her sister before?' Torj asked.

'She said Wren would want to be alone, and that she'll see her when she's won the damn thing.'

Torj gave a dark laugh. That sounded like Thea, alright.

Wilder gave him a knowing look. 'She also said it might be my turn to repay the favour . . .'

'What are you talking about?'

'When Thea went to undertake the Great Rite, you gave me some advice.'

Torj raked his hands through his hair with a noise of frustration. 'What the fuck did I know? Save it, Hawthorne—'

But his fellow Warsword stood, placing himself between Torj and the door, as though he knew Torj was mere seconds away from throwing it open and going to Wren.

'You told me this: *the closer you get to true happiness, the more you fear it.* You said it's the what-ifs that eat you alive . . . *What if it all goes wrong? What if you lose it all?*'

'I can feel her terror!' Torj roared, clenching his fists as his anger surged. 'And that was just the start. She's been gone for hours—'

His friend simply stared at him. 'You think it was easy for me to watch Thea walk into the Great Rite? You think I didn't want to go tearing after her and rip apart everything that tried to hurt her?'

Torj looked at the floor. He knew the love between Wilder Hawthorne and Althea Embervale was nothing short of legendary; he knew the lengths they would go to for one another, what they had endured together and apart. Theirs was a love that had torn down the Scarlet Tower, that had spanned kingdoms, battles and the entire shadow war.

Understanding flashed in Wilder's gaze as Torj met it once more. He gripped Torj by the shoulder, as Torj had once done to him in the Singing Hare in Aveum. 'You told me I was asking all the wrong questions . . . That the one to ask instead was this: *what if you got everything you ever wanted?*'

Shrugging off Wilder's grip, Torj paced the room furiously. 'I did. And now . . .'

'Now your woman is fighting to achieve something she has wanted her whole life. Your role, your *only* fucking role here, is to support her. Fail to do that, and your fears of losing her will come true. Succeed, and it will be better than you ever dreamed.'

Torj braced himself against his desk, knocking over a pile of books, watching them spill across the surface. 'I don't like this wise version of you.'

'I can return to my old ways of using my fists, if you like. Your nose was always too straight for my liking.'

'No one could ever land a hit. Yours, on the other hand . . .'

'Fuck off,' his friend muttered. 'Can I trust you won't do something stupid?'

'I'm not making any promises,' Torj grunted.

There was a gleam of amusement in Wilder's silver eyes. 'Not so easy, is it, when it's you on the other side of that fear? But you can't be her shield in this, brother.'

Torj forced himself to take a steadying breath. At last, he nodded. He pictured the determined gleam in Wren's stormy eyes and knew: the Gauntlet was hers for the taking, and by the Furies, she would take it.

CHAPTER 77

Wren

'With my body as a shield, my mind as a blade,
I will not hesitate to sacrifice'

– *Drevenor Academy Oath of Secrecy*

WREN'S BLOOD RAN cold.
The Gauntlet?

If this was the Gauntlet, then where were Zavier and Dessa? If this was the Gauntlet, what had happened to the other teams? To the points system and the staggered start times?

Wren was suddenly moving, stumbling down the dark passageway outside her cell. She reached for her belt and pulled out more dried iruseed, chewing the bitter substance quickly. She couldn't afford to pass out, not now.

A scream sounded, but the echo was disorientating, bouncing off the wet walls and adding to the pounding in Wren's head. The dank, musty smell of the crypt filled her nostrils, and she fought the urge to gag. She had to act quickly if they were to have any chance of continuing. She had to find Dessa and Zavier.

All around her were iron doors, a small window at the top of each. *Empty. Empty. Empty*, she realized as she passed, her hands trembling violently at her sides.

A scream sounded again, this time far sharper and closer than the last.

Dessa.

Wren ran, following the sound, ignoring the dizziness that flooded her vision.

At last, she reached the right cell. Peering through the bars, she spotted Dessa slumped against the wall, her face bruised, her clothes torn. The cell's door was ajar, and there was no one else inside.

'Dessa,' Wren whispered urgently, 'it's me. It's Wren. I'm here to get you out.'

Dessa lifted her head weakly, her eyes struggling to focus. 'Wren? How did you . . . ?'

'No time to explain,' she interrupted, pushing the door open with a creak. 'Can you stand?'

Dessa nodded, leaning heavily on Wren for support. 'Zavier?' she asked.

'Right here,' came his voice from the doorway.

Wren's gaze snapped up to spot his lean figure braced against the frame. He was bleeding heavily from a cut in his brow.

'Did you say anything?' Wren asked. 'About—'

Zavier shook his head. '*Six hours and not a word of Drevenor's secrets . . .*' he said darkly.

Wren turned back to Dessa. 'Did you tell them anything?'

'No,' her friend croaked.

Wren dragged Dessa upright, towards Zavier. 'We're in the—'

'Gauntlet, I know,' he told her, looping Dessa's other arm around his shoulder. 'I know the way out.'

'Shit,' Dessa muttered between them.

'Sums up my feelings on the matter,' Zavier grunted, hauling her from the cell.

Wren pushed a piece of dried iruseed into Dessa's mouth as Zavier navigated the winding passageways of the crypt, the terrain inclining as they went.

'Not far now,' he said.

It wasn't long before soft light glowed at the end of the tunnel, and the trio limped towards it. As they reached the end, they came upon a gate.

'It's locked,' Wren muttered, rattling it by the bars.

'It's timed,' Zavier told her. 'Remember? The team ahead of us gets a ninety-second head start . . . If they passed the secrecy test—'

As if in answer, something deep in the gate groaned, and the door swung outwards.

'Let the Gauntlet begin,' Zavier murmured, stepping forwards.

As they crossed the threshold, Wren's breath caught in her throat. For beyond it was a forest.

The trees closed in around them, the canopy hanging heavy with an eerie stillness. Wren's heart was still racing, and a wave of goosebumps rushed over her arms as she and her companions moved deeper into the glade. She thought she heard a cry in the distance, but neither Zavier nor Dessa showed any sign of hearing it, so she pressed on. The plants were so dense that they had to climb over roots and bushes, and Wren's heart shot into her throat as she brushed against hairy leaves that she was sure would elicit some sort of horrific reaction.

'We need to treat our injuries,' she said, eyeing their cuts and bruises in the dappled moonlight.

Zavier nodded to her belt. 'Got anything in there?'

'A lot of it was taken during . . .' she trailed off. She wasn't ready to talk about her interrogation yet. 'But there should be some basics we can use with whatever the forest holds.'

Zavier's head was still oozing blood. 'Not looking too good, is it?'

'I've seen worse,' Wren told him, scanning the ground for anything that might staunch his bleeding.

Dessa pointed behind Wren. 'There's some yarrow by that tree over there.'

Giving her a grateful nod, Wren took several cuttings of both the leaves and the flowers, passing them to Zavier. 'Those should help it clot.'

He gave her a wry smile. 'I know.'

Wren dug through the remainder of the herbs at her belt, dishing out the last of her dried iruseed. 'That won't fix anything, but it'll stop you losing consciousness. The Warswords have been using it for centuries in battle.'

Together, they patched themselves up as best they could.

'What now?' Wren asked, looking around at the dense treeline.

'Look,' Zavier said, pointing.

Around the trunks of several trees, black ribbons had been tied, creating a path to follow.

'They're heading south-west,' Zavier said. 'Drevenor lies in the same direction. I say we follow them.'

As the trio moved deeper into the dense forest, the eerie silence enveloped them. The towering trees seemed to close in around them, their gnarled branches reaching out like ghostly fingers, making the hair on the back of Wren's neck stand on end.

A twig snapped beneath Zavier's boot, and Wren whirled around, her hand instinctively reaching for her dagger. Dessa placed a reassuring hand on her shoulder, but her eyes darted nervously through the shadows.

'We need to pick up the pace,' Wren whispered, her voice barely audible above the rustling of leaves.

They pressed forwards, each step more cautious than the last, while the forest seemed to watch them, as if the very trees had eyes. Wren's senses were on high alert, her ears straining for any sound that might signal danger.

As if on cue, distant screams echoed through the dense foliage.

An icy chill raked down Wren's spine, her heart pounding.

Suddenly, the screams weren't so distant. The cries grew louder, more panicked, more hysterical, until the very ground seemed to vibrate with their intensity.

Wren locked eyes with Zavier and Dessa. '*Run*,' she hissed.

Branches whipped at Wren's face as she sprinted, her lungs and injured ribs burning with each ragged breath. She could hear her teammates' footsteps beside her, their own desperate gasps for air mingling with the sound of their pursuers.

The forest blurred around them, a kaleidoscope of green and brown as they dodged trees and leapt over fallen logs. Wren's mind raced as fast as her feet, trying to form a plan, a way to escape the relentless pursuit while each scream behind them pierced the air like a dagger, fuelling their urgency as they navigated deeper into the forest.

A horrific snarling noise had Wren whirling on her feet. Between the trees, she saw them: two women and a man emerged from the shadows, their faces contorted with madness. Wren recoiled as she recognized the telltale signs: eyes glazed with inexplicable rage, slight foaming at their mouths, hands curled at their sides, animalistic noises . . .

All symptoms of mad honey disease.

'Stay back,' she cautioned the others. 'They're—'

'Mad honey disease,' Zavier cut in, palming a dagger and sizing up their opponents. 'Nectar of rhododendron has fucked them up good. You think they were force-fed the honey?'

'There's no way to tell,' Wren replied, not taking her eyes off the trio that stalked towards them, menace in their stares.

'We can't fight them,' Dessa argued. 'They don't know what they're doing. They're—'

'They knew what they were doing when they signed up for Drevenor,' Zavier said. 'It's every alchemist for themselves.'

Wren plucked two vials from her belt and braced herself, muscles tense with anticipation.

Dessa hesitated. 'I don't think—'

But with feral growls, the afflicted group lunged forwards, their movements erratic and unpredictable. Like a caged animal, one of the women swiped at Wren as though she had claws, and Wren sprang into action. All those lessons with Torj came flooding back and her body moved instinctually, blocking the blows and the onslaught of fists, twisting out of any grip before she could be immobilized.

She moved with more fluidity than she ever had, leaning into the rhythm her body set as she parried the frenzied attacks from her peers. Zavier and Dessa fought beside her, their movements echoing her own in a deadly dance.

With a flick of her fingers, Wren popped the corks on the two vials she'd drawn from her belt. 'Stay back,' she warned her companions as she flung the contents at their opponents.

A cloud of darkness exploded between them, and Wren lurched forwards, grabbing Zavier and Dessa by the arms and hauling them back.

'Come on,' she panted. 'It won't keep them for long.'

'What was that?' Zavier looked astounded.

'Soot root powder,' she replied, pulling them through the undergrowth, desperate to put distance between them and the mad team.

As they moved through the forest, Wren realized it seemed to be narrowing around them. Soon, they were on a path that led into a steep decline, taking them beneath the surface of the forest. Damp earth formed a narrow tunnel, leading them down, down, down . . .

Wren's thoughts turned as dark as the earthen walls closing in around them.

All paths lead to the underworld.

CHAPTER 78

Torj

'Every shadow is a potential threat, every sound a harbinger of danger'

– *Mastering the Craft of Close Protection*

Time lost all coherence. Seconds, minutes, and hours stretched into eternity as Torj waited for news of Wren, alone now that Wilder was following orders elsewhere. Her fear lanced through his chest like a blade: sharp, cutting to the bone. He could taste her terror on his tongue.

Unable to stand the quiet and the faint lingering scent of Wren in his rooms, Torj found himself back in the dining hall. He paced jagged lines between the rows of tables, each restless step only fuelling the turmoil within. Somewhere out there in the Gauntlet, Wren was facing something horrific, and there was nothing he could do to help her.

Around him, the academy masters, the newly arrived royals and their guards, the Warswords and scholars engaged in hushed conversations, their words lost beneath the weight of his panic.

'Easy there, Bear Slayer,' said a voice from behind him. 'You'll wear a track through the floor.'

Althea Embervale was leaning against one of the tables, cleaning her fingernails with her Naarvian steel dagger, pinning him with a celadon gaze that matched her sister's. In Wren's absence, the sisters' similarities made Torj's heart wrench: hair the same shade of bronze, those piercing green eyes, the same dark features, Thea's currently drawn taut in a fiery expression.

'You don't worry for her?' Torj asked.

'No,' Thea said simply.

Torj stared at her. 'How can you not? Knowing what she's up against? Knowing the danger—'

Thea gave a harsh laugh. 'Wren knows danger intimately. It's the danger that should be concerned.'

How long ago had it been that he'd said something similar to Audra?

Thea gave him a sympathetic look. 'Have faith.'

But Thea wasn't feeling what he was. She didn't have her sister's panic spearing through her, nor her surges of power. Torj rubbed at his sternum with his fist as it coursed through him again. It went against his very nature not to be by her side, not to be protecting her.

He felt sick. Bracing himself on the edge of the table, he inhaled measured breaths, waiting for the brutal onslaught to subside.

When he looked up again, Thea was watching him with narrowed eyes. 'What aren't you telling me, Bear Slayer?'

He wanted to tell her it was nothing, that he was merely concerned for Wren, as any rational person would be. But with each passing moment, the foreign pulse of fear reverberated through his body, a relentless drumbeat of dread that threatened to consume him.

'Torj?' Thea pressed, brow crinkling. 'What is it? And if you tell me "nothing" I'll blast you with lightning – and it won't be the kind that inspires the phrase *"storm-kissed"*.'

The bolt of power Wren had hit him with at Thezmarr had hardly been gentle, but he kept that detail to himself.

'I'd save yourself the trouble and just tell her, brother,' Wilder said, taking his place beside Thea, an arm sliding around her waist.

Torj tracked the movement: casual and familiar, yet still a subtle claiming for the whole world to see. It made his chest ache.

His friends waited, their expressions open, their eyes full of understanding.

Torj glanced around. 'Not here,' he said.

He took them away from the prying eyes and eager ears of the dining hall to the archives and the private space he'd often occupied over the last few months. When they were seated and he was certain they wouldn't be overheard, he met their gazes.

'I can feel her,' he told them, pulling his shirt aside to reveal the web of scars there.

'What do you mean?' Thea said slowly.

'Right now, I can feel her fear, and when she uses her magic . . . It pulses right here. I consulted Farissa, and I've been investigating magical wounds, accidental curses, the effects of sovereign magic – all to understand what this is . . .'

'And?' Wilder asked.

'And I don't have the answers. I have read dozens of books. I have researched for hours on end. I have talked to others with injuries resulting from magic. But I am not sick. The scars haven't spread. I feel like myself, only . . . *more*. In the years after the war, I felt it only occasionally. A thrum of power, like an echo left over from the battle, but . . .' He dragged his fingers through his hair, pushing back the stray lock that fell into his eyes. 'Since I saw Wren again, it's been different.'

'Different how?' Thea demanded, her eyes locked on his scars.

'It's as though we're linked. I can sense her power, her emotions. We're . . . in tune with one another.'

Thea folded her arms across her chest and glanced at Wilder. 'She allowed you to wield her power in the battle for Thezmarr. We both witnessed it.'

Wilder nodded. 'I've never seen anything like it.'

'That kind of magic leaves more than a mark, surely . . . ?' Thea ventured.

'That's what I've been trying to determine,' Torj said. 'What happens to someone who has hosted power that doesn't belong to them – that they were not made to wield? Does some sort of delayed reaction occur? Does the wound heal over, only to fester from within?'

Thea unsheathed her dagger and spun it on the table. 'Why *wound*?' she asked.

'What do you mean?'

'I mean, has this link caused you pain? Do the scars ache?' she pressed, continuing to spin her dagger, her brow furrowed.

Torj hesitated. When Wren's power had first hit him in the battle, he had thought he was going to die, but had it been from pain? Had he suffered as the lightning coursed through him?

'No,' he said quietly. 'It has never hurt me.'

'Then why the discussion of magical wounds and injuries?'

Beside her, Wilder looked thoughtful. 'It's natural, isn't it? What comes before a scar? Pain.'

'And yet, our Bear Slayer here felt none.'

'Perhaps he just doesn't remember?' Wilder said gently. 'Trauma does that to the best of us . . .'

But Thea shot to her feet.

'Where are you going?' Torj asked.

'Just wait here,' she commanded, already halfway out the door.

To Torj's surprise, Wilder hadn't moved a muscle. He simply offered a shrug. 'I find it's just best to run with it.'

With his elbows on the table, Torj rested his head in his hands, tensing as another surge of storm magic assaulted him. The walls of the study chamber seemed to close in.

'It's that intense?' Wilder asked quietly.

'This isn't the half of it,' Torj replied, not looking up.

He wasn't sure he could bear the agony of uncertainty for much longer. He was just about to return to the dining hall to see if there was any word when a thick book dropped onto the table before him with a thud.

'Here,' Thea said, throwing herself back into her chair. 'That was in Kipp's room. I saw it when I arrived and thought nothing of it, but now . . .'

Frowning, Torj turned the title towards him.

Tethers and Magical Bonds Throughout History.

'You kept saying you were *linked*. That's not an injury – it's a connection. And the fact that Kipp had this in his room tells me he's thinking something similar,' Thea supplied. 'I hate to break it to you, but you've been researching the wrong thing, Bear Slayer.'

A strange, creeping sensation swept across Torj's skin as he opened the hefty tome, turning to its contents page.

Definitions of magical bonds

Causes of magical bonds

Classifications of magical bonds

His gaze caught on the list beneath the latter: *Parental and inherited magical connections. Sibling bonds. Animal telepathy. Fated enemies. Seers and subjects. Bonds and magical objects. Alchemical connections.*

Soul bonds.

A breath shuddered out of him as he read, forgetting Thea and Wilder as he leafed through the pages to the correct chapter.

'Soul bonds . . .' he murmured, tracing the title before reading aloud. '*Also referred to as: soul-bonded, bonded, fated pairing, twin flames, surge binding, soul ties . . .*'

Thea cleared her throat. 'Looks like you have some reading to do.'

Torj didn't even look up as the couple left the chamber. Instead, he pored over the words before him, each more damning than the next.

⁂

If Audra was surprised to find Torj on the other side of her door, she didn't show it.

'You knew.' The accusation came out in a growl.

Audra's expression remained unreadable as she opened the door further and motioned him inside. Only when the door clicked shut did she dip her head in acknowledgement. 'I suspected.'

'Since when?' he demanded.

'Since I saw that bolt of lightning hit you on the battlefield.'

'Five fucking years ago.'

'Yes.'

He made a sound of pure rage. 'What the fuck, Audra?'

Audra's eyes narrowed. 'Calm yourself, Elderbrock.'

'Calm myself?' He shook his head in raging disbelief. 'How do you expect me to calm myself? I have no idea what this means.'

'Exactly what part don't you understand?'

'To start with – the part where I might be connected to Wren's *soul*?'

Audra sighed heavily. 'A soul bond is a rare and powerful form of magic that is fated by the gods themselves. A gift. It was always simmering beneath the surface for you and Elwren, lying dormant, but I suspect that moment during the final battle awoke it.'

Torj tossed the book Thea had found onto Audra's desk with a thud. 'This says there have been no records of soul bonds for centuries. So, how? *How* the fuck is this possible? And how could you possibly have known?'

Audra pushed her spectacles to the bridge of her nose with barely a glance at the tome. 'The power Wren displayed at Thezmarr could have only been withstood by something ancient . . . a magic no longer of this world – until now. You should have died. You were not built to wield power like it, and yet . . . you did. Because you are a part of her, and she a part of you.'

Torj clenched his fists at his sides, suppressing the urge to hit something. 'What are you saying, Audra? Speak plainly for once in your fucking life.'

Unperturbed, Audra continued. 'Often in moments of great emotional intensity, or in the face of a life-altering event, the bond makes itself known. Wren's power unlocked it between you. The fall of the Veil soon after only gave way to more old magic in the world.'

'If you knew all of this, why did you encourage my research on the wrong fucking subject? I've been toiling away reading text after text about magical wounds, for fuck's sake. Interviewing poor victims of sovereign magic—'

'I needed to be sure it wasn't an injury that would send you mad like others who've faced the might of such power. A mad Warsword is a dangerous thing.'

He spoke his next words through gritted teeth. 'And how can you be sure?'

'I can't. Only *you* can.'

'How?' he demanded.

Audra glanced at the book on the table. 'The ancient texts I have read report that a soul bond can be *seen* by the bonded. When it falls into place for the fated pair, there is a visible representation – a golden thread between them. Have you seen such a thing?'

Torj took a steadying breath, fighting to rein his emotions back in. 'No.'

'Then perhaps I'm wrong,' Audra offered.

'But you don't think you are.'

'No,' she replied. 'I believe it has to play out . . .'

'We're not pawns in some fucking game,' Torj snapped.

'We are all pieces on life's chessboard, Elderbrock.'

No longer able to stand still, he moved about the room like an incensed beast. He wanted to destroy things, wanted to tear Audra's space apart for what she'd done. But he needed to know, needed to understand.

'How does it work?' he ground out.

She eyed him warily. 'What starts as a seemingly simple connection grows into something all-consuming. The two individuals become linked in ways that defy understanding. They can sense each other's emotions, share dreams, and even experience the other's physical sensations as if they were their own . . .'

Torj's throat went dry, each revelation hitting him hard in the chest. And yet he couldn't believe it – wouldn't.

'The bond grows stronger with time and proximity.'

Torj glared at her, his heart rate spiking. 'You paired me as her bodyguard deliberately.'

'Everything I do is deliberate, Bear Slayer,' she said. 'But not even I am a match for the will of the Furies, and the fates they lay at our feet. Whether I put you and Elwren together or not, you would have found your way back to one another.' She thrust her chin towards the book on the table. 'How much of that have you read?'

'Enough to confront you about your horseshit mind games.'

'But not all of it,' she surmised with an arched brow. 'I suspect that the bond has been sliding into place for some time, perhaps since your reunion at the fortress? Though I imagine it's amplified since you became . . . intimate.'

Torj balked, rage simmering to a boil. 'Are you *spying* on us, Guild Master?'

Audra scoffed. 'It was inevitable, Bear Slayer. And whether it was the physical act or something more emotional, a trigger set it in motion. Some ancient texts cite the soul bond as a gift from the gods, a testament to the power of love and destiny, something that can strengthen and heal. Others see it as a curse, a burden that strips away free will and binds two souls together for eternity.'

'And?' he pressed.

'It is not without its dangers. Just as the bonded individuals can share their triumphs, they also share each other's pain and suffering. If one is wounded, the other feels the wound as if it were their own. In times of war or strife, this connection can be a double-edged sword, making the bonded vulnerable to their enemies.'

'And so . . . if this far-fetched story is true . . . you put me in a position where I would willingly die for her? I literally threw myself in front of a spear for her, only to now discover it could have killed her too.' He couldn't breathe, not as the image of Wren suffering the same agony flashed before him.

But Audra ploughed on. 'You haven't *seen* the thread between you, so perhaps this isn't what I think. Or – the bond is not fully in place. Until it is, that cannot happen. Though no doubt your sacrifice only made your connection that much stronger.'

'Are you mad?' Torj was shaking. 'Are you actually insane?'

'No,' Audra replied. 'Far from it. You have always been stronger together. And you will be, when you are soul-bonded for life.'

A laugh of disbelief escaped Torj then. 'You expect me to believe that there is some sort of mystical ancient magic between me and Wren?'

'Yes,' Audra said plainly. 'And you must believe it, for it may pose a danger to you both. If anyone discovers this bond when it falls into place, it can be exploited. You can be used against each other, hurt one to hurt the other . . .' She pinned him with a meaningful look. 'I do not deny that she will be vulnerable through you. The connection between you can be abused. A strike against you is a strike against her.'

'Well, if by some stroke of the Furies this is true . . . No one knows. No one has to know,' Torj argued, his impatience rising. He should have been out there looking for her, and he was standing here, listening to Audra talk nonsense. There was no *gold thread* linking him and Wren, no so-called *soul bond*. Their connection was natural, shaped by over a decade of knowing one another, of facing a war together.

But Audra was frowning. 'Secrets such as these never remain hidden for long. Tell me, how did you finally uncover the concept?'

He pointed to the volume on the table. 'Thea found that book in Kipp's room. She brought it to me.'

Audra raised a brow. 'So . . . I know. Farissa suspects. Thea, and, naturally, Hawthorne, know. Kristopher knows. Already it is no longer a secret.'

'There is nothing to know,' Torj countered. 'And even if there was, I would trust them with my life.'

'But do you trust them with *hers*?'

Torj hesitated. Of course he trusted his friends. They had been through the war together; they had saved each other time and time again. But Audra had a point. Secrets could so quickly unravel.

'You see?' Audra said, watching the realization dawn on his face.

Torj swallowed the lump in his throat. 'If it were real . . . What then? Is there a way to . . . stop it? To cut the tie?'

'If there is, I do not know it. But this connection between you runs soul-deep, Elderbrock. To meddle with it would be to interfere with the will of the gods, with fate itself.'

Torj shifted on his feet, eyes narrowing. 'What's in this for you, Audra? Are you hoping that if this is true, I'll wield Wren's storms at your command? That you'll somehow benefit from one of your soldiers being soul-bonded to the future Queen of Delmira? Has it been a power play all along for you?'

'Watch your tone, Bear Slayer.'

'I'll watch my tone when you stop hiding your real agenda.' Audra had always been known for her scheming and secrets, but this? He would not have her using Wren in her games.

'Everything I do is for the good of the midrealms, Warsword. You'd do well to remember that.' The Guild Master gathered herself. 'During those seconds on the battlefield, Elwren saved you. She tethered you to this world, and to herself for life. Your fates have always been entwined.'

Ready to throw the damn book in the fire, Torj snatched it from the table, surging for the door. He turned back to level Audra with a hard stare. 'We're the makers of our own fucking fates, Guild Master.'

CHAPTER 79

Wren

'There is nothing so poisonous as that which the mind conjures'

— *The Poisoner's Handbook*

As Wren and her companions descended into the dark depths of the tunnel, the air grew thick with the scent of wet stone. Any faint light from the forest canopy vanished behind them as the path wound deeper still.

'Any guesses as to what's next?' Zavier mused, turning another corner, where torches illuminated the path ahead.

'A flood of poisoned water?' Wren offered. 'A cursed mountain drake?'

Zavier snorted. 'What about an arachne nest?'

'Or plague of some kind?'

'That's not funny,' Dessa said sharply. 'We've already been abducted, tortured and nearly killed by our own peers.'

Wren exchanged a look with Zavier, and they stifled unhinged laughter.

The number of torches increased as they moved further into the strange cavern, casting a golden glow across what greeted them at the end of the tunnel. The passageway widened into what appeared to be a sprawling maze of stone, its corridors stretching out before them – an array of options, all likely housing their own unique brand of doom. Columns of ancient granite loomed overhead, their surfaces etched with markings Wren didn't recognize, languages and runes she didn't understand.

'Where is everyone?' Wren murmured, staring into the maze, her skin crawling. She'd been sure some of the cohort would have caught up with them by now, and that they themselves might have happened upon Selene, Alarik and Gideon . . . The ninety-second intervals between teams were a mere eye-blink in the scheme of the horrors they had faced so far.

The trio followed the stone path, sticking close together as the maze offered various twists and turns – diversions from the main route, or so it felt. With each step, Wren scanned her surroundings, her senses alert and honed to a keen razor's edge, her blood still roaring in her ears from her exertions in the forest.

It was only when they came to a strange circular opening in the labyrinth that they drew to a stop. Slowly, they approached the centre.

'Do you think this is the heart of the maze?' Dessa asked quietly. 'Does this mean we've finished the Gauntlet?'

The floor was covered in elaborate carvings, which were almost dizzying to look upon.

Unease roiled in Wren's gut. 'I don't—'

Something clicked. Wren lurched, arms flailing as the floor shifted, turning beneath them like a dial. Both Dessa and Zavier stumbled as well, the three of them fighting to stay upright as the centre of the labyrinth turned.

A strange mist released from the carvings.

'Cover your mouth and nose!' Wren shouted as the white fog drifted up between them.

But she was too late. A smoky, bittersweet smell tickled her nose.

Dessa surged for the archway on the far side. Wren grabbed her arm. 'Dessa—'

'I can hear my father,' she rasped, struggling against Wren's hold. 'He's calling me, he needs me—'

To Wren's shock, Zavier, too, was moving towards another arched tunnel that had appeared beyond the centre.

'Zavier? What are you doing?'

'My brother . . .' he murmured, reaching the threshold as though in a trance.

Still holding on to Dessa, Wren listened. She could hear no one calling her friends, could hear nothing but the drip of moisture down the stone walls and the hiss of the vapour as it was released at their feet.

Suddenly, Dessa shoved her, and Wren went toppling back. Dessa disappeared into the tunnel beyond. Wren whipped her head around in time to see Zavier glance back at her before he, too, sprinted into the passage before him, calling out to his brother.

Wren got to her feet and paced the circular space, wondering where the rest of the cohort was –

Then, she heard them.

Sam.

Ida.

Anya.

'Wren!' Sam called from one of the tunnels. 'Wren, where are you?'

Sam was nearby. The note of panic in her voice spurred Wren into action.

Without thinking, she surged for the passageway just as her friends had done before her. She sprinted down the path, cool air whipping around her, her bun coming loose from its pin.

It was dark in the tunnel, but she didn't care. She ran, her friends' and her sister's voices growing stronger with every stride.

'Sam!' she shouted, heart hammering against her sternum. 'Ida! Anya! I'm coming!'

As Wren rounded another corner, she skidded to a halt, a broken sob on her lips.

For there they stood.

Sam and Ida, wearing their grey Thezmarr aprons, baskets of herbs and flowers hanging from the crooks of their elbows.

And Anya, her green eyes bright, her scythe held loose at her side.

'Come with us,' Anya said, smiling as she motioned towards the other end of the tunnel.

Ida reached for her. 'You're finally here . . .'

'We've been waiting for you,' Sam added.

Tears stung Wren's eyes. 'I've missed you,' she croaked, stumbling towards them. 'I've missed you all so much.'

'We know,' Anya replied, her voice gentle, more than it ever had been in life. 'You don't have to miss us any more. We're nearly there.'

'Where?' Wren asked, closing the gap between them.

'Far away from this awful place,' Ida told her.

Wren didn't remember the last time she'd cried. Not truly. Not since she'd lost herself in the Bloodwoods all those years ago in the Bear Slayer's arms. But now, she let her tears fall, feeling them track through the grime on her face. She let that dam within burst, grief spilling over its banks in a colossal wave.

A whimper escaped her as she looked upon her friends, her sister. They had not aged a day, not even after half a decade. Those years had been robbed from them; they would never be as old as she was, and Wren struggled to breathe against the weight of it all, unable to fill her lungs with enough air, no matter how hard she gasped.

'All will be well, Wren,' Anya said. 'You just have to come with us.'

Ida's smile was nothing but kindness and reassurance. 'It's not far . . .'

Wracked with sobs, Wren shook her head. 'You're all dead. You're not really here . . .'

Sam was still smiling. 'But we are.'

'No,' Wren rasped, choking back her cries. 'You died five years ago. And I have grieved for you ever since.'

With trembling hands, she palmed away her tears, her heart pounding against her ribcage like a desperate prisoner seeking escape, each beat reverberating in her ears like the drums of the war she'd survived – the war that held her last memories of them all.

There on the spiked walls of Thezmarr, she saw the brutalized severed heads of Sam and Ida: eyes plucked out, faces streaked with blood, cries of terror frozen on their open mouths.

Anya's broken body flashed before her next, the light leaving her sister's eyes.

Each inhalation was a struggle, Wren's chest rising and falling in erratic spasms. 'You've been gone a long time,' she told them hoarsely.

There were countless concoctions, thousands of plants that could produce hallucinations, that could bring one's darkest moments to the surface. This was one of them; Wren knew it in her bones. And yet she couldn't help but drink in the sight of them, whole and unharmed.

It had been so long. So painful without them.

'You're not real,' she whispered, pressing a hand to her aching chest before reaching for her belt of potions.

All her dried iruseed was gone. But she needed something far more potent to bring herself out of this mirage. Wren grasped desperately for something, anything, to anchor her fraying mind.

That presence in her chest, that kernel of shared magic pulsed, a calling from somewhere far away.

She had to go back.

Her fingertips found a small vial she hadn't dared use yet. A powerful combination of powdered guarana, ephedra and cassine . . .

Fighting back the overwhelming urge to collapse, to double over into her grief, Wren poured the fine dust onto the back of her hand and inhaled it sharply.

Sam, Ida and Anya watched her wordlessly.

Their forms suddenly flickered.

'Goodbye,' Wren murmured, not tearing her eyes from the women she'd loved and lost.

As she swayed, she could smell the lavender scent drifting from Sam and Ida's baskets. She followed that pull within her chest, that strange power guiding her elsewhere, taking her home . . .

She pictured sea-deep blue eyes, a lock of silver hair.

And slowly, agonizingly, Wren began to claw her way back to the surface, fighting against the suffocating tide of grief and panic with every ounce of willpower she possessed.

Her friends and her sister faded. And as the darkness began to recede, Wren closed her eyes and grounded herself in her surroundings, using her senses as moorings to the present moment. The rich scent of damp earth. The coolness of the stone walls as she pressed her fingertips to them. The soft glow of the torchlight as she opened her eyes at last.

When she did, she was with Zavier and Dessa once more. Dessa was tipping a small vial of something clear to her lips.

'We're alright,' her friend said. 'You're alright.'

Lavender, Wren realized. She could still smell lavender. Her eyes focused, meeting Dessa's.

'You told me it has a calming effect,' Dessa explained, glancing over at Zavier, who was on his knees, wiping the sweat from his brow.

'Hallucinations,' he panted, spitting on the ground. 'I preferred the torture chamber.'

Wren staggered to her feet, and together she and Dessa helped Zavier up.

There was a loud, metallic groan, and a few feet away, a new passageway opened. This time, when the light flooded the chamber and Wren blinked the world back into focus, there were no more Gauntlet trials beyond. Instead, she saw the great hall of Drevenor.

Together, the trio limped towards it.

Wren felt that same surge of magic in her chest. But it was not from within. It was from somewhere beyond.

And yet it was familiar. In a way that she knew deep in her soul.

Wren and her team burst into the hall. But it was not the masters she sought with her gaze.

Ignoring the long tables adorned with silverware and goblets, the cloches gleaming in the centre beneath the glowing chandeliers, her eyes went to the towering figure at the heart of it all.

Bear Slayer. Warsword.

Lightning-kissed. Storm-blessed.

Ancient power long forgotten . . .

It was *him*, she realized. She felt it in her life's blood.

Forgetting the Gauntlet, forgetting the entire world around her, Wren surged for Torj Elderbrock and leapt into his arms.

His handsome face was bright with pride and triumph for her as he lifted her into his arms, her legs wrapping around his waist.

And there, before the masters and her fellow alchemists, Wren Embervale kissed the man she loved.

CHAPTER 80

Torj

'In the light of the Furies, I swear my allegiance, my loyalty, to casting the evil from these lands. I will hunt. I will punish. I will kill. Any and all who threaten these kingdoms'

— *Warsword oath to the Furies upon the Great Rite*

WREN WAS IN his arms, whole, beautiful, and *his*. Not just his to protect, but his to love. She was a part of him, and with her mouth on his, he felt it through every fibre of his being: coursing through his veins, crackling beneath his skin, thundering through his heart.

Somewhere in the distance, he heard Thea wolf-whistle, and a smattering of applause followed.

'Congratulations, Elwren, Odessa, and Zavier,' the High Chancellor's voice boomed. 'Not only have you passed our great Gauntlet, but you have won first place.'

A more dignified round of applause echoed between the rafters and the sound of glasses clinking rang out across the hall. Attendants rushed to Zavier and Dessa, who stumbled further into the hall, looking more dazed than celebratory, an assortment of injuries covering them.

It was then that Wren buckled beneath Torj, and he pulled back to survey her properly.

He froze.

A deep cut slashed through her right cheek, dried blood caking that side of her face. The sleeves of her gown were ripped, mottled welts swelling on her arms. A familiar pair of manacles were slung over her shoulder. Torj looked to her wrists. They were pink and raw, blood crusting the skin there too.

Every breath he took seared his lungs. Every nerve in his body was alight with the call for vengeance.

Behind her, Dessa and Zavier were in similar states. A blur of movement told him that the masters had gone to their aid. But Wren's teammates were not his concern.

He didn't look anywhere except at his poisoner, and the wounds that marked her. He took in every bruise, every stitch of torn fabric, every smear of blood across her body. He didn't touch her. Instead, he catalogued every wince, the slight favouring of her less injured side, and that cut, that brutal slice to her beautiful face . . .

When he met her gaze, five words spilled from his lips: '*Who did this to you?*'

Wren stared back at him, and her eyes were a beacon of defiance. 'We were tortured. To see if we would break before the Gauntlet. To test our oath of secrecy . . .'

Torj couldn't stop himself touching her then. He cupped the uninjured side of her face, feeling the kiss of lightning beneath his palm. He exhaled slowly, as a means of restraint. 'Tell me,' he said simply. 'Tell me so I can end them all.'

He felt her jaw clench as her eyes flicked to the High Chancellor. 'You can't. I took the oath. We were warned we'd be tested. I passed.' Her eyes moved about the room, clearly noting the lack of other students. 'And then I faced the Gauntlet. And won.'

Torj dropped his hand. In three strides he was before the High Chancellor, that same hand wrapping around the fragile column of Belcourt's throat. His mind was blank. All that filled him was an inferno, roaring with the rage of a thousand storms as he began to squeeze the life out of the High Chancellor. Everything else faded around him, and all he could feel was the tension in his own muscles, coiled tight and ready to unleash devastation on the piece of filth who spluttered beneath his grip.

'Let's see how long you last.' Torj's voice was cold and cruel. He lifted the High Chancellor bodily from the ground so his feet kicked the air in desperation and his nails clawed at Torj's hand.

With one ounce of added pressure, Torj knew he could crush Remington Belcourt's windpipe, snap his neck. He would relish the sound. He would savour the light leaving the bastard's eyes. It was only the second time in his life he had felt rage as he did now, a primal, searing torrent. And when he peered at the purpling face before him, he saw his father.

Torj was no longer a Warsword, no longer a man. He was the embodiment of wrath itself, a force that would obliterate anything and anyone that lay a hand on Elwren Embervale—

'Torj.' A gentle hand rested on his arm.

He blinked, turning from the mottled face of the High Chancellor to find Wren at his side.

'Enough,' she said.

Torj's grip did not loosen. 'He had you hurt. *Tortured*.'

'Yes, he did.'

'And yet you'd let him live?' Torj's heart still pounded like a war drum, the blood pumping through his veins still full of fire.

'I will not let it have been for nothing,' Wren said, her voice unwavering. 'Enough.'

Torj let go. The High Chancellor collapsed to the floor like a sack of grain, clutching his throat and gasping.

Wren looked at him coldly. 'You're welcome, High Chancellor.'

She seemed to be holding herself upright with sheer willpower alone, but soon, she swayed, and Torj locked his body to hers, supporting her.

Farissa was suddenly there as well. 'Let's get you looked at, Elwren.'

'You knew,' Wren croaked, a note of betrayal lacing her voice. 'You knew what they were going to do.'

Farissa looked grief-stricken. 'I didn't know,' she murmured, reaching for Wren. 'I swear it.'

'Testing the oath was a new addition with your cohort,' the High Chancellor wheezed as Hardim and Nyella helped him to his feet. 'My idea for an added measure of security, given all the unrest we have faced of late.'

Farissa whirled around to face him. 'You *tortured* our students! How could you—'

'I did what was required. As did those novices who passed, your former apprentice included.'

Feeling Wren trembling against him, Torj had heard enough. He made to guide her away from the masters, a protective arm around her shoulders, careful of any wounds that might be hidden by her dress. Molten fury still coursed through him, but he had to get Wren away from these monsters, had to make sure she was alright. Then, and only then, would he take his vengeance.

But Wren paused in front of Master Belcourt. 'How many?' she asked hoarsely. 'How many broke? How many passed?'

'Only time will tell.'

She shook her head. 'I never thought I'd see the day where I was ashamed of this place, but today? I will remember it for the rest of my life.' Her words were a warning, a threat. Torj felt it in the thunder that thrummed in his chest as Wren looked to her bruised and battered teammates. 'And so will they.'

She straightened and made for the door. Torj rushed after her, Thea on his heels.

In the foyer, Thea gripped Wren's shoulder. 'You look awful,' she said with a grimace. 'Can I do something?'

'Leave me in peace.' Wren brushed her off with a forced smile. 'I'll manage.'

'Are you sure—'

'Thee,' Wren cut her off. 'Later.'

Torj was about to step in when Thea nodded stiffly. 'Later, then,' she said, leaving them.

It was only when Wren and Torj were alone that Wren's mask faltered. She stumbled in the hallway. Torj caught her, holding her upright once more, only to find tears tracking down her cheeks.

'I need your help,' she whispered, voice cracking.

'Anything you need, Embers, it's yours.'

Her throat bobbed. 'I need you to carry me.'

CHAPTER 81

Torj

'Bound by a vow of protection, a bodyguard's oath extends beyond the realm of defence to the pursuit of justice. Should their charge suffer harm, they become an instrument of retribution'

– *The Protector's Manual: A Practical Guide for Safeguarding Nobility and Royalty*

WITHOUT ANOTHER WORD, he scooped her up in his arms. She buried her face in his chest, and his heart fractured for her.

As Torj took Wren to her rooms, Cal and Kipp rushed after them. Cal's face paled when he saw Wren. 'What happened?' he breathed, unlocking the door for Torj.

'She'll tell us when she's ready,' Torj replied. 'I need you to get hot water. Medical kits. Food. Drinking water.'

'I'll get something to dull the pain,' Kipp said.

Cal stared at Wren for a moment longer, his lips moving but no words coming out. Then he sprang into action, closing the door as he and Kipp left.

Wren was limp in Torj's arms. As much as he wanted to lay her on the comfortable bed, he needed to know the extent of her injuries first. As gently as he could, he placed her in her chair and knelt before her.

'Tell me where it hurts, Embers,' he murmured, lacing his fingers through hers and peering into her eyes.

Wren pressed a hand to her chest. 'Here.'

Like a heavy blanket draped over his shoulders, despair weighed down his movements as he took her hand in his and pressed a gentle kiss to the back of it. 'I know.'

And he did. For he could feel her pain as acutely as if it were his own.

A strained breath shuddered out of Wren. 'On the bench, there's the beginnings of a salve . . . The same one I made for you—'

'Tell me who to send for,' he pleaded. 'Tell me who can help.'

'You,' she said weakly. 'Only you.'

Torj swallowed. 'I'm no healer.'

'I can talk you through it.'

'But—'

'Please, Torj. I think it will help keep my mind off the pain.'

He swallowed the lump in his throat, suppressing that instinct that had him burning for vengeance, that made him want to rip those responsible limb from limb. 'Alright,' he said. 'Tell me what to do.'

Wren closed her eyes, sagging with relief. 'The salve. It's a light green colour. It should already be in the mortar . . .'

Torj forced himself to stand, to step away from her to do her bidding. 'I've got it.'

'You'll need to add clove. Use the pestle to grind it together.'

It was only when Torj went to pick up the ingredients that he realized his hands were shaking. Every one of his senses was attuned to hers, the shallow rhythm of her breath, the flutter of her heartbeat in sync with his own. It engulfed him with a wave of raw emotion, and he had to brace himself against the workbench.

He allowed himself a second, no more. And then he did as she asked.

While he worked, Cal and Kipp returned with all that he had requested. They set the pails of steaming water by Wren and Cal held a canteen to her lips, helping her drink.

Torj had to force down the urge to knock Cal aside. He didn't want anyone near her. He wanted to be the one to tend to her, to comfort her. But that was his overprotective streak sweeping in, and he had to fight it back as best he could. Wren didn't need him crowding her like that.

'They're still waiting on two teams to return,' Cal told them. 'But they're already planning the graduation ceremony. It seems like they want it dealt with within a fortnight or so . . .'

'Torj has it from here, Cal,' Wren said, gently pushing the canteen away. 'Same to you, Kipp.'

'You're sure?' Cal asked. 'I could get Farissa—'

'I don't want Farissa,' Wren told him. 'If you want to help, please go check on Dessa and Zavier. See who else returned.'

'If that's what you want . . .'

'It is. Thank you.' The dismissal was clear.

Cal and Kipp each gave Torj a nod before they left again.

Torj brought the mortar to Wren and showed her.

'That's good,' she said, shifting in her chair with a wince. 'You'll need to wash your hands first. Hot water and soap.'

As he turned towards the bathing room, Torj hesitated. He didn't want to let her out of his sight.

Wren gave a weak smile. 'I'm not going anywhere, Bear Slayer.'

Clenching his jaw, he went to wash his hands. When he returned to her, slightly more composed than before, he said, 'We should clean your wounds first.'

'I taught you well.'

'That one doesn't take a genius alchemist's tutelage to know.'

Wren huffed a pained laugh. 'You'd be surprised. Thea needed some thorough instructions.' She jerked her chin towards the steaming buckets. 'Water first. Then cleanse with alcohol. Then apply the salve. Unless something needs stitching.'

'Kipp brought something for the pain.'

'I feel nothing.'

'You will.' He held out the small flask. 'Please. I can't stand to cause you pain.'

To his relief, Wren took it with trembling fingers and put it to her lips, taking a decent slug and grimacing. 'They make it taste awful on purpose,' she muttered, leaning back in her chair with a sigh. 'Face first, Warsword. I can feel it festering.'

Torj lowered himself to his knees and dipped a fresh linen bandage into the steaming water. Tilting Wren's wounded cheek to the light, he wiped away the dried blood and dirt as gently as he could.

He could barely keep his voice even as he asked, 'What made this mark?'

Wren's throat bobbed. 'A cane.'

Torj rinsed the linen and continued to clean the cut. 'I should have been there.'

'No. You shouldn't have. Don't you dare say otherwise.' She was exhausted to the bone; he could hear the strain in her voice, but through that was the uncompromising strength of steel. 'This was no failure on your part. You are not responsible for these marks.' Her blood-stained hand gripped his chin and forced his gaze to hers. 'Do you hear me, Warsword?'

He lost himself in her stormy eyes. 'I hear you.'

Seemingly satisfied, Wren turned her face again, allowing him to cleanse the cut with alcohol. When he was done, she reached for the bottle and took a long swig, eyes watering as she swallowed the harsh liquor down. Torj did the same, hoping it would steady his hands.

He applied the salve as instructed, hoping it would draw the heat from the wound as it had his. He could already feel the flame of her skin.

'There are scissors on the bench,' Wren said as he placed the mortar on the floor.

'Scissors?'

'You're going to have to cut this gown off me. The fabric around my middle . . . It's stuck to my skin. I must have a few cuts and scrapes, and I'm not sure if my ribs are bruised or broken . . .'

Locating the scissors on Wren's desk of chaos proved difficult, but when he found them, his chest tightened. He removed her belt, noting just how many vials were empty. She had put up a fight with everything she had.

Fitting the twin blades to the top of her gown, he started cutting downwards. It would have been quicker for him to tear the dress straight down the middle, but he was worried the motion would jolt her, and so he worked slowly, cutting away the fabric diligently. Even so, every wince, every stifled gasp she gave pierced his soul, that raw helplessness driving him to the brink.

Finally, he had cut the gown open down the front. He peeled it away from her as gently as he could, noting where the fabric had stuck to her skin with dried blood. Wren wore only her undergarments now, a thin camisole and a pair of satin shorts. Sweat beaded on her brow and Torj paused to press a cool washcloth there.

'Nearly over,' he told her. 'Then you can rest.'

As gently as he could, he lifted the hem of her camisole, sliding the fabric up to bunch just below her breasts. Mottled bruising covered her ribcage, along with various cuts and scrapes.

His brow furrowed as he ghosted his fingertips over the marks, probing delicately for signs of more serious injury. Wren sucked in a sharp breath at his touch, and he paused, glancing up at her face.

But she bit her lip and gave him a stiff nod. 'Keep going.'

His hands were steady now, because they had to be. Applying gentle pressure, he took stock of her wounds and their severity with a measured care that belied the thunder raging within him.

Wren kept still as his hands mapped out her ribs, feeling for irregularities, monitoring her breathing. 'I don't think anything is broken . . .' His voice was low, his words tender. 'What do you think? You're the expert.'

'A fracture or two at most,' she sighed. 'There's salve on the bench.'

Torj retrieved the jar and scooped out a generous amount, smoothing it over her skin with a featherlight touch, his callused fingers gentle as he worked the soothing balm over her injuries.

To his surprise, she reached for him, brushing a stray lock of hair from his eyes. 'Thank you,' she said.

Torj stilled, the air heavy with all the unspoken words between them. But he sighed and leaned forwards, resting his forehead against hers. 'I've never been more scared in all my life, Embers.'

'I know. But I made it out of there . . .'

Steeling himself, Torj pulled away and reached for more pain tonic, tipping it to her lips. She drank it without argument.

At long last, he carried her to the bed and laid her down. Her lashes fluttered against the tops of her cheeks.

'It was worth every minute,' she said hoarsely.

Torj stroked her hair. 'To pass the Gauntlet?'

'No,' she whispered. 'To get back to you.'

CHAPTER 82

Wren

'All things are connected
in the grand tapestry of existence'

– *Alchemy Unbound*

TWO WEEKS PASSED in a blur of pain tonics and fitful sleep. Visits from Thea, Cal, and Kipp punctuated the hours, but the one constant was the Warsword at her bedside.

Wren often woke in a daze, wondering if it had all been a terrible nightmare. But as her room came into focus, the memories grew sharper.

She had passed the Gauntlet. She had *won*.

And she had all but declared her love for the Bear Slayer before the whole academy.

Over the past few days, she'd found her feet again. She'd moved about a little, regaining her strength, talking quietly with Torj into the evenings, sharing meals with him. Her friends visited as well, each of them recovering in their own way from the trials.

Soon, the official date for their graduation ceremony was set.

That morning, Wren came back to herself, waking for the first time with a clear head, and the worst of the pain gone from her body. At her bedside, Torj was asleep in a chair, his hammer resting across his lap, as though he needed the comfort of its weight in his hands as he guarded her.

Wren tentatively drew herself up into a sitting position, still expecting to feel the pull of her injured ribs. But she felt nothing. Not a single twinge of pain.

She shifted again, her eyes catching the beam of sunlight filtering in through her window, reflecting off her box of trinkets on the sill. Distantly, she realized that she hadn't opened it in weeks, hadn't sought out the reassurance of her mementos of vengeance for a long while. Somewhere along the road, she'd left the Poisoner behind, and become an alchemist once more.

Months ago, that thought would have bothered her; enraged her, even. But now . . .

With a glance at the sleeping Warsword, she peeled back the blankets and lifted her camisole, where Torj had routinely bandaged her middle. Slowly, she unwrapped the fabric.

Where Torj had applied the salve every evening, the skin was smooth. Only a faint discoloration lingered in the wake of the deep, mottled bruises that had been there after the Gauntlet.

She lifted a hand to her face, where she could feel the dried residue of the salve, but again, no pain.

Quietly, careful not to wake Torj, Wren slipped from her bed and padded to the bathing chamber. When the door closed behind her, she studied herself in the mirror for the first time in weeks. Across her cheek was a pink line of scarring; the deep slash had healed nicely . . . and as Wren's fingers traced it, she smiled. It reminded her of Anya. Her eldest sister had sported a brutal scar right through her eye, from above her brow to midway down her cheek. If Wren's new scar made her look half as fierce as Anya, she'd wear it proudly. There was nothing quite like making men quake in their boots at the sight of them – something they'd both agreed on.

Wren looked down, turning her hands over. The manacle marks around her wrists were faint. All her open cuts had scabbed; some were already healed, small pink lines of new skin littering her flesh. The beating she'd taken was a distant memory, at least to her body.

At long last, feeling more herself than she had in a long while, she washed, scrubbing the remnants of salve from her skin. Wiping a soapy washcloth around her midsection, her thoughts went to the Warsword asleep beside her bed. Upon her return to Drevenor, she had felt his turmoil in her own chest. She had felt that animal fury as though it were her own as he'd nearly killed the High Chancellor . . . and he hadn't left her side since. Warmth bloomed within her at the thought.

As Wren dried herself, she glimpsed her reflection in the mirror again. Though traces of her hardships remained, she was herself. Healed. Whole.

A restlessness took hold of her then, a readiness to face the world once more. She had been cooped up too long, and there was so much she wanted to do.

Starting with the Warsword in her room.

When she emerged from the bathing chamber, wearing her towel tucked under her arms, Torj was awake, on his feet, war hammer in hand.

'You shouldn't be up. You should—'

'Torj,' she said gently. 'I'm alright . . . I've been in bed more than long enough. I feel good . . . *Better* than good.'

He dropped the hammer with a resounding thud and closed the distance between them in two strides. His hands came up to cradle her face, tilting it by the jaw to examine the pale pink slash across her cheek.

'See?' she prompted.

His brow furrowed as he scanned her exposed arms and legs, assessing, before his gaze met hers. 'Are you sure?'

Wren smiled. 'I'm sure.'

The Bear Slayer's shoulders dropped with relief. 'Thank the Furies. Wren, I—'

But Wren pressed a finger to his lips. 'We've talked enough, don't you think?'

Her hands went to the knot of her towel between her breasts. She pulled it loose, taking a deep breath as the material fluttered to the floor, leaving her utterly bare before him.

A muscle trembled in his neck as his gaze dropped from her face, down the length of her torso and below . . .

She heard him gulp as his attention shifted from her breasts to her navel, where small pink scars littered the skin and the bruising had all but faded.

Torj's hand brushed across them. 'Embers . . .' he said hoarsely.

'I want you,' Wren told him. 'I have wanted you for as long as I can remember.'

As he cupped her bare hip, Torj's jaw clenched, the muscle twitching beneath his dark stubble. He wet his lips, the internal struggle drawing his features together. 'I don't want to hurt you.'

'You'd never hurt me.' That simple touch at her hip was doing something to Wren, the heat of his fingertips alone turning her molten. This time, she was the one who was naked, and he was still fully clothed. 'I want this.'

Wren took his hand and placed it between her legs.

Torj groaned at the dampness he found there. 'You're killing me, Embers . . . You're still healing. I'm trying to be decent—'

'Forget decent,' she said, pushing against his hand. 'Give me wicked and unleashed.'

Desire darkened the Warsword's stare, and he slid his fingers through her wetness, finding her centre. 'You're sure you've recovered?' He traced a circle around her clit, the touch possessive, demanding. 'I won't ask you again.'

A desperate whimper escaped Wren as she nodded.

She didn't know who moved first, only that they came together in a frenzy. Her mouth was on his, and he lifted her bodily from the ground, crushing her naked body to his as he kissed her back. She moaned at the taste of him, at the way his tongue moved with hers and sent spirals of anticipation from her head to her toes.

Every part of her ached for contact, her skin singing beneath the rough press of his clothes, at the touch of his fingers between her legs. Her hands flew to the buttons of his shirt, practically pawing at him, desperate to feel the heat of him against her bare palm.

Torj caught her hands. 'This isn't how I imagined it, Embers . . .' he murmured.

Her gaze shot up. 'What?'

'A bustling academy outside our door, listening to every sound you make . . . This time, those noises belong to me and me alone.'

Wren blinked up at him, suddenly very aware of how naked she was.

'You said you wanted to know what it was like,' he said. 'With someone like me.'

'I do.'

'Then get dressed.'

Though it seemed counterproductive, with trembling hands, Wren did as the Warsword bid. When she was done, he took her hands in his.

'Do you trust me?' he asked.

She didn't hesitate. 'Yes.'

He kissed her. It was gentle, but full of dark promise. Weeks ago, Torj had said there was no going back, but this . . . Wren knew she was on the precipice of something far deeper than she'd ever known.

When the Bear Slayer tugged her hand, she followed.

She was ready for what came next.

To her surprise, he led her through the adjoining door into his chamber, where he grabbed a pack from beneath his bed and went to the map mounted on the far wall. There, he hooked his fingers behind the frame and dragged them down. Something clicked, and the framed map swung open, revealing a dark passageway beyond.

Shouldering his pack, Torj gave her a mischievous grin and held out his hand. 'There's something I want to show you.'

Wren reached for him, his strong fingers entwining with hers and pulling her into the tunnel after him. He pulled a cord on the wall and the map closed after them.

'How long have you known about this?' she asked in wonder as he lit a lantern and led her towards a narrow spiral staircase.

'Since we arrived.'

'Is it not a security risk?'

He huffed a laugh. 'Now you're thinking like a Warsword. The passage only opens from the inside. It's an escape route, should something go wrong. I was assured that only the High Chancellor knows of its existence. This way, Embers. Watch your step.'

Wren's heart was racing as she followed him into the near darkness, still clutching his hand. Their footsteps echoed softly in the cool, damp air, and Wren could feel the pulse of power in her chest, curious and ready to explore.

'Where are you taking me?'

His hand tightened around hers. 'You'll see.'

'I don't do well with cryptic, Warsword.'

Another laugh. 'I'm taking you somewhere I can make you moan loud enough to make the ground tremble.'

Wren's breath hitched at that.

'How many places does this lead to?' she managed to ask.

'Three. But don't go getting any ideas about using these passages without me. They're for emergencies only.'

'And this is an emergency?'

'Gods, yes.' Torj squeezed her hand. 'It's a matter of life and death.'

At last, they emerged into a secluded courtyard – one Wren didn't recognize, enveloped by ivy-clad stone walls and adorned with a pair of elaborate iron gates.

'Not much farther,' Torj told her, pulling her through the gates.

Beyond them was a meadow.

A vast, rolling meadow, full of wildflowers, so unlike the neat and tidy rows of the academy gardens. A canvas painted by nature's hand.

Untamed, beautiful, just like the Warsword at her side.

CHAPTER 83

Wren

'An alchemist's greatest wisdom is intuition. Follow it'

— *Arcane Alchemy: Unveiling the Mysteries of Matter*

A GENTLE BREEZE rippled across the emerald-green grass and the blooms, carrying a whisper of fragrant jasmine and orchids.

'Where are we?' Wren asked.

'The far northern border of the academy. I found it when I did my initial security sweep of the grounds. Only the masters know of it, and now you. I was told there are rare plants here that are not accessible in the main gardens, but this place isn't used for anything at the moment. I've wanted to bring you here for a long time.'

Tears stung Wren's eyes, but she blinked them back. 'Thank you,' she murmured, drinking in the sight. She could already see the rich violet of dragon's breath orchid peeking out from the verdant fronds, and the subtle glow of moon lilies . . .

She turned to the Warsword to find him staring at her in the same way she was staring at the meadow, a gleam of awe in his eyes, his mouth slightly parted. The space between them was suddenly heavy with anticipation, with those vows he'd made in her rooms, in that tunnel . . .

Torj was moving again, leading her by the hand through the wild blooms that blanketed the land, towards a towering willow tree that fractured the horizon. There, he took a blanket from his pack and laid it out atop the fallen leaves.

Wren took in the secluded spot, the sprawling hills of wildflowers. 'You're not worried about our safety out here? That we'll get into some sort of trouble?'

Torj closed the gap between them, gripping her chin with strong, warm fingers and lifting her face to his. 'I was in trouble the moment I met you, Embers.'

And then he kissed her.

She surrendered to him, opening her mouth and losing herself in the intoxicating taste, in the strokes of his tongue. Her hands slid up into his hair, tugging him closer to her in desperation.

He kissed her passionately, a wild hunger sweeping them both up in its midst. She moaned against his lips, gasped as he captured her lower lip between his teeth and whimpered as he licked over the flash of pain, deepening the kiss again.

Wren's body went molten beneath him, arousal pooling between her legs, her breasts aching for his touch. Her hands went to the buttons of his shirt, and this time, he didn't stop her. Gods, how she wanted him.

Under trembling fingers, the fabric came apart, revealing that golden skin, scarred and tattooed. She broke away to press a kiss to the marred flesh there, feeling the thrum of power beneath. As she traced the scars with her lips and tongue, Torj let out a pained groan.

'Do you mean to kill me, Embers?'

His powerful frame was rigid with tension – with restraint, she realized.

'Because if you're to be the end of me, it's an end I'll greet with open arms.'

He peeled off his shirt, revealing every inch of that sculpted torso and broad shoulders before his hands were at her laces and his lips were at her neck, teeth scraping the fragile column of her throat.

Wren cried out as her bodice loosened and he slipped his hands beneath the fabric of her dress, cupping her breasts in rough palms. A strained noise escaped Torj, as though the feel of her alone might send him hurtling over the edge. Just as frenzied, Wren pushed off her boots and helped him with the rest of her laces and dress, at last letting it slide down her body to pool at her feet.

She heard Torj's breath catch as his gaze raked over her naked form, lingering, as though committing every inch of her to memory. He traced the lines of her body with reverent, featherlight fingers – the arch of her hip, the swell of her breast – before they brushed down to her navel, and lower.

A tempest bloomed inside her, and Wren couldn't wait any longer. She clawed at Torj's leathers, sliding them down his muscular thighs, the hard length of him springing free.

Her mouth went dry at the sight.

Furies save her, he was glorious. Every inch of him the war-honed warrior she'd come to know and—

He kissed her fiercely again, taking her in his arms and laying her down on the blanket he'd brought for them. She touched the soft fabric.

'How long have you been planning this?' she asked between breathless kisses.

'For ever,' he panted. 'It feels like for-fucking-ever.'

His hand slid between her thighs and her legs fell open for him, completely and utterly exposed. Cold air kissed the most intimate part of her as he traced her clit, eliciting a gasp from her as sparks burst across her skin.

She rolled her hips, moving with him, before his mouth closed over her nipple.

With a moan, she took him in her hand, learning the shape and granite feel of him, imagining it buried deep inside her. She explored him from base to crown, swiping her thumb over the moisture she found there, causing him to buck beneath her touch with a quiet curse.

She smiled against his lips and stroked his length again, adding more pressure and watching in awe as his head tipped back with a groan.

'We should talk about protection,' he gritted out, thrusting with the motion of her hand, echoing the rhythm with his fingers on her. 'Against pregnancy.'

'I take a tonic,' she breathed.

'As do I,' he told her. 'So there's nothing standing in our way?'

'Nothing.'

When he looked at her again, his eyes were glazed with lust. He brought two fingers to his mouth and sucked her desire from them before sliding them back between her legs, pushing them inside her.

'Oh, gods,' she gasped, opening wider for him as he pumped those fingers in and out of her, circling her clit with his thumb in a way that had her writhing beneath him.

Torj's mouth descended, painting her with kisses down her neck, across her breasts, and down her stomach, his beard grazing her skin.

He withdrew his fingers and she made a noise of protest – only to feel him replace them with his tongue.

That wicked, talented tongue.

He held her thighs open as he feasted on her, sucking on her clit, sliding his tongue inside her, until she was riding his face with utter abandon.

'Torj . . .' she cried out, her fingers tangling in his hair, trying to draw him back up her body.

Torj obliged her, capturing her mouth in a devastating kiss as he dragged the head of his cock through the wet heat of her.

They both moaned, loud and guttural.

'I want you drenched for me, Embers.'

'Torj,' she warned, her nails digging into the muscles of his arms. 'Please.'

He looked into her eyes in a way that stole the breath from her lungs. 'I wasn't meant to fall for you,' he said hoarsely, pressing the tip of his cock to her entrance. 'I wasn't meant to want this, to want you. But Furies save me, I do. I do want you. And I'll never let you go.'

With those words, he thrust inside her, sheathing himself to the base.

Wren cried out, stars bursting across her vision. She clung to him as a powerful surge of storm magic rocked her to the core.

'Fuck . . .' Torj murmured, moving with long, luxurious rolls of his hips, hitting a spot deep inside her that had her panting. He kissed her brutally, claiming her lips as he claimed her body. 'Gods, you were made for me.'

His fingers threaded through hers and pinned them above her head as he thrusted, drawing out long spirals of rapture. She arched beneath him, wrapping her legs around his back, tilting her own hips up to meet his.

A blazing fire of need coursed through her, and she felt Torj's heart pounding against her own as he moved inside her. She broke away from his kiss, staring up at him as a palpable current surged between them, locking them together in a cascade of sensations that transcended all else. He was everywhere, setting her senses alight, awakening the storm within.

He braced himself on his elbow as he fucked her, long and deep, reaching between them to roll her clit beneath his thumb. Pure ecstasy unravelled then. A strangled sob broke from her, and she clamped around him, the swell of her climax rising and rising.

Arching beneath him, she scored his back with her nails, bit down on his shoulder, became more animal than woman: marking him, claiming him as he did her. They were tethered together. She could feel it like a physical bond growing taut between them.

'Wren . . .' Torj growled against her lips. A note of desperation, of trembling restraint wavered in his voice, his kisses becoming rougher, more demanding, leaving her smouldering for him.

She moaned as she felt the first ripples of her climax start at the base of her spine. 'Don't stop,' she panted.

Torj leaned back on his knees, holding her by her thighs, finding a deeper angle as he sank into her again and again. She was so full, so stretched, and she wanted every inch of him.

He pressed his thumb against her clit once more, adding to the explosions taking hold of her whole body. She met every one of his wild thrusts with a tilt of her hips, desperate for release, desperate to see him completely and utterly unleashed, all the while losing herself to his body, his touch. Higher and higher into oblivion she climbed, and there was no coming back down to reality now.

'Go up in flames with me, Embers,' Torj murmured.

Everything Wren was feeling, body and soul, exploded then and there, as he pushed into her and pinched her clit at the same time.

Wren's orgasm ripped through her like a wild storm. She cried out, shattering into a thousand pieces, cresting in the most intoxicating, devastating way. Her body was not her own as it came apart beneath him, his cock driving into her, dragging out every last ounce of insane pleasure.

Wren came with his name on her lips, each stroke of his cock erasing everything but the two of them, and the power thrumming between them.

CHAPTER 84

Torj

'There is little known of the veil between the tangible nature of scars and what lies beyond'

— Magical Transference

As Wren climaxed beneath him with his name on her lips, Torj lost control. With his heart about to punch a hole through his chest, he erupted with a shout, his release spilling into her with the primal urge to claim, the sensation nearly unbearable.

A moan broke from him as he shuddered in rapture that had him quaking above her in awe. Wren was flushed and damp with sweat, her eyes wide and lips parted.

Torj didn't trust himself to speak, not when every feeling roiling through him was so raw. Instead, he leaned down and kissed her, a long and deep exploration of her mouth.

Then, he slid out of her, a soft gasp breaking from her as he did, as though she mourned the loss of him inside her already. Torj bit back another moan of his own as he watched his release spill from her, suppressing the urge to push it back in with his fingers, his cock already hardening again at the sight.

Wren made a noise of disbelief. 'How . . . How are you ready again so soon?'

Smug pride bloomed in his chest. 'Hasn't anyone ever told you about Warsword stamina, Embers? I want you, always.'

Wren stared at him. 'So that's what it's like . . .'

Torj's gaze inched up her body, where he met her stare with a heated one of his own. 'What what's like?'

'Sex, real sex . . . Sex with you.'

Heart still racing, he lay down beside her, propping himself up on his elbow so he could survey her fully. 'Embers, that was beyond sex.'

'You mean it's not always like that for you?'

A breath shuddered out of him, and he fought to contain the swell of emotions gathering in his chest, stirring the tempest beneath his scars. 'It's *never* like that,' he told her. 'Only with you.'

Wren inhaled sharply. 'Oh.'

Torj rubbed at his scars, a strange pressure building there.

'What is it?' she asked, covering his hand with hers.

Torj warred with himself. He wanted to be honest, to pour his feelings out and give her everything he had, but . . . he didn't want to scare her, didn't want the intensity to be too much.

She seemed to sense his hesitation. 'You can tell me anything.'

He cradled her head in his hands and kissed her, fresh waves of desire washing over him, stronger than any drug. He was drowning in her. He hauled her into his lap, his fingers lacing through her hair, the kiss becoming more urgent, more fevered. He moaned as he felt the slick heat of her core against his cock. One shift of his hips and he'd be sheathed inside her again. Wren ground against him, seeking that friction too.

But no matter how deeply he kissed her, or how passionately she kissed him back, there was no holding it in any longer.

He broke away from her, the words spilling out.

'I'm in love with you. So fucking in love with you, Embers.'

Wren froze in his arms, breath catching as his cock lined up perfectly with her. Gods, his skin was alive with lightning everywhere they touched, all his senses heightened.

'Love?' she said quietly.

'Yes,' he told her fiercely. If he was going to offer her his wretched, dark heart, then he would do it right. 'In love. With you. And I'm done denying it. Done fighting it.'

Wren stared at him, a blush staining the tops of her cheeks.

And then, oh so slowly, she sank down onto the length of him.

A low, carnal sound escaped from Torj's lips, and his hands shot to Wren's hips.

'You're in love with me,' she repeated, shifting herself experimentally.

Torj's head tipped back, arousal pulsing at his cock, a delicious kind of torture. 'Yes,' he said, grabbing her hand and setting it to his scars. 'You feel it here, Embers. You have since that day on the battlefield. It's you. Furies save me, it's always been you.'

Giving himself over to the dark frenzy, Torj gripped her arse, hard, and moved her over him, so he could hit that spot inside her.

But Wren slowed. 'I—'

'You don't have to say it,' he said hoarsely. 'I just want you to know that I'm yours. That even when I'm nothing but ash, I'll still be yours.'

Wren let out a cry as she rode him, sliding up and down his cock, her head thrown back, her hands reaching up to cup her breasts and pinch her nipples.

Gods, this woman was lightning and fire.

When she looked at him, he eased his thrusts, drawing them out beneath her, long and steady enough to capture her mouth with his, to brand her with a kiss that she'd feel deep in her soul.

For he felt it in his. An alignment of the very magic that she'd poured into him once.

'Torj?' she said, breaking away.

'Hmm?'

'I'm yours as well.'

'Well, thank fuck for that,' he muttered. All notion of restraint snapped, his chest swelling as he flipped her onto her back and drove into her.

She was his.

His balls tightened at the thought, begging to empty into her again. She arched up to meet him, and he revelled in the way her body responded to his.

He moaned with her, holding both their pleasure in the palm of his hand, never wanting it to end, but desperate to come.

Torj didn't hold himself in check, not this time. He kissed her, deep and dominating, claiming her with every stroke of his tongue and every savage thrust of his hips. He couldn't contain himself, not when it came to what was his.

And Elwren Embervale belonged to him, mind, body and soul.

Her nails scored his chest, and wildly, he hoped she'd break skin, so he could wear her marks proudly.

'Torj . . .' she rasped as his fingers found her clit and he drove her to that intoxicating crest. He felt her clenching around him, succumbing to the waves of ecstasy he was wringing from her.

'Break apart for me,' he told her through the haze of his own longing, his own climax charging straight for him.

Wren writhed beneath him. 'Yes . . .'

With a broken gasp, she trembled beneath him, her whole body tensing as the force of her orgasm took hold. He felt it around his cock, and her cries set off his own release.

He came inside her again with a roar, slowing his strokes to luxurious glides into that drugging heat, drawing out both their climaxes until they were both trembling.

In the aftermath of the war, where the world was muted in ash, Wren was a burst of colour.

The words spilled from his lips between breathless kisses. 'I love you.'

A storm sang between them. And in the whisper of breath between the best orgasm of his life and the world coming back into focus . . .

He thought he saw a glimmer of gold.

CHAPTER 85

Wren

'An alchemist's duty is to
embrace the cycles of creation and chaos'

– *Transformative Arts of Alchemy*

SOMETHING SHIFTED DEEP within Wren, and it altered the very fabric of her soul. She felt the change, both in herself and in Torj, as they came together, and came apart in each other's arms.

She breathed him in, so that his scent became a part of her.

'I . . .' The words felt inadequate for the storm taking hold of her entire being. But she said them anyway. 'I love you, too.'

Torj's answering smile was radiant, tugging that thread within her chest.

She kissed him, slowly and thoroughly, savouring the taste and feel of him. 'I never want to leave this meadow,' she whispered against his lips.

He tucked her hair behind her ear, most of it having come loose from her bun. 'Nor I, Embers. But I doubt your academy waits for love. The Gauntlet is over, and I imagine there are all manner of proceedings to attend to now . . . Your graduation, for one?'

Wren groaned as reality came crashing down around her. Reluctantly, she reached for her dress, only to realize she needed a washcloth before she could—

'Here,' Torj said, dropping a kiss on her bare shoulder and tearing a scrap of material from the blanket beneath them. He poured water from a canteen over it and handed it to her.

Ignoring the heat in her cheeks, she turned her back to him and cleaned herself up as best she could.

'You don't need to be embarrassed, Embers. Not with me. It's my mess.'

'Our mess,' she said, smiling faintly.

His arms came around her from behind. 'I intend to make a lot more messes with you . . .'

A laugh burst from her. 'Careful, or I won't be able to walk.'

A low chuckle rumbled against her neck. 'Then I've done my job right.'

Something bloomed in her chest, and she felt lighter than she had in five long years. It had her wanting to throw caution to the wind and stay out here in the meadow with Torj. She was always so set on moving to the next task, and the next, that she rarely stopped to appreciate the smaller moments.

Like now, where Torj had managed to get his shirt stuck over his head, a sliver of that ridged abdomen showing above his unlaced leathers.

She reached out and traced the contours of his stomach, and those two deep grooves that pointed beneath his waistband. 'You're at my mercy now, Bear Slayer,' she said playfully.

He huffed a laugh, managing to tug his shirt over his shoulders at last. 'I've been at your mercy for a long while.'

She felt drunk. Not Kipp-level drunk, but that contentment and ease that came with the first drink or two of the night: the sensation that she might float away, and everything would be alright.

Torj stuffed the blanket back into his pack and shouldered it while Wren tugged her boots on with a heavy sigh.

As they made their way through the meadow, she picked wildflowers.

'Planning another poisoning any time soon?' Torj said with a gentle smile, watching her move through the bushes for the best blooms.

'Not this time, Warsword. These . . . these are just because they're beautiful.'

'I know the feeling,' he told her, his gaze lingering on her face as he took the flowers from her so that her hands were free to pick more.

Her cheeks ached from smiling. She couldn't remember the last time she'd done so for so long.

Torj's expression softened. 'It looks good on you.'

'What does?'

He leaned in, pressing a gentle kiss to her lips. 'Happiness.'

Wren's eyes pricked with tears, but she blinked them back. This man had ruined her. All those hard edges she had honed, all those walls she had built . . . She was defenceless against him, and surprised to find herself glad to be so. A little voice in her head chimed like a bell, telling her that there was no way something like this could last, that all good things were fleeting. But the man beside her had not wavered. Not during the war, not in its aftermath.

'How does this work between us now?' she heard herself ask, hoping she didn't sound too vulnerable.

But the Warsword didn't look perturbed. Instead, he took her hand and kissed her knuckles. 'We'll work it out,' he told her. 'But know this . . . From here on, you belong in my arms, in my bed, in my life. You belong with me, no matter what.'

Wren's stomach swooped. 'You promise?'

'I swear it, Embers.'

'And all the rest? The guild? The academy? What if the world doesn't—'

'Then I'll tear it in two,' he vowed, wrapping an arm around her shoulders. 'It's me and you. Always.'

CHAPTER 86

Torj

'The study of magical bonds throughout the ages reveals a complex tapestry of power, control and the eternal struggle between the self and the other'

– *Tethers and Magical Bonds Throughout History*

ALL THE WAY back to the academy, Torj warred with himself. He couldn't deny it: there had been a flicker of gold. But it had to have been a trick of the light, or perhaps he'd been momentarily blinded by his climax . . . And it had gone as quickly as it had come – a figment of his imagination. There had been no *thread*, either, not as Audra had described it.

Regardless of what he had or had not seen, he needed to tell Wren about his conversation with Audra. He should have told her the first chance he got, before what had transpired in the meadow. But he'd been so caught up in her, so overwhelmed by his love for her that nothing else had mattered.

As the academy building came into view, he glanced at her: the smiling curve of her lips, the brightness of her willow-green eyes. He had never seen her more beautiful, more content than she was now.

Yet Audra's words came back to him with a pulse of dread.

You can be used against each other: hurt one to hurt the other . . . I do not deny that she will be vulnerable through you.

He had to tell Wren what he'd learned, and together they could decide what it meant. That was the only way.

When they reached the foyer steps, hand in hand, he halted her. 'I have to tell you something.'

Wren's face fell, and it broke his heart to see it, to be the cause of it. 'What is it?' she asked, tensing. The afternoon sun gilded her, highlighting every beautiful feature.

'Torj?' Wren's voice wavered. 'Is something wrong?'

She deserved to know what Audra suspected, what had been discussed while she was in the Gauntlet. He cupped her face and peered deep into her eyes.

Steeling himself, Torj stroked her jaw. 'That depends . . .'

'On . . . ?'

'On how you feel about—'

'*There* you are!' Dessa's voice exclaimed from the top of the stairs.

Torj reluctantly let his hands fall away from Wren as Dessa rushed down to greet them, but her eyes were still on him.

'Later,' he told her.

Worry etched lines across Wren's brow. 'But—'

'Wren!' Dessa clasped her shoulder. 'Where have you been? We're meant to be preparing for the graduation ceremony.'

Sure enough, beyond the entrance, Torj could see the flurry of activity in the foyer.

Dessa was already tugging Wren up the stairs. 'You have to be fitted for your robes, and we *have* to do something about your hair,' she added, plucking a twig from Wren's bronze tresses.

Wren resisted, trying to wrench her arm free of her friend's hold. 'Dessa, we were just in the middle of something—'

'It can wait,' Torj heard himself say, spying Thea waiting in the doorway. 'Go and get ready for the ceremony. You've earned this.'

'But—' Concern flashed in Wren's eyes as Dessa renewed her attempts to get her up the stairs.

Torj smiled. 'I meant every word I said, Embers. We'll talk later. For now, it's time to celebrate what you've achieved.'

Her throat bobbed. 'It's me and you?' she said.

'Always.'

⁂

With Wren swept away by Dessa and guarded by Thea, Torj went to the great hall, which had been transformed into a grand amphitheatre. Rows of wooden benches had been arranged in a semicircle facing the raised platform at the far end. Banners bearing the symbols of the four pillars – healing, lifelore, warfare and design – hung from the rafters, their vibrant colours catching the light that streamed through the high windows.

'How's Wren?' a voice said from behind him.

Torj turned to see Wilder Hawthorne approaching, a smug smile on his face.

'She's good,' Torj said as his friend came to stand beside him.

'You finally talked? About what you found in that book?'

'We . . .'

Wilder barked a laugh. 'Did more than talked.'

Heat crept up Torj's neck. 'That's between us.'

'Glad to hear it, brother,' Wilder replied. 'I'm happy for you . . . Both of you. And it's about time.'

'That's rich, coming from you,' Torj scoffed.

But Wilder grasped his shoulder firmly. 'I mean it, Torj. You deserve happiness. You have for a long while. I'm glad you've found it.'

'Thank you,' Torj managed, his thoughts drifting to Wren, picturing her preparing for the ceremony with the other novices. It felt like only moments ago that he had finally found the words to confess his feelings for her. The memory of her smile and the warmth of her embrace still lingered on his skin.

For a moment, Torj stood with Wilder, the pair watching the servants scurry about the hall, placing intricately woven cushions on the benches. The scent of incense wafted through the air, mingling with the fragrance of fresh flowers that adorned the walls and pillars. An audience began to take their places – academy staff and students, the loved ones of the novices . . . The alchemy masters gathered at the front of the hall, including the High Chancellor, whose robes of deep blue brought out the mottled bruising still prominent around his throat.

'Your doing?' Wilder asked, noting the same thing.

'He got off easy,' Torj muttered.

'I'll say. I'm surprised you didn't rip his head clean off.'

'I wanted to, believe me.'

'Wren stopped you?' Wilder asked with a note of amusement.

'Yes.'

Wilder chuckled. 'They have a way of doing that.' Then, he pointed to the front of the hall. 'Look . . .'

A sudden hush fell over the bustling hall. Torj followed Wilder's gaze to where a procession of royal guards and Warswords marched through the entrance, their armour glinting in the late sunlight that streamed through the high windows.

In the lead was King Leiko, his shoulders draped in a regal cloak of claret trimmed with bronze thread, a rearing horse embroidered on the back. Beside him walked Queen Reyna, her graceful steps barely disturbing the hem of her flowing gown. The fabric shimmered with hues of silver and blue, like the surface of the great frozen lake of Aveum. Her long auburn hair was braided with strands of pearls, and a delicate silver tiara rested upon her brow.

Behind them, Lady Liora, the regent of Harenth, followed closely. Her raven hair was pulled back into an intricate knot, held in place by a hairpin adorned with a single blood-red ruby.

'They're all here,' Torj murmured to Wilder. 'When was the last time the rulers of the midrealms gathered in the same halls?'

'The memorial at Thezmarr,' Wilder replied, his voice equally awed as the royal guests took their seats on the elevated platform.

'I suppose their attendance speaks to their newfound respect for alchemy,' Torj mused.

Wilder made a noise of agreement. 'That and their investments in Drevenor. I think they've finally realized the role the newly minted adepts will play in shaping the future of the midrealms . . .'

Torj turned back to the entrance of the great hall, where the novices would soon make their appearance. The seats had filled, and the anticipation in the room was palpable, the air thick with a mix of excitement and apprehension.

For of the original cohort of fifty, only twenty-five would go on to graduate to adept. Besides Wren and her team, Torj didn't know who else had made it through the Gauntlet. His thoughts had only been of her.

He tensed as High Chancellor Belcourt stood at the podium, his aged hands gripping the edges of the lectern as he surveyed the gathered crowd. As the murmurs of the audience faded into silence, he began to speak, his voice deep and resonant, filling the great hall.

'Esteemed guests, royal dignitaries, masters of alchemy, and most importantly, our brave novices. It is my great honour to welcome you all to this momentous occasion – the graduation ceremony of our most promising alchemists. Please be upstanding.'

The High Chancellor gestured to the back of the hall, where the novices were gathered. The crowd stood to await their entrance.

Torj's eyes went straight to Wren. The bond between them made it easy to spot her in a sea of others. Her gaze met his across the hall, as though she, too, had followed that tether to him. She was standing beside Dessa and Zavier, resplendent in emerald-green robes.

And when she smiled . . . it was the most breathtaking thing he had ever seen.

CHAPTER 87

Wren

'Advancing from novice to adept marks a true milestone in an alchemist's journey. It signifies not just expanded knowledge, but a deeper connection to the mysteries of our sacred art'

– *Drevenor Academy Handbook*

DESSA ELBOWED HER. 'Quit staring at your Bear Slayer,' she hissed. 'We're about to be called.'

Thea, who was standing guard behind Wren, snorted loudly.

Flushing, Wren tore her gaze away from the lightning-kissed Warsword with a smile and forced her attention back to the High Chancellor.

Belcourt scanned the faces of the novices, and then the larger crowd across the rows of benches. 'Today, we bear witness to the culmination of hard work, dedication, and sacrifice. The path of an alchemist is not an easy one, for it demands not only a mind sharp as a blade, but also an unwavering loyalty, and a true heart. The novices who stand before us have proven themselves worthy of this calling, having endured the rigorous training and trials that have shaped them into the individuals they are today.'

Goosebumps broke out across Wren's skin as his words washed over what remained of their cohort. This was the first chance she'd had to see who had made it through the Gauntlet. She scanned the familiar faces, trying to work out who was missing – besides Blythe, of course. A tremor of guilt ran through her. Blythe might have passed the Gauntlet too, if she hadn't looked quite so much like Wren.

The High Chancellor's voice grew more solemn as he continued. 'To our novices, I say this: remember the lessons you have learned within these hallowed halls. Remember the bonds you have forged with your fellow alchemists, for they will be your greatest strength in the years to come. And above all, remember the sacred oath you have taken . . .'

The High Chancellor turned to face the royal guests, bowing his head in respect.

'To our esteemed guests, the rulers of the midrealms, we thank you for your presence here today. Your support and recognition of the alchemical arts are a testament to the vital role that our graduates will play in shaping the future of our lands. May their knowledge and their dedication serve you and your people well in the years to come.' He cleared his throat. 'And so, without further ado, let us begin the graduation ceremony. Novices, come forth!'

Wren squared her shoulders and approached the podium with her friends. As she did, she thought of Ida and Sam, wishing they were here to see her now, wishing that they, too, were climbing the stage to accept their adept medallions. Tears burned her eyes, and for once, she didn't blink them back. Not as her name was called, not as she bowed her head to accept her own medallion from the High Chancellor. The gold-and-silver disc gleamed in the torchlight.

'Congratulations, Elwren,' High Chancellor Belcourt said. 'You surpassed even my high expectations.'

He shook her hand in a dry, warm grip before she continued across the podium, where Farissa was beaming at her.

'You did it,' her former mentor whispered.

For a moment, Wren forgot the tension between them, forgot that Farissa had tried to stop her from attending Drevenor. Instead, she remembered the years of tutelage, the hours of patience, and the unwavering kindness Farissa had shown her from the very beginning.

She threw her arms around the older woman's shoulders.

After a moment of shock, Farissa relaxed, returning the embrace firmly. 'Ida and Sam . . . They would be proud,' she murmured. 'Unsurprised, but proud.'

Fresh tears tracked down Wren's face. Farissa's words meant more than she could ever say.

'Thank you,' she said. 'For everything.'

Farissa smiled warmly. 'I always knew this day would come.'

Wren gave her a final squeeze before following Dessa and Zavier to the side of the stage to await the rest of the graduates. She found Torj's sea-blue gaze in the crowd once more, his presence anchoring her to the moment, his pride for her so clear on his handsome face.

Dessa bumped her hip against Wren's. 'Could he be any more obvious?' she whispered. 'He's so in love with you.'

Wren wiped the tears from her cheeks and grinned. 'I know.'

Dessa grinned right back.

The evening couldn't have been more perfect. Despite everything that had led to this moment, Wren knew she wouldn't take it back for the world—

An explosion rumbled in the distance.

All around her, whispers and gasps broke out. People surged towards the windows.

'Get back!' Cal called from the fringes of the hall, forcing his way to the stained glass and peering beyond.

A horn blasted in warning.

'There's an unknown force at the gates,' Cal's voice echoed across the hall. 'Audra?'

The Guild Master did not hesitate. 'Lead the unassigned Warswords and two units of guards to the academy entrance,' she ordered.

'Whoever this force is, they're not to step foot on these grounds, are we clear?'

'Crystal.' Cal was already moving, shouldering his bow and quiver. The doors were thrown open, and Cal led the charge for the main gates, his fellow warriors of Thezmarr behind him. Wilder barred the main hall doors, the timber and iron rattling after them.

Wren watched on in shock as her fellow students huddled together, eyes wide, hands shaking as they clutched their newly awarded medallions. The royal guards had surrounded their monarchs, weapons drawn.

'We need to get the rulers out of here,' Thea shouted across the crowd.

A towering figure warmed Wren's side. Torj was there. 'There's an antechamber behind the stage,' he told her, his knuckles white around the grip of his war hammer. 'Take the others, get inside, and lock the door.'

But Wren threw her robes over her head, heart hammering, hands palming several vials at her belt. 'I don't fucking think so, Bear Slayer. We stay together.'

Torj opened his mouth to argue, but his words were drowned out by a deafening blast. The very foundations of the hall shook as the eastern wall exploded inwards, showering the room with dust and debris. Screams of terror filled the air as people scrambled for cover.

Through the gaping hole, Wren glimpsed dozens of armed figures pouring into the hall, weapons gleaming in the torchlight. Their faces were obscured by dark masks, revealing only cold, merciless eyes.

The People's Vanguard.

The Warswords and rulers had thought the threat stamped out.

But there was no denying it: they had been wrong.

A bloodcurdling scream pierced the air as the masked men advanced.

Wren's heart pounded as she prepared to unleash her alchemy and storms upon them. With Cal and the bulk of the forces gone, they were outnumbered . . . but she'd be damned if she didn't go down swinging.

CHAPTER 88

Wren

'Gold will turn to silver in a blaze of iron and embers, giving rise to ancient power long forgotten'

– *Prophecy from the Seer Queen of Aveum*

A WAVE OF violence washed over the hall as the alchemists, guards, and Warswords sprang into action, their weapons and potions at the ready. Shrieks of panic echoed between the rafters, mingling with the sudden clash of steel.

Magic crackled in Wren's veins, threatening to overwhelm her, demanding to be released. But the conflict was too close, and her control still questionable. By her side, she could feel the same power radiating from Torj, and somewhere nearby, from Thea as well.

Wren reached for her potions instead, her fingers closing around the familiar vials as she hurled herself into the chaos.

Her movements were a blur of precision and deadly intent. With a flick of her wrist, she hurled a vial of explosive black powder at the feet of the advancing attackers. It shattered, igniting a blinding flash and a concussive blast that sent the masked figures flying backwards.

Using the momentary distraction, she darted forwards, already reaching for the next vials at her belt. She lobbed a series of concoctions into the fray – a smokescreen to obscure vision, a sticky slime to ensnare feet, a corrosive acid to eat through armour.

Torj was right beside her, his war hammer singing as it crushed bones, shattered weapons, and broke men apart.

But for every enemy they felled, two more seemed to take their place. Wren gritted her teeth, realizing they were being steadily pushed back towards the royals.

'Wren, look out!' Torj's shout rang out above the clamour, and Wren spun just in time to see a black-clad figure lunging towards her, wicked-looking blade in hand.

She ducked and rolled as the Warsword himself had taught her, feeling the kiss of air as the blade passed over her head. Coming up on one knee, she hurled a potion at the attacker's feet, watching with grim satisfaction as the vial shattered and a cloud of choking vapour enveloped them.

Torj was at her side again in an instant, his war hammer swinging. Skulls caved beneath its iron, blood spraying as he shouted orders. 'Guard the rulers! To the royals!' he bellowed, carving a path through the enemy.

The warm glow of the graduation ceremony was gone.

The great hall became a battleground.

Poisoner and Warsword moved together in unison, felling anyone who stood in their path as they made their way towards the royals, who had huddled at the front of the hall.

A horn blasted from the entrance, where Audra stood, attempting to call their forces back. Glancing to the main gates, Wren saw that Cal and the other Warswords were dealing with a large force there, smoke pluming into the air from the fence. She leapt over bodies on the ground, the scene all too familiar to the memories she'd been trying to escape for half a decade. But she couldn't stop. The rebels were closing in on the royals, and she saw King Leiko locked in combat with two of the attackers, his sword flashing in the wavering light as he fought to defend himself and his fellow rulers.

She started as balls of fire shot from his hands, only to fizzle out before impact. When was the last time he'd used his power in combat?

With Torj, Wren reached the front of the hall just as one of the black-clad figures made a grab for Queen Reyna, his hands closing around her arm. Wren didn't hesitate to use her magic this time. She drew on the well of power within her, the same energy she sensed in Torj and Thea. With a cry of effort, she thrust out her hand, hurling a bolt of lightning at the attacker, watching as he convulsed and fell to the ground, his body smoking.

Torj charged towards the centre, where Thea and Wilder were fighting back-to-back, defending the cowering regent of Harenth. Nearby, another Warsword had reached King Leiko and was shielding him with her body, her sword a blur of silver before her.

All around Wren, blades clashed and people screamed, a symphony she knew like the back of her own hand. From the lectern on the podium, the High Chancellor's voice rang out above the commotion.

'The mind is a blade! Use it, for Furies' sake!'

'Dessa!' Zavier shouted. 'Now!'

Glass vials glinted as they spun through the air.

The pungent scent of chemicals and smoke filled the hall as the alchemists of Drevenor came to its defence.

Zavier led the attack, a sword whirling in one hand as he cast handfuls of strange powder at the enemy with the other. Some fell to their knees, choking, while others clutched at their eyes with panicked shrieks, blinded. The powder seemed to have a mind of its own, seeking out gaps in armour and exposed flesh. Where it touched skin, it left angry red welts and blisters.

Wren gaped at her teammate, distantly wondering if it was a chemical of his own design. Zavier threw her a wild grin as he continued his assault. He moved through the chaos with the grace of a dancer, his sword flashing in a deadly arc. Each strike found its mark, leaving a trail of broken bodies in his wake, while behind him, the alchemists of Drevenor rallied.

The metallic tang of blood was thick in the air and bile rose in Wren's throat as the acrid smell of burning hair filled her nostrils, too. The sounds of shattering glass and screams of terror assaulted her ears, making it hard to think, hard to breathe.

But she had lived through battle before. And she knew the only option was to keep going.

She hurled another potion at an approaching attacker, watching as the vial exploded in a burst of blinding light and searing heat. The figure stumbled back, clutching at their eyes, and Wren took the opportunity to send a bolt of storm magic crackling towards them, the energy surging through her veins like liquid fire.

Beside her, Torj was a whirlwind of motion, his war hammer smashing through the ranks of the black-clad figures like a battering ram. He was surrounded, and only his Furies-given strength kept him in the battle against the overwhelming odds. But they kept coming, wave after wave of them.

The Bear Slayer's face was a mask of grim determination, his eyes blazing with a fierce protectiveness that made Wren's heart ache. She knew in her bones that he would die to protect her, to protect all those he had sworn to defend. And that knowledge terrified her more than any of the horrors unfolding around them.

That was what made her do it.

'Torj!' She threw her hand out, summoning lightning to her fingertips.

She sent the bolt soaring for his hammer.

Embers sparked as storm power channelled through iron, setting the ancient runes aglow with blue light. The air crackled with energy, raising the hairs on Wren's arms, stealing the breath from her lungs.

Torj's eyes widened as he felt the surge of power, his grip tightening on the haft of the hammer. Tendrils of magic danced along its surface.

With a roar that shook the very stones beneath their feet, Torj raised the hammer high, the brilliance of a captured tempest swirling around its head. He brought it down in a mighty swing, slamming it against the ground at the feet of their enemies.

The impact unleashed a shockwave of pure wrath. Lightning exploded outwards in a blinding flash, engulfing the masked attackers in searing light and thunderous sound. Men screamed as they were flung through the air like rag dolls, their weapons and armour melting and twisting beneath the onslaught.

When the glare faded, Wren blinked spots from her vision, her ears ringing in the sudden silence. Where moments before there had been a sea of enemies, now only smouldering bodies and scorched stone remained.

Torj stood at the centre of the devastation, his hammer still crackling with residual energy. He turned to Wren, his eyes alight with a fierce intensity.

Wren stared, her breath catching in her throat.

Gold will turn to silver in a blaze of iron and embers, giving rise to ancient power long forgotten.

The premonition from long ago came back to her in a powerful wave, goosebumps racing across her skin. In that moment, she saw Torj as the legends painted him – a force to be reckoned with, unstoppable and utterly fearsome.

The lightning-kissed Bear Slayer.

But the battle was not done. As they pushed the enemy towards the rear of the hall, Wren caught sight of High Chancellor Belcourt, his robes stained with blood as he fended off a group of attackers with a flurry of potions. She saw Farissa and Hardim locked in a deadly dance with a black-clad figure wielding a pair of curved blades, their movements a blur.

'Wren!' Thea's voice cut across the chaos.

Wren was already moving towards her, blasting attackers from her path with bolts of lightning. Everywhere, she saw the bodies of those who had already fallen – fellow students, guards and alchemists alike. The floor was slick with blood and gore.

The fury that rose up in Wren was uncontainable.

As she reached her sister's side, they joined forces, as they had in the war.

Storm magic met storm magic, and together they forced back a unit of thirty. A sob rose in Wren's throat, but she choked it back, forcing herself to maintain her connection to Thea. But even as they pushed forwards, Wren couldn't shake the feeling that she was missing something.

And then, through the haze of smoke and chaos, she saw him.

A figure clad in black like the others, his face obscured by a mask . . . but his eyes glinted with a cold, calculating intelligence, and his presence thrummed with the alchemy they had all come to fear.

Alchemy that made Wren's blood run cold.

CHAPTER 89

Torj

'A soul bond only strengthens with time,
in the presence of the bonded'

– Tethers and Magical Bonds Throughout History

THE GUILD HAD been wrong. So incredibly wrong. Whoever they had captured and interrogated had fed them false information. And as Torj watched in horror as the enemy's ranks parted, it became clear that Thezmarr had never had their true leader in custody.

For now, standing at the rotten core, was a man cloaked in black. A man who was a commander in every respect. Like his subordinates, he wore a mask, but that was where the similarities ended. His presence demanded acknowledgement; the fighting around him slowed in his shadow.

He stood tall, a simple shield braced across one arm, a small vial of purple liquid clutched in his other hand. The mask concealing his face was a work of art in itself: a masterpiece of blackened metal and polished obsidian, the eyeholes narrow and elongated, giving the unsettling impression of a predator's unblinking stare.

As he surveyed the battle unfolding before him, the masked leader remained utterly still, save for the slight tilting of his head as he observed the ebb and flow of the conflict. His underlings swarmed forwards at some unseen signal, their movements coordinated, a testament to the discipline he must have instilled in them.

A bolt of lightning carved through the air, shooting straight for him—

He raised his shield in answer.

The storm magic hit, and a strange energy pulsed through the air around them as the shield's centre point seemed to absorb the power.

Torj looked back to Wren, who was studying her fingertips and looking to Thea in shock. Thea looked just as surprised.

'What the fuck . . . ?' Wren muttered.

Torj edged closer to her, adjusting the grip on his hammer, but Wren rolled her shoulders and met the enemy's gaze. Lightning gathered once more in her palms; outside, thunder clapped. Torj could taste the rain on his tongue.

Wren unleashed herself.

The air around her crackled with energy. The hairs on Torj's arms stood on end as she summoned her storm magic, her eyes flashing with fierce determination. He had seen her use her powers before, had watched on in awe as she called down lightning from the sky and summoned it from within, sending it arcing towards her enemies with a flick of her wrist.

But this was different.

The leader wielded his shield like a weapon itself, and that was exactly what it was. It gleamed with some sort of substance – *alchemy*, Torj realized. The polished metal surface absorbed Wren's attacks like a sponge, the energy dissipating harmlessly into the air. Frustration flashed across her face as she redoubled her efforts, her attacks coming faster and more furiously than ever before. Her movements were fluid and graceful, her body twisting and spinning as she dodged the leader's attacks.

The masked figure thrust his shield forwards, and a jet of sizzling emerald liquid sprayed from its centre, hissing as it ate through the stone floor where Wren had been standing mere moments before. The acrid stench of melting rock filled the air.

The enemy pressed forwards, his shield now pulsing with an angry red glow. He slammed it against the ground, a crimson mist expelling from its surface, cracking the flagstones and sending jagged shards flying in all directions.

Torj surged towards Wren, but she was two steps ahead, sending bolts of lightning sizzling through the air, the smell of the storm mingling with the tang of smoke and blood that already hung heavy in the great hall. Sparks flew in the wake of her power.

No one intervened. No one dared, not as the leader's shield began to glow again with an eerie, sickly glint, the metal warping and buckling under the onslaught of Wren's magic. She advanced, Thea at her back and Torj at her side. A glimmer of hope rose in Torj's chest, his grip tightening on the haft of his hammer as she pressed her advantage.

'Who are you?' she demanded, her magic raging around them.

But behind his shield, the enemy leader uncorked the small glass vial he was holding with a flick of his thumb, bringing it to his lips beneath his mask. He tipped the contents down his throat, his eyes never leaving Wren's face.

Torj tensed as the tonic visibly raced through the leader's body, his muscles bulging and rippling beneath his black armour, seeming to grow before their very eyes. His stare glowed with an unnatural, almost feverish light.

He let out a pained roar of pure, unbridled power that made the very stones of the Great Hall tremble.

Beside him, Torj felt Wren falter as the leader lunged towards her.

Torj himself braced for impact, readying to throw himself between them, as Wren's storm magic vanished.

But in its place was an explosion of alchemy.

Wren threw everything she had in her belt at him – glass shattering, colourful powders and potions bursting across the enemy's shield as he lifted it again. The air crackled with the force of their clashing alchemies, a maelstrom of reactions that threatened to tear the hall apart.

The man gave a shout as he danced away from the onslaught and misted Torj with a disorientating substance. He then staggered towards Wren and struck her with his shield.

Torj heard the gasp of pain that tore from her lips as she was sent flying backwards through the hall. Her body slammed into the wall with a heavy thud.

Around them, both allied and enemy forces spilled in from the smouldering grounds outside. It was pandemonium. Cal shot arrows in a blur; Wilder was dual wielding his Naarvian steel blades against a trio of men. The rest of the Warswords returned to the fold, gathering around the royals and defending the students. Thea sent throwing stars flying and opened enemy throats with her dagger as she fought her way to Wren.

The masked leader lurched forwards, poised to strike the sisters.

At last, the strange substance clearing from his senses, Torj stepped into the enemy's path, placing himself in front of Wren, war hammer raised. 'You won't touch her again,' he growled, voice laced with the promise of violence.

Torj swung first, his hammer cleaving through the air with all his Furies-given strength behind it. But when it hit the enemy's shield, he knew something was wrong. For neither the shield, nor its bearer, faltered beneath his blow. The enemy's strength was unnatural, enhanced by whatever elixir he'd consumed.

Torj struck again, and was blocked, again. The masked figure retaliated with a series of swift, powerful strikes, his shield moving with a speed and precision that belied its size and the strength of its wielder. Torj sensed cruel calculation in every movement. This was certainly no mere foot soldier, but a true master of whatever dark alchemy he employed.

The enemy leader pressed his advantage. The concoction that coursed through his veins had transformed him into something more than human, a being of pure malice and power. Torj was forced back with a relentless barrage of blows.

He risked a glance at Wren, who Thea was helping to her feet.

Could she channel her magic through his hammer again? He needed all the help he could get.

But blood matted her hair and dripped down her face, and Torj's heart clenched painfully at the sight. He wanted desperately to go to her, but he couldn't. He needed to end this.

And so, with a roar of defiance and a final, desperate surge of strength, Torj threw himself at the masked leader, his hammer singing through the air as he brought it down with all the force he could muster. For Wren, for the kingdom, for everything they had fought and bled for, he would not fail—

But the leader lunged, the movement impossibly fast, and pain lanced through Torj's chest.

He looked down.

A small dagger protruded from his breastbone.

Staring at it, Torj watched as blood pulsed from the wound, and he staggered forwards, dropping his hammer, falling to his knees.

His breath rattled in his chest, and he found he could not move, his strength seeping out of him along with his blood.

A long shadow cast across him as the enemy leader closed in, shield and sword raised to make the killing blow—

A lean figure stepped into his path, placing himself between Torj and the enemy.

Zavier.

He twirled an elegant rapier, a gleam of silver in the flickering light, its tip pointed at the enemy's heart.

'You shouldn't have come here,' the alchemist said.

'And *you* have chosen the losing side,' the masked man replied.

Zavier's grip tightened on his blade; his jaw clenched. For a moment, the two men faced each other, locked in a silent battle of wills.

Then, Zavier's rapier flashed forwards, a blur of steel aimed at the leader's throat. At the same time, the masked figure thrust his shield before him, a wall of impenetrable alchemy.

The pieces clashed, sparks flying from the point of impact. But even as they struggled against each other, Torj saw a flicker of movement, a subtle shift in stance.

Both men reached out with their free hands, their fingers splayed wide. And with a blinding flash of light and a thunderous boom, an invisible force flung them backwards, their bodies hurtling through the air like rag dolls. They slammed into opposite walls with bone-shattering force, the stone cracking and crumbling beneath the impact.

Shock masking his own agony, Torj struggled towards Wren as slowly, painfully, the two men staggered to their feet. The leader cast a final, inscrutable glance at Zavier, his mask concealing any hint of emotion. Then, without a word, he turned and limped over to Torj.

'It appears,' the leader said, his voice quiet as he eyed the poisoner a few feet away, 'that I can get to her through you.'

And that was when Torj heard Thea scream.

Despite his own searing agony, his gaze snapped up.

He saw Wren on her knees, blood blooming just above her heart.

'No,' he croaked, staggering towards her.

The air was stolen from his lungs as a golden thread materialized between them. It was the same hue as that shimmer he'd glimpsed in the meadow.

And that could mean only one thing: Audra had been right.

He was not going mad.

The scars at his chest were no wound.

They connected him to Wren.

A *soul bond*.

Around him, no one moved or pointed; no one acknowledged the gold thread at all. But to Torj, it grew brighter with every breath, humming with an otherworldly energy that echoed in his chest. Gilded hues danced along its shimmering length as it grew taut between them—

'Wren!' Thea shouted, holding her sister's shoulders. 'What the fuck?'

Torj collapsed. He began to crawl to his soul-bonded through the blood and gore – but heavy footsteps sounded at his side.

'We got what we came for,' the voice of the masked leader sounded, as he lingered a moment longer. Then he retreated, his black cloak billowing, his forces falling into place behind him.

Torj barely noticed their withdrawal from the hall, barely registered as the battle subsided around them. Wren looked down at the stain of blood across the top of her shirt, panting through the pain that Torj felt in his own flesh, agony radiating in waves.

He crawled to her, the bond between them shining brighter, though Wren didn't seem to see it. As he drew closer, he heard her laborious breaths matching his own. She was feeling every pulse of pain he did.

Torj's vision blurred with tears as he wrenched the dagger from his chest, Wren crying out as he did. The sound cut him more deeply than the blade had.

Gasping, Torj reached her side, blood flowing from his searing flesh. Gritting his teeth, he fought to stay conscious, to cling to that cord that burned between them, that bound him to her—

'Embers,' he managed, tearing at her shirt to get a look at her wound – the very same as his own.

The connection between you can be abused. A strike against you is a strike against her.

Through the haze of pain, he was distantly aware of the final throes of chaos unfolding around them. Of Wilder and Cal taking on a lingering masked unit with a group of Guardians from Thezmarr.

Oblivious to the golden thread linking them, Wren was still staring down at the blood spreading quickly across her shirt, the crimson so stark against the white fabric.

Her lips turned ashen.

'No . . .' Torj pleaded, reaching for her.

For a moment, he had had everything. Everything he had ever wanted.

In the pocket of silence between life and death, what could have been flashed before his eyes. What they could have been together.

He was always meant to be hers, and whatever happened here, he always would be. But his pain was her pain, and her pain was his.

Bonded, they were vulnerable.

Tethered to one another, they were dying.

And that made things simple.

'Is there a way to . . . to stop it? To cut the tie?' he had asked Audra. He could feel it pulsing between him and Wren, and through the haze, he could feel her anguish, her desperation to live.

Through whatever ancient magic filled him, Torj knew what he had to do.

She was his to protect.

She would *always* be his to protect.

There was no rulebook, only the fierce urge to keep her safe, and he let it guide him. Torj focused all his remaining strength on the tether between them, pulling the shimmering cord between his heart and Wren's taut, drawing her close. He poured every ounce of his love, his devotion into that connection.

With a gasp, he felt the bond begin to vibrate, made up of a thousand strands weaving together, one by one . . .

To meddle with it would be to interfere with the will of the gods, with fate itself . . .

But Torj knew his fate.

It was her.

It always had been.

Before his eyes, the bond glowed brighter, the connection between him and Wren growing stronger for one brief, shining second.

A final surge of iron-clad determination rippled through him.

He grasped the golden thread in both hands, pulling it taut. It was warm and silken against his fingers, pulsing with a sense of rightness, of finally finding where he belonged. A sanctuary in a world of chaos. A dawn chasing away the darkness.

'I love you,' he whispered into Wren's hair.

And then, with a single, violent wrench, Torj Elderbrock severed the soul bond.

CHAPTER 90

Wren

'Understanding people is akin to
mastering poisons and antidotes.
One must discern between cure and affliction'

– Elwren Embervale's notes and observations

12 years ago

THE EARTH WAS damp beneath Wren's knees, staining her skirts as she took her harvesting knife to the stems of a yarrow plant. Careful to keep the densely packed petals intact, she took what she needed, laying several bundles down in her basket, along with the hollyhock she had already collected.

Not many knew that some of the best medicinal flowers grew along the edges of the Mourner's Trail, the only way in and out of Thezmarr. She liked to keep it that way, for her foraging hours were the only ones that were truly her own. Humming to herself, she dusted off the dirt and made for her final stop: a patch of lemon balm by the foot of a great weeping oak. There was a fever making its way through the fortress, and Farissa had asked her to gather ample supplies—

A twig snapped on the trail. Wren whirled on her heel, brandishing her harvesting knife, her heart pounding.

A riderless horse was on the Mourner's Trail, an arrow protruding from its flank.

'What in the midrealms . . .' Wren sheathed her knife in her belt and approached the poor beast cautiously. She wasn't the best with horses, but she hated to see any creature in pain. 'What happened to you?' she asked, stroking its neck.

The horse groaned, and Wren spotted more dried blood across its dusty coat.

'It's alright.' She kept her voice low and soft as she reached for the reins. But the horse – a stallion, she realized – gave a whinny of protest and darted forwards, taking off at a gallop towards the fortress.

Frowning, Wren ignored the unease that had settled over her and turned back to where she'd left her basket – only to find an enormous figure now braced against the tree.

She started, her hand flying to her chest. 'Who are you?' she demanded.

'I usually don't need an introduction,' he said roughly, pain lacing his words.

Even hunched over, with his forearm resting against the oak, the man was huge – imposing. His golden hair had fallen across his brow, matted with blood, and his features were drawn taut with discomfort. Despite his injuries, there was no mistaking the hardened physique of a seasoned warrior, perhaps nearly a decade past her eighteen years.

'Someone thinks highly of himself.' Wren stepped forwards, noting the warrior's chest rising and falling with short, laboured breaths. 'Sit down before you fall down,' she ordered, reaching for the kit she kept at her belt.

He glanced up at the sharpness in her tone. 'You know, most people wouldn't dare talk to me like that.'

Wren laid her medical supplies atop the leaves and took hold of the warrior's arm, forcing him down to the ground. 'Most people don't know their head from their arse.'

The man huffed a laugh, which was followed by a wince and a groan of pain as she settled him on the forest floor.

'Did you fall off your horse?' Wren asked.

'Fall?' He made a noise of indignation. 'Of course not. I didn't want to aggravate Tucker's wound. Sent him ahead to find the stable master. Figured I'd manage the rest of the way on my own.'

Wren snorted. 'How's that working out for you?'

The man scowled. 'Just fine until the bossy likes of you came along.'

'Not what it looked like to me.' Wren peeled back the top of the man's shirt, revealing a broad, blood-slicked chest—

'What are you doing?' he protested.

'You warriors are all brawn and no brain. What's it look like?' she muttered, swatting his hands away so she could get a better look at the wound. 'How did this happen?'

'Arrow,' he grunted.

Wren shook her head as she located her vial of rubbing alcohol. She needed to cleanse the wound before she could stitch it. 'And you pulled it out?'

'It was in the way.'

'You didn't think to keep it in to stop the bleeding? You could have at least just snapped the fletching off—'

Abruptly, the warrior made to stand. 'I'm heading back to the fortress.'

But Wren pushed him down by the shoulder and he grunted as his backside hit the ground once again.

'You'll stay there until I've tended to that gaping hole in your chest,' she told him firmly. She tore away the collar of his shirt, revealing more of the damage at the juncture of his pectoral and shoulder. 'Absolute fools, the lot of you. Don't they teach you how to care for injuries during your Guardian training?'

'I'm not a Guardian.' His husky voice sent a wave of goosebumps across her skin, just as her fingers brushed against something around his bicep.

Slowly, she took in the symbol on the armband fastened there. Not the two crossed blades indicating the rank of a Guardian, but three . . .

'You're a Warsword,' she breathed, her heart stuttering. The man before her was one of only three elite warriors left in the midrealms. A man who had passed the Great Rite. A man who had been gifted with strength from the gods themselves.

'Did the giant war hammer not give it away?' he quipped, thrusting his chin towards a massive weapon discarded in the leaves a few feet away.

'The arrogance should have,' Wren replied, trying to school her shocked features into something more neutral while she busied herself wiping the grime away from the injury.

He laughed, the sound warm and rich. 'I suppose we deserve that reputation.'

'Among others.' She scanned his golden hair and the aforementioned hammer on the ground. 'You're the one they call the Bear Slayer.'

'Guilty,' he replied with a note of amusement. 'Or Torj, if we're friendly.'

'We're not.'

His gaze met hers, more amusement gleaming there. 'And what do they call you?'

'Wren,' she said simply, and applied the rubbing alcohol.

Torj swore, his breath hissing between his teeth at the pain. Wren knew the burn of application from her own cuts and scrapes over the years, but without proper cleaning, the wound would fester.

'Hold still,' she chastised as she readied the needle and thread.

'So you're not squeamish, then?' he grunted.

'No. Are you?' But she didn't wait for his answer. Instead, she pierced the skin and threaded the needle through, ignoring his cursing. 'Here I was thinking someone called the Bear Slayer might have a higher pain tolerance.'

'Here I was thinking healers were meant to be kind. Or at least have a decent bedside manner.'

'I'm not at your bedside, and I'm not a healer,' she told him, concentrating on the push and pull of the needle. His skin was warm beneath her fingers, and she couldn't stop her gaze from dipping to the whorls of dark ink adorning his muscular chest.

'Then why in the midrealms am I letting you poke me with that damn torture device?'

'You're a bit dramatic, aren't you?' she mused, finding her rhythm.

The Bear Slayer shook his head in disbelief. 'Again . . . no one talks to me like that.'

'Perhaps it's time someone did.'

Wren could feel the intensity of his stare on her, hot as a brand. Though she was confident her expression remained professional, she couldn't stop her breath from catching as the warrior reached out, his large fingers brushing the bare skin of her neck—

She started, her stomach fluttering. 'What are you—'

But between his fingers, he held a leaf. 'This was in your hair.'

'Oh.'

He let it fall between them. 'If you're not a healer, dare I ask what you are?'

Wren returned to finishing her sutures. There would be a scar, but it would be small and neat thanks to her steady hands. 'I'm an alchemist.'

'Is that so . . .' Torj said thoughtfully.

'Yes.'

The air between them felt charged, the silence broken only by the soft rustle of fabric as Wren shifted closer to inspect her handiwork. She was increasingly aware of how close they were, of how he hadn't looked away from her once. Beneath the metallic tang of blood, the scent of him was rich and warm – black cedar, perhaps, and a hint of oakmoss. She had to stop herself from leaning in.

'And where might I find you?' Torj's chest vibrated beneath her touch with his words. 'For . . . follow-up care?'

'You won't need any,' Wren replied brusquely. 'Just keep it clean and dry.'

'What about removing the stitches?'

'I'm sure someone of your . . . experience can figure out how to remove a few stitches.'

He gave a wry smile. 'Are you calling me old?'

She clicked her tongue in annoyance. 'I'm sure there are other things I could call you.'

'No doubt . . .' There was a playful note in his tone. 'How old are you, anyway?'

'None of your business.' Tying off the thread, Wren cleared her throat. 'There,' she said, leaning back with a satisfied nod. 'That should hold, as long as you don't do anything stupid to tear the stitches.'

Torj raised an eyebrow. 'And what qualifies as stupid, in your expert opinion?'

Wren shot him a look as she packed away her kit. 'Anything that lands you back in my care, Bear Slayer. I've got better things to do than patch up reckless warriors who don't know when to quit.'

'Wren?'

Her name on his lips was like a song. She met his gaze, and his rugged handsomeness hit her like a blow.

'Just so you know . . .' The Bear Slayer grinned. 'I never quit.'

Wren got to her feet, needing to put distance between them. 'Good luck and good riddance, Bear Slayer,' she told him, heading for the road.

'You can't get rid of me that easily,' he called out.

'Whatever you say, Warsword.' But as she walked away, Wren felt his gaze on her back, warm as summer sun, and a strange spark, right in the centre of her chest.

※

Wren was falling.

First, through every moment she had shared with Torj Elderbrock. A labyrinth of their time together. His hand in hers. His tongue tracing her lips. The weight of his body braced over her own.

'I'm so in love with you . . . So fucking in love with you, Embers.'

He was in her blood, in her magic – part of him living inside her, reverberating through the very marrow of her bones.

Then a torrent of agony blinded her. The pain was endless, electric, as though it were channelling right through the lightning in her veins.

'You belong in my arms, in my bed, in my life. You belong with me, no matter what.'

Someone was screaming.

'You promise?'

'I swear it, Embers.'

Wren was made of fire. She'd forgotten what it felt like not to burn. All she knew was the searing of her insides, the tearing of her soul.

'It's me and you. Always.'

On and on it went. Seconds stretched into eternity as Wren relived those moments, and all those that had come before. Every nerve ending, every fibre of her being screamed for reprieve, for respite from the relentless onslaught that threatened to engulf her. The stripping of some unknown part of her; the endless fall through agonizing oblivion.

Until she was burned down to those final threads.

'Even when I'm nothing but ash, I'll still be yours.'

CHAPTER 91

Wren

'It has been decades since the magical might of the five kingdoms has been felt across the midrealms'

– *The Midrealms Chronicles*

WHEN WREN CAME to, she saw that her wound was gone. Red stained her skin, but there was no mark, no blemish where a ragged slash had been only moments before. Sticky with blood, a strange pain still lingering, Wren looked up at Torj in wonder.

But she didn't recognize the Warsword before her.

There was no warmth or love in that stormy sea-blue gaze.

Only cold, unflinching iron.

She reached for him, and he stepped away.

A hollowness yawned wide inside her, a chasm that could not be filled. It left her breathless, her hands trembling. Something deep in her chest had fractured, the ache in its wake like the pulse of a phantom limb.

With utter bedlam around her, and her front still wet and warm with blood, Wren sought Torj again, but he would not meet her eyes. That chasm within unfurled wider, deeper, until she could barely contain the short, shallow gasps that escaped her.

'What happened?' she whispered.

'Wren!' Dessa shouted from a few feet away. 'Wren, we need you!'

It was Thea who helped Wren to her feet. The hall spun as she stood. The enemy's leader was nowhere in sight, nor were the remains of his forces that weren't dead on the ground with their own.

'What happened?' Wren croaked at her sister.

'They used the smoke again and retreated,' Thea explained. 'But they've taken Queen Reyna—'

'Wren!' Dessa cried out. 'Hurry!'

Wren leaned on Thea as she left Torj behind, hobbling to Dessa's side, where Zavier was keeled over, clutching his abdomen.

'He said he wasn't hurt,' Dessa blurted. 'He said it was just a scratch, but—'

Wren's gaze fell to the wound that was already festering at Zavier's stomach, blood pulsing from a thin slice there. The hair on the back of her neck prickled as she crouched beside her teammate.

'Which weapon?' she asked him, scanning the various blades scattered across the floor.

With a ragged gasp, Zavier pointed.

A prickle of unease crept up Wren's spine as she picked up the sword in question, noting the gleam of chemicals on the steel. Swallowing, she looked from the blade to Zavier, who was sweating profusely, doubled over in pain.

'This is treated with the enemy's alchemy . . . It only affects those with magical blood.' She knelt beside Zavier once more. The wound was shallow, superficial, and yet . . .

Realization slammed into Wren, sending a wave of shock coursing through her body.

Zavier looked up at her, but said nothing, a vein pulsing in his neck.

'You're a royal,' she murmured. 'This alchemy wouldn't affect you otherwise . . . Not like this. That was your magic back there . . .'

She reached for her belt, for the vial she had meant to give Farissa.

'I've only tested this on myself,' she explained. 'There's every chance it won't work—'

'Just do it.' Zavier was panting in pain as he eyed the tiny glass bottle in her hand. His body convulsed and he gave a stifled cry as the wound at his gut opened further.

Wren hesitated over the vial, just for a second.

If she was wrong, it could kill him.

If she was right and didn't use it, he would die anyway.

Zavier seized, white spittle foaming at his mouth, his eyes rolling back into his head.

Wren threw herself into action. She tipped the vial to his lips, pouring the clear liquid into his mouth, watching his throat bob as he swallowed. Zavier's whole body convulsed in a series of violent fits.

Wren's blood went cold. With Dessa's help, she held him down, placing someone's cloak under his head.

He stopped moving.

And around them, the hall fell silent.

Wren held her breath. The tonic was untested, save for herself . . . There were a million factors that could change the results, that could hinder the remedy, that could make things *worse* . . . But what was worse than dead?

A lot of things, she thought grimly, checking Zavier's pulse. It was so faint she could hardly feel it.

He was dying. And there was no knowing if she'd been the one to push him across the line into the underworld.

All paths lead to the underworld, novices . . .

'Wren . . .' Dessa whispered, her voice laced with terror. 'What have you done?'

'I—'

Suddenly, Zavier shot up with a ragged gasp for air, his eyes wide and bloodshot. He clutched his stomach, which was still wet with blood, and looked around wildly until his gaze locked with Wren's.

'What the . . .' he wheezed, perspiration still beading at his brow, his mouth agape in shock.

Wren became increasingly aware of all the eyes boring into her back, of the masters staring at the trio huddled on the floor.

But her attention didn't leave Zavier. '*Who are you?*' she demanded.

Her teammate fought to catch his breath, gulping at the air as though it couldn't fill his lungs fast enough.

Finally, he levelled her with a stare. 'Zavier Terling, Highness. Prince of Naarva.'

A ripple of shock passed over the hall. But Wren stared back as the pieces fell into place. The flicker of power she'd felt during breakfast in the great hall. His vast knowledge of the Kingdom of Gardens and lifelore. His resentment towards her from the start . . .

'Zavier Terling . . .' she murmured, feeling his magic unfurl from him as the haze of pain left his eyes.

He offered a sly smile. 'Pleased to officially make your acquaintance, Poisoner.'

CHAPTER 92

Wren

'An alchemist cannot ignore the lessons of failure, for it is through adversity that a novice finds mastery'

— *Elwren Embervale's notes and observations*

WHEN WREN LOOKED for the one person with whom she wanted to share her complete and utter disbelief, the Bear Slayer was nowhere to be found.

Instead, it was Farissa who rushed to Wren and Zavier, nearly spilling her healing supplies as she dropped to the ground at their sides.

'I saw what happened,' she whispered as she examined Wren first, wiping away the dried blood on her chest.

Wren looked down. Her skin was smooth, no scar there to commemorate the pain she'd felt – no tell-tale sign of the strange agony that still thrummed within, far worse than the wound itself.

With trembling hands, Farissa cleaned the gore away. 'Do you . . . understand this?'

Dazed, Wren shook her head, still scanning the blood-stained halls for Torj. Her memory of what had happened was distant: her chest opening beneath an invisible blade, her name on Torj's lips. 'Not even a little,' she managed.

Farissa nodded, more to herself than to Wren. 'You will. For now, you're in one piece.'

Wren's breath seemed to rattle in her chest. 'Am I?'

Farissa reached out and squeezed her hand before she turned to Zavier's wound and surveyed it critically. 'This was a big risk, Elwren.'

'I know.'

'But it worked,' Zavier said, voice hoarse. 'Do you have more?'

'This was just a sample, but I have all my notes,' Wren replied, rubbing her chest, hoping to alleviate the empty ache there. It persisted.

She excused herself to wander the hall. The air was thick with the coppery smell of blood and the acrid tang of smoke. Everywhere she looked, she saw the bodies of the fallen, eyes staring lifelessly at the vaulted ceiling. The wounded were being treated beside the dead, some moaning in pain, others shivering in shock. The sight was too familiar to Wren, and panic stalked the edges of her mind. The world she had known, the fragile peace they had built in the wake of the shadow war, had been shattered in the space of a few short hours. And now, everything hung in the balance . . .

Her body ached from the enemy leader's brutal attack. She didn't know how she was still standing. But the pain of her injuries paled in comparison to the emptiness that now pulsed within. She followed it around the hall, searching, searching, to no avail.

'He's not here,' Thea's voice sounded at her side.

Bone-weary, Wren turned to her sister. 'Where, then?'

'Wilder saw him head across the grounds, towards the gardens.'

Thea was looking at her with pity, and Wren couldn't stand it. 'I'm alright,' she said.

'You're not,' Thea said firmly. 'But you will be.'

⁂

At last, Wren found the Bear Slayer by the lavender bushes, his fingers trailing over the purple florets. At the sight of him, the chasm in her chest did not close, nor did the pain abate.

As though he felt it too, Torj's hand went to the web of scars across his heart. He tensed, seeming to brace himself against something.

'Torj?' Wren asked quietly, tearing her eyes from the sliver of ruined tattoo beneath his tattered shirt. She followed his gaze to the rows of blooms that shivered in the evening breeze.

He didn't respond immediately. When he did, his voice was detached, cold. 'This can't continue, Wren.'

'What?' Her lungs constricted, her stomach sinking.

His words were like ice. 'We're done. It's over.'

Wren searched his face for that warmth, that kindness that she'd come to know, come to love.

She found nothing but iron.

Her eyes narrowed, fists clenching at her sides. 'I don't believe you.'

Torj shook his head, still not meeting her eyes. 'We were fooling ourselves, thinking this could work.'

The fresh memory of the agony lancing through her entire being left her breathless again. Panic clawed at the fringes of her mind, its cold talons raking at that hollowness within. There had been something between them; she had felt it in her magic, in her heart, in the very depths of her soul.

It's me and you. Always.

'What happened between our time in the meadow and here?' she demanded. 'What changed?'

He drew himself up to his full height. 'You made me weak in that battle. You made me someone I'm not. I'm a fucking *Warsword*, Embervale. I'll *always* be a Warsword.'

Not once had she felt *weak* in the Bear Slayer's presence; not once had she felt anything but right with him at her side.

Until now.

But they had come too far for it to end like this. They had faced years of uncertainty, of stolen moments and longing glances. They had stood side by side through a war that threatened to tear their world apart, their bond forged in the crucible of battle and tempered by everything else they had shared.

And now, just when they thought they might finally have a chance, a new enemy had emerged from the shadows. An enemy that, until this moment, Wren had believed they would face together, as they had faced everything else.

'Torj . . .' She reached for him.

'Don't,' he growled, twisting away from her grasp as though he couldn't bear her touch.

'How can you throw away everything we've been through?' she said, hating how her voice had grown thick with emotion. 'Every battle we've fought, every obstacle we've overcome?'

Torj's stoic facade cracked for just a second, a flicker of pain crossing his features before the mask slammed back into place. 'The past isn't enough to build a future on.'

Wren felt each syllable like a physical blow. 'So that's it?'

'That's it.'

'You said it was me and you. Always.'

A muscle feathered in the Bear Slayer's jaw as he looked away. 'I was wrong. There is no "always" for people like us. I'm doing what I have to do.'

Wren flinched. 'Because that's your job,' she heard herself say.

'Exactly. I didn't want it. I never wanted it.'

'Didn't want *what*?'

'*This*. I never asked for any of it. It's too hard.'

Wren's hands had begun to shake. She blinked up at the Warsword, not sure she was hearing him correctly. 'You said . . . You said that I *saved you*. Whatever we have . . . It's a *gift*.'

'It's a *curse*, Embervale.' His tone was cold and hard, so unlike the warm and husky voice that had murmured her name against her skin.

A beat of silence passed, and Wren wasn't sure she trusted herself to speak, but the words tumbled from her lips all the same. 'You don't mean that.'

'I do. With all my heart.'

Wren stared into those dark sea-blue eyes she no longer recognized. She refused to acknowledge the splintering feeling in her chest, refused to let the tears burning in her eyes fall. Instead, she clung to the rage she knew so well.

'You're not the man I thought you were,' she said.

'I'm *exactly* the man you thought I was.'

For a moment, Wren stared at him, her heart still pounding, her breaths still shallow, before she returned her gaze to the rows of lavender. She pretended they'd never knelt in the dirt together, that she'd never shown him how to take cuttings in the place where they now stood. She told herself she'd never seen those dried florets on his windowsill.

Tilting her chin to the canvas of darkening sky, Wren closed her eyes and forced herself to take a long, measured breath, inhaling the crisp evening air as her lightning crackled beneath her skin.

When she looked at Torj again, she closed the gap between them and brushed her fingers over the lightning-shaped scars beneath the folds of his shirt.

'I gave you this,' she said quietly. 'That day at Thezmarr. When I thought I'd lose you.'

Torj's jaw clenched, but he remained silent.

'I thought . . . I thought it meant something,' Wren continued, her hand still resting over his heart. She felt his pulse quicken beneath her palm, saw the anguish in his eyes. For a moment, she thought he might break, might tell her what was really going on.

But then his expression hardened once more.

Wren dropped her hand, taking a step back. Dark clouds gathered above as she steeled herself. Above them, thunder clapped.

'Well,' she said, her voice low as she turned back towards the gates. 'It's the last piece of me you'll ever have.'

CHAPTER 93

Torj

'The rare phenomena of the soul bond has not been recorded for centuries'

— *Tethers and Magical Bonds Throughout History*

TORJ WATCHED AS Wren passed beneath the iron gates, her head held high, her steps never faltering. A tempest circled overhead, the wind whipping through the lavender, ripping flowers from the stems and sending them hurtling through the darkening sky. She was a queen calling the storm, a phoenix rising from the ashes, a bolt of lightning in the deep night.

She was everything he had ever wanted, everything he had ever needed.

And he had just broken her heart.

He wanted to call out to her, to beg her to come back, to forgive him. But instead, he watched her go. For theirs was a story written in scars. A tale of what could have been, shattered by his own hand.

He knew he was right. It was the worst thing he'd ever done, but he'd had to do it – had to sever the bond to save her life; had to hurt her, to save her from himself. Even if it meant losing her. Even if it meant facing a lifetime without her by his side. He would gladly bear that agony, that gaping void in his chest, if it meant she would be safe. If it meant she would live.

A murky version of the future formed before him. One where Audra still allowed him to travel abroad, and he could put as much distance between himself and his former soul-bonded. High seas and flying drakes circling. It was a hollow image. One without meaning, without purpose.

He would go anyway. It was the best course of action for everyone.

Therein lay the irony. He didn't want to live without her – had been ready to die so she would not. But when he'd gone back to the book about magical bonds, he'd found a passage that read:

The selfless act of severing the bond to save one's soul-bonded can trigger an ancient magic. A magic that recognizes sacrifice and grants its wielder a second chance at life, healing them enough to survive.

It explained his miraculous recovery from such a wound. How there was no new scar added to his already marred flesh.

He would live.

A half-life, without her.

He could still feel the echo of her, the warmth of her presence that had filled the cracks and crevices of his battle-worn heart. That pain told him all that he needed to know.

That, soul-bonded or not, he would always carry a piece of her with him.

With her storm magic still raging around him, Torj watched on as Wren walked away, as she disappeared beyond the dip of the hill.

And it was like taking a war hammer to the fucking heart.

CHAPTER 94

Wren

'I hereby pledge myself to Drevenor'

– *Drevenor Oath of Secrecy*

THREE DAYS LATER, Wren found herself cornered by Remington Belcourt and Audra in the High Chancellor's private quarters. They confirmed that it was as Thea had told her: Queen Reyna had been captured by the enemy – an enemy who was a Master Alchemist in their own right.

'We need to know how you made that cure,' Audra demanded. 'The one that saved our long-lost prince's life.'

Wren took a deep breath, still reeling from the events of the battle. 'As I told Farissa, I've been experimenting with what might counter the alchemy's effects throughout the semester. I had very few samples to work with, and I used myself as a test subject.'

'But it worked,' the High Chancellor said. 'Zavier is living proof.'

'And I used the last of it on him.'

'Then you will make more,' he replied. 'We will give you whatever resources you need. The fate of the midrealms depends on it.'

Audra pushed her spectacles to the bridge of her nose. 'Agreed. The cure is paramount. Can you make more?'

Wren shifted on her feet, trying to ignore the emptiness that attempted to swallow her from within. Slowly, she met Audra's eyes. 'On one condition.'

Audra's nostrils flared. 'Oh? You'd use our desperation to your advantage?'

But Wren didn't flinch beneath her scrutinizing stare. 'I will reproduce the cure. On the condition that Torj Elderbrock is removed as my bodyguard, effective immediately.'

The following silence was stifling. But Wren did not yield.

'I do not want the Bear Slayer in my service for a moment longer. My sister, Thea, can take his place in the interim, until I find a suitable replacement of my choice.'

Audra's eyes narrowed. 'You do not get to make demands, Elwren—'

But Wren lifted her chin in defiance. 'Those are my terms, Guild Master. Take them or leave them.'

༄

Afterwards, Wren nearly collapsed as Thea's arms encircled her in the hallway. 'We're getting the fuck out of here,' her sister muttered. 'Let's hit something. Or drink. Or both.'

'Both,' Wren said instantly. But the smile didn't quite reach her eyes as Thea tried to spar with her, Cal and Kipp all at once on the way to the Mortar and Pestle. Zavier and Dessa walked with them as well, Dessa interrogating the Naarvian prince to no avail.

'How could you say nothing, all this time? We're your *teammates*!'

'I'm afraid it was top-secret information,' Zavier replied.

Wren tried her hand. 'Did *anyone* know who you were?'

Zavier offered an infuriating smile. 'Audra,' he allowed. 'I approached her before the semester began, told her who I was. It was her idea to put me on your team. She and Farissa orchestrated the whole thing.'

Wren stared at him. 'What? Why?'

Zavier shrugged. 'The heirs to two fallen kingdoms? Guess she thought we might need each other.'

'Unbelievable . . .' Wren shook her head. 'I guess she was right. You did need me, in the end.'

Zavier shrugged. 'What's a debt between friends, Poisoner?'

'Is that what we are now?' Wren scoffed.

'I'm afraid so.'

Dessa laughed at that and linked her arm through Zavier's, doubling down on her barrage of questions.

A hand grasped Wren's elbow and pulled her back so that she fell behind the others. Kipp produced a crumpled scroll from his pocket.

'As requested, Your Queenliness,' he said with his usual mischievous grin. 'It was incredibly hard to come by.'

When she'd first broached the topic back at the Mortar and Pestle, she'd honestly thought her friend wouldn't remember come morning. Surprised, Wren made to take the parchment, but Kipp didn't release it immediately.

'You need to be careful with this information,' he warned.

Wren tugged it from his grasp. 'Thank you.'

He wiggled his brows at her and gave her a weighted look. 'Just remember our deal.'

'Kipp, we were drunk out of our skulls . . .'

The strategist shrugged. 'A deal's a deal.'

Wren sighed and tucked the scroll into her satchel. 'Suppose it is, *Professor*.'

As she crossed the grounds with her sister and their friends, she felt the absence of a shadow in their wake.

The Warsword who had been hers for a few fleeting moments.

Wren clung to the lightning that was solely her own, the power that coursed through her veins, matching the drumbeat of her heart.

She had survived her first semester at Drevenor.

She had survived the Gauntlet.

And she had survived *him*.

She didn't look behind her, to where he'd once been. She vowed she never would again.

For knowledge was the victor over fate, and love, just like the mind, was a blade: beautiful, until its sharp edge found its mark.

Then, there was nothing but blood.

Alchemist. Poisoner. Lover . . . Wren had been a hundred women before this moment, but now she shed their skins.

As though sensing the storm that simmered so close to the surface, tangling with Wren's dark mood, Thea came to her side. 'What is it?'

Wren considered her sister before she spoke. 'I was just thinking . . . about war.'

'What about it?'

'That the shadow war was made for you, one of monsters and steel. The next one . . . The next one is mine. A war of minds and alchemy.'

Thea glanced at the storm clouds on the horizon ahead, her expression hard. 'I hate that you might be right . . . That there's another reckoning coming. It feels like last time . . .'

'It won't be like last time,' Wren vowed.

Thea gave her a sad smile and threaded her fingers through Wren's. 'Whatever happens, I'll be glad to be with you at the end.'

'End?'

Wren followed Thea's gaze to where lightning split the sky.

'Sister,' she said. 'It's only the beginning.'

ACKNOWLEDGEMENTS

THIS BOOK WAS the most challenging one yet ... I'm not exaggerating. *Iron & Embers* was written and edited during one of the most turbulent periods of my life so far; both as its predecessor series, *The Legends of Thezmarr*, truly found its readership, and as I bought and moved into my first home, which was something that for so long felt completely out of reach. As someone who thrives on routine and discipline, the beginning of 2024 was nothing but chaos to say the least. When it came to this manuscript, there were plenty of moments where I couldn't see the light at the end of the tunnel, where it all felt just too hard. At times I questioned whether this book would ever be finished – whether it would make it into your hands at all ...

But as always, there were wonderful people who cheered me on, who stopped me from throwing in the towel entirely.

Gary, thank you for pushing me to make this book better, even when I was done, even when I wanted to give up. Without your encouragement and reasoning, this story would not have made it into its current form.

Claire Wright, fellow author, incredible editor and an even better friend. Thank you for your patience with my constant deadline changes and listening to my panicked memos.

To my beta readers, Sacha Black and Jenny Hickman ... I was so embarrassed to send the first draft of this to you, knowing how fractured and messy it was. Thank you for pulling out the good, and encouraging me to keep going.

Thank you to a very special group of authors who kept me entertained and (relatively) sane throughout the final stages of this book: Tay Rose, V. B. Lacey, Sheila Masterson, Penn Cole, Kara Douglas, Nicole Platania and Emilia Jae.

To more of my wonderful author friends: Meg, Simone, Angelina . . . thank you for your ongoing support and cheerleading. And thank you to Melissa Wright for working your blurb magic!

Thank you to Anne Sengstock, my wonderful PA, proofreader and friend. Making you a part of my team has been one of the best decisions of my career.

Thank you to my agents, Ezra and Ethan, for all your hard work in getting my books to the rest of the world.

To Gillian Green and the rest of the team at Tor Bramble UK, thank you for believing in this story, and for welcoming me into the Pan Macmillan fold.

A massive thank you to my street team, both past and present. Launching books would be a lonely business without you, and I appreciate each and every one of you. Your efforts are inspired and the conversations in Discord bring me so much joy from afar.

As always, thanks to my mum, Bronwyn, for doing a final proof pass on these pages, and for your love and support. And all my love and thanks to the rest of the Scheuerer fam back home in Sydney.

Thank you to my wonderful friends who continue to show their support in numerous ways: Eva, Lisy, Aleesha, Ben, Hannah, Natalia, Fay, Erin, Danielle, Phoebe, Maria and Joe.

And as always, last, but never least . . . thank *you*, dear reader. For your support, for giving another wild idea of mine a chance. This next season of epic romantic adventures is for you.

Much love,
Helen

Read on for
an Exclusive Bonus Chapter
for FairyLoot Readers

Torj

Torj grimaced against the searing pain just below his collarbone, the arrow wound throbbing with each step. It had been a damn ambush between two villages, and he'd somehow managed to get caught in the middle. Dealing with monsters was preferable to humans sometimes.

He'd sent his stallion, Tucker, ahead to the fortress, not wanting to aggravate the horse's injury, but now he was staggering along the Mourner's Trail back to the fortress of Thezmarr, Torj regretted that decision.

'Fuck,' he cursed between clenched teeth, wondering if the arrow had been tipped with poison. He didn't usually let flesh wounds get the better of him. Or maybe he was just getting old - a fact Wilder continued to remind him about every chance he got. The prick.

Torj pushed on. There was a shortcut through the woods that he'd known since he was a teenager, he just needed to—

The trees swam before him, his vision blurring at the edges as he braced himself against a giant weeping oak.

That's when he heard it - a horse's whinny, and a soft voice, carried on the breeze. Torj tensed, his warrior instincts kicking in despite his weakened state. He peered around the trunk of the oak, squinting to focus his vision.

It was Tucker, who suddenly bolted in the direction of the fortress.

And a young woman, shaking her head as she turned back to the woods, towards Torj. Her bronze hair was piled atop her head, held messily in place by a pin, and her skirts were stained dark with dirt.

Too late, Torj spotted the basket of herbs at his feet and looked up.

The woman saw him at the same time, starting in alarm, and within seconds was brandishing a small knife at him. Her wide willow-green eyes met his, and for a moment, Torj forgot about the pain.

'Who are you?' she demanded, her voice surprisingly steady.

Torj couldn't help the twitch in his lips, even as he struggled to remain upright. 'I usually don't need an introduction,' he said.

The woman's eyes narrowed, taking in his bloodied state. 'Someone thinks highly of himself,' she retorted, stepping closer. Her gaze swept over him, assessing critically. 'Sit down before you fall down,' she ordered, sheathing her blade and reaching for a kit at her belt.

Torj raised an eyebrow, amused despite himself. 'You know, most people wouldn't dare talk to me like that.'

It was true. He could scarcely remember a time where the answer to anything he said hadn't simply been, *'yes, Warsword Elderbrock'*. There was always an element of awe and fear when people dealt with him now.

He gaped at the woman as she grabbed his arm without preamble and pushed him down to the ground.

'Most people don't know their head from their arse,' she said bluntly.

A laugh bubbled from Torj at that. Then he was wincing again as she adjusted his position on the forest floor, apparently having no qualms with laying hands on an injured warrior all alone in the woods. Who was this storm of a woman?

'Did you fall off your horse?' she asked.

'Fall?' He didn't think he'd ever been more offended. A Warsword? Falling off his damn horse? Never. 'Of course not. I didn't want to aggravate Tucker's wound. Sent him ahead to find the stable master. Figured I'd manage the rest of the way on my own.'

A very unladylike noise escaped her. 'How's that working out for you?'

Gods, this woman had *some nerve*. 'Just fine until the bossy likes of you came along,' he retorted.

'Not what it looked like to me.' And then she was pulling the top of his blood-soaked shirt away from his wound.

'What are you doing?' he hissed, tensing against the pain and trying to stop her.

'You warriors are all brawn and no brain. What's it look like?' She batted his hands away and peered curiously at the gash. 'How did this happen?'

'Arrow.'

The woman had taken out a belt of tools and vials and laid it down upon the leaf litter. Shaking her head, she snatched something up and uncorked it. 'And you pulled it out?' He didn't miss the chiding note in her voice.

'It was in the way,' he muttered.

'You didn't think to keep it in to stop the bleeding? You could have at least just snapped the fletching off—'

That was it. He was a fucking Warsword of Thezmarr. He didn't have to sit here being scolded by some forest nymph, no matter how pretty.

'I'm heading back to the fortress.' He surged upwards, trying to get back on his feet—

Firm hands gripped his shoulders, shoving him back down so he landed hard on his backside. For a little thing, she was surprisingly strong.

'You'll stay there until I've tended to that gaping hole in your chest.'

Torj recognized an order when he heard one, and Furies save him . . . he found himself obeying. He had fought monsters and men alike all over the midrealms for over a decade, but this woman . . . she was a force to be reckoned with all on her own. Without batting an eye at the blood and gore, she ripped away the collar of his shirt.

'Absolute fools, the lot of you. Don't they teach you how to care for injuries during your Guardian training?' she chided.

Ah. That was it. She didn't know who he was. 'I'm not a Guardian,' he told her, waiting for the shoe to drop, for her to ramble off a bunch of apologies.

'You're a Warsword,' she said quietly, surveying the armband around his bicep: three crossed swords that marked him as one of the most elite warriors in the midrealms.

'Did the giant war hammer not give it away?' he mused, nodding towards his weapon lying on the ground nearby.

'The arrogance should have,' she replied, not bothering to look up as she cleaned his wound.

A surprised laugh burst from him. 'I suppose we deserve that reputation.'

'Among others.' The woman did look up then, her gaze shifting between his golden hair and his war hammer on the ground. Her expression was guarded. He saw none of the awe that usually accompanied the realization of who he was.

'You're the one they call the Bear Slayer,' she surmised.

'Guilty.' He gave her a winning smile. 'Or Torj, if we're friendly.'

'We're not.'

Oh, he liked her. He liked her a lot. Finally a sparring partner worthy of a round or two. Still smiling, he waited until she locked eyes with him once more. 'And what do they call you?'

'Wren.'

He was going to ask her something else, but then she pressed what he could only assume was liquid torture on his wound—

'Fuck,' he hissed, as the searing sensation of rubbing alcohol burned through his battered flesh.

'Hold still,' she said without an ounce of sympathy. Gods, her bedside manner could use some work. He opened his mouth to say as much but she was busy threading thread through a needle.

'So you're not squeamish, then?' he grunted.

'No. Are you?'

Before he could reply, she stuck the needle through his skin and a stream of curses left his lips. He could handle pain. That had been ingrained in him from a very young age. But there was something about the pinch and pull of a needle and thread that set his teeth on edge.

Wren looked more amused than empathetic. 'Here I was thinking someone called the Bear Slayer might have a higher pain tolerance.'

'Here I was thinking healers were meant to be kind. Or at least have a decent bedside manner,' he quipped. Her touch was light and practiced, and for a fleeting moment Torj imagined what her hands might feel like trailing along his skin in a different context.

'I'm not at your bedside, and I'm not a healer,' she said.

He stared at her. 'Then why in the midrealms am I letting you poke me with that damn torture device?'

Wren's lips quirked to the side. 'You're a bit dramatic, aren't you?'

He suddenly wanted to see what she looked like with a real smile on her face, he found himself fascinated. 'Again . . . no one talks to me like that.'

'Perhaps it's time someone did.'

As she worked, he took in the sight of her . . . her simple clothing did nothing to detract from her beauty, which was astounding. If anything, it only made it more obvious. Loose strands of hair framed her face, her dark brows furrowed in concentration while she stitched him. There was a light smattering of freckles across her nose, her lower lip caught between her teeth. As she moved, more hair fell into her eyes and, without thinking, he reached to tuck it behind her ear—

She jerked back. 'What are you—'

Torj came back to himself with a rush of embarrassment. But he'd learned to think on his feet long ago. Schooling his features into some semblance of indifference as he spotted a leaf sticking out from her tresses. He snatched it between his fingers and presented it to her smoothly. 'This was in your hair.'

'Oh.'

A delicious blush stained her cheeks as he let the leaf fall between them.

'If you're not a healer, dare I ask what you are?' he said, still struggling to take his eyes off her. He was almost grateful for the sharp sting of the needle stopping him from saying or doing something reckless. *Again*. She couldn't be older than twenty, which would put some solid years between them . . .

'I'm an alchemist,' she replied, her stitches approaching the last few inches of his wound.

And still, he couldn't stop looking at her. 'Is that so . . .'

'Yes.'

She was one of Farissa's students then . . . it was no wonder that she was good with injuries in that case, Farissa was a Master Alchemist of healing and had been long before Torj had ever walked the fortress halls.

'And where might I find you?' he heard himself ask like an absolute fool. 'For . . . follow-up care?'

Wren's voice was all business. 'You won't need any. Just keep it clean and dry.'

No, Torj decided, she wasn't brushing him off so easily. 'What about removing the stitches?'

She raised a brow. 'I'm sure someone of your . . . experience can figure out how to remove a few stitches.'

'Are you calling me old?'

'I'm sure there are other things I could call you.'

'No doubt . . .' He heard the stupidly flirtatious note in his voice, but couldn't stop himself. 'How old are you, anyway?'

'None of your business.' Wren tied off the final thread. 'There,' she said, sounding satisfied. 'That should hold, as long as you don't do anything stupid to tear the stitches.'

'And what qualifies as stupid, in your expert opinion?'

'Anything that lands you back in my care, Bear Slayer,' she warned. 'I've got better things to do than patch up reckless warriors who don't know when to quit.'

He was already planning on tearing his stitches, realizing he'd gladly suffer the needle again just to spend a few more minutes with her. *What are you doing out here alone?* He wanted to ask, anything to keep the conversation going. Which was unlike him. Sure, he was friendly enough. He talked to lots of people. But . . . no one like her.

'Wren?' he said instead.

Heat flared in her eyes, he saw it, right before she hid it with a scowl.

Torj knew he was grinning like a prized idiot, but he didn't care. Her berating words told one story, but her flushed cheeks and parted lips told another.

'Just so you know . . . I never quit,' he assured her.

No one had ever scrambled to their feet faster. He watched as she snatched up her things and hooked her basket in the crook of her elbow.

'Good luck and good riddance, Bear Slayer,' she declared, making for the trail, her hips swaying.

'You can't get rid of me that easily,' he yelled after her.

'Whatever you say, Warsword,' came her reply.

Torj watched her go, smiling to himself, a strange warmth blooming in his chest. Shifting his shoulder experimentally, the stitches pulled painfully.

It wouldn't be the last time he saw the beautiful alchemist, he'd make sure of it.

ABOUT THE AUTHOR

Helen Scheuerer is the author of the bestselling fantasy series The Oremere Chronicles, the Curse of the Cyren Queen quartet and The Legends of Thezmarr. Her work has been highly praised for its strong, flawed female characters and its action-packed plots. Helen's love of writing and books led her to pursue a creative writing degree and a Master's in Publishing. She has been a full-time author since 2018 and now lives among the mountains in New Zealand, where she is constantly dreaming up new stories.